GRUBBS

By
Max Weaver
and
Ted Dawson

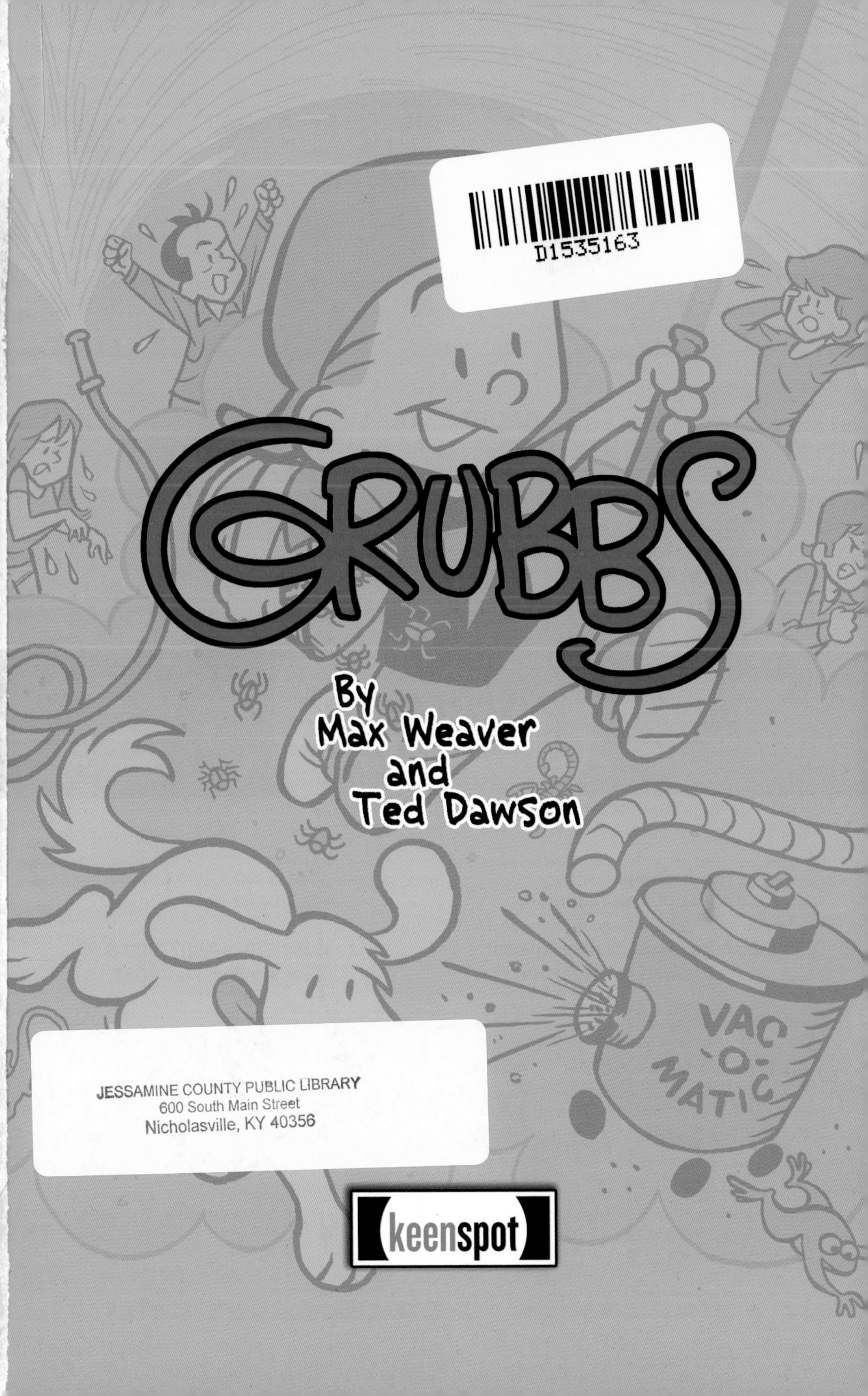
VAC-O-MATIC

keenspot

GRUBBS VOL. 1

GRUBBS and all related characters are © and ™ 2021 by Max Weaver.

Published by
Keenspot Entertainment
Apple Valley, CA
E-Mail: keenspot@keenspot.com
Web: www.keenspot.com

For Keenspot
CEO & EIC Chris Crosby
PRESIDENT Bobby Crosby

ISBN 978-1-932-77599-0
First Printing, May 2021
Printed in USA

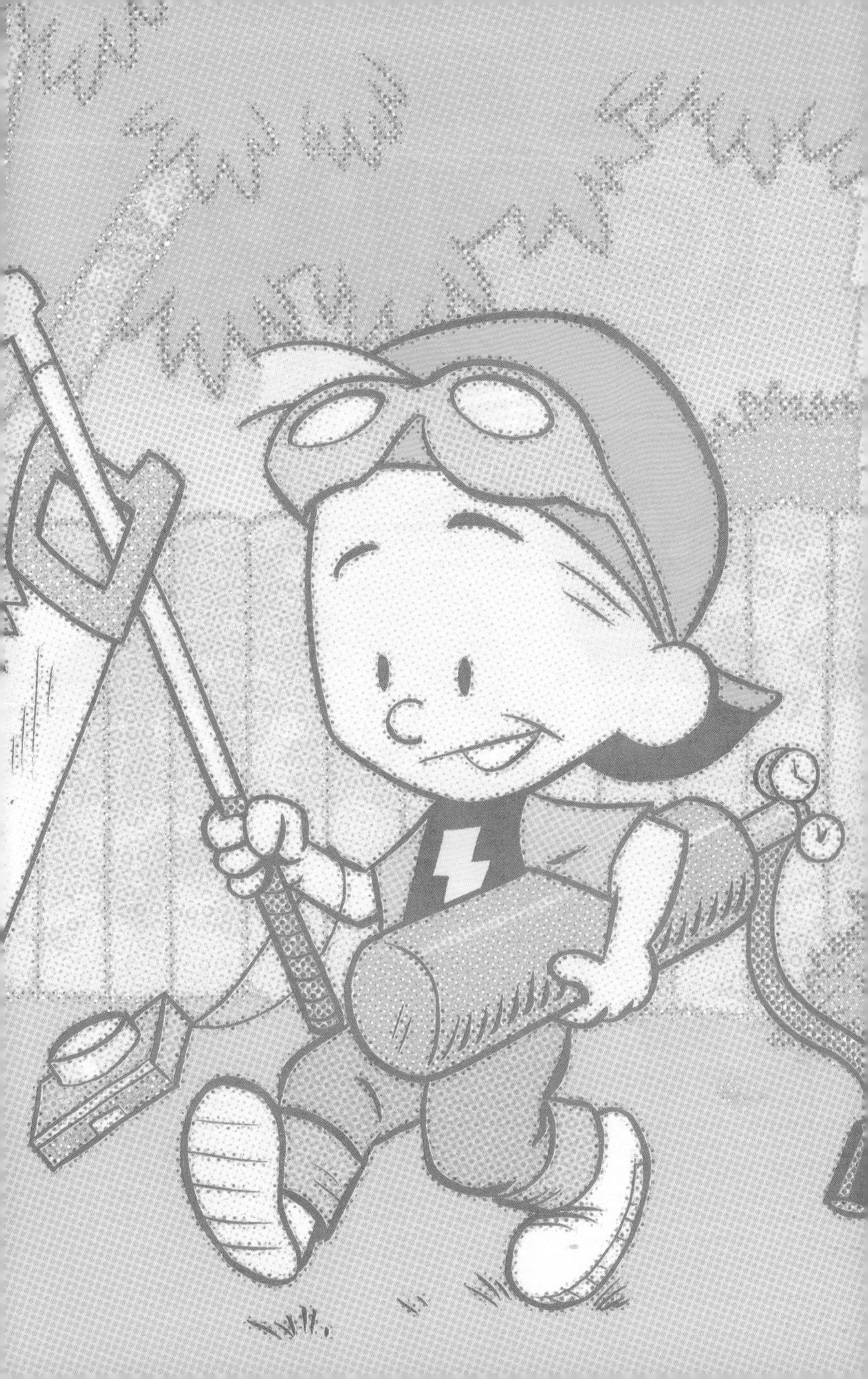

MEET GRUBBS

ZANE

TYLER

COURTNEY

CIGAR

ALLISON & AMY

MOM

DAD

by
MAX WEAVER
&
TED DAWSON

Billy Watson is an eight-year-old boy who received the unwanted nickname "Grubbs" from his older brother Zane. In the following pages you'll have a front row seat watching Grubbs at his favorite past time, tormenting Zane and his older sister, Courtney. And it doesn't stop there...

Grubbs' best pal is his imaginary friend, Tyler. Tyler is Grubbs' confidante and adviser as Grubbs concocts his schemes to get even, get ahead, and just get by. Join in with Mom, Dad, the twins Amy and Allison, and Cigar the dog for all the fun!

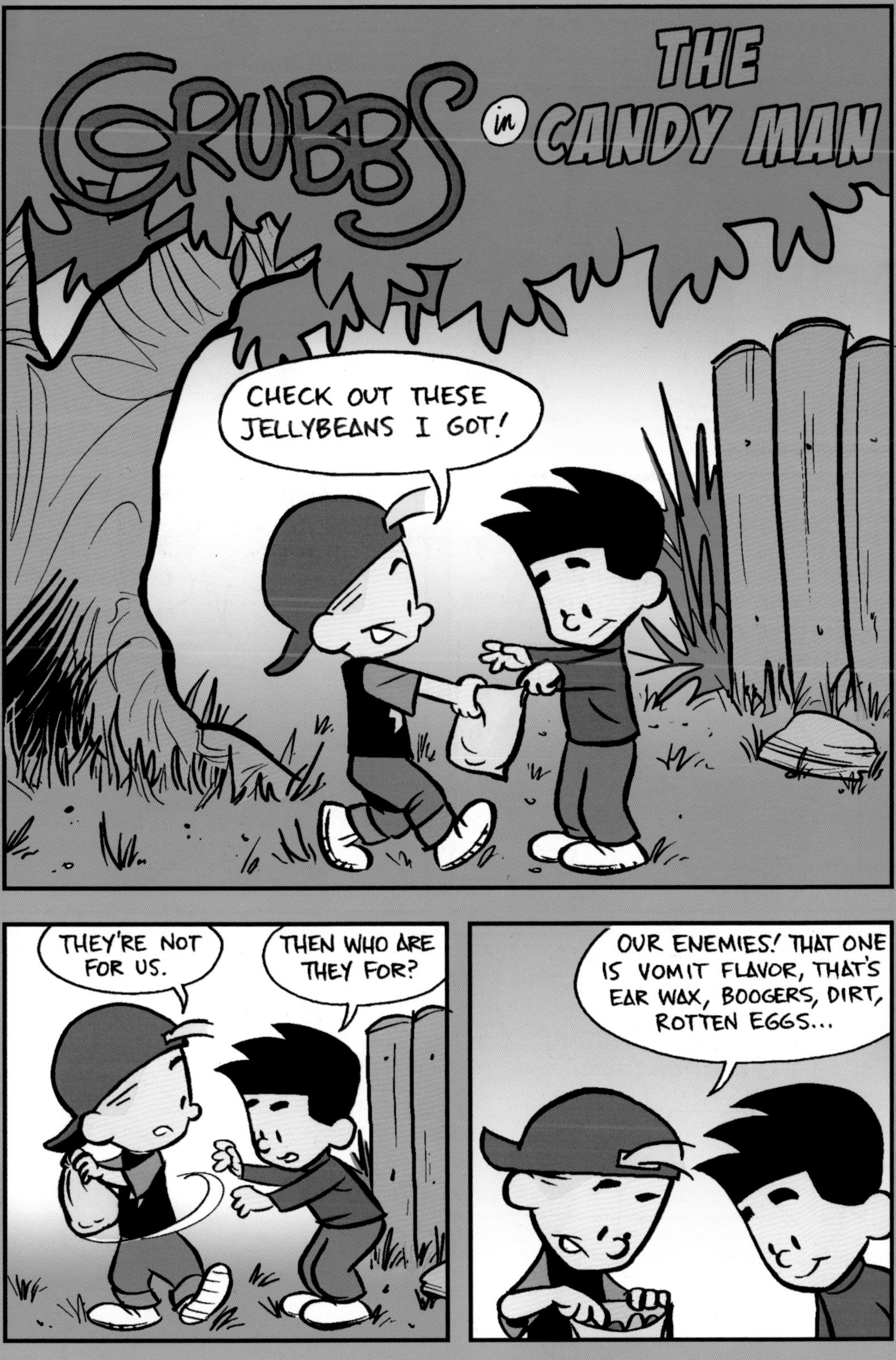
GRUBBS in THE CANDY MAN
CHECK OUT THESE JELLYBEANS I GOT!
THEY'RE NOT FOR US.
THEN WHO ARE THEY FOR?
OUR ENEMIES! THAT ONE IS VOMIT FLAVOR, THAT'S EAR WAX, BOOGERS, DIRT, ROTTEN EGGS...

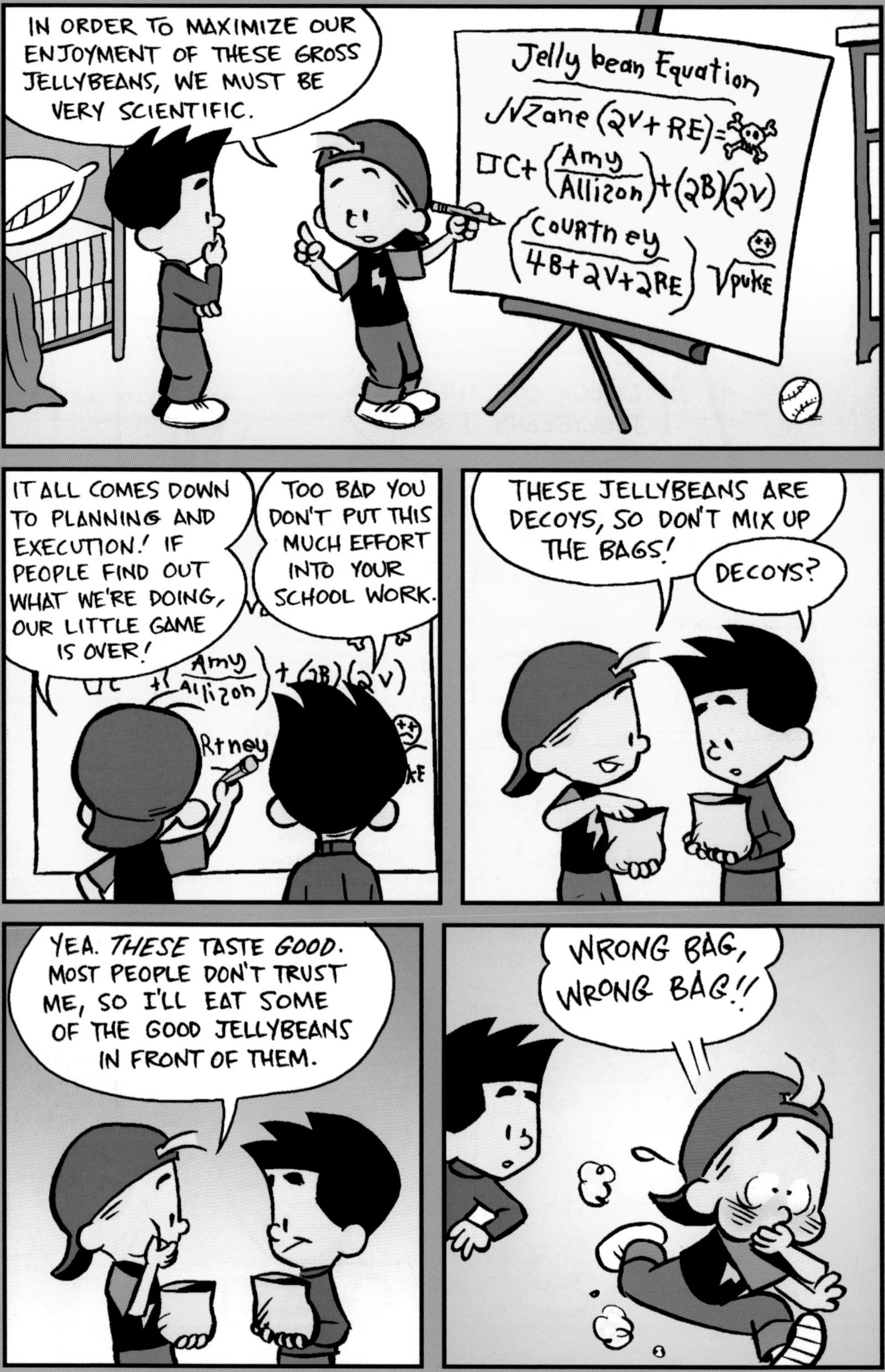
IN ORDER TO MAXIMIZE OUR ENJOYMENT OF THESE GROSS JELLYBEANS, WE MUST BE VERY SCIENTIFIC.
Jelly bean Equation
IT ALL COMES DOWN TO PLANNING AND EXECUTION! IF PEOPLE FIND OUT WHAT WE'RE DOING, OUR LITTLE GAME IS OVER!
TOO BAD YOU DON'T PUT THIS MUCH EFFORT INTO YOUR SCHOOL WORK.
THESE JELLYBEANS ARE DECOYS, SO DON'T MIX UP THE BAGS!
DECOYS?
YEA. *THESE* TASTE *GOOD*. MOST PEOPLE DON'T TRUST ME, SO I'LL EAT SOME OF THE GOOD JELLYBEANS IN FRONT OF THEM.
WRONG BAG, WRONG BAG!!

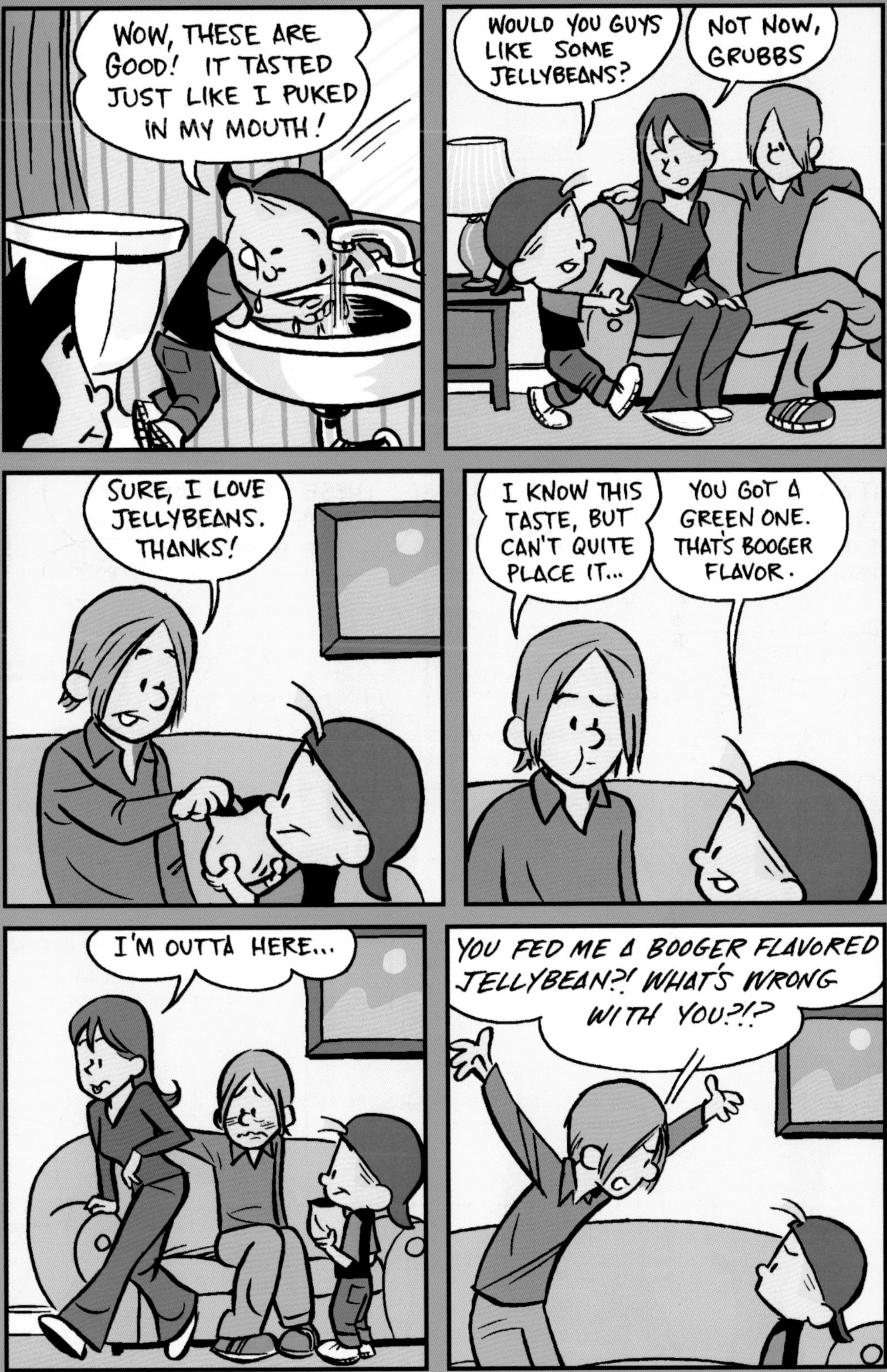
WOW, THESE ARE GOOD! IT TASTED JUST LIKE I PUKED IN MY MOUTH!
WOULD YOU GUYS LIKE SOME JELLYBEANS?
NOT NOW, GRUBBS
SURE, I LOVE JELLYBEANS. THANKS!
I KNOW THIS TASTE, BUT CAN'T QUITE PLACE IT...
YOU GOT A GREEN ONE. THAT'S BOOGER FLAVOR.
I'M OUTTA HERE...
YOU FED ME A BOOGER FLAVORED JELLYBEAN?! WHAT'S WRONG WITH YOU?!?

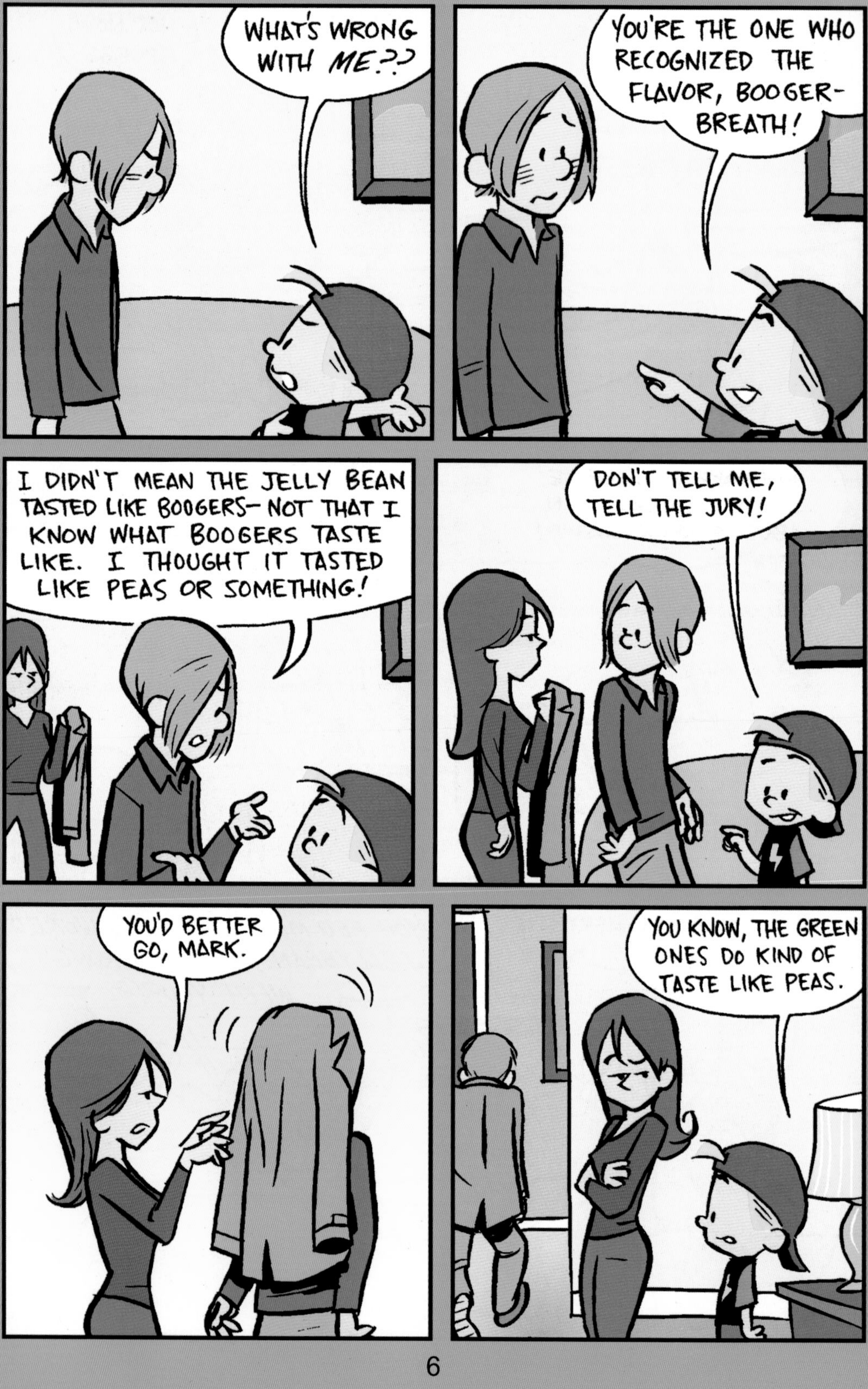
WHAT'S WRONG WITH ME??
YOU'RE THE ONE WHO RECOGNIZED THE FLAVOR, BOOGER-BREATH!
I DIDN'T MEAN THE JELLY BEAN TASTED LIKE BOOGERS— NOT THAT I KNOW WHAT BOOGERS TASTE LIKE. I THOUGHT IT TASTED LIKE PEAS OR SOMETHING!
DON'T TELL ME, TELL THE JURY!
YOU'D BETTER GO, MARK.
YOU KNOW, THE GREEN ONES DO KIND OF TASTE LIKE PEAS.

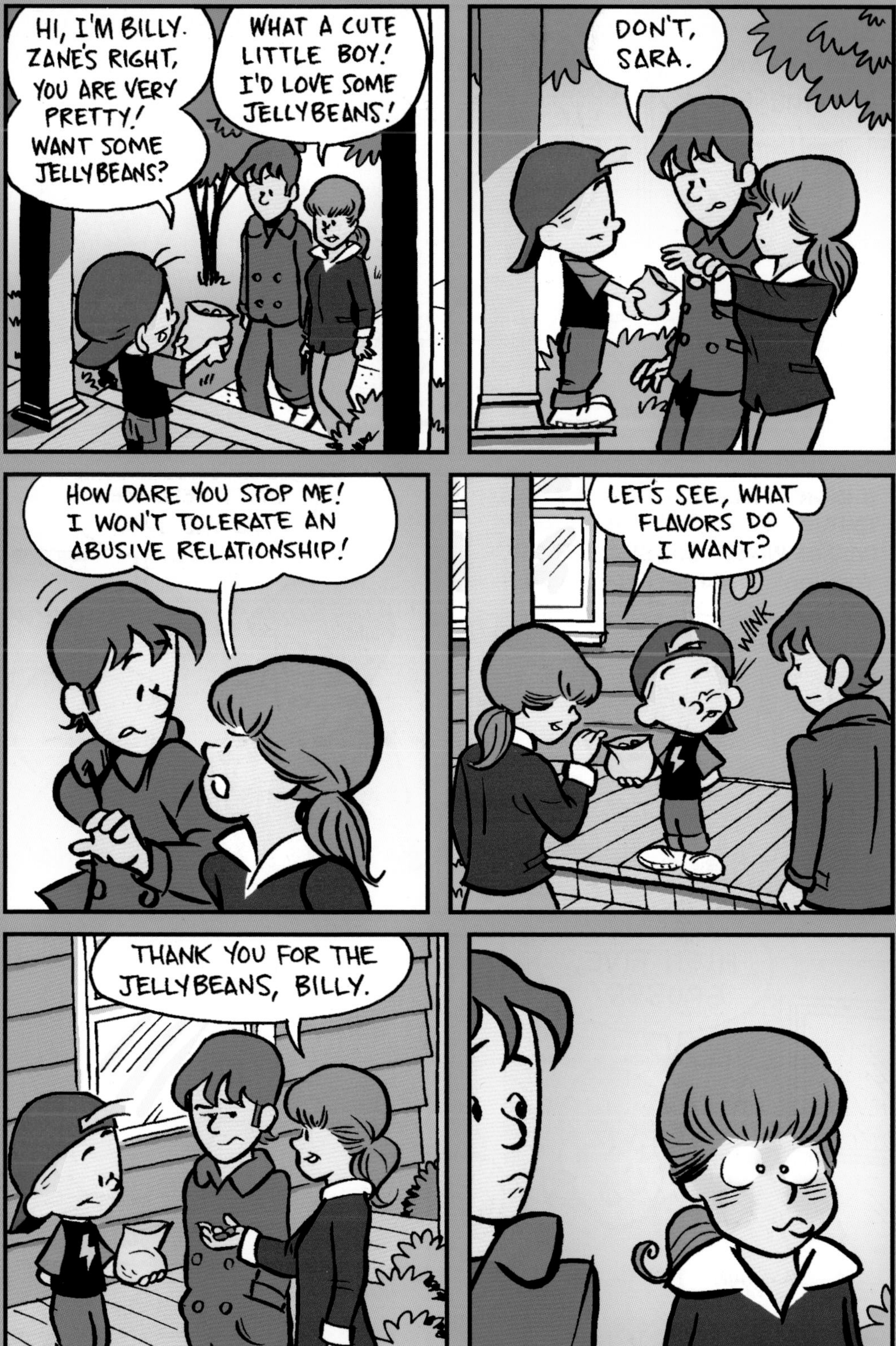
HI, I'M BILLY. ZANE'S RIGHT, YOU ARE VERY PRETTY! WANT SOME JELLYBEANS?
WHAT A CUTE LITTLE BOY! I'D LOVE SOME JELLYBEANS!
DON'T, SARA.
HOW DARE YOU STOP ME! I WON'T TOLERATE AN ABUSIVE RELATIONSHIP!
LET'S SEE, WHAT FLAVORS DO I WANT?
WINK
THANK YOU FOR THE JELLYBEANS, BILLY.

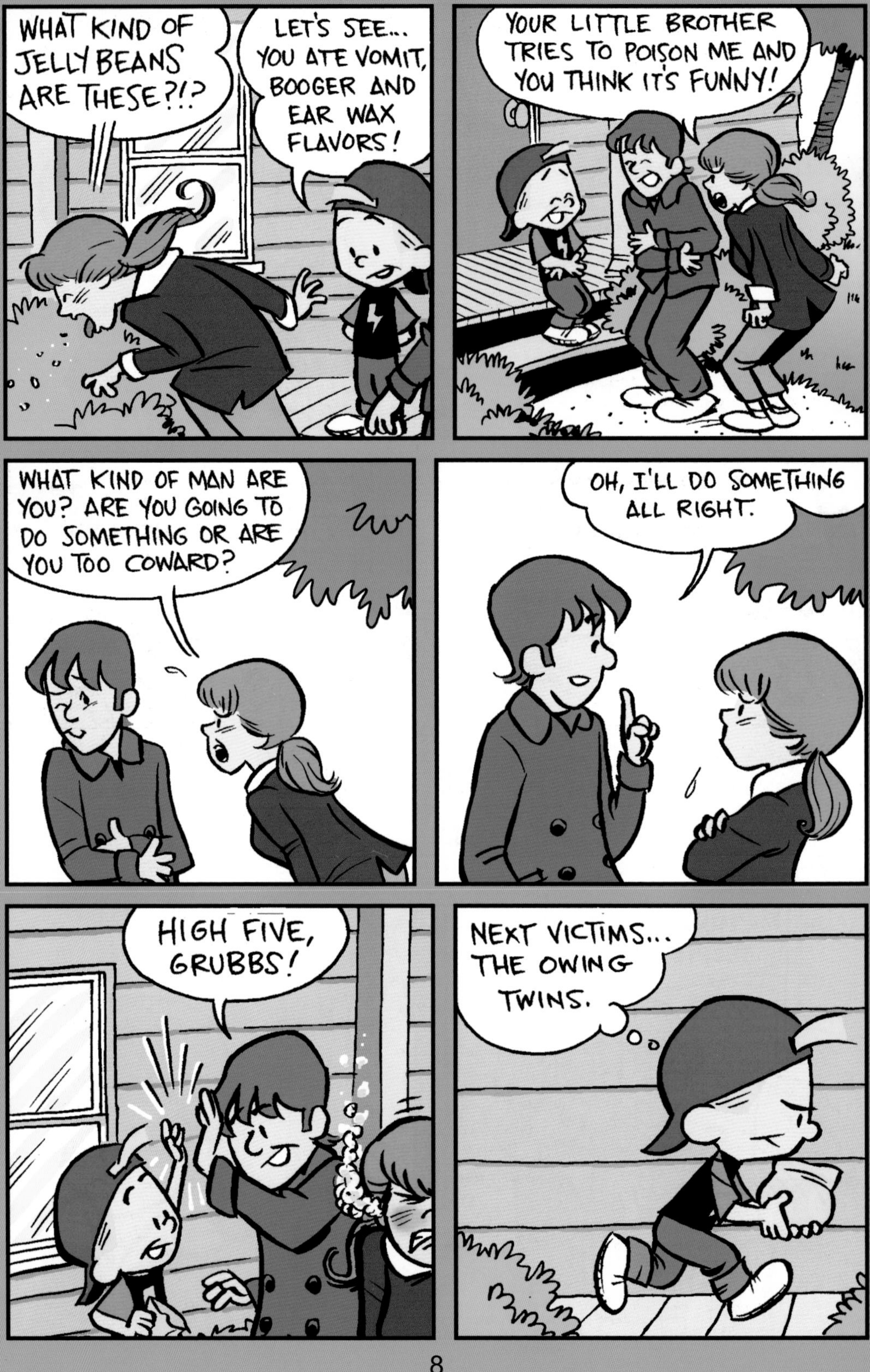
WHAT KIND OF JELLY BEANS ARE THESE?!?
LET'S SEE... YOU ATE VOMIT, BOOGER AND EAR WAX FLAVORS!
YOUR LITTLE BROTHER TRIES TO POISON ME AND YOU THINK IT'S FUNNY!
WHAT KIND OF MAN ARE YOU? ARE YOU GOING TO DO SOMETHING OR ARE YOU TOO COWARD?
OH, I'LL DO SOMETHING ALL RIGHT.
HIGH FIVE, GRUBBS!
NEXT VICTIMS... THE OWING TWINS.

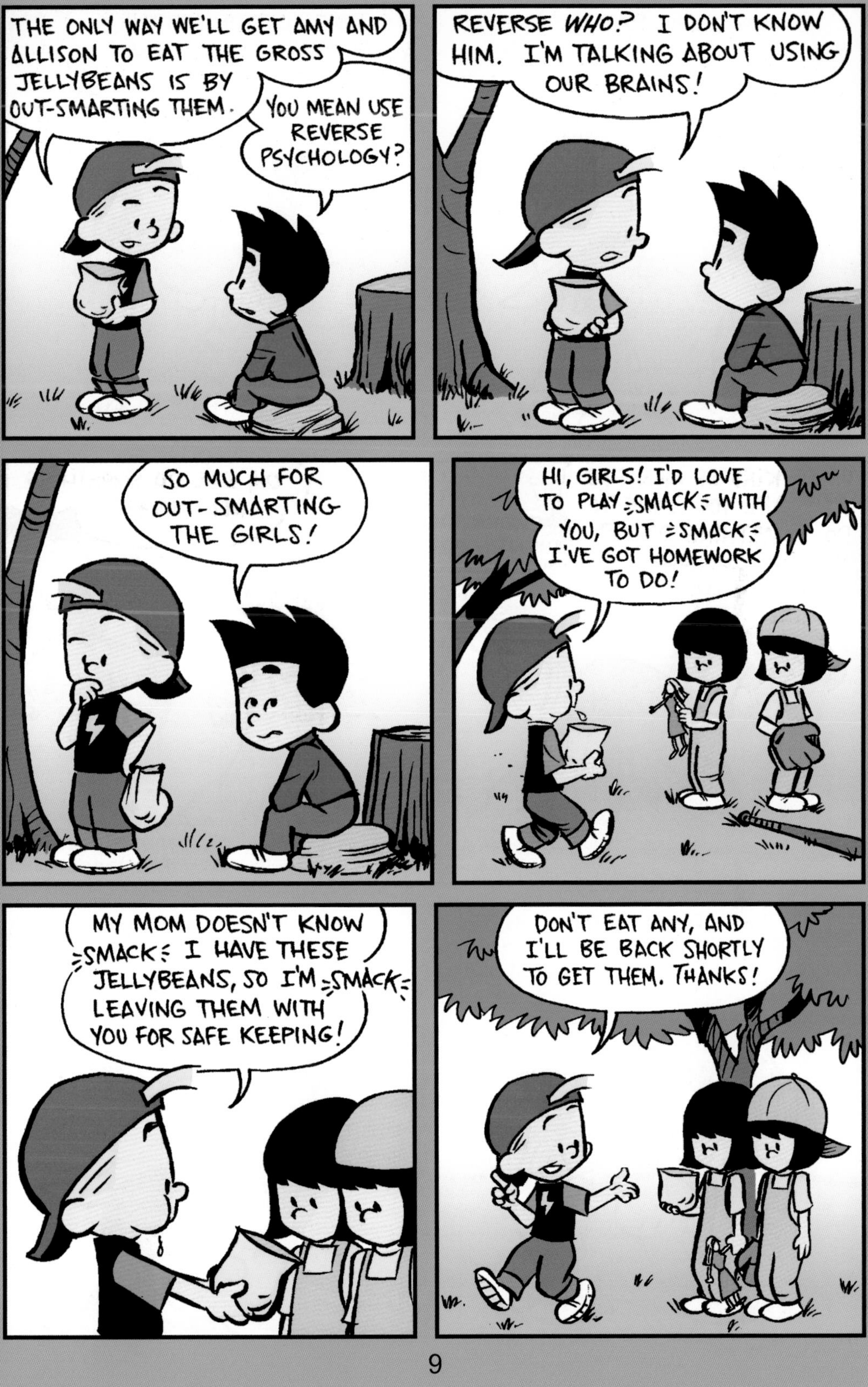
THE ONLY WAY WE'LL GET AMY AND ALLISON TO EAT THE GROSS JELLYBEANS IS BY OUT-SMARTING THEM.
YOU MEAN USE REVERSE PSYCHOLOGY?
REVERSE WHO? I DON'T KNOW HIM. I'M TALKING ABOUT USING OUR BRAINS!
SO MUCH FOR OUT-SMARTING THE GIRLS!
HI, GIRLS! I'D LOVE TO PLAY SMACK WITH YOU, BUT SMACK I'VE GOT HOMEWORK TO DO!
MY MOM DOESN'T KNOW SMACK I HAVE THESE JELLYBEANS, SO I'M SMACK LEAVING THEM WITH YOU FOR SAFE KEEPING!
DON'T EAT ANY, AND I'LL BE BACK SHORTLY TO GET THEM. THANKS!

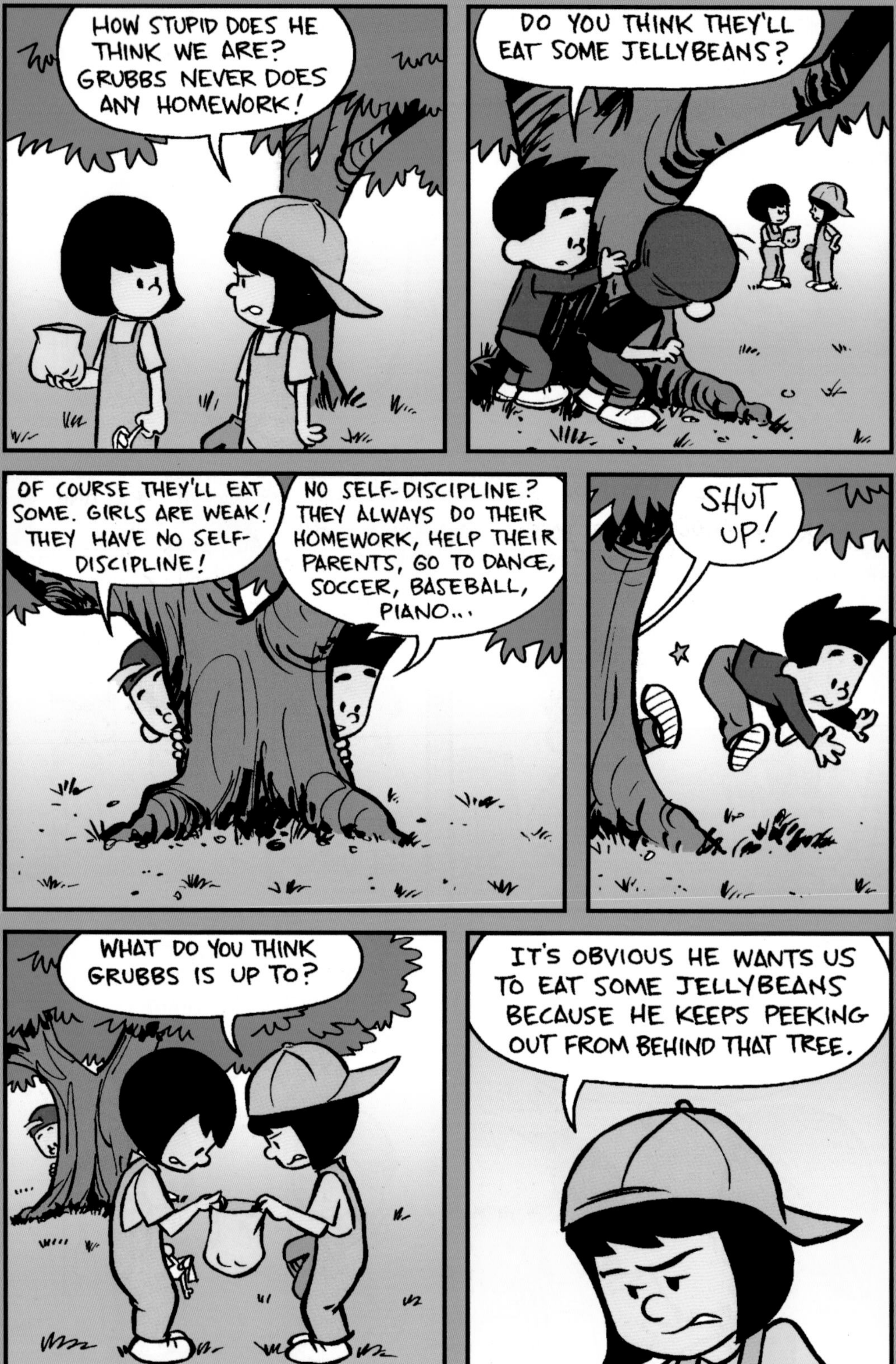
HOW STUPID DOES HE THINK WE ARE? GRUBBS NEVER DOES ANY HOMEWORK!
DO YOU THINK THEY'LL EAT SOME JELLYBEANS?
OF COURSE THEY'LL EAT SOME. GIRLS ARE WEAK! THEY HAVE NO SELF-DISCIPLINE!
NO SELF-DISCIPLINE? THEY ALWAYS DO THEIR HOMEWORK, HELP THEIR PARENTS, GO TO DANCE, SOCCER, BASEBALL, PIANO...
SHUT UP!
WHAT DO YOU THINK GRUBBS IS UP TO?
...
IT'S OBVIOUS HE WANTS US TO EAT SOME JELLYBEANS BECAUSE HE KEEPS PEEKING OUT FROM BEHIND THAT TREE.

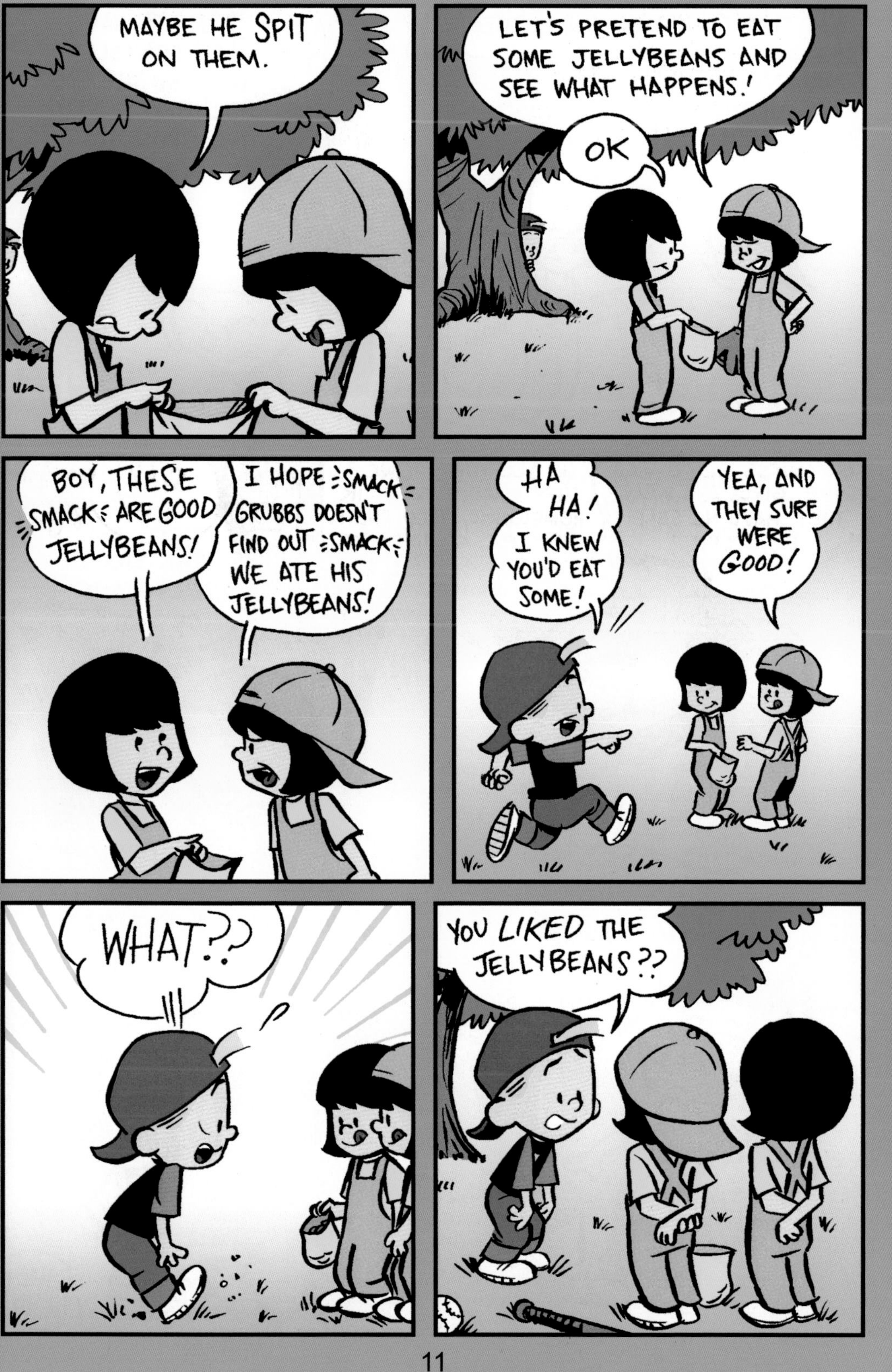
MAYBE HE SPIT ON THEM.
LET'S PRETEND TO EAT SOME JELLYBEANS AND SEE WHAT HAPPENS!
OK
BOY, THESE SMACK ARE GOOD JELLYBEANS!
I HOPE SMACK GRUBBS DOESN'T FIND OUT SMACK WE ATE HIS JELLYBEANS!
HA HA! I KNEW YOU'D EAT SOME!
YEA, AND THEY SURE WERE GOOD!
WHAT??
YOU LIKED THE JELLYBEANS??

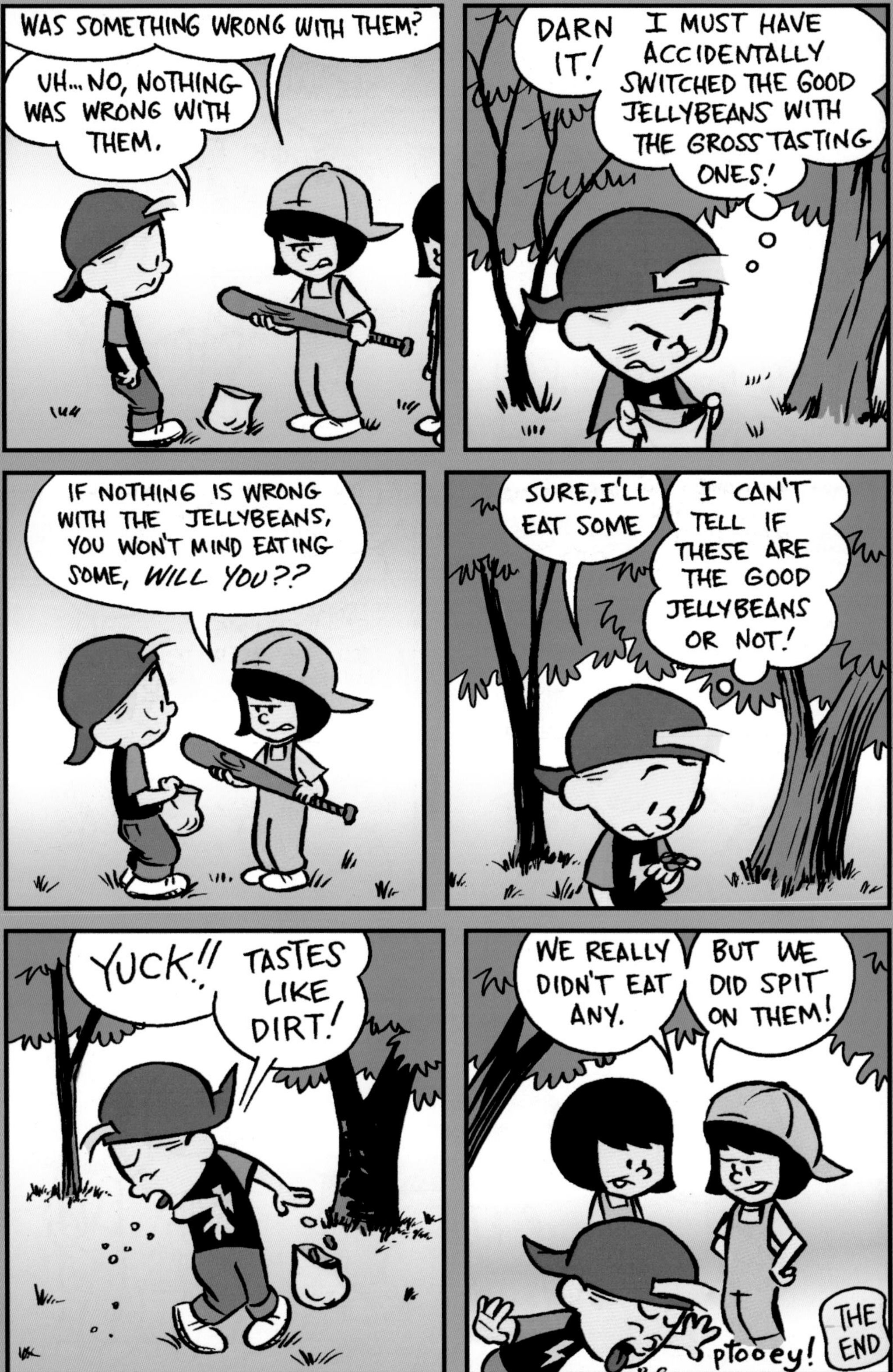
WAS SOMETHING WRONG WITH THEM?
UH... NO, NOTHING WAS WRONG WITH THEM.
DARN IT!
I MUST HAVE ACCIDENTALLY SWITCHED THE GOOD JELLYBEANS WITH THE GROSS TASTING ONES!
IF NOTHING IS WRONG WITH THE JELLYBEANS, YOU WON'T MIND EATING SOME, WILL YOU??
SURE, I'LL EAT SOME
I CAN'T TELL IF THESE ARE THE GOOD JELLYBEANS OR NOT!
YUCK!!..
TASTES LIKE DIRT!
WE REALLY DIDN'T EAT ANY.
BUT WE DID SPIT ON THEM!
ptooey!
THE END

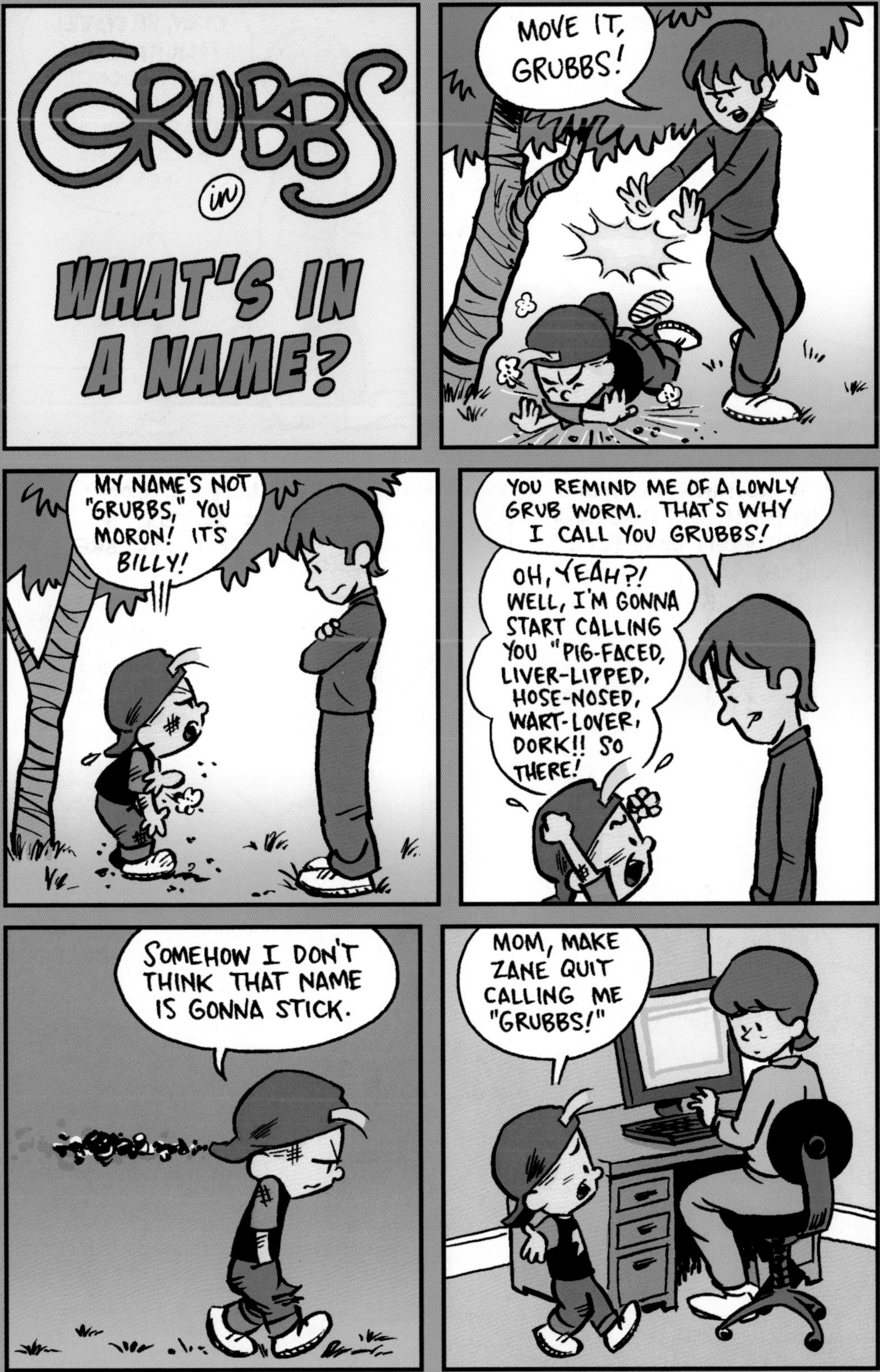
GRUBBS
in
WHAT'S IN A NAME?
MOVE IT, GRUBBS!
MY NAME'S NOT "GRUBBS," YOU MORON! IT'S BILLY!
YOU REMIND ME OF A LOWLY GRUB WORM. THAT'S WHY I CALL YOU GRUBBS!
OH, YEAH?! WELL, I'M GONNA START CALLING YOU "PIG-FACED, LIVER-LIPPED, HOSE-NOSED, WART-LOVER, DORK!! SO THERE!
SOMEHOW I DON'T THINK THAT NAME IS GONNA STICK.
MOM, MAKE ZANE QUIT CALLING ME "GRUBBS!"

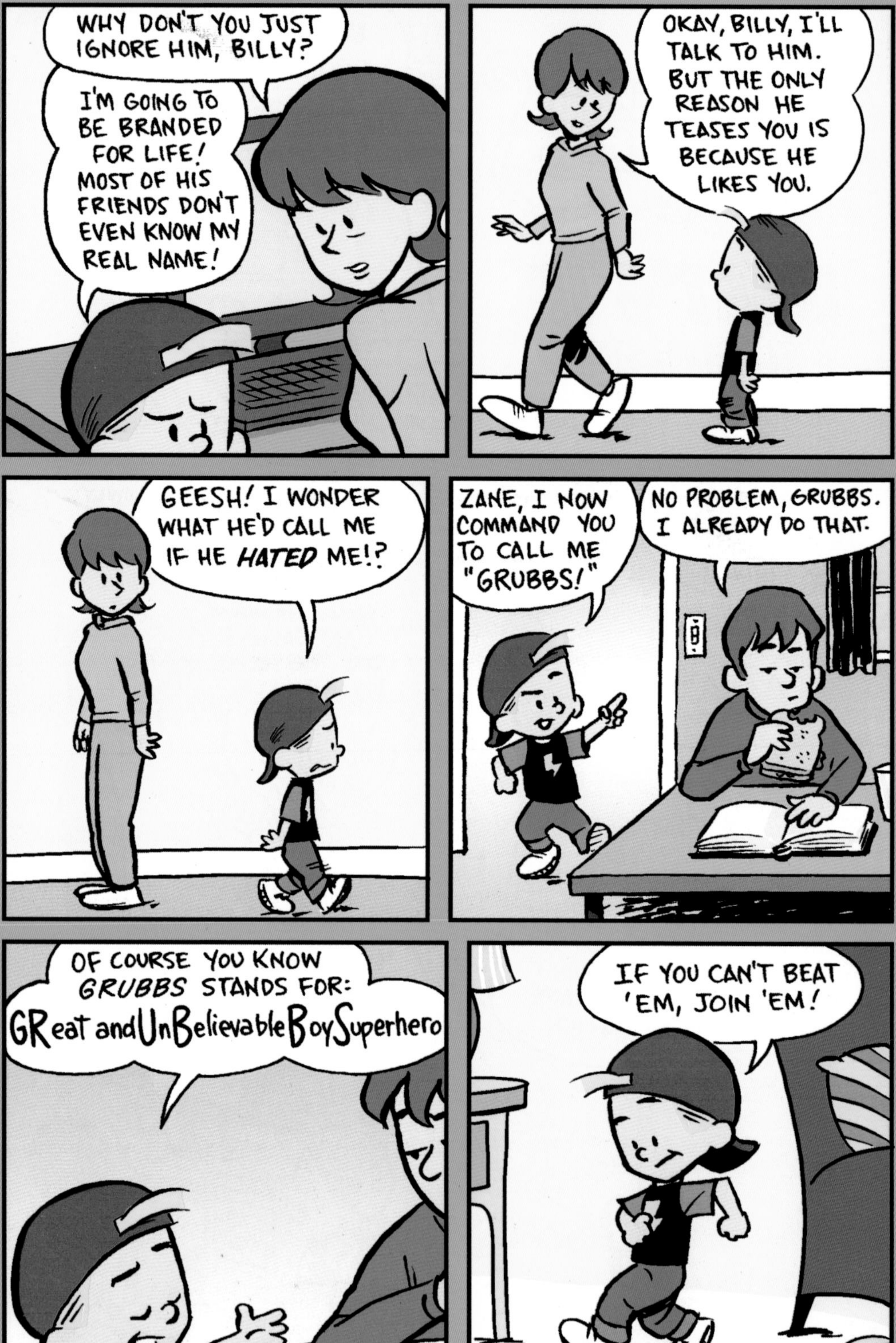
WHY DON'T YOU JUST IGNORE HIM, BILLY?
I'M GOING TO BE BRANDED FOR LIFE! MOST OF HIS FRIENDS DON'T EVEN KNOW MY REAL NAME!
OKAY, BILLY, I'LL TALK TO HIM. BUT THE ONLY REASON HE TEASES YOU IS BECAUSE HE LIKES YOU.
GEESH! I WONDER WHAT HE'D CALL ME IF HE *HATED* ME!?
ZANE, I NOW COMMAND YOU TO CALL ME "GRUBBS!"
NO PROBLEM, GRUBBS. I ALREADY DO THAT.
OF COURSE YOU KNOW *GRUBBS* STANDS FOR:
GReat and UnBelievable Boy Superhero
IF YOU CAN'T BEAT 'EM, JOIN 'EM!
END

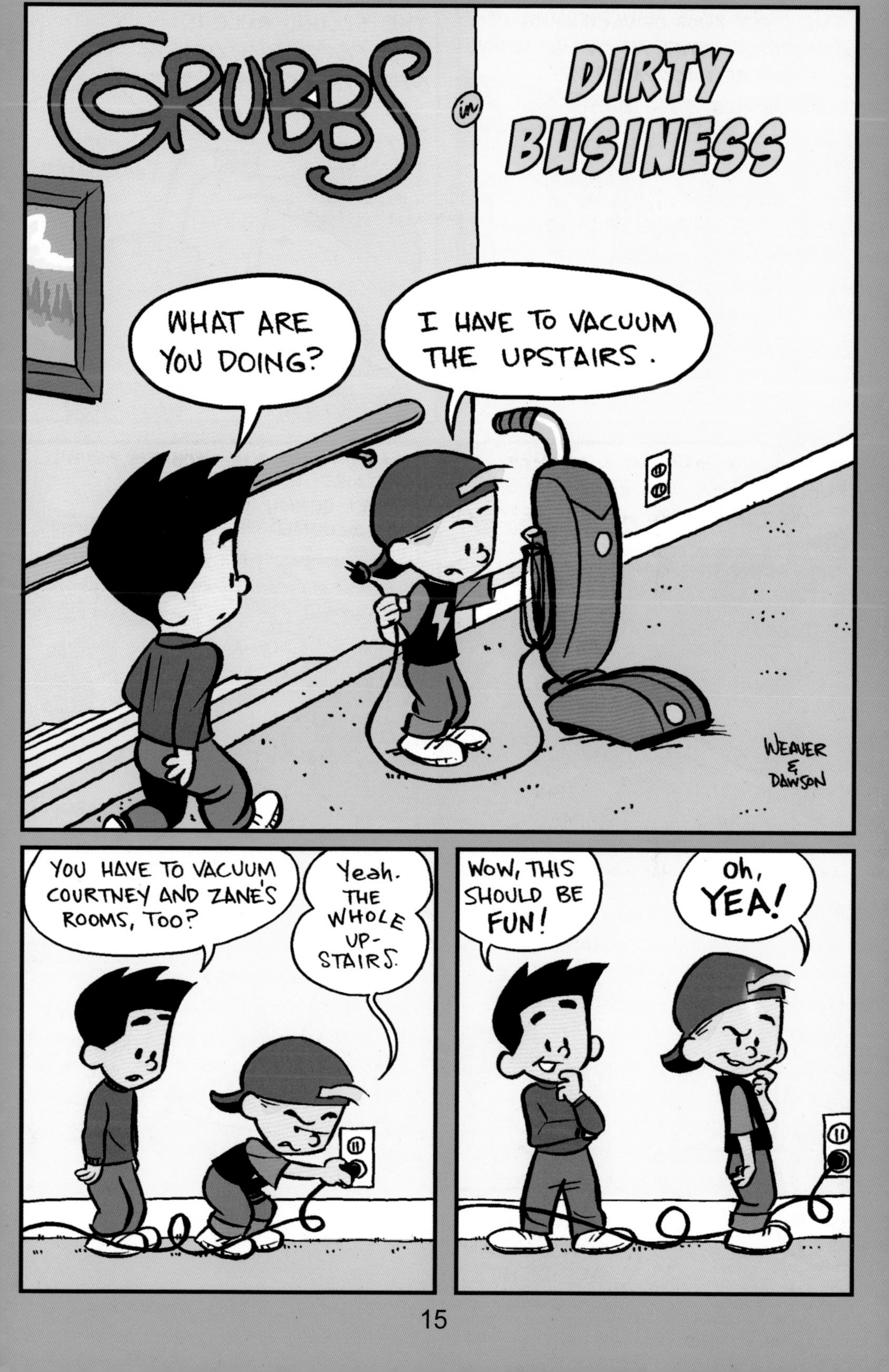
GRUBBS in
DIRTY BUSINESS
WHAT ARE YOU DOING?
I HAVE TO VACUUM THE UPSTAIRS.
WEAVER & DAWSON
YOU HAVE TO VACUUM COURTNEY AND ZANE'S ROOMS, TOO?
Yeah. THE WHOLE UP-STAIRS.
WOW, THIS SHOULD BE FUN!
Oh, YEA!

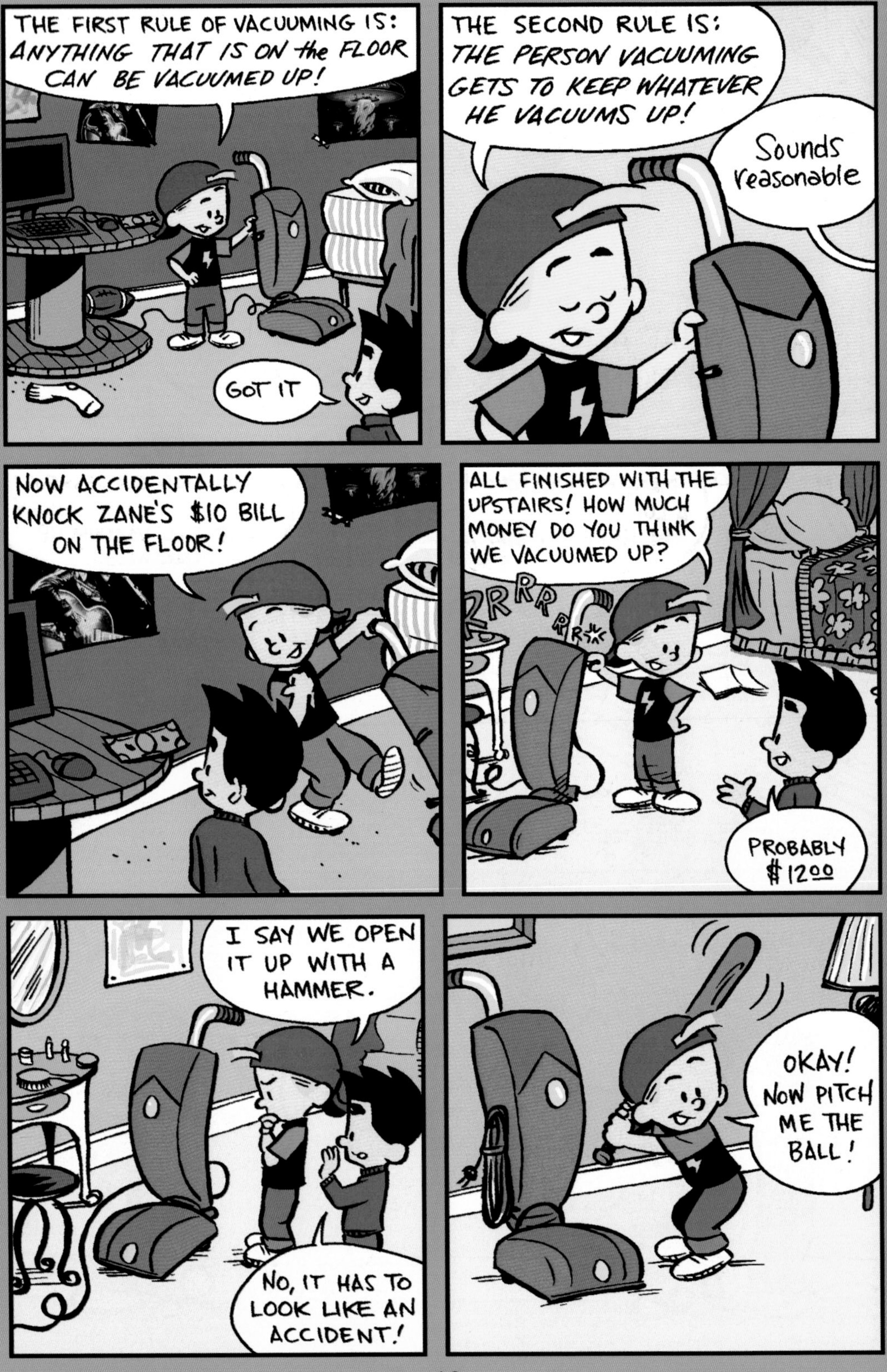
THE FIRST RULE OF VACUUMING IS: ANYTHING THAT IS ON the FLOOR CAN BE VACUUMED UP!
GOT IT
THE SECOND RULE IS: THE PERSON VACUUMING GETS TO KEEP WHATEVER HE VACUUMS UP!
Sounds reasonable
NOW ACCIDENTALLY KNOCK ZANE'S $10 BILL ON THE FLOOR!
ALL FINISHED WITH THE UPSTAIRS! HOW MUCH MONEY DO YOU THINK WE VACUUMED UP?
RRRRRRR
PROBABLY $12.00
I SAY WE OPEN IT UP WITH A HAMMER.
NO, IT HAS TO LOOK LIKE AN ACCIDENT!
OKAY! NOW PITCH ME THE BALL!

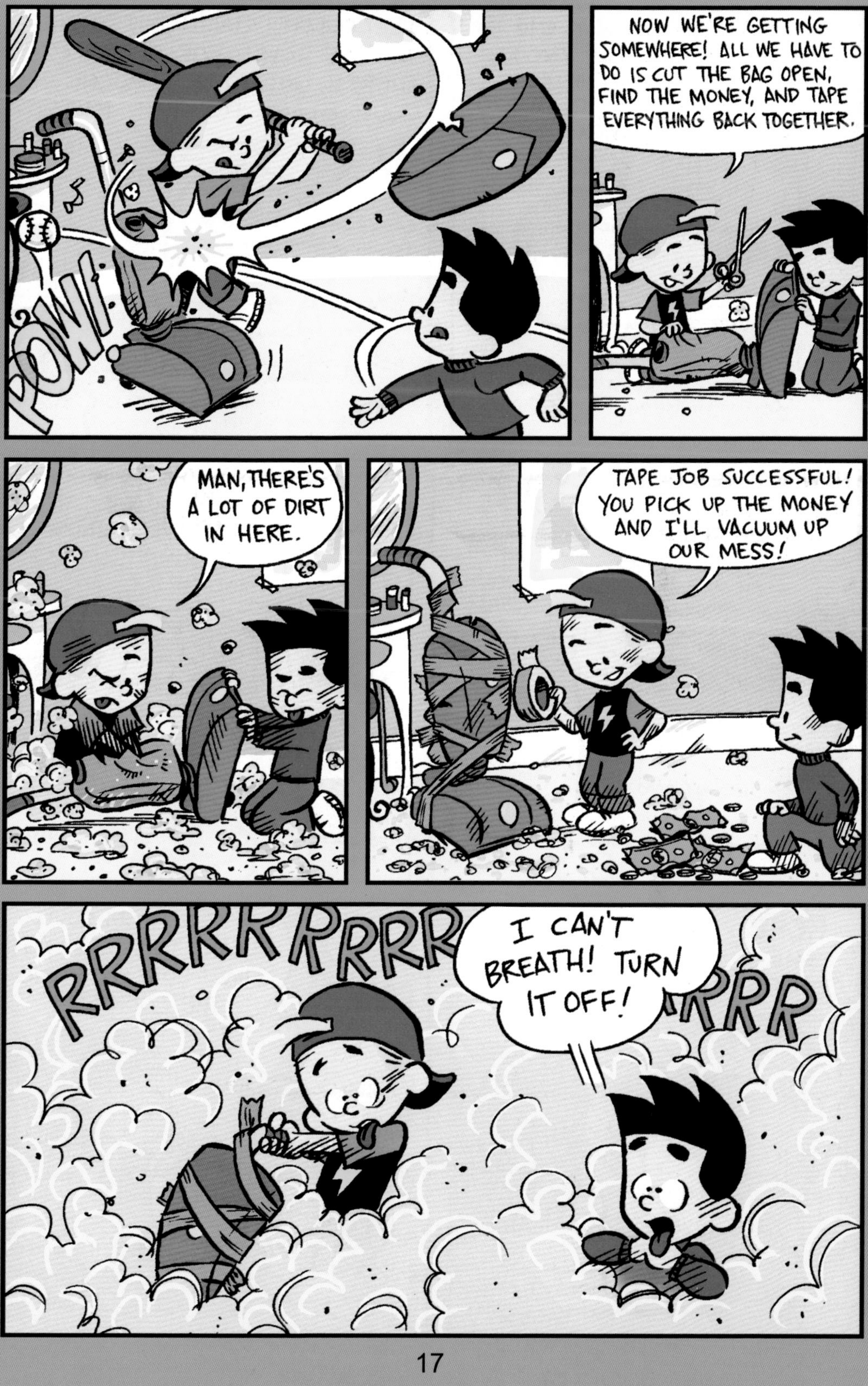
POW!
NOW WE'RE GETTING SOMEWHERE! ALL WE HAVE TO DO IS CUT THE BAG OPEN, FIND THE MONEY, AND TAPE EVERYTHING BACK TOGETHER.
MAN, THERE'S A LOT OF DIRT IN HERE.
TAPE JOB SUCCESSFUL! YOU PICK UP THE MONEY AND I'LL VACUUM UP OUR MESS!
RRRRRRRRRR
I CAN'T BREATH! TURN IT OFF!
RRRR

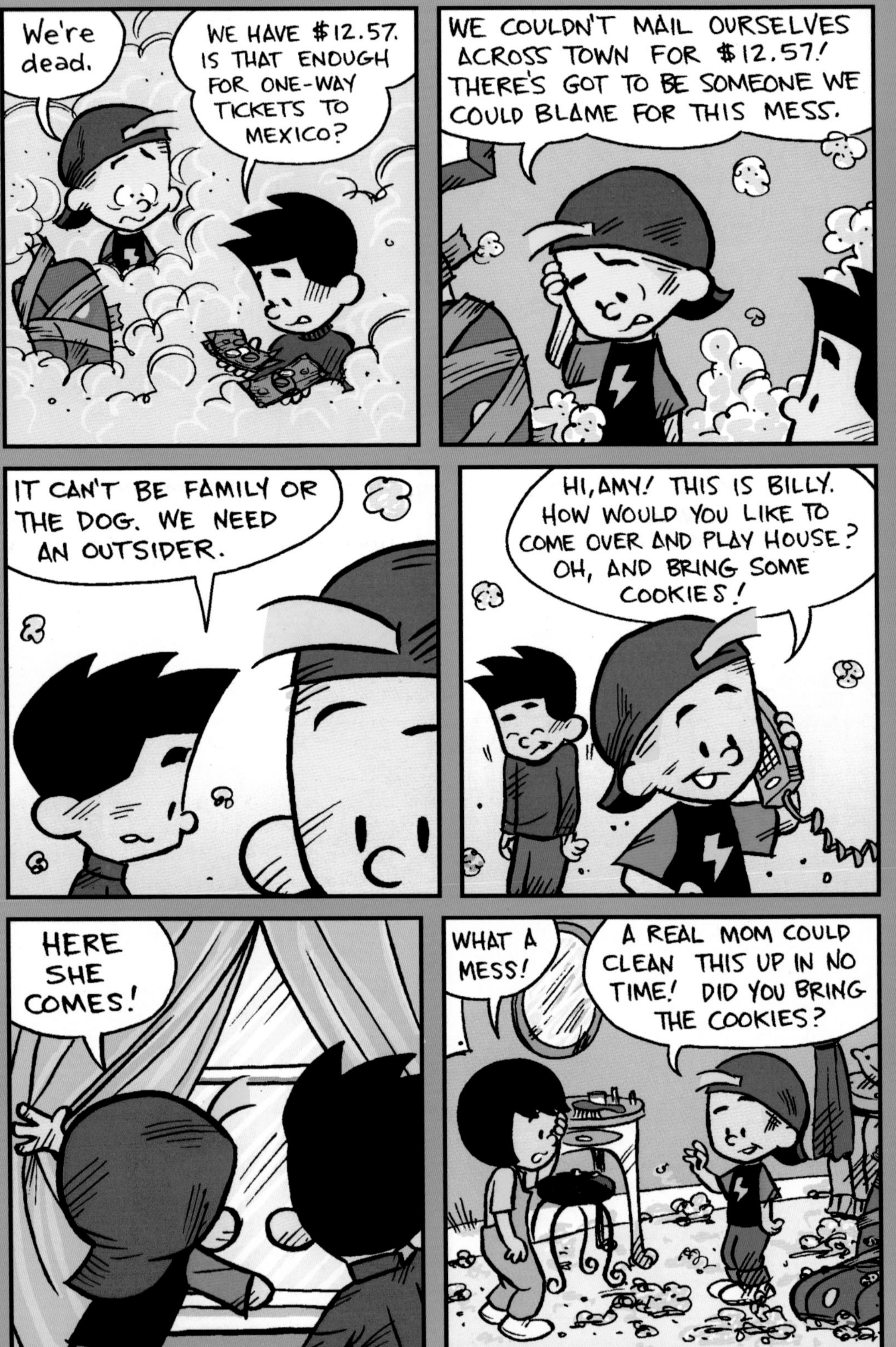
We're dead.
WE HAVE $12.57. IS THAT ENOUGH FOR ONE-WAY TICKETS TO MEXICO?
WE COULDN'T MAIL OURSELVES ACROSS TOWN FOR $12.57! THERE'S GOT TO BE SOMEONE WE COULD BLAME FOR THIS MESS.
IT CAN'T BE FAMILY OR THE DOG. WE NEED AN OUTSIDER.
HI, AMY! THIS IS BILLY. HOW WOULD YOU LIKE TO COME OVER AND PLAY HOUSE? OH, AND BRING SOME COOKIES!
HERE SHE COMES!
WHAT A MESS!
A REAL MOM COULD CLEAN THIS UP IN NO TIME! DID YOU BRING THE COOKIES?

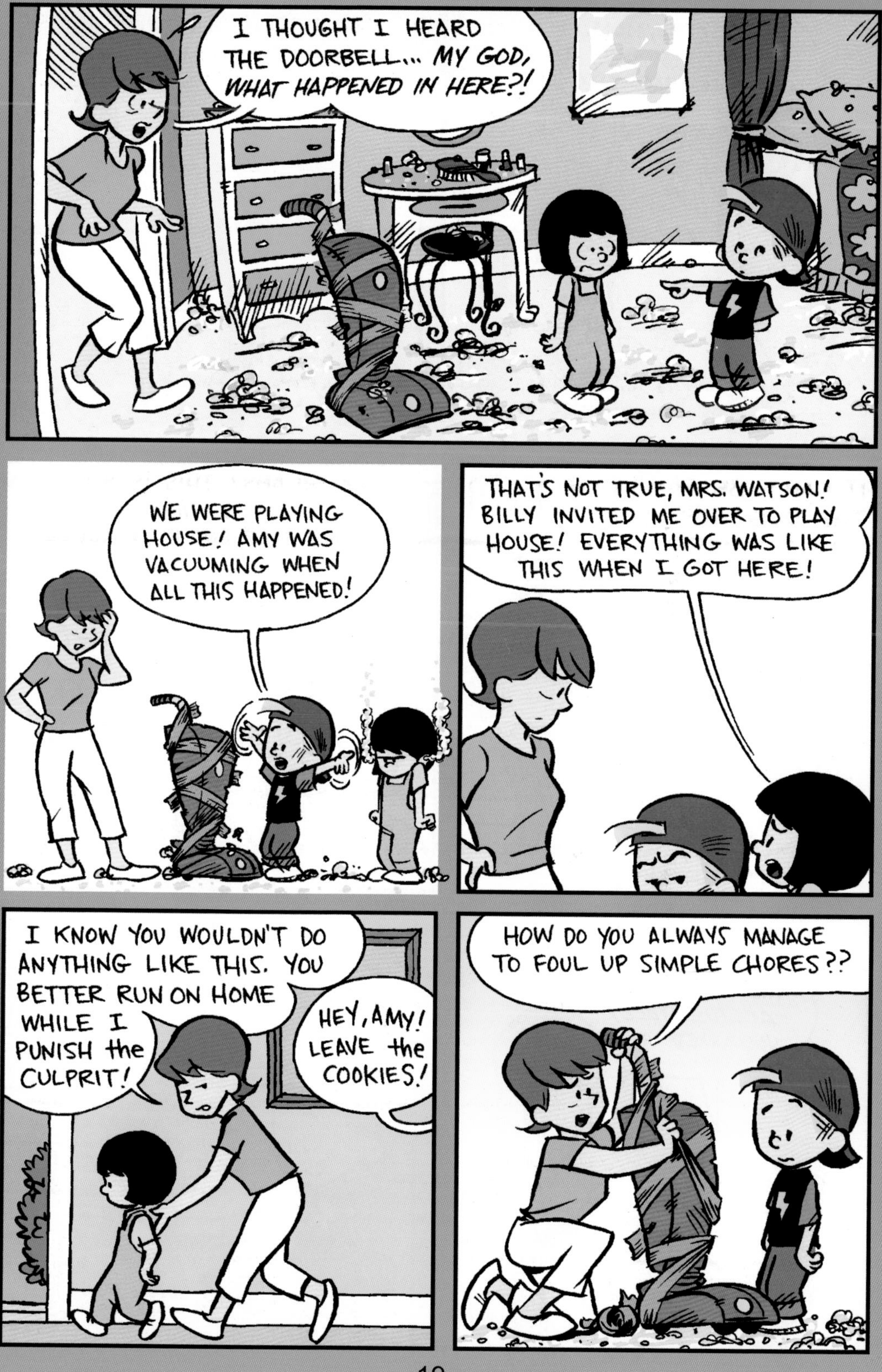
I THOUGHT I HEARD THE DOORBELL... MY GOD, WHAT HAPPENED IN HERE?!
WE WERE PLAYING HOUSE! AMY WAS VACUUMING WHEN ALL THIS HAPPENED!
THAT'S NOT TRUE, MRS. WATSON! BILLY INVITED ME OVER TO PLAY HOUSE! EVERYTHING WAS LIKE THIS WHEN I GOT HERE!
I KNOW YOU WOULDN'T DO ANYTHING LIKE THIS. YOU BETTER RUN ON HOME WHILE I PUNISH the CULPRIT!
HEY, AMY! LEAVE the COOKIES!
HOW DO YOU ALWAYS MANAGE TO FOUL UP SIMPLE CHORES??

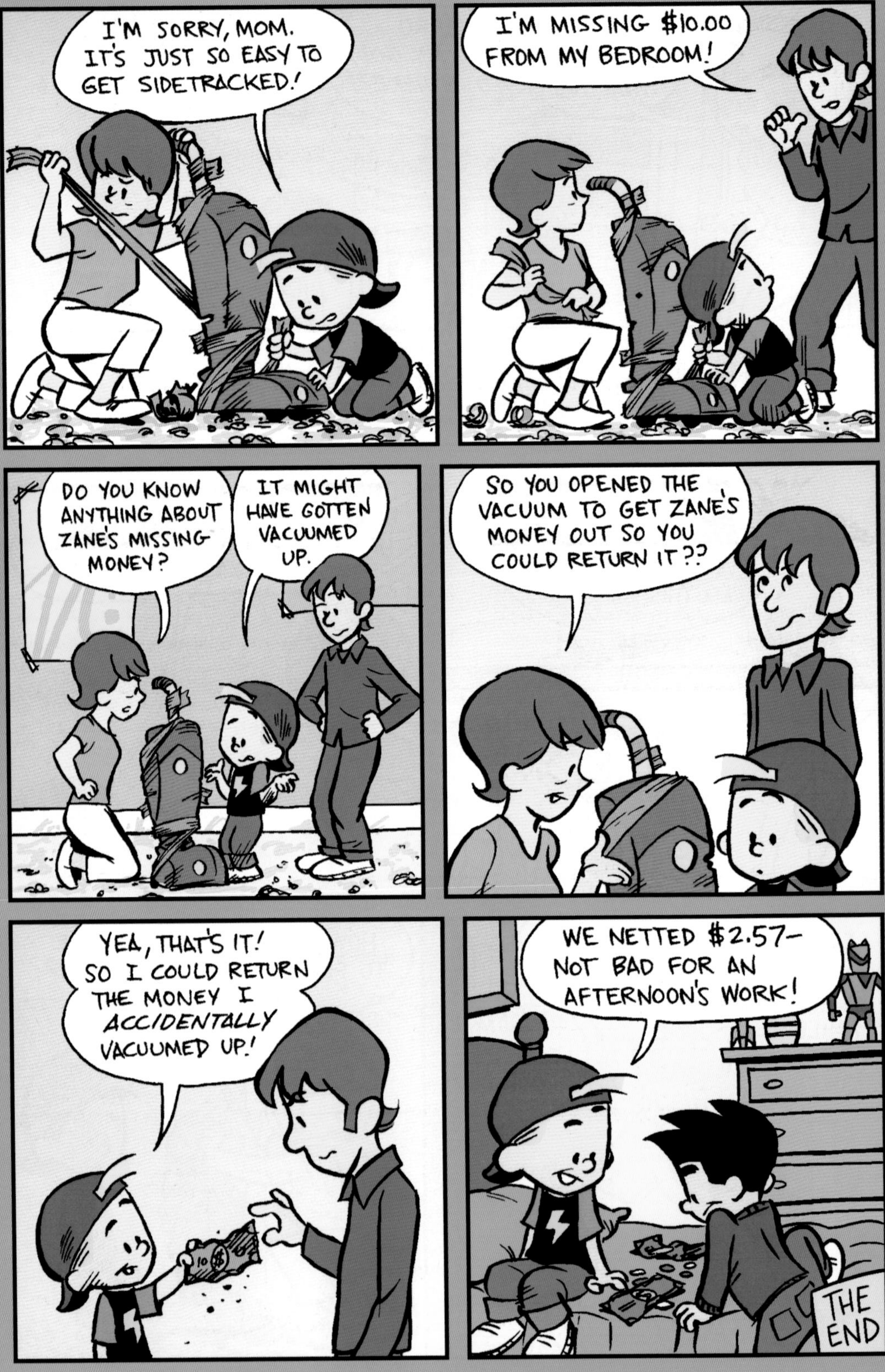
I'M SORRY, MOM. IT'S JUST SO EASY TO GET SIDETRACKED!
I'M MISSING $10.00 FROM MY BEDROOM!
DO YOU KNOW ANYTHING ABOUT ZANE'S MISSING MONEY?
IT MIGHT HAVE GOTTEN VACUUMED UP.
SO YOU OPENED THE VACUUM TO GET ZANE'S MONEY OUT SO YOU COULD RETURN IT??
YEA, THAT'S IT! SO I COULD RETURN THE MONEY I *ACCIDENTALLY* VACUUMED UP!
WE NETTED $2.57– NOT BAD FOR AN AFTERNOON'S WORK!
THE END

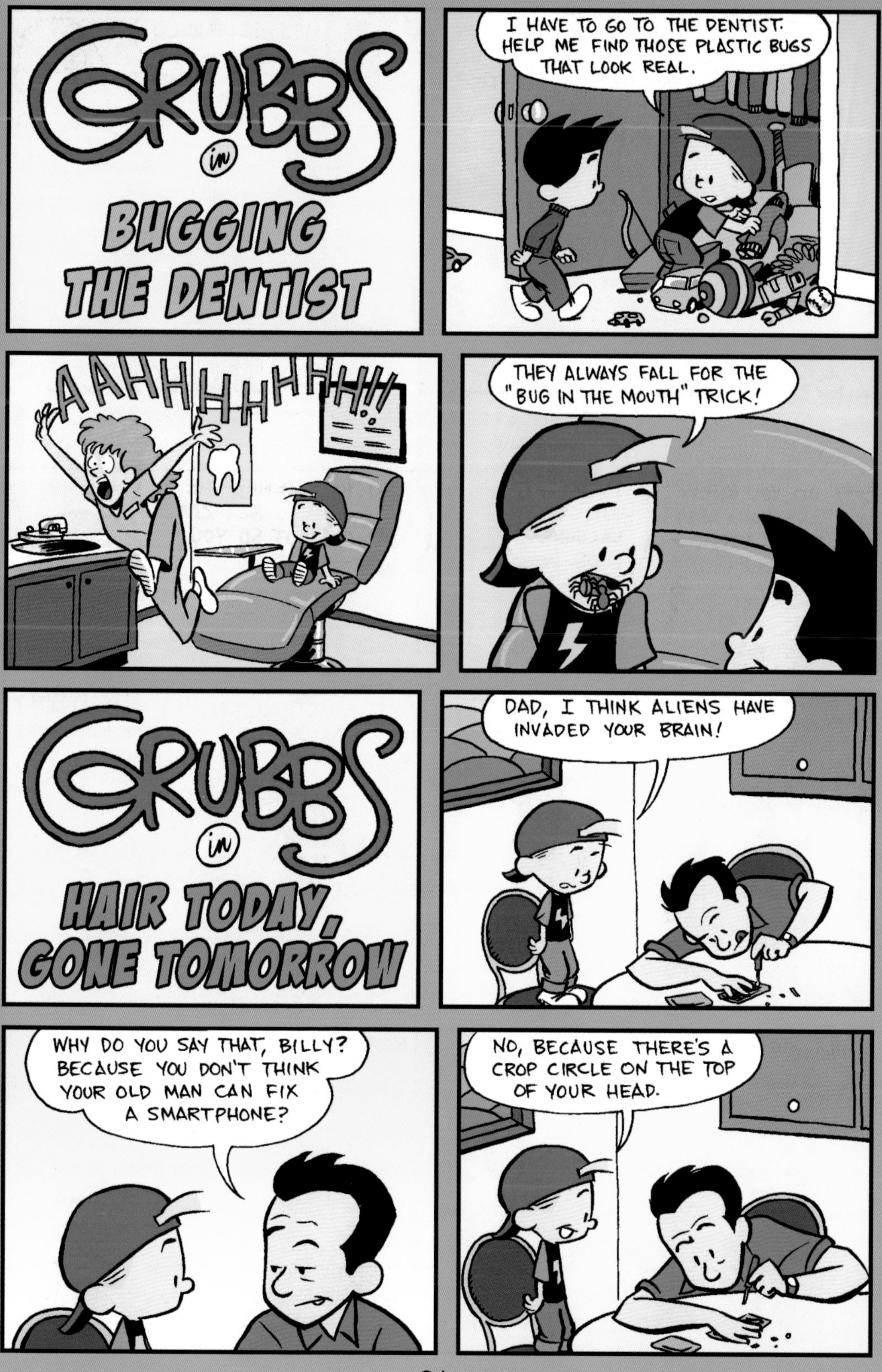
GRUBBS
in
BUGGING THE DENTIST
I HAVE TO GO TO THE DENTIST. HELP ME FIND THOSE PLASTIC BUGS THAT LOOK REAL.
AAHHHHHHHH!!
THEY ALWAYS FALL FOR THE "BUG IN THE MOUTH" TRICK!
GRUBBS
in
HAIR TODAY, GONE TOMORROW
DAD, I THINK ALIENS HAVE INVADED YOUR BRAIN!
WHY DO YOU SAY THAT, BILLY? BECAUSE YOU DON'T THINK YOUR OLD MAN CAN FIX A SMARTPHONE?
NO, BECAUSE THERE'S A CROP CIRCLE ON THE TOP OF YOUR HEAD.

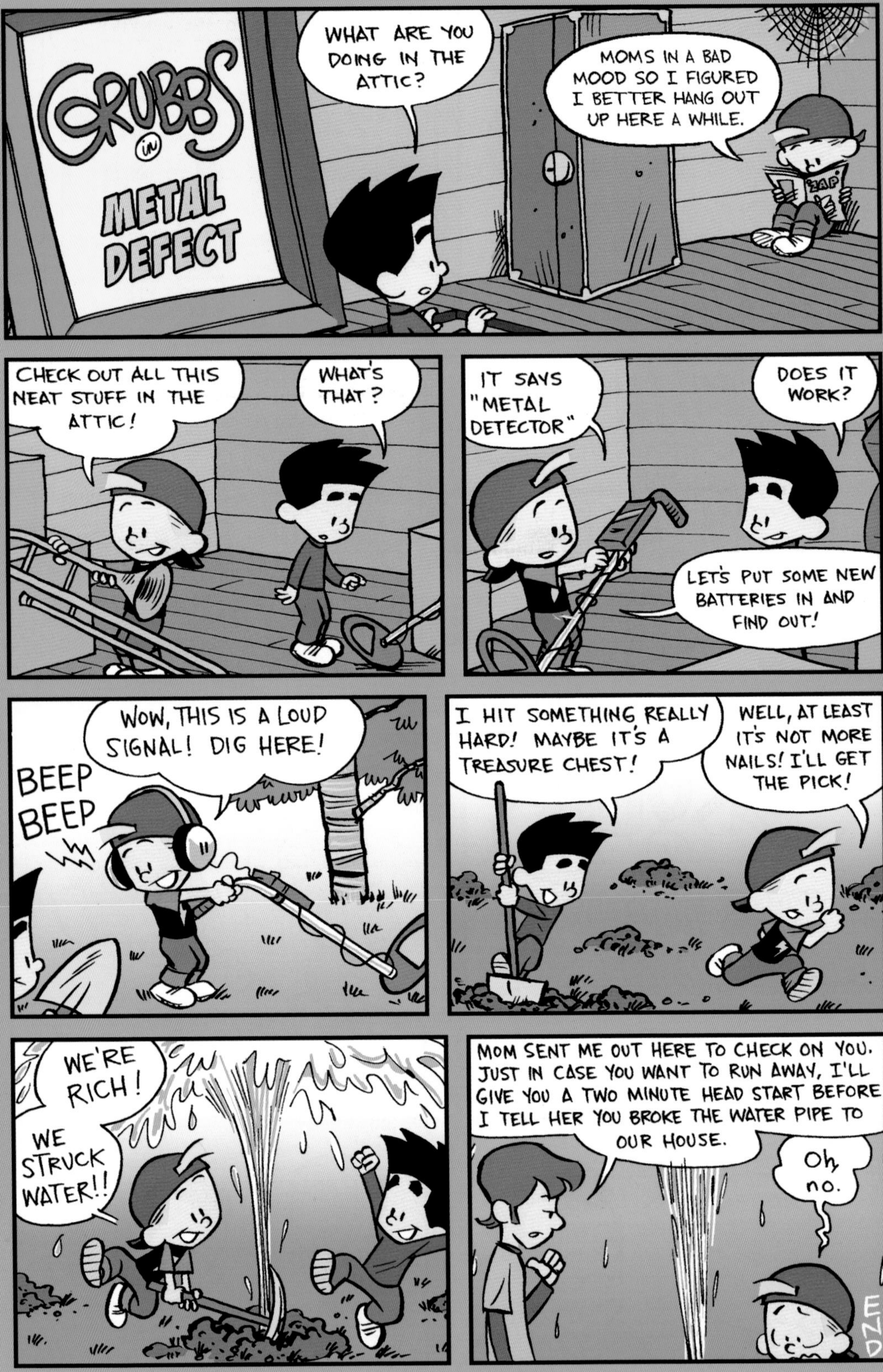
GRUBBS in METAL DEFECT
WHAT ARE YOU DOING IN THE ATTIC?
MOMS IN A BAD MOOD SO I FIGURED I BETTER HANG OUT UP HERE A WHILE.
ZAP
CHECK OUT ALL THIS NEAT STUFF IN THE ATTIC!
WHAT'S THAT?
IT SAYS "METAL DETECTOR"
DOES IT WORK?
LET'S PUT SOME NEW BATTERIES IN AND FIND OUT!
WOW, THIS IS A LOUD SIGNAL! DIG HERE!
BEEP BEEP
I HIT SOMETHING REALLY HARD! MAYBE IT'S A TREASURE CHEST!
WELL, AT LEAST IT'S NOT MORE NAILS! I'LL GET THE PICK!
WE'RE RICH!
WE STRUCK WATER!!
MOM SENT ME OUT HERE TO CHECK ON YOU. JUST IN CASE YOU WANT TO RUN AWAY, I'LL GIVE YOU A TWO MINUTE HEAD START BEFORE I TELL HER YOU BROKE THE WATER PIPE TO OUR HOUSE.
Oh, no.
END

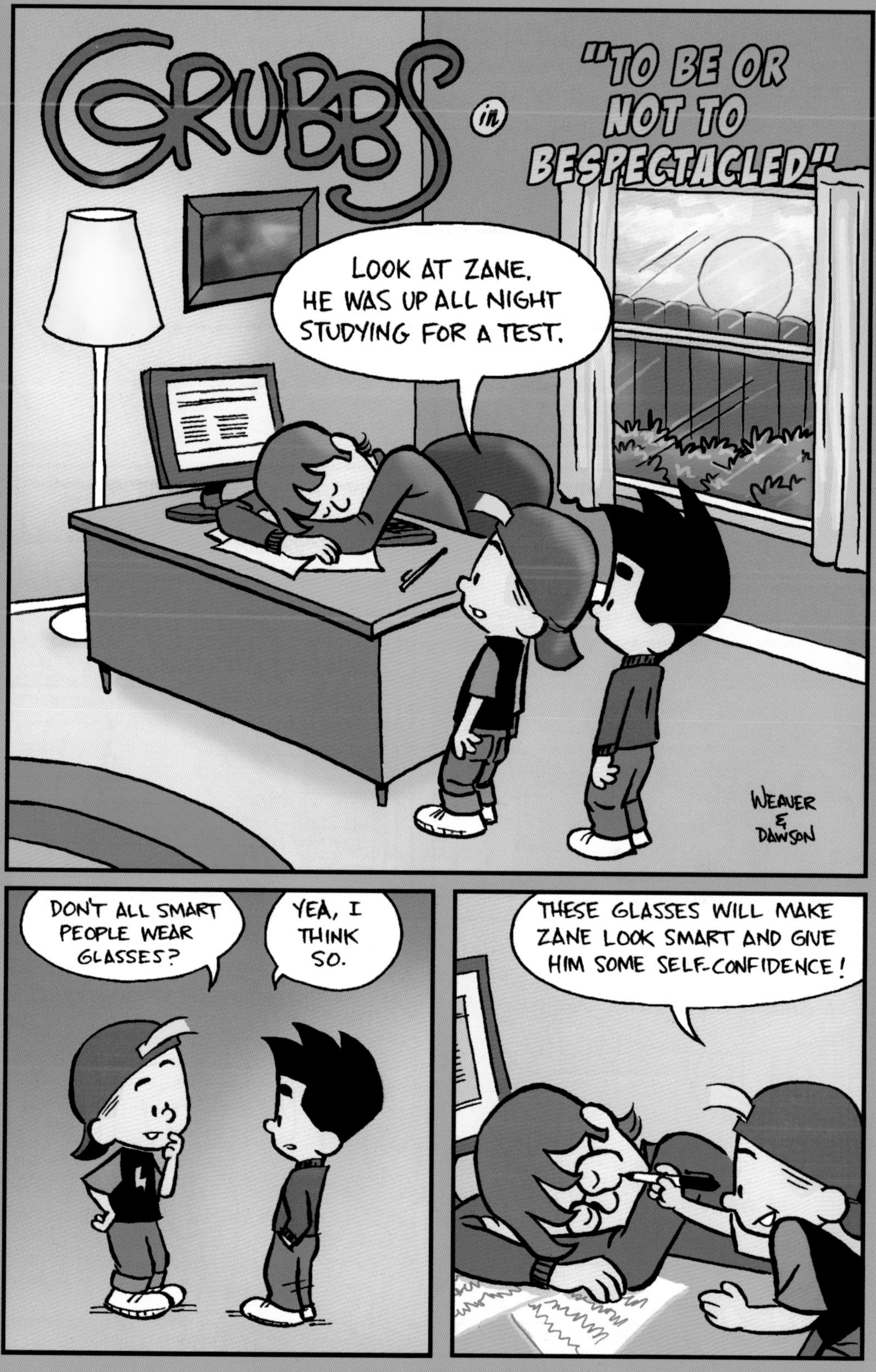
GRUBBS in
"TO BE OR NOT TO BESPECTACLED"
LOOK AT ZANE. HE WAS UP ALL NIGHT STUDYING FOR A TEST.
WEAVER & DAWSON
DON'T ALL SMART PEOPLE WEAR GLASSES?
YEA, I THINK SO.
THESE GLASSES WILL MAKE ZANE LOOK SMART AND GIVE HIM SOME SELF-CONFIDENCE!

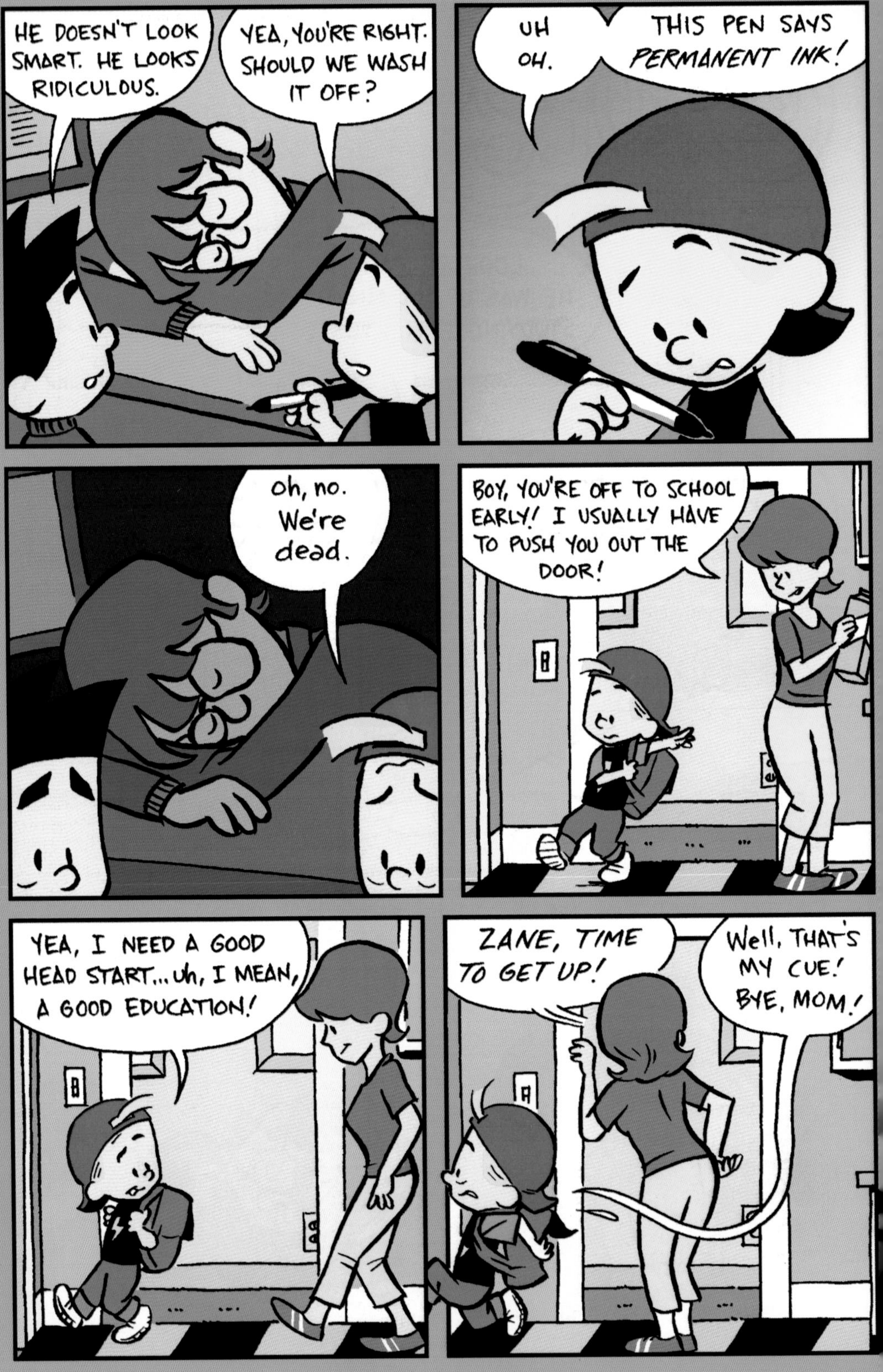
HE DOESN'T LOOK SMART. HE LOOKS RIDICULOUS.
YEA, YOU'RE RIGHT. SHOULD WE WASH IT OFF?
UH OH.
THIS PEN SAYS PERMANENT INK!
oh, no. We're dead.
BOY, YOU'RE OFF TO SCHOOL EARLY! I USUALLY HAVE TO PUSH YOU OUT THE DOOR!
YEA, I NEED A GOOD HEAD START... uh, I MEAN, A GOOD EDUCATION!
ZANE, TIME TO GET UP!
Well, THAT'S MY CUE! BYE, MOM!

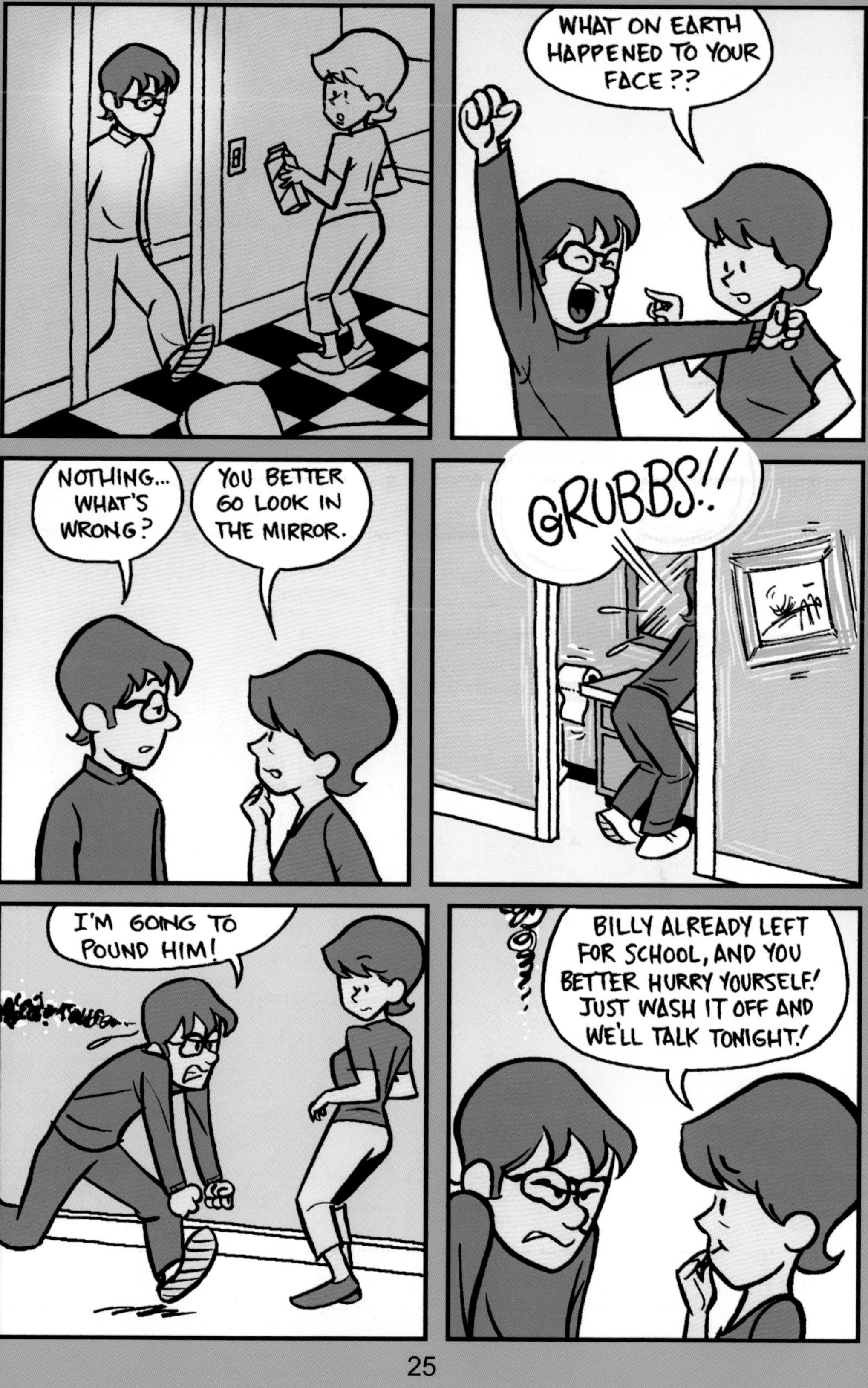
WHAT ON EARTH HAPPENED TO YOUR FACE??
NOTHING... WHAT'S WRONG?
YOU BETTER GO LOOK IN THE MIRROR.
GRUBBS!!
I'M GOING TO POUND HIM!
BILLY ALREADY LEFT FOR SCHOOL, AND YOU BETTER HURRY YOURSELF! JUST WASH IT OFF AND WE'LL TALK TONIGHT!

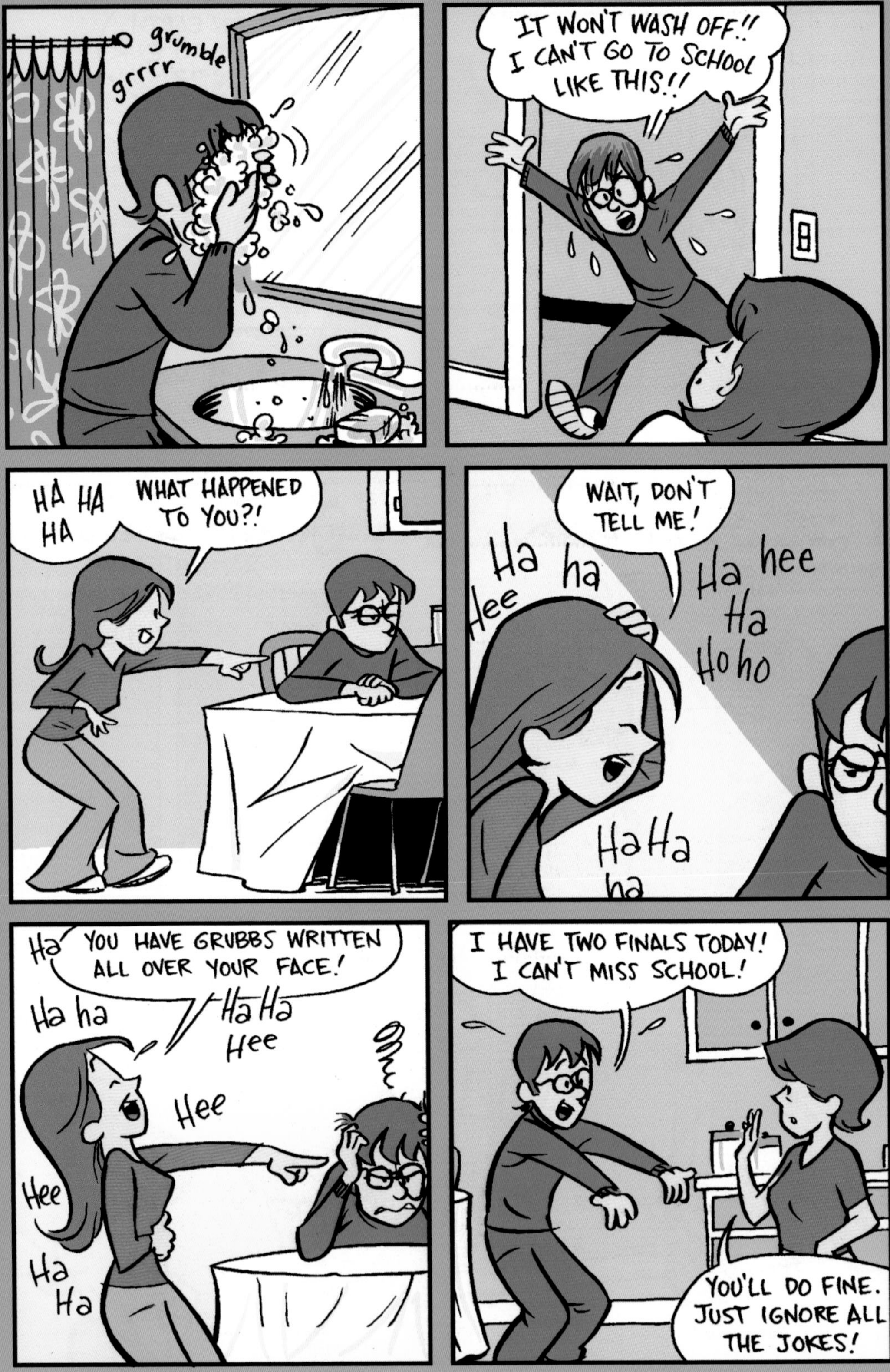
grumble
grrrr
IT WON'T WASH OFF!! I CAN'T GO TO SCHOOL LIKE THIS!!
HA HA HA
WHAT HAPPENED TO YOU?!
WAIT, DON'T TELL ME!
Ha Hee ha
Ha hee Ha Ho ho
HaHa ha
Ha
YOU HAVE GRUBBS WRITTEN ALL OVER YOUR FACE!
Ha ha
Ha Ha Hee
Hee
Hee
Ha Ha
I HAVE TWO FINALS TODAY! I CAN'T MISS SCHOOL!
YOU'LL DO FINE. JUST IGNORE ALL THE JOKES!

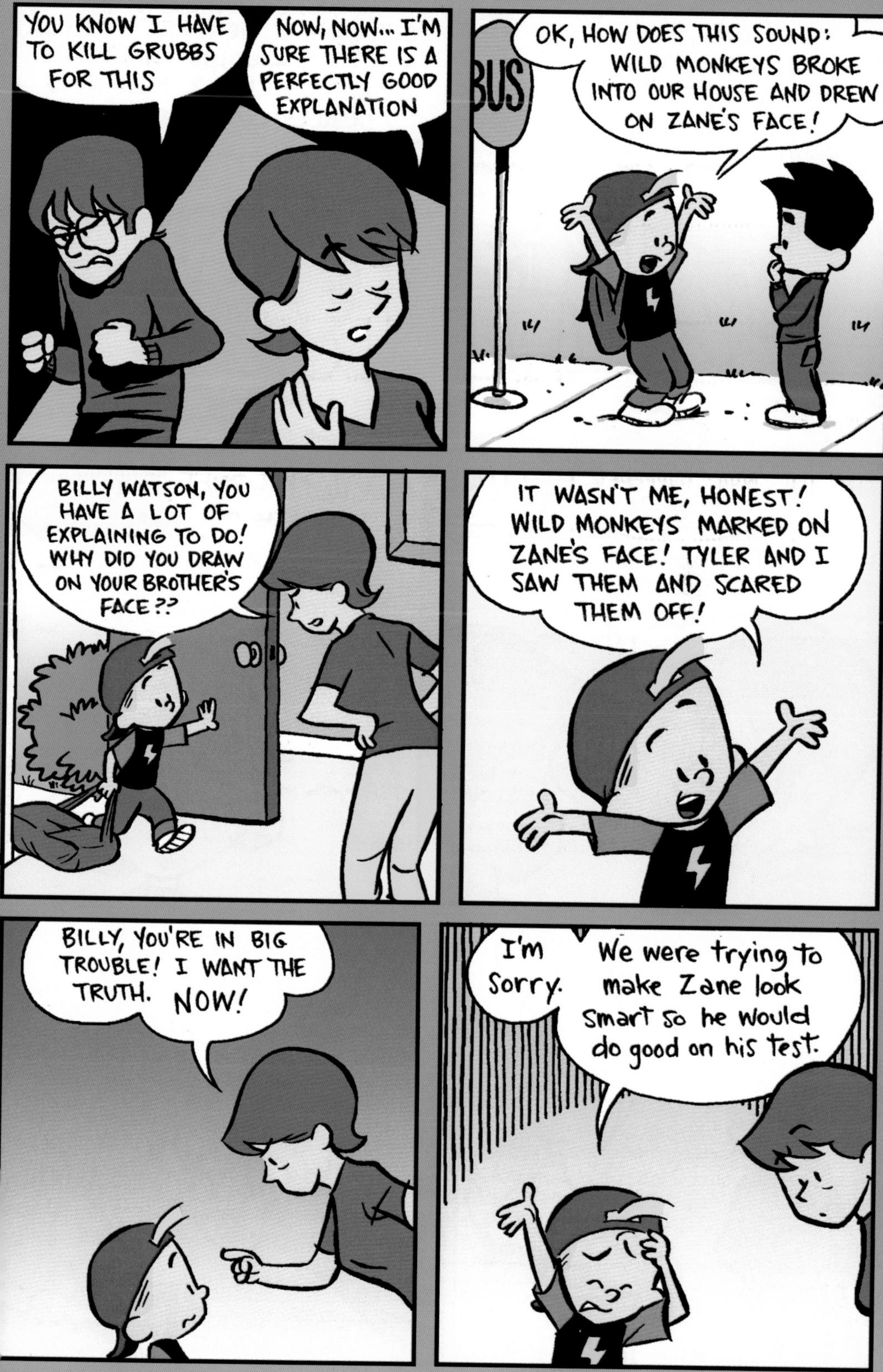
YOU KNOW I HAVE TO KILL GRUBBS FOR THIS
NOW, NOW... I'M SURE THERE IS A PERFECTLY GOOD EXPLANATION
OK, HOW DOES THIS SOUND: WILD MONKEYS BROKE INTO OUR HOUSE AND DREW ON ZANE'S FACE!
BUS
BILLY WATSON, YOU HAVE A LOT OF EXPLAINING TO DO! WHY DID YOU DRAW ON YOUR BROTHER'S FACE??
IT WASN'T ME, HONEST! WILD MONKEYS MARKED ON ZANE'S FACE! TYLER AND I SAW THEM AND SCARED THEM OFF!
BILLY, YOU'RE IN BIG TROUBLE! I WANT THE TRUTH. NOW!
I'm Sorry.
We were trying to make Zane look smart so he would do good on his test.

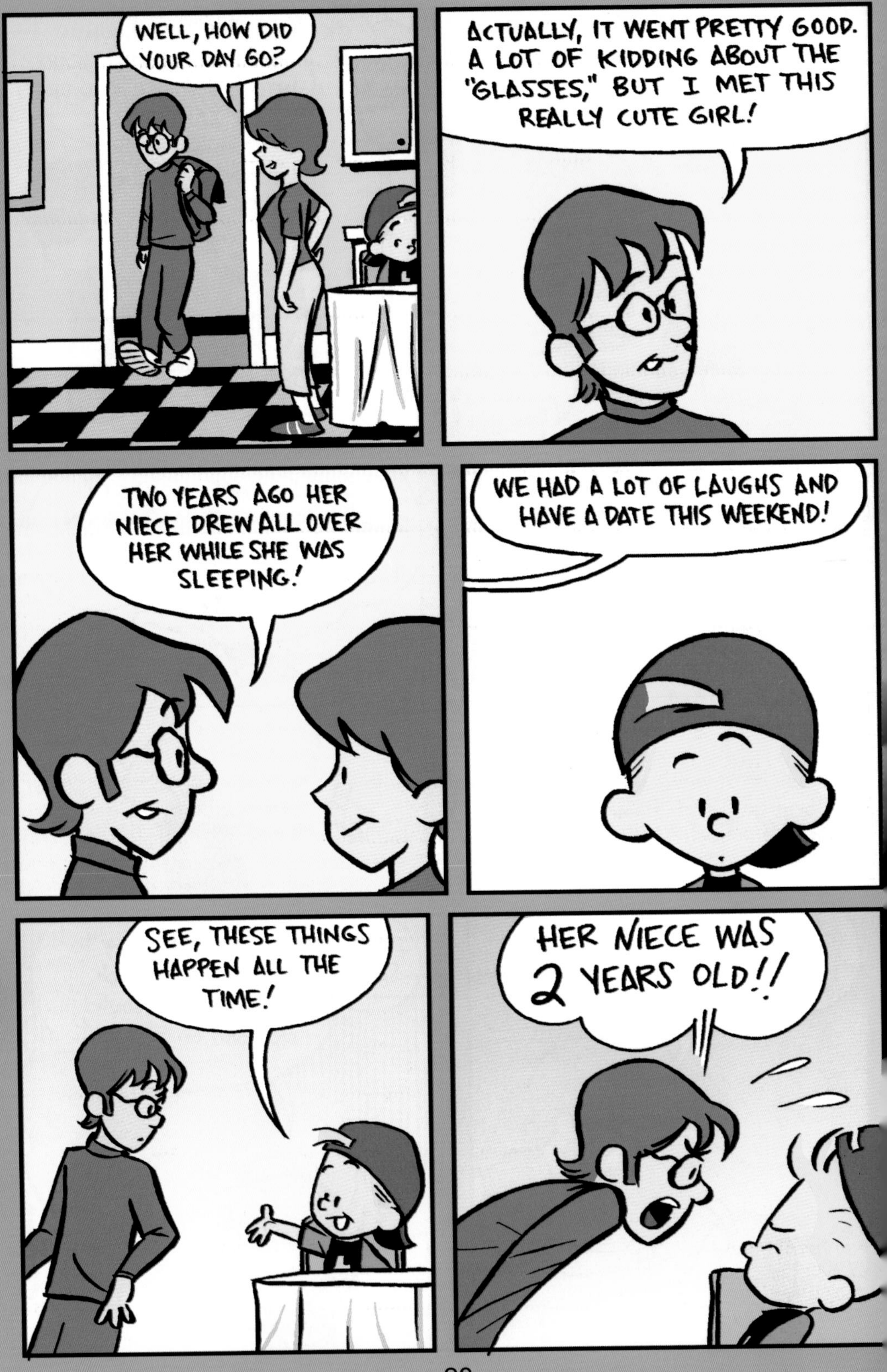
WELL, HOW DID YOUR DAY GO?
ACTUALLY, IT WENT PRETTY GOOD. A LOT OF KIDDING ABOUT THE "GLASSES," BUT I MET THIS REALLY CUTE GIRL!
TWO YEARS AGO HER NIECE DREW ALL OVER HER WHILE SHE WAS SLEEPING!
WE HAD A LOT OF LAUGHS AND HAVE A DATE THIS WEEKEND!
SEE, THESE THINGS HAPPEN ALL THE TIME!
HER NIECE WAS 2 YEARS OLD!!

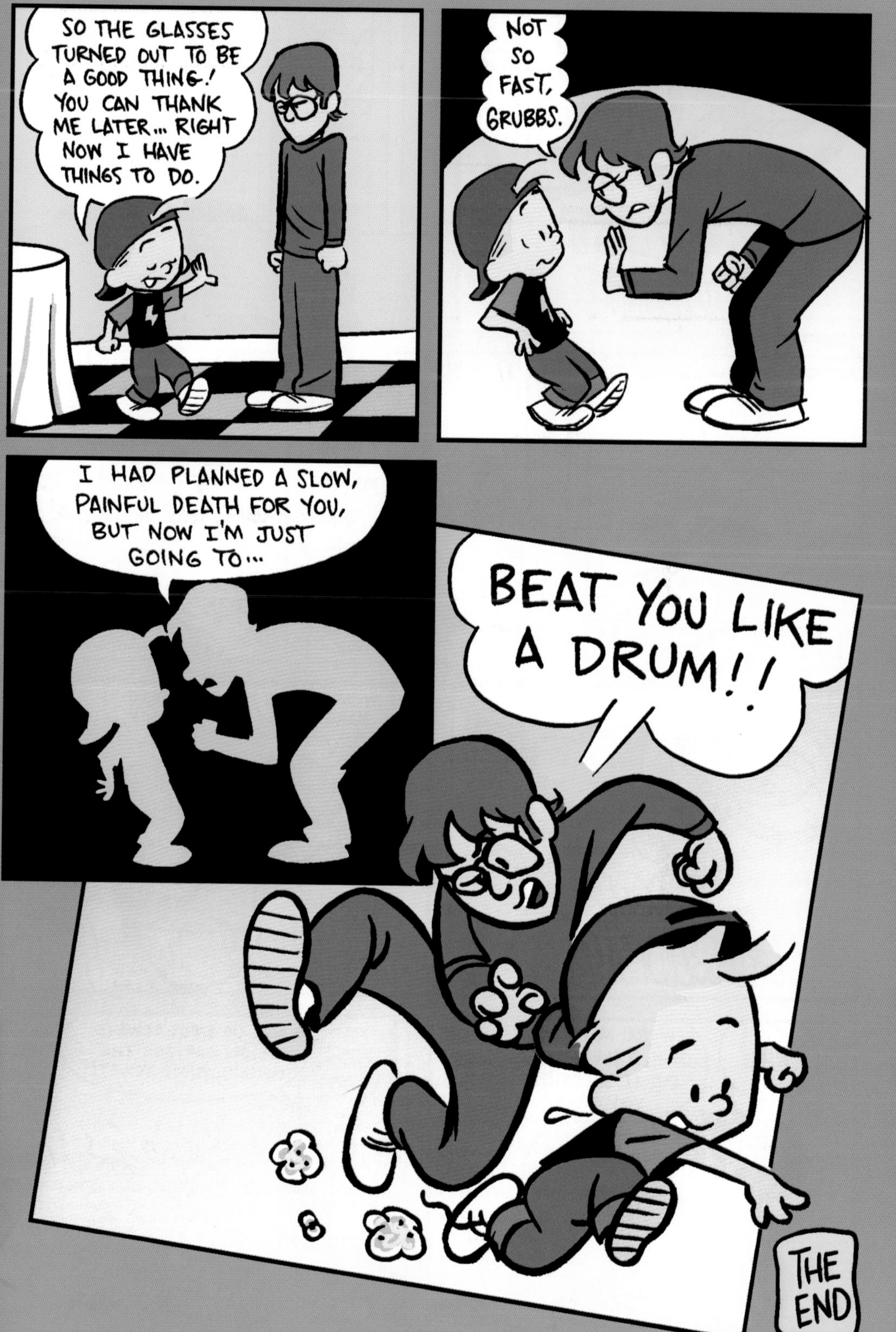
SO THE GLASSES TURNED OUT TO BE A GOOD THING! YOU CAN THANK ME LATER... RIGHT NOW I HAVE THINGS TO DO.
NOT SO FAST, GRUBBS.
I HAD PLANNED A SLOW, PAINFUL DEATH FOR YOU, BUT NOW I'M JUST GOING TO...
BEAT YOU LIKE A DRUM!!
THE END

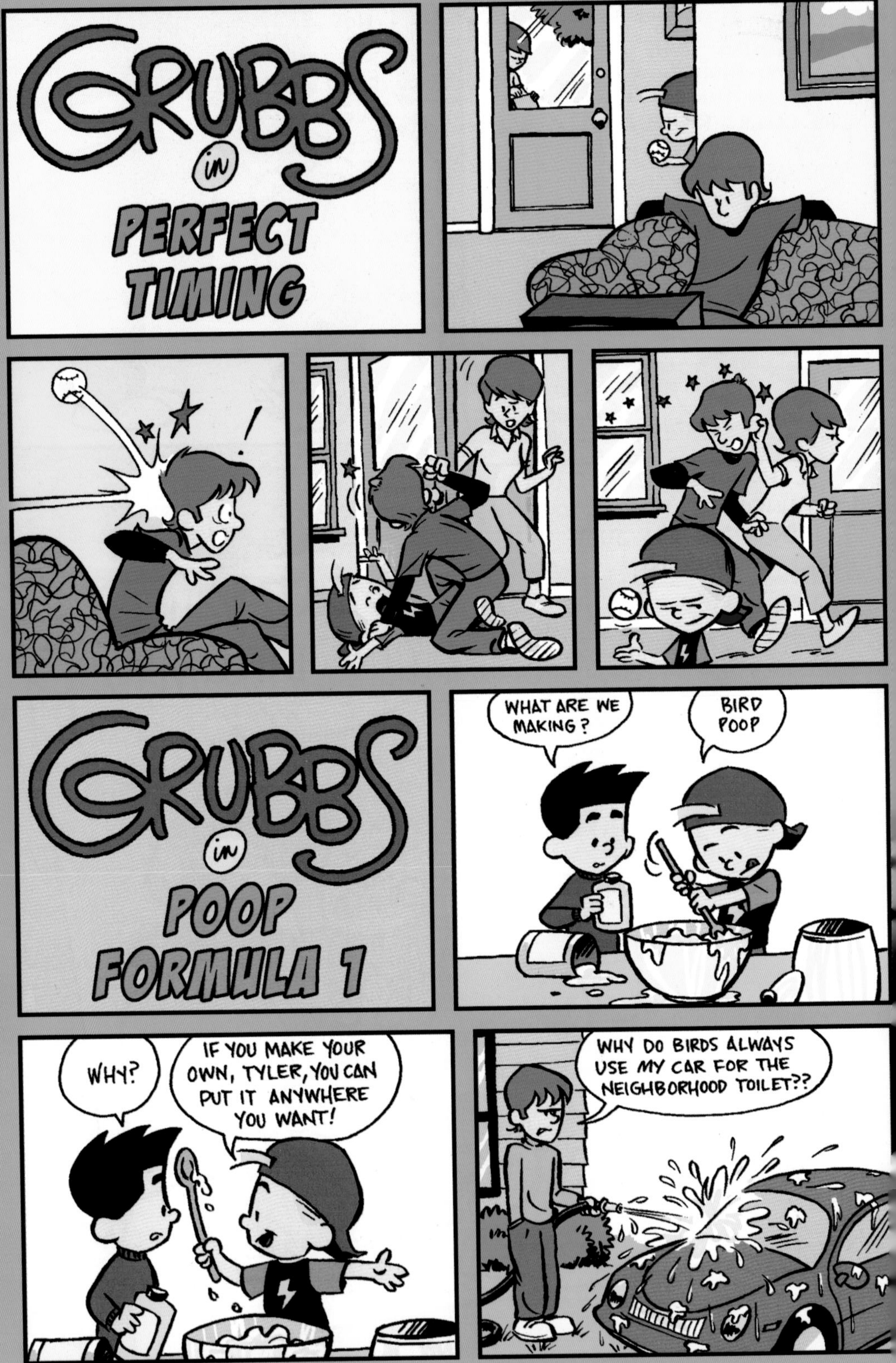
GRUBBS
in
PERFECT TIMING
!
GRUBBS
in
POOP FORMULA 1
WHAT ARE WE MAKING?
BIRD POOP
WHY?
IF YOU MAKE YOUR OWN, TYLER, YOU CAN PUT IT ANYWHERE YOU WANT!
WHY DO BIRDS ALWAYS USE MY CAR FOR THE NEIGHBORHOOD TOILET??

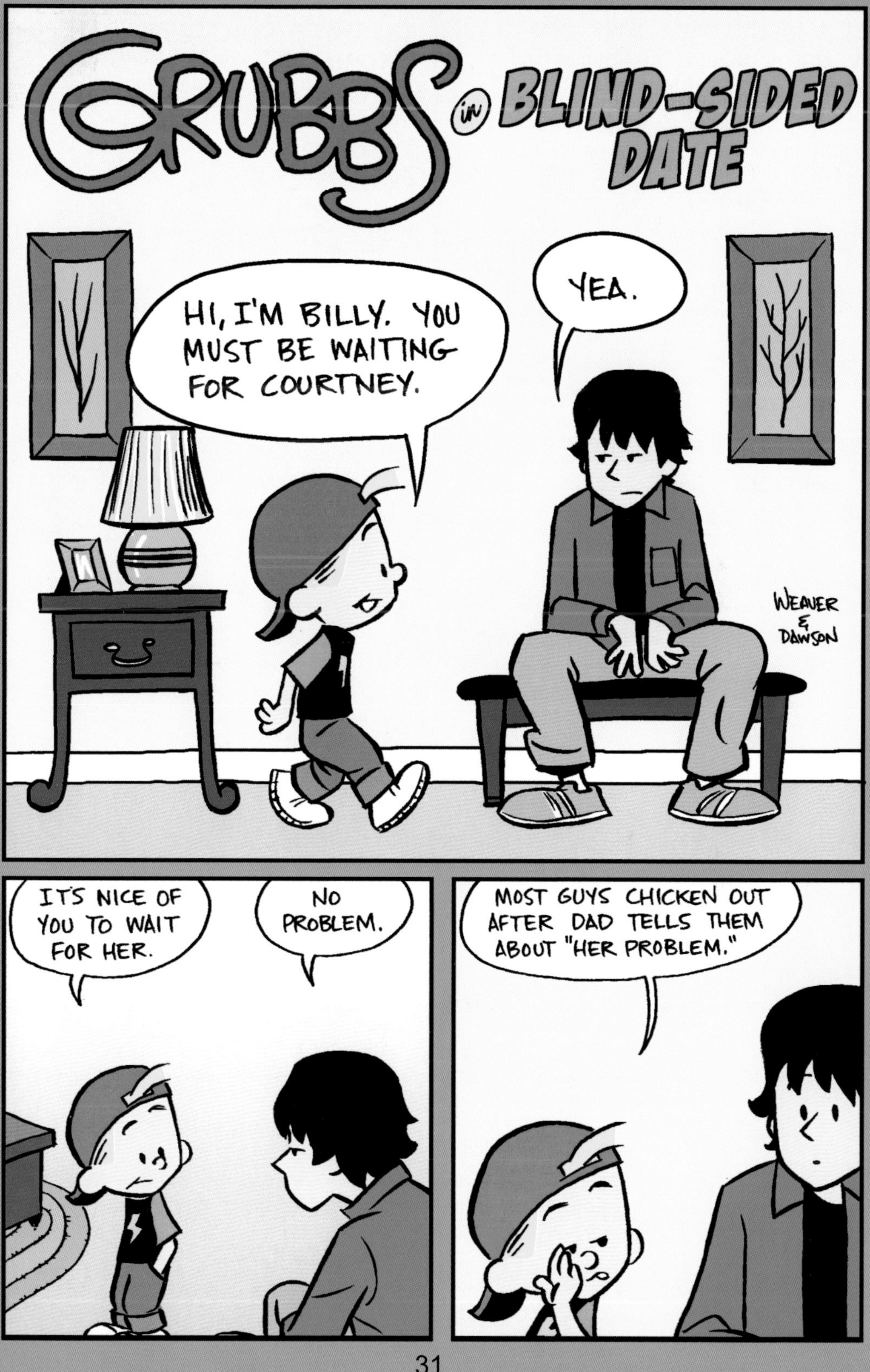
GRUBBS in BLIND-SIDED DATE
HI, I'M BILLY. YOU MUST BE WAITING FOR COURTNEY.
YEA.
WEAVER & DAWSON
IT'S NICE OF YOU TO WAIT FOR HER.
NO PROBLEM.
MOST GUYS CHICKEN OUT AFTER DAD TELLS THEM ABOUT "HER PROBLEM."

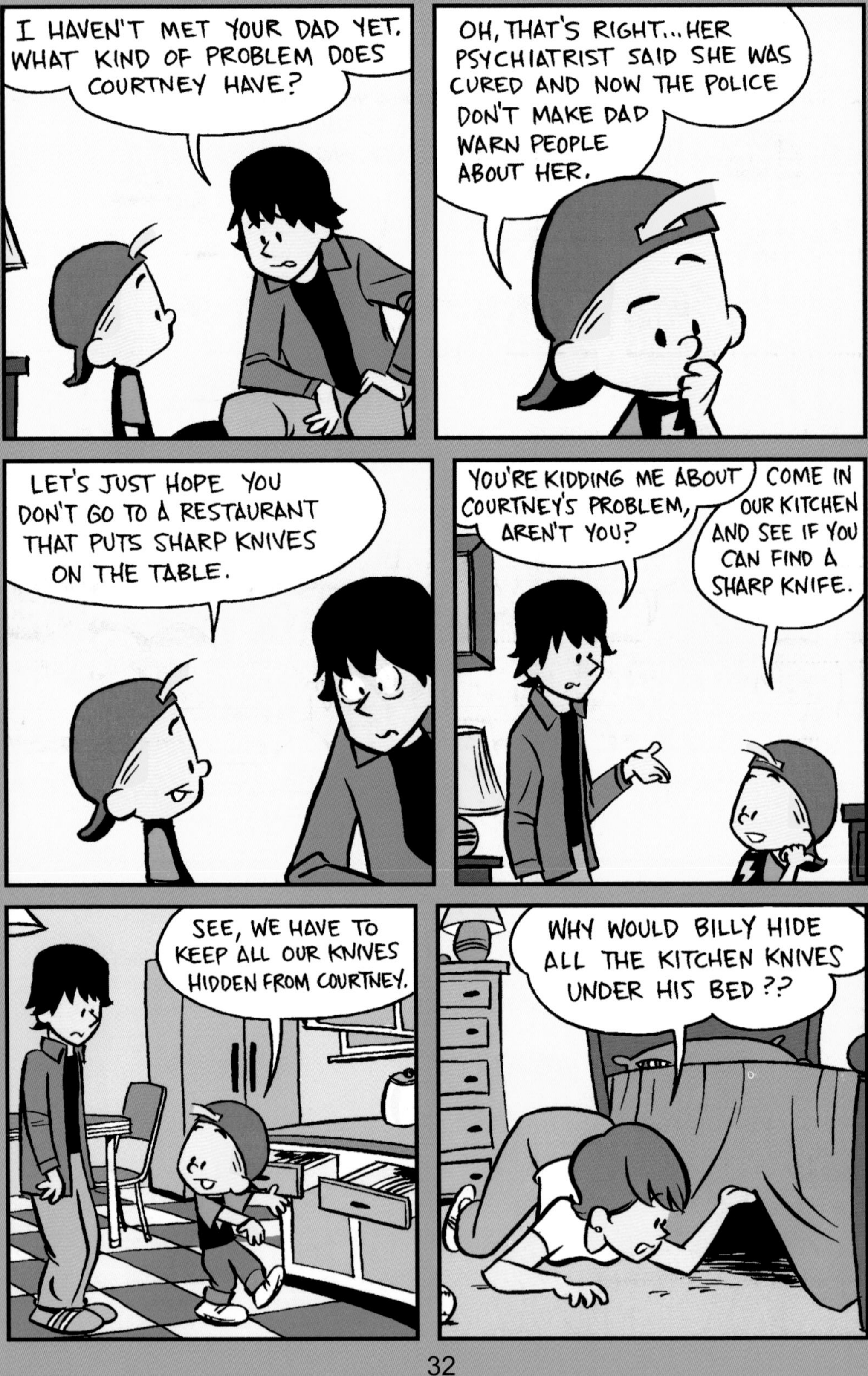
I HAVEN'T MET YOUR DAD YET. WHAT KIND OF PROBLEM DOES COURTNEY HAVE?
OH, THAT'S RIGHT... HER PSYCHIATRIST SAID SHE WAS CURED AND NOW THE POLICE DON'T MAKE DAD WARN PEOPLE ABOUT HER.
LET'S JUST HOPE YOU DON'T GO TO A RESTAURANT THAT PUTS SHARP KNIVES ON THE TABLE.
YOU'RE KIDDING ME ABOUT COURTNEY'S PROBLEM, AREN'T YOU?
COME IN OUR KITCHEN AND SEE IF YOU CAN FIND A SHARP KNIFE.
SEE, WE HAVE TO KEEP ALL OUR KNIVES HIDDEN FROM COURTNEY.
WHY WOULD BILLY HIDE ALL THE KITCHEN KNIVES UNDER HIS BED ??

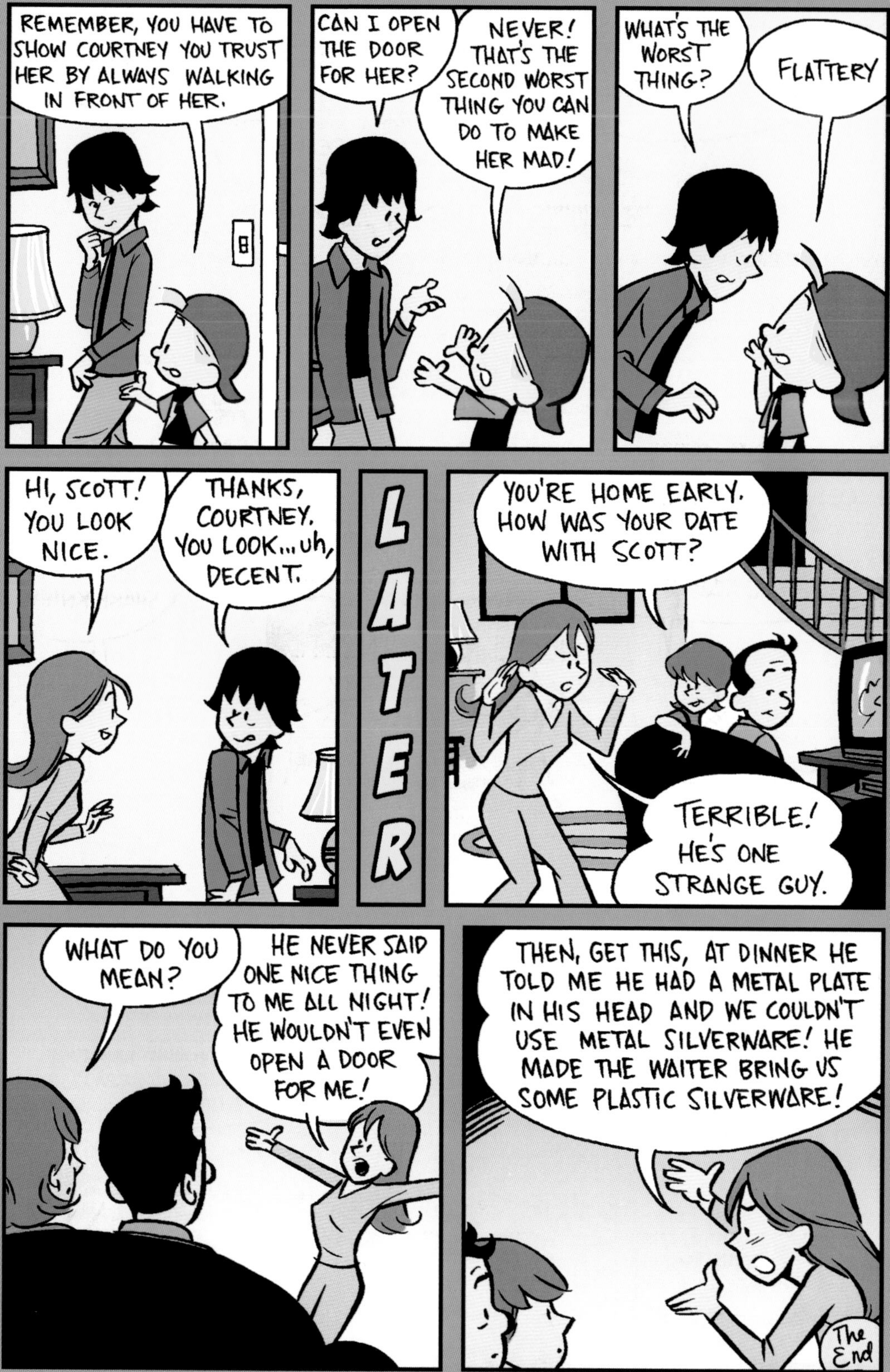

REMEMBER, YOU HAVE TO SHOW COURTNEY YOU TRUST HER BY ALWAYS WALKING IN FRONT OF HER.
CAN I OPEN THE DOOR FOR HER?
NEVER! THAT'S THE SECOND WORST THING YOU CAN DO TO MAKE HER MAD!
WHAT'S THE WORST THING?
FLATTERY
HI, SCOTT! YOU LOOK NICE.
THANKS, COURTNEY. YOU LOOK...uh, DECENT.
LATER
YOU'RE HOME EARLY. HOW WAS YOUR DATE WITH SCOTT?
TERRIBLE! HE'S ONE STRANGE GUY.
WHAT DO YOU MEAN?
HE NEVER SAID ONE NICE THING TO ME ALL NIGHT! HE WOULDN'T EVEN OPEN A DOOR FOR ME!
THEN, GET THIS, AT DINNER HE TOLD ME HE HAD A METAL PLATE IN HIS HEAD AND WE COULDN'T USE METAL SILVERWARE! HE MADE THE WAITER BRING US SOME PLASTIC SILVERWARE!
The End

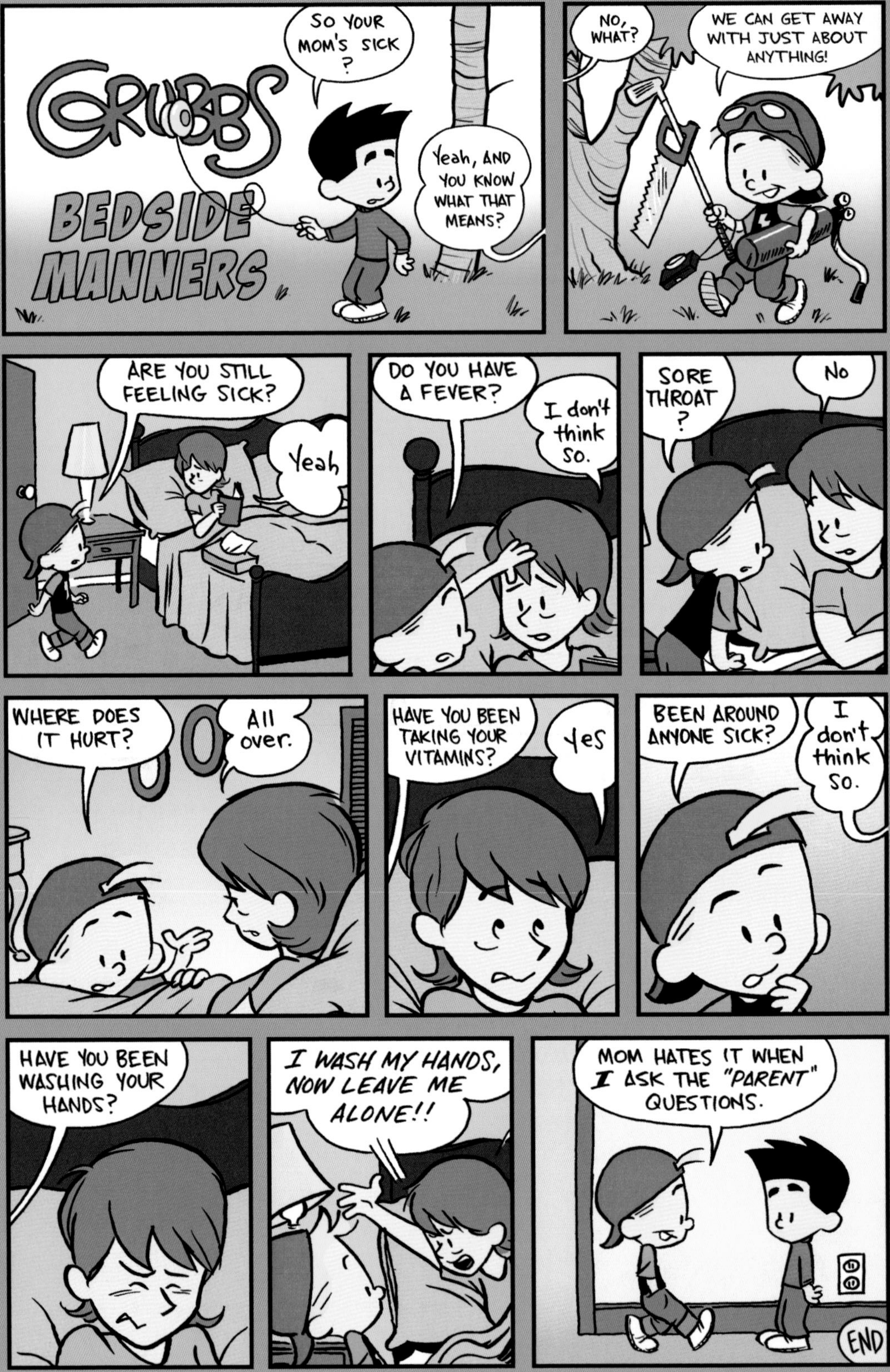
GRUBBS
BEDSIDE MANNERS
SO YOUR MOM'S SICK ?
Yeah, AND YOU KNOW WHAT THAT MEANS?
NO, WHAT?
WE CAN GET AWAY WITH JUST ABOUT ANYTHING!
ARE YOU STILL FEELING SICK?
Yeah
DO YOU HAVE A FEVER?
I don't think so.
SORE THROAT ?
No
WHERE DOES IT HURT?
All over.
HAVE YOU BEEN TAKING YOUR VITAMINS?
Yes
BEEN AROUND ANYONE SICK?
I don't think so.
HAVE YOU BEEN WASHING YOUR HANDS?
I WASH MY HANDS, NOW LEAVE ME ALONE!!
MOM HATES IT WHEN I ASK THE "PARENT" QUESTIONS.
END

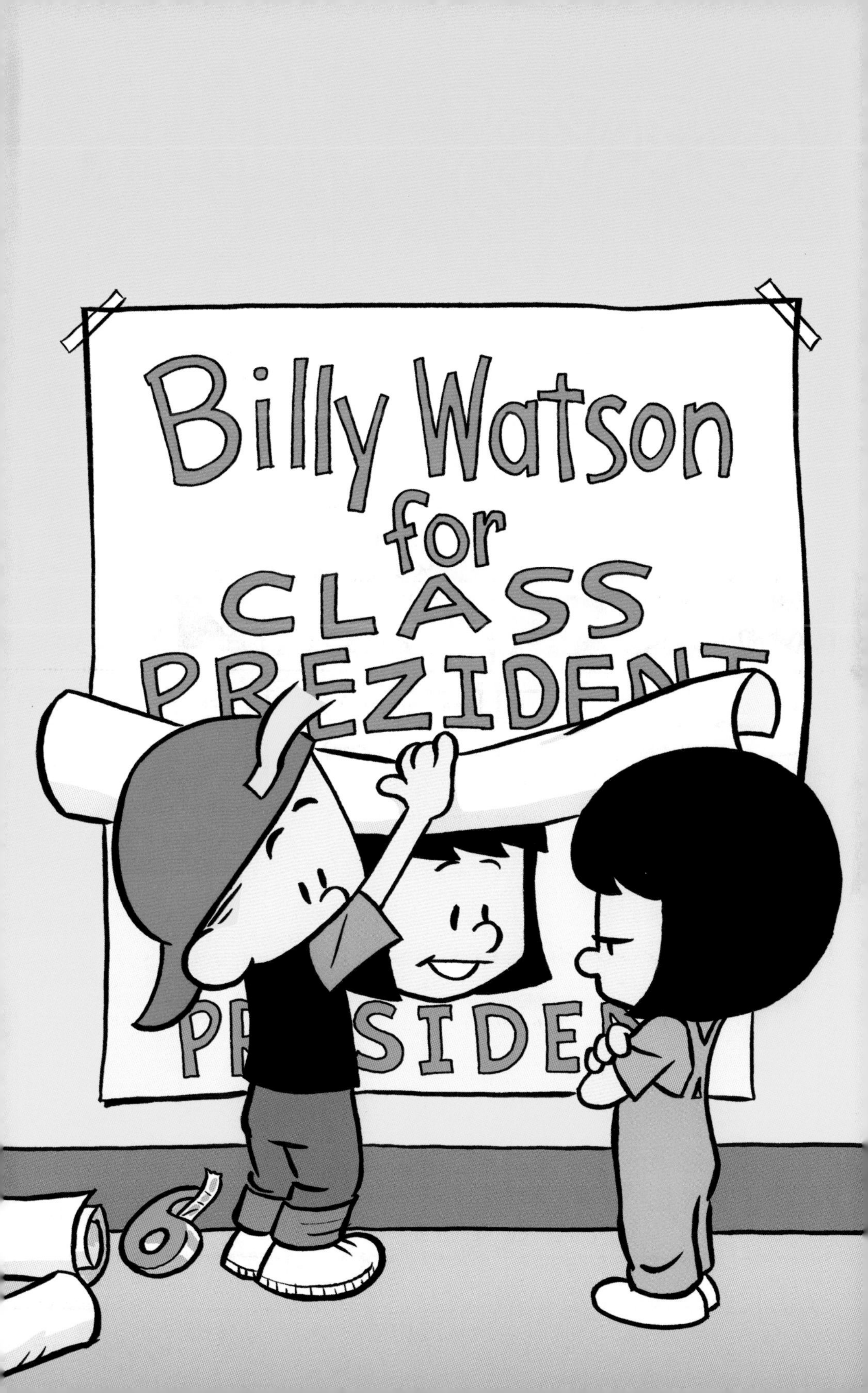
Billy Watson
for
CLASS

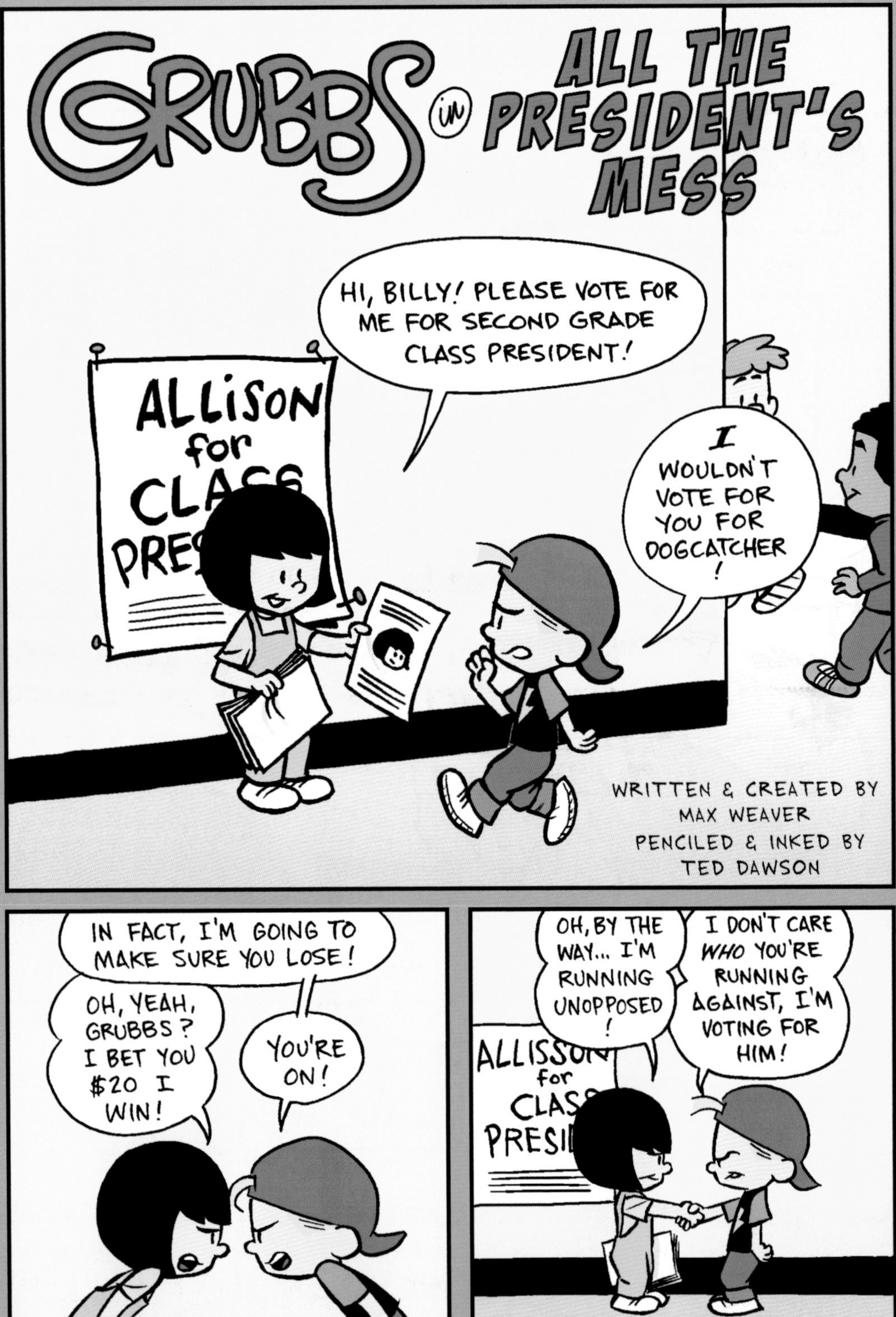
GRUBBS in ALL THE PRESIDENT'S MESS
HI, BILLY! PLEASE VOTE FOR ME FOR SECOND GRADE CLASS PRESIDENT!
ALLISON for CLASS PRES
I WOULDN'T VOTE FOR YOU FOR DOGCATCHER!
WRITTEN & CREATED BY MAX WEAVER
PENCILED & INKED BY TED DAWSON
IN FACT, I'M GOING TO MAKE SURE YOU LOSE!
OH, YEAH, GRUBBS? I BET YOU $20 I WIN!
YOU'RE ON!
OH, BY THE WAY... I'M RUNNING UNOPPOSED!
I DON'T CARE WHO YOU'RE RUNNING AGAINST, I'M VOTING FOR HIM!
ALLISON for CLASS PRESI

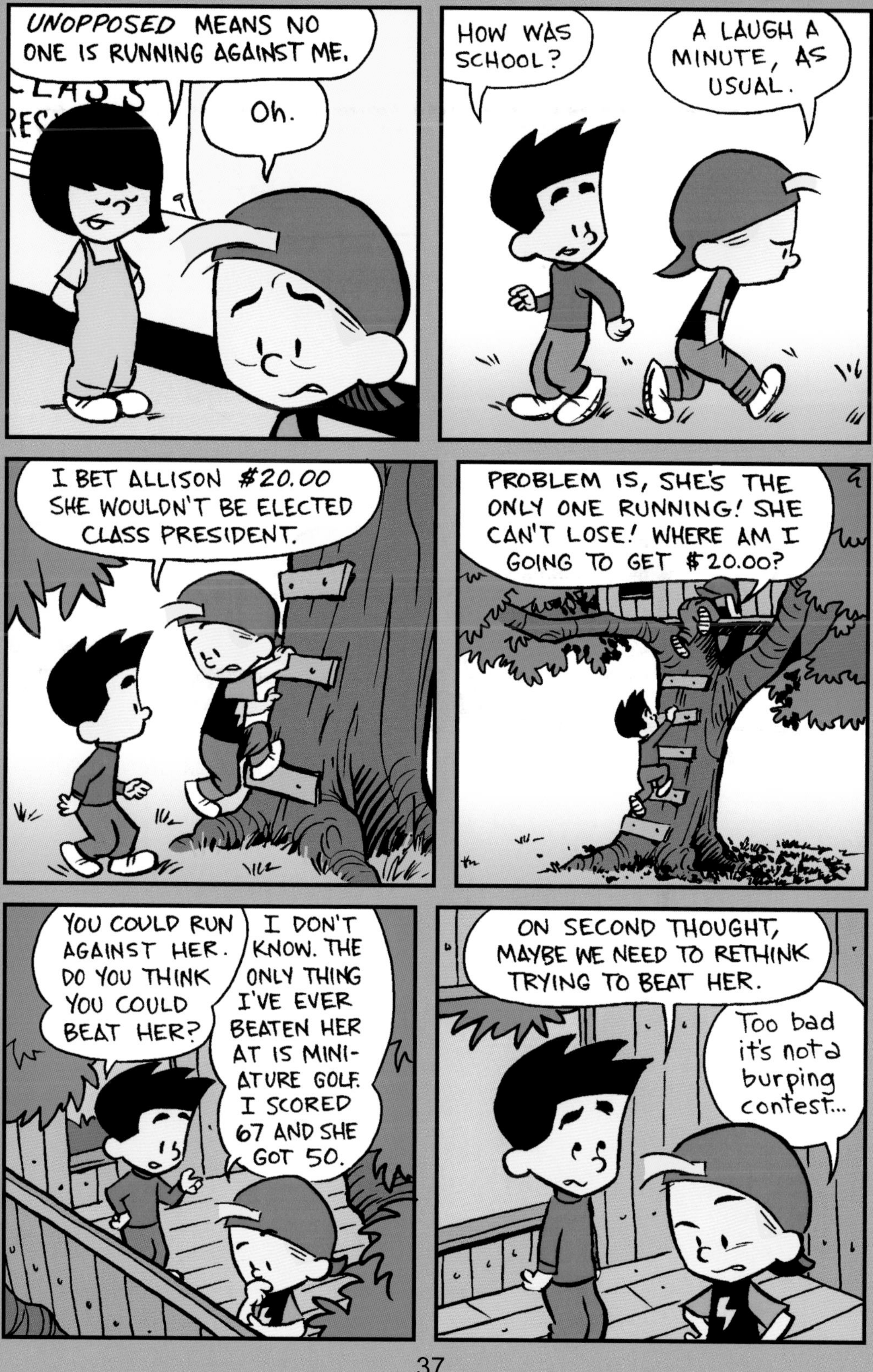
UNOPPOSED MEANS NO ONE IS RUNNING AGAINST ME.
Oh.
HOW WAS SCHOOL?
A LAUGH A MINUTE, AS USUAL.
I BET ALLISON $20.00 SHE WOULDN'T BE ELECTED CLASS PRESIDENT.
PROBLEM IS, SHE'S THE ONLY ONE RUNNING! SHE CAN'T LOSE! WHERE AM I GOING TO GET $20.00?
YOU COULD RUN AGAINST HER. DO YOU THINK YOU COULD BEAT HER?
I DON'T KNOW. THE ONLY THING I'VE EVER BEATEN HER AT IS MINI-ATURE GOLF. I SCORED 67 AND SHE GOT 50.
ON SECOND THOUGHT, MAYBE WE NEED TO RETHINK TRYING TO BEAT HER.
Too bad it's not a burping contest...

OK, I'VE GOT A PLAN. I TELL MOM I'M RUNNING FOR CLASS PRESIDENT AND I NEED $50.00 FOR CAMPAIGN SUPPLIES!

WE BUY A FEW SUPPLIES AND SAVE THE REST TO PAY OFF THE DEBT!

LET'S MAKE A LIST OF CAMPAIGN SUPPLIES WE'LL NEED... POSTERS, PENS, SODA, CANDY, GUM...

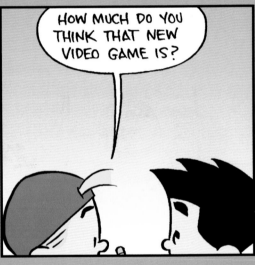

HOW MUCH DO YOU THINK THAT NEW VIDEO GAME IS?

BOY, MOM WAS EASY! SHE REALLY LIKED THE IDEA OF ME RUNNING FOR CLASS PRESIDENT!

I'VE DONE SOME RESEARCH. SECOND GRADE HAS EIGHT MORE BOYS THAN GIRLS. IF YOU GET ALL THE BOYS TO VOTE FOR YOU, YOU CAN'T LOSE!

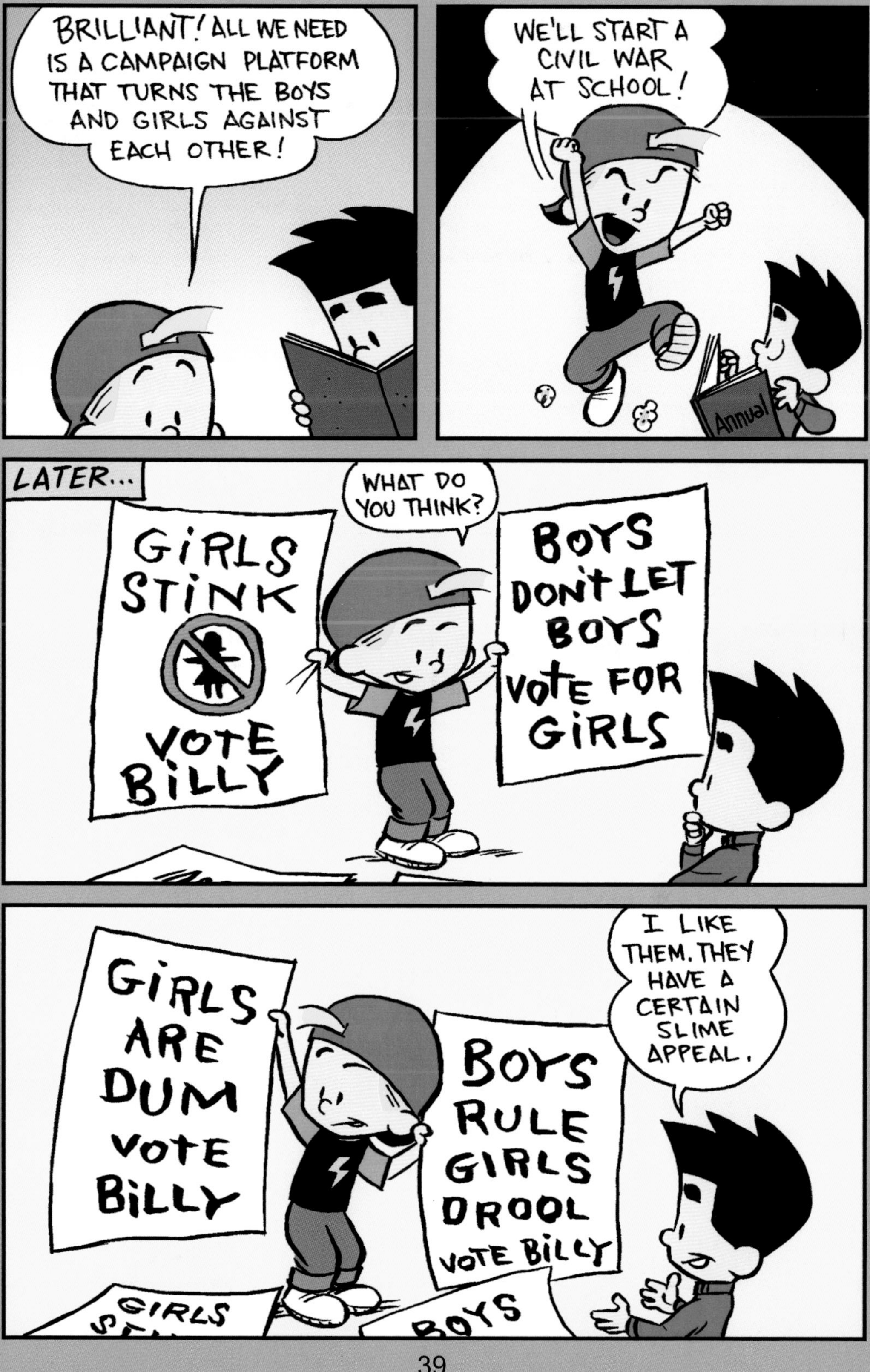
BRILLIANT! ALL WE NEED IS A CAMPAIGN PLATFORM THAT TURNS THE BOYS AND GIRLS AGAINST EACH OTHER!
WE'LL START A CIVIL WAR AT SCHOOL!
Annual
LATER...
WHAT DO YOU THINK?
GIRLS STINK VOTE BILLY
BOYS DON'T LET BOYS VOTE FOR GIRLS
I LIKE THEM. THEY HAVE A CERTAIN SLIME APPEAL.
GIRLS ARE DUM VOTE BILLY
BOYS RULE GIRLS DROOL VOTE BILLY
GIRLS
BOYS

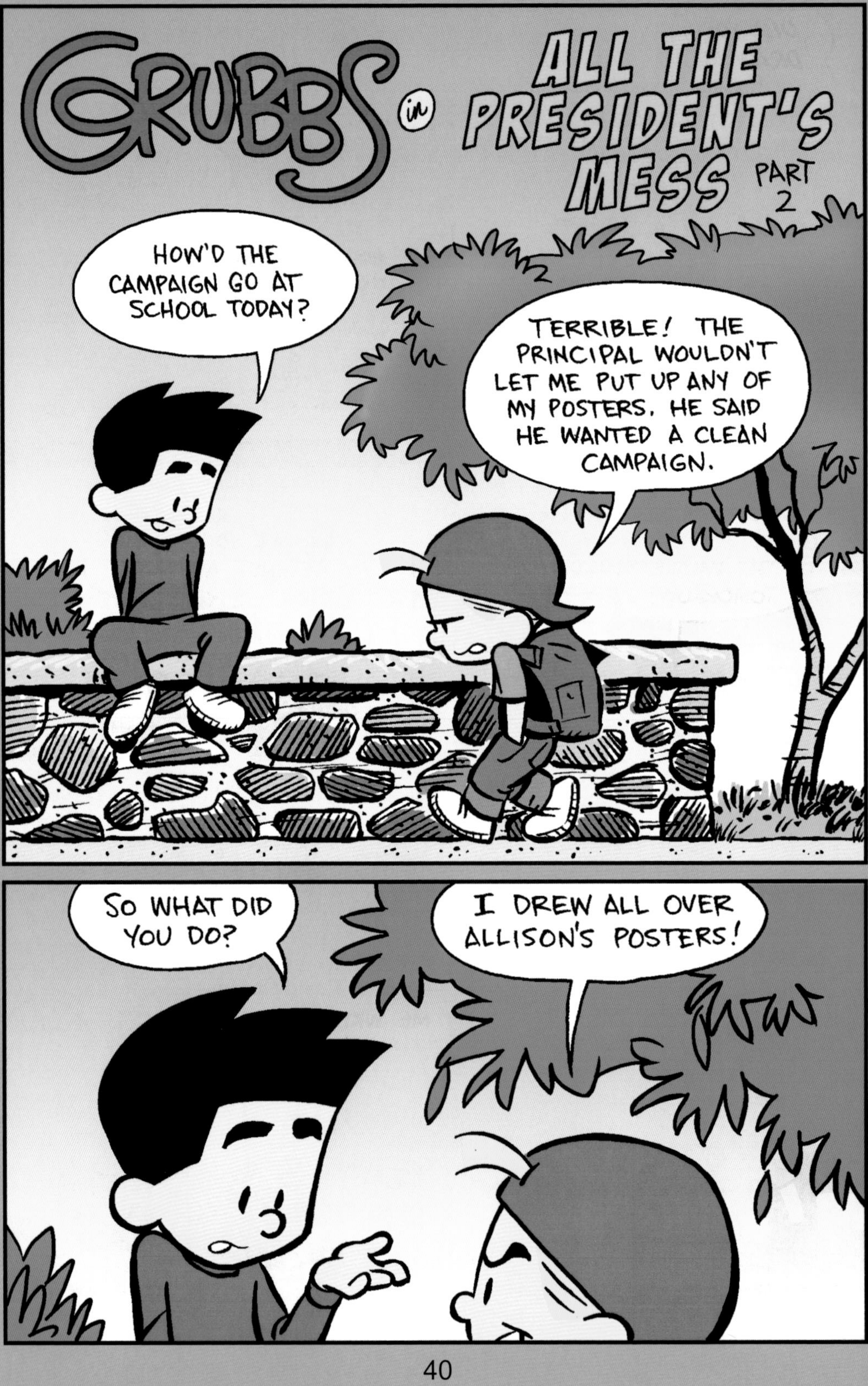
GRUBBS in ALL THE PRESIDENT'S MESS PART 2
HOW'D THE CAMPAIGN GO AT SCHOOL TODAY?
TERRIBLE! THE PRINCIPAL WOULDN'T LET ME PUT UP ANY OF MY POSTERS. HE SAID HE WANTED A CLEAN CAMPAIGN.
SO WHAT DID YOU DO?
I DREW ALL OVER ALLISON'S POSTERS!

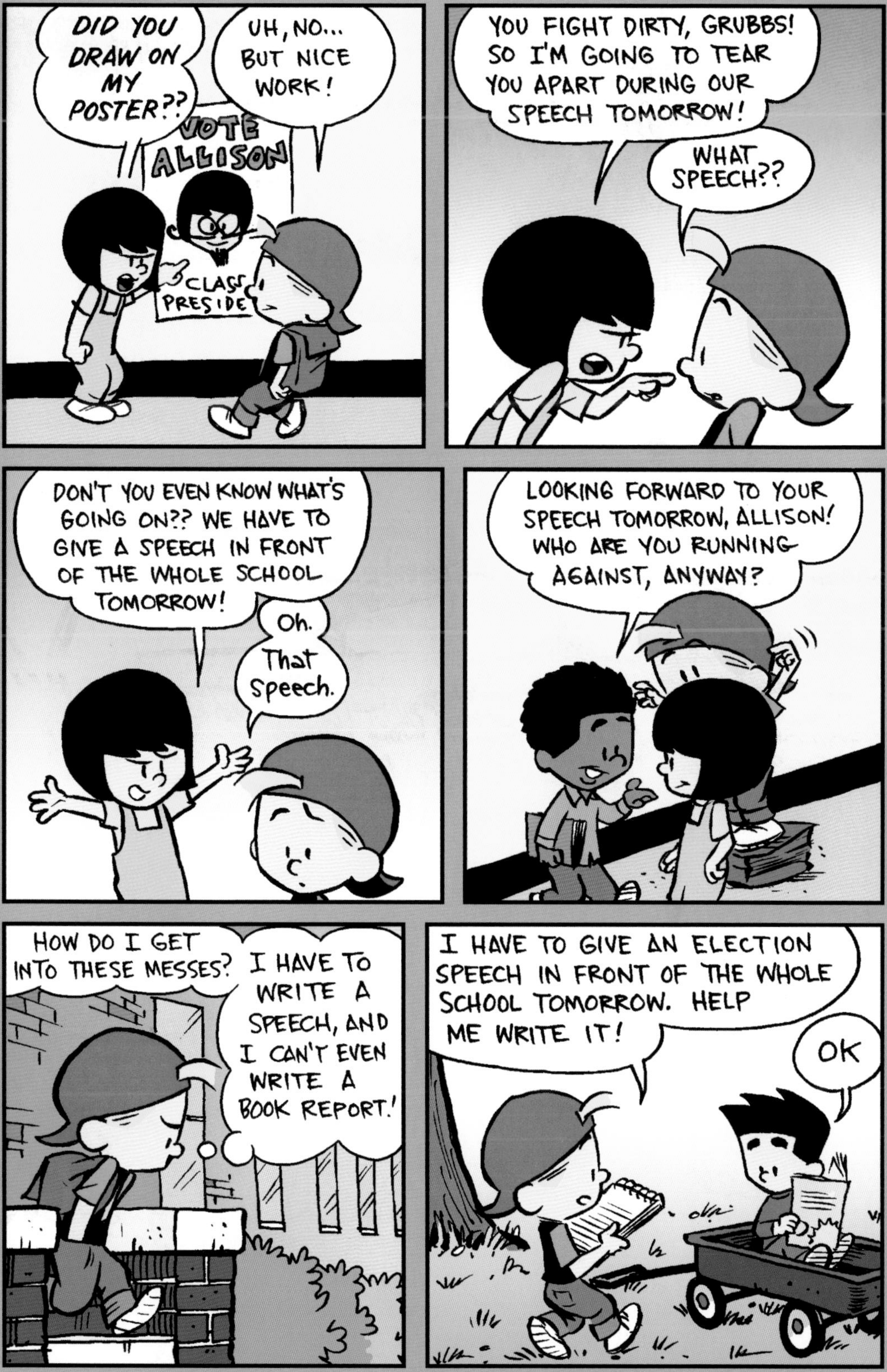
DID YOU DRAW ON MY POSTER??
UH, NO... BUT NICE WORK!
VOTE ALLISON
CLASS PRESIDE
YOU FIGHT DIRTY, GRUBBS! SO I'M GOING TO TEAR YOU APART DURING OUR SPEECH TOMORROW!
WHAT SPEECH??
DON'T YOU EVEN KNOW WHAT'S GOING ON?? WE HAVE TO GIVE A SPEECH IN FRONT OF THE WHOLE SCHOOL TOMORROW!
Oh. That Speech.
LOOKING FORWARD TO YOUR SPEECH TOMORROW, ALLISON! WHO ARE YOU RUNNING AGAINST, ANYWAY?
HOW DO I GET INTO THESE MESSES?
I HAVE TO WRITE A SPEECH, AND I CAN'T EVEN WRITE A BOOK REPORT!
I HAVE TO GIVE AN ELECTION SPEECH IN FRONT OF THE WHOLE SCHOOL TOMORROW. HELP ME WRITE IT!
OK

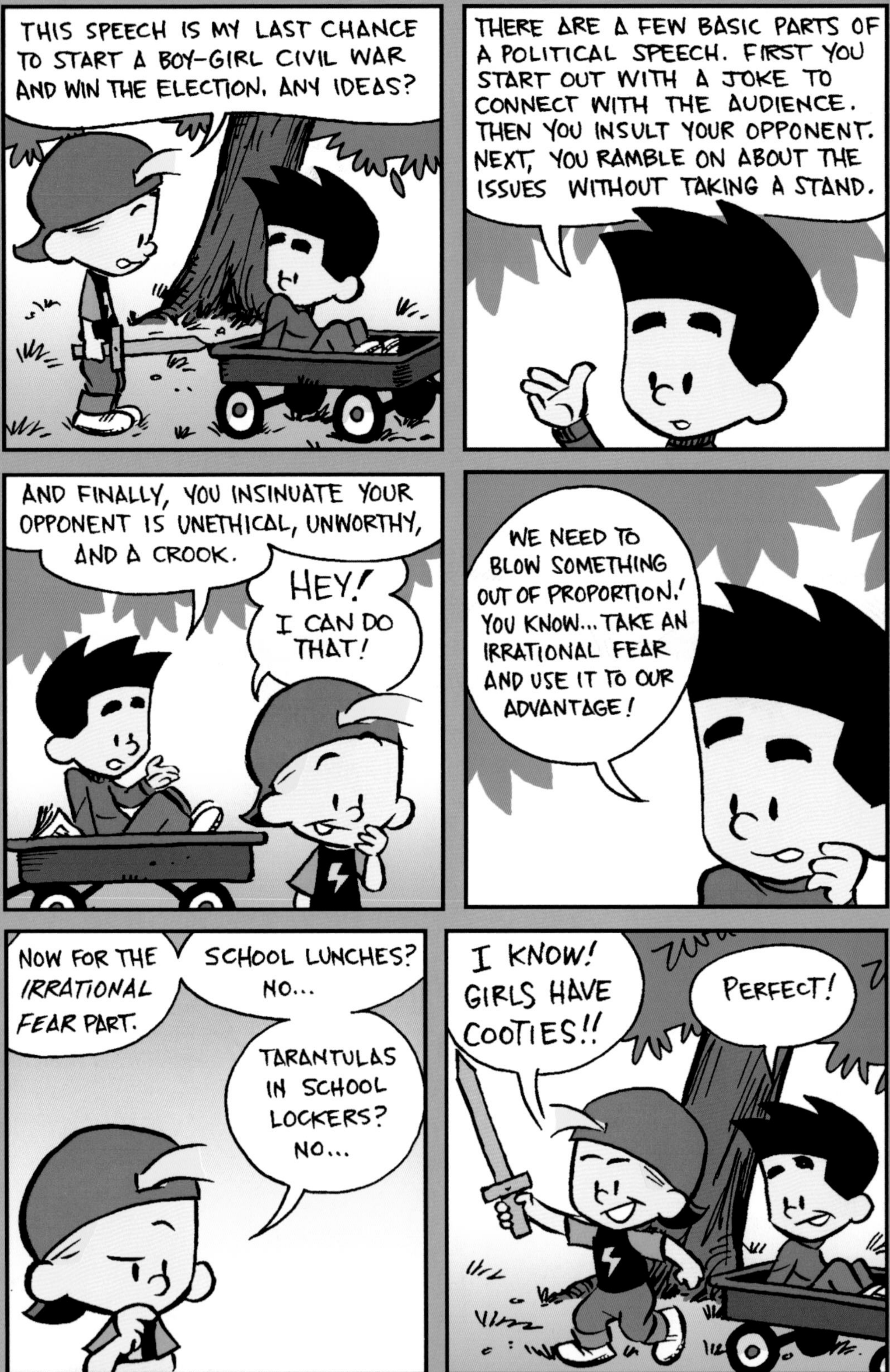
THIS SPEECH IS MY LAST CHANCE TO START A BOY-GIRL CIVIL WAR AND WIN THE ELECTION. ANY IDEAS?
THERE ARE A FEW BASIC PARTS OF A POLITICAL SPEECH. FIRST YOU START OUT WITH A JOKE TO CONNECT WITH THE AUDIENCE. THEN YOU INSULT YOUR OPPONENT. NEXT, YOU RAMBLE ON ABOUT THE ISSUES WITHOUT TAKING A STAND.
AND FINALLY, YOU INSINUATE YOUR OPPONENT IS UNETHICAL, UNWORTHY, AND A CROOK.
HEY! I CAN DO THAT!
WE NEED TO BLOW SOMETHING OUT OF PROPORTION! YOU KNOW... TAKE AN IRRATIONAL FEAR AND USE IT TO OUR ADVANTAGE!
NOW FOR THE *IRRATIONAL FEAR* PART.
SCHOOL LUNCHES? NO...
TARANTULAS IN SCHOOL LOCKERS? NO...
I KNOW! GIRLS HAVE COOTIES!!
PERFECT!

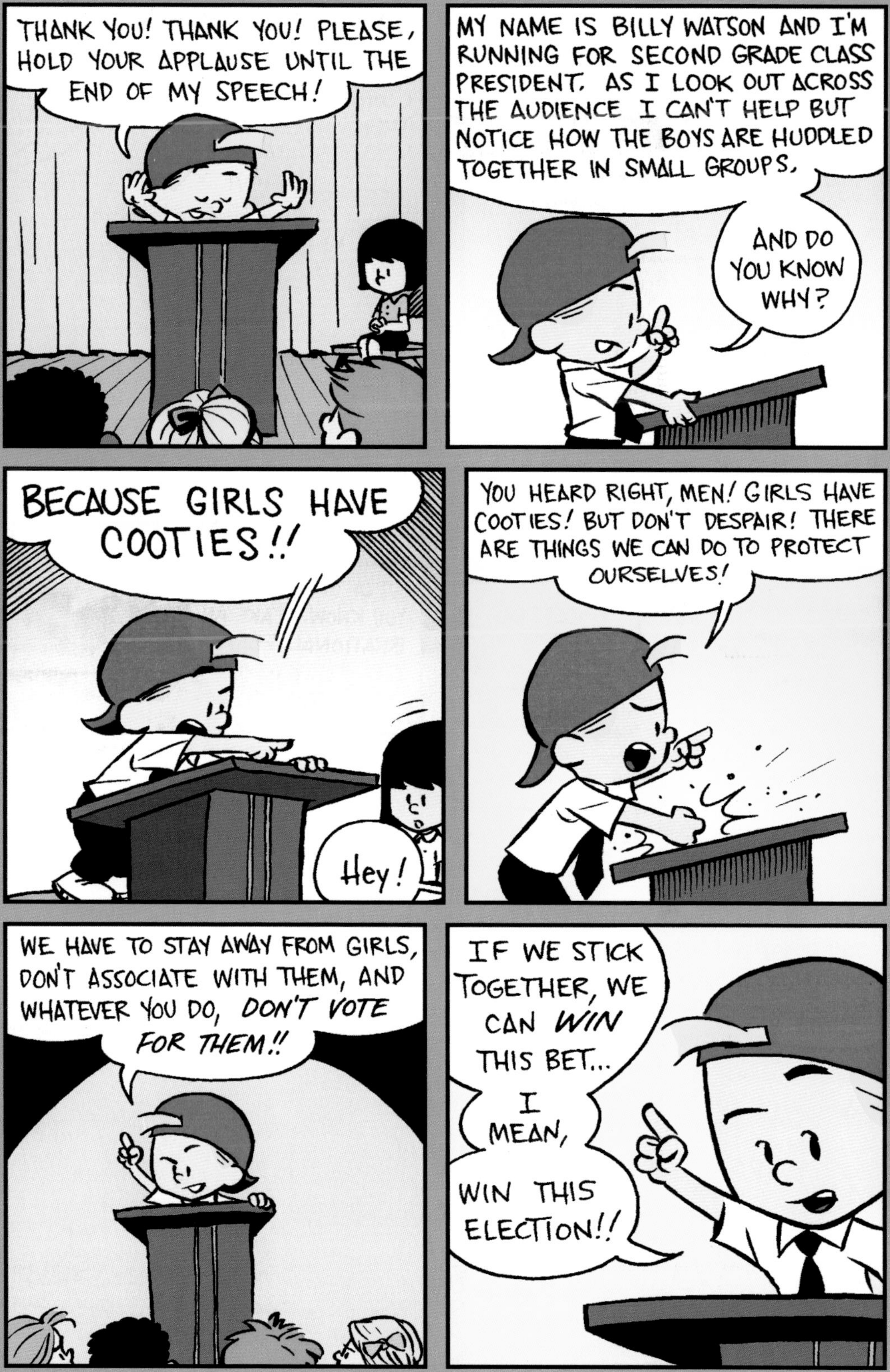
THANK YOU! THANK YOU! PLEASE, HOLD YOUR APPLAUSE UNTIL THE END OF MY SPEECH!
MY NAME IS BILLY WATSON AND I'M RUNNING FOR SECOND GRADE CLASS PRESIDENT. AS I LOOK OUT ACROSS THE AUDIENCE I CAN'T HELP BUT NOTICE HOW THE BOYS ARE HUDDLED TOGETHER IN SMALL GROUPS.
AND DO YOU KNOW WHY?
BECAUSE GIRLS HAVE COOTIES!!
Hey!
YOU HEARD RIGHT, MEN! GIRLS HAVE COOTIES! BUT DON'T DESPAIR! THERE ARE THINGS WE CAN DO TO PROTECT OURSELVES!
WE HAVE TO STAY AWAY FROM GIRLS, DON'T ASSOCIATE WITH THEM, AND WHATEVER YOU DO, *DON'T VOTE FOR THEM!!*
IF WE STICK TOGETHER, WE CAN *WIN* THIS BET...
I MEAN,
WIN THIS ELECTION!!

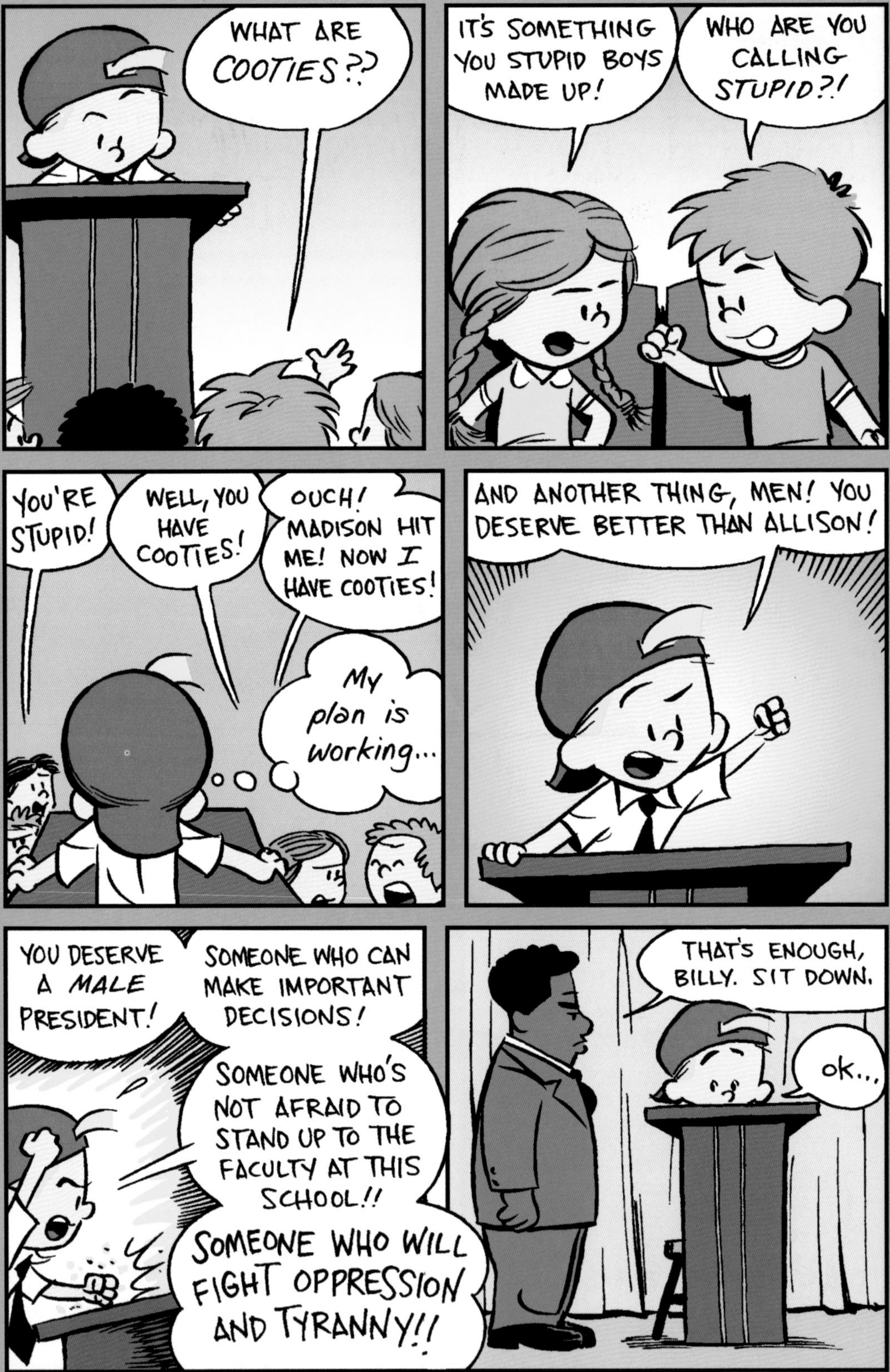
WHAT ARE *COOTIES*??
IT'S SOMETHING YOU STUPID BOYS MADE UP!
WHO ARE YOU CALLING *STUPID*?!
YOU'RE STUPID!
WELL, YOU HAVE COOTIES!
OUCH! MADISON HIT ME! NOW I HAVE COOTIES!
My plan is working...
AND ANOTHER THING, MEN! YOU DESERVE BETTER THAN ALLISON!
YOU DESERVE A *MALE* PRESIDENT!
SOMEONE WHO CAN MAKE IMPORTANT DECISIONS!
SOMEONE WHO'S NOT AFRAID TO STAND UP TO THE FACULTY AT THIS SCHOOL!!
SOMEONE WHO WILL FIGHT OPPRESSION AND TYRANNY!!
THAT'S ENOUGH, BILLY. SIT DOWN.
ok...

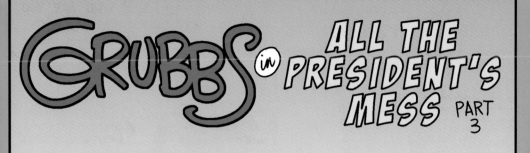

GRUBBS in ALL THE PRESIDENT'S MESS PART 3

AND NEXT, WE'LL HEAR FROM ALLISON OWINGS.

BILLY, I WANT TO SEE YOU IN MY OFFICE WHEN WE'RE DONE HERE.

I WANT TO SEE YOU AFTER SCHOOL!

ME, TOO! AND I SUGGEST YOU BRING SOME BANDAGES!

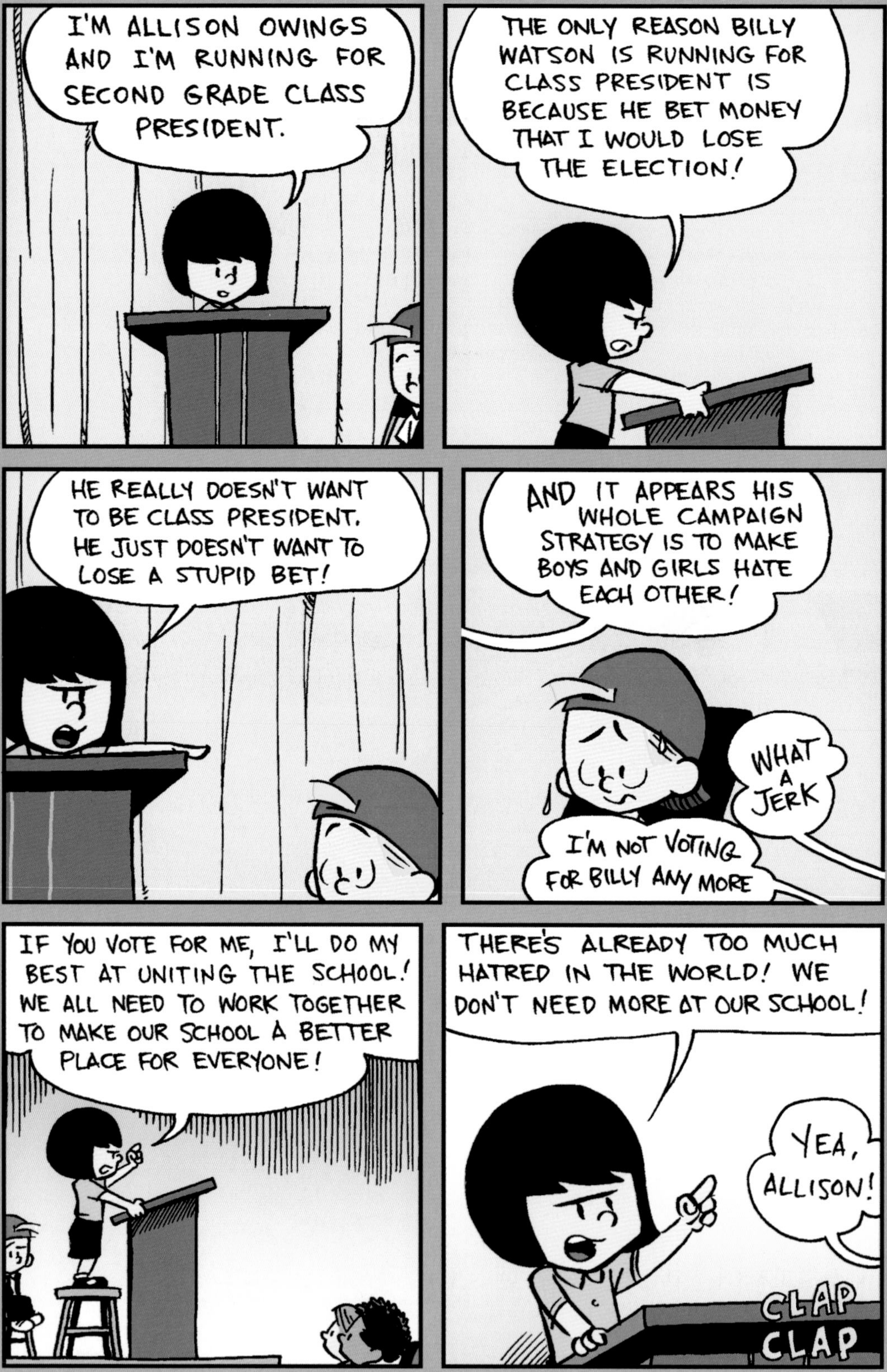
I'M ALLISON OWINGS AND I'M RUNNING FOR SECOND GRADE CLASS PRESIDENT.
THE ONLY REASON BILLY WATSON IS RUNNING FOR CLASS PRESIDENT IS BECAUSE HE BET MONEY THAT I WOULD LOSE THE ELECTION!
HE REALLY DOESN'T WANT TO BE CLASS PRESIDENT. HE JUST DOESN'T WANT TO LOSE A STUPID BET!
AND IT APPEARS HIS WHOLE CAMPAIGN STRATEGY IS TO MAKE BOYS AND GIRLS HATE EACH OTHER!
WHAT A JERK
I'M NOT VOTING FOR BILLY ANY MORE
IF YOU VOTE FOR ME, I'LL DO MY BEST AT UNITING THE SCHOOL! WE ALL NEED TO WORK TOGETHER TO MAKE OUR SCHOOL A BETTER PLACE FOR EVERYONE!
THERE'S ALREADY TOO MUCH HATRED IN THE WORLD! WE DON'T NEED MORE AT OUR SCHOOL!
YEA, ALLISON!
CLAP
CLAP

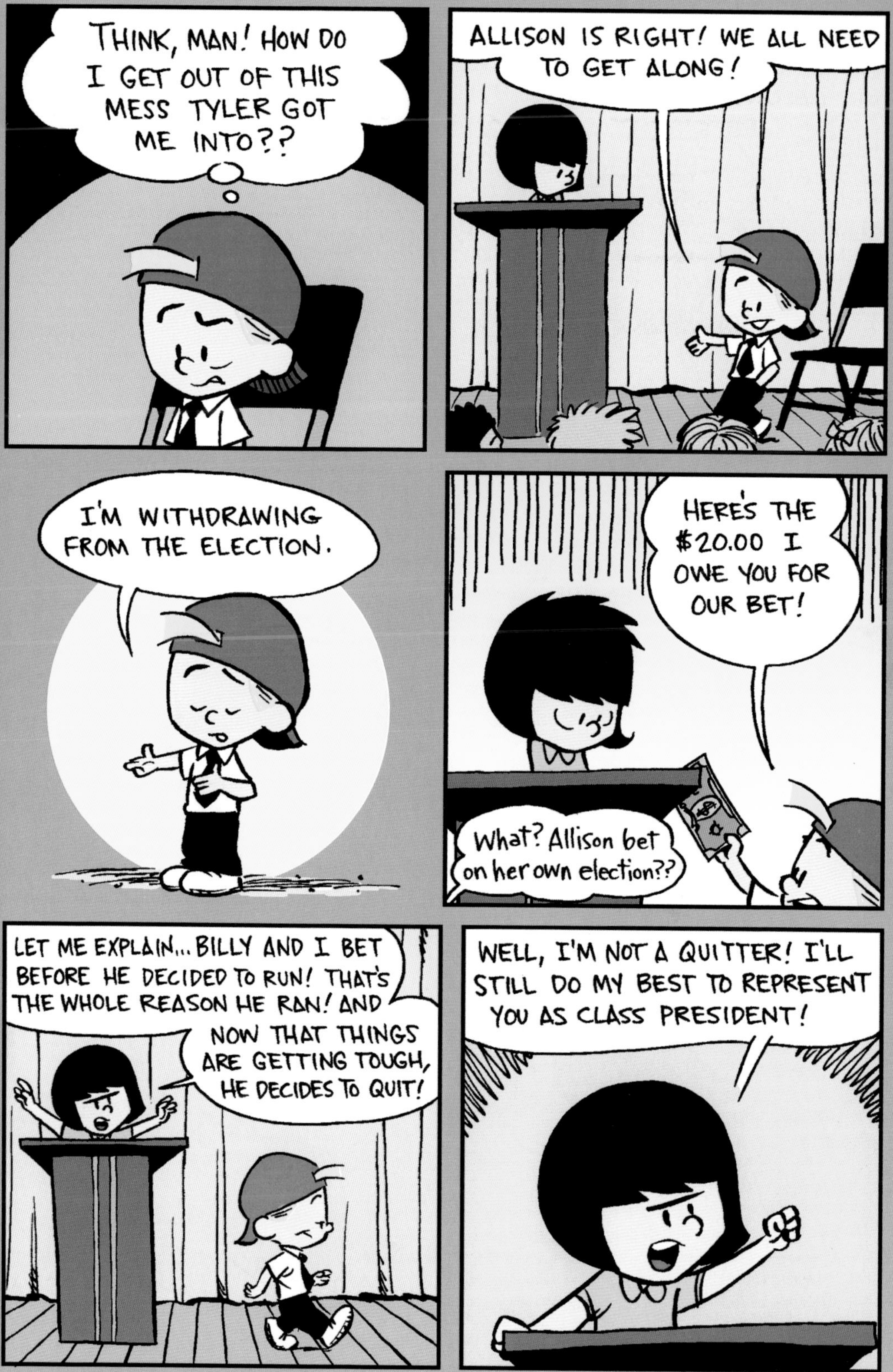
THINK, MAN! HOW DO I GET OUT OF THIS MESS TYLER GOT ME INTO??
ALLISON IS RIGHT! WE ALL NEED TO GET ALONG!
I'M WITHDRAWING FROM THE ELECTION.
HERE'S THE $20.00 I OWE YOU FOR OUR BET!
What? Allison bet on her own election??
LET ME EXPLAIN... BILLY AND I BET BEFORE HE DECIDED TO RUN! THAT'S THE WHOLE REASON HE RAN! AND
NOW THAT THINGS ARE GETTING TOUGH, HE DECIDES TO QUIT!
WELL, I'M NOT A QUITTER! I'LL STILL DO MY BEST TO REPRESENT YOU AS CLASS PRESIDENT!

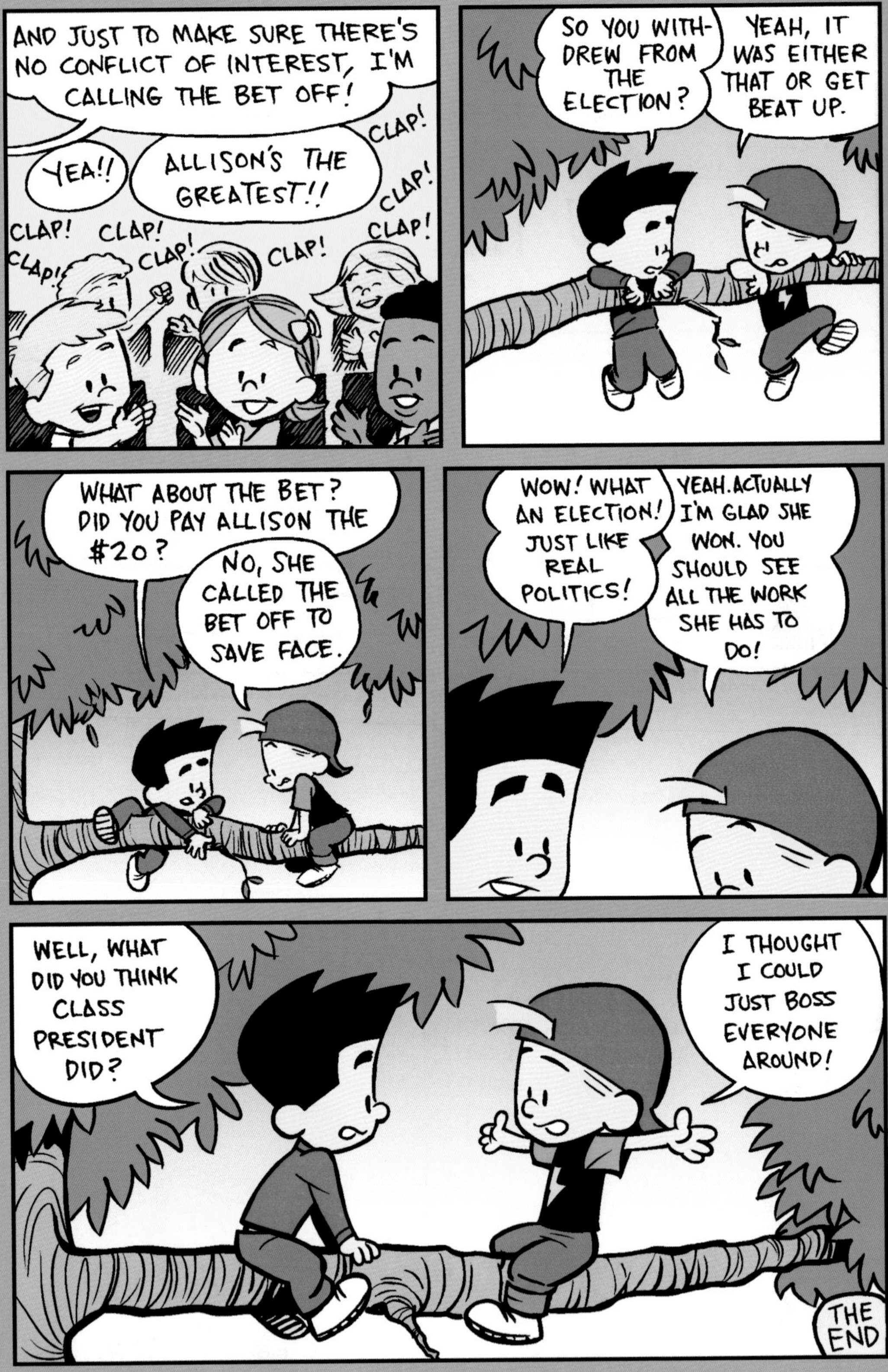
AND JUST TO MAKE SURE THERE'S NO CONFLICT OF INTEREST, I'M CALLING THE BET OFF!
YEA!!
ALLISON'S THE GREATEST!!
CLAP! CLAP! CLAP! CLAP! CLAP! CLAP! CLAP! CLAP!
SO YOU WITH-DREW FROM THE ELECTION?
YEAH, IT WAS EITHER THAT OR GET BEAT UP.
WHAT ABOUT THE BET? DID YOU PAY ALLISON THE $20?
NO, SHE CALLED THE BET OFF TO SAVE FACE.
WOW! WHAT AN ELECTION! JUST LIKE REAL POLITICS!
YEAH. ACTUALLY I'M GLAD SHE WON. YOU SHOULD SEE ALL THE WORK SHE HAS TO DO!
WELL, WHAT DID YOU THINK CLASS PRESIDENT DID?
I THOUGHT I COULD JUST BOSS EVERYONE AROUND!
THE END

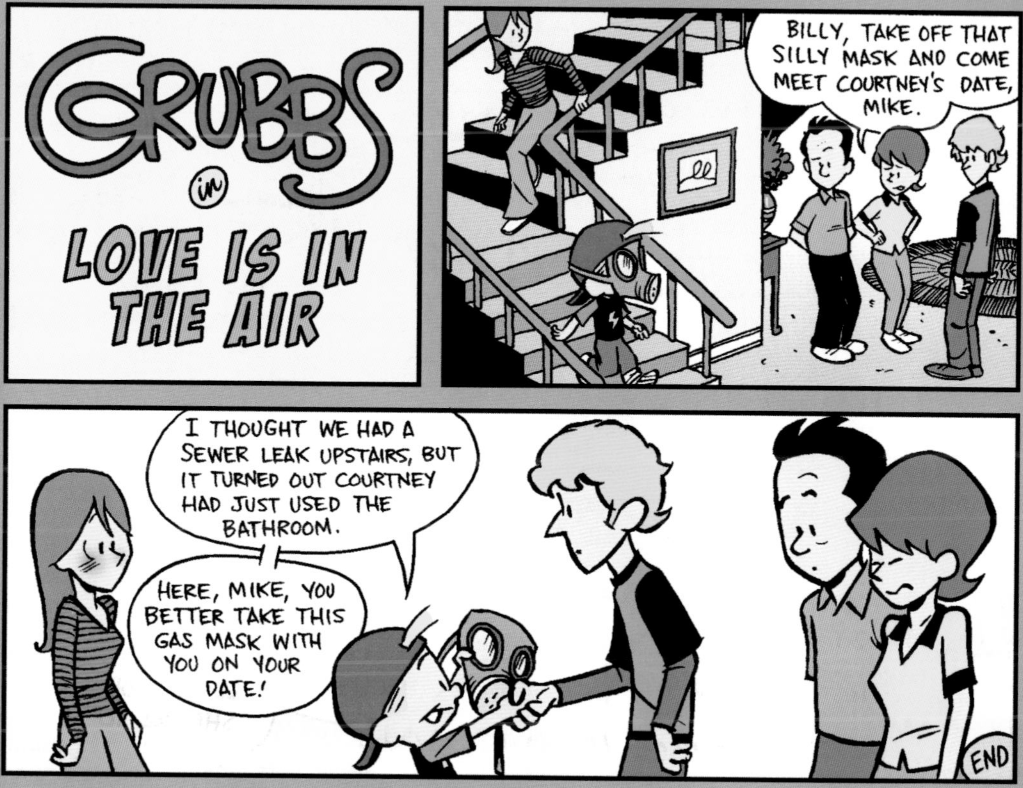
GRUBBS
in
LOVE IS IN THE AIR
BILLY, TAKE OFF THAT SILLY MASK AND COME MEET COURTNEY'S DATE, MIKE.
I THOUGHT WE HAD A SEWER LEAK UPSTAIRS, BUT IT TURNED OUT COURTNEY HAD JUST USED THE BATHROOM.
HERE, MIKE, YOU BETTER TAKE THIS GAS MASK WITH YOU ON YOUR DATE!
END

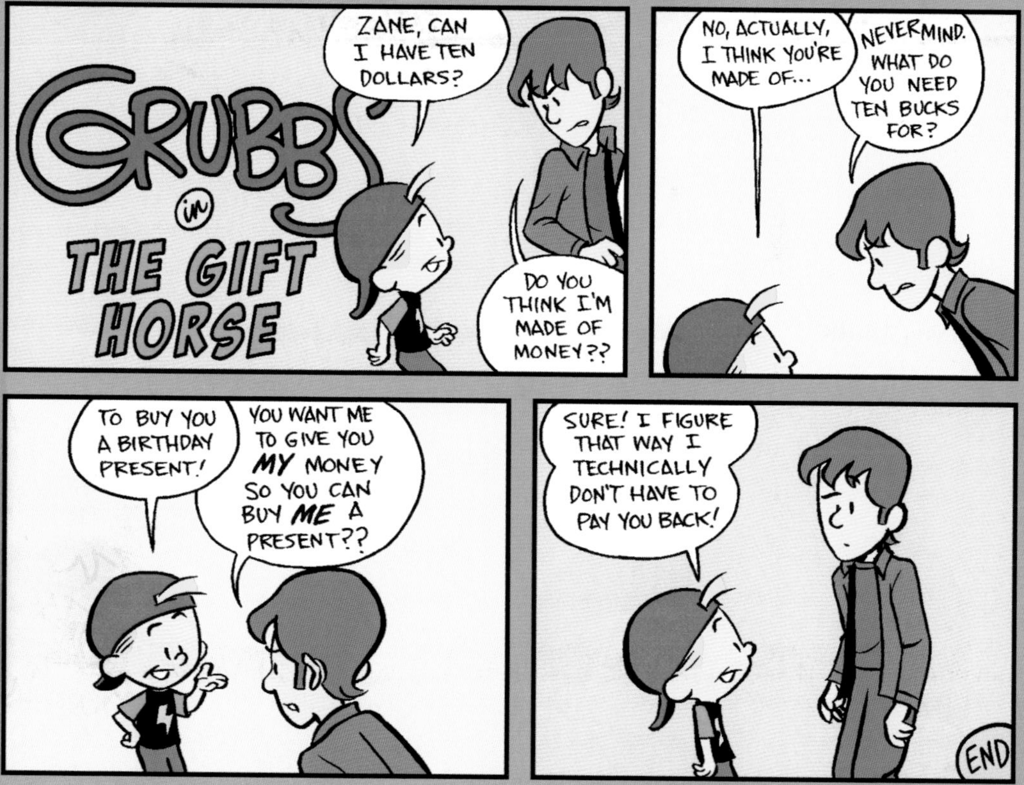
GRUBBS
in
THE GIFT HORSE
ZANE, CAN I HAVE TEN DOLLARS?
DO YOU THINK I'M MADE OF MONEY??
NO, ACTUALLY, I THINK YOU'RE MADE OF...
NEVERMIND. WHAT DO YOU NEED TEN BUCKS FOR?
TO BUY YOU A BIRTHDAY PRESENT!
YOU WANT ME TO GIVE YOU MY MONEY SO YOU CAN BUY ME A PRESENT??
SURE! I FIGURE THAT WAY I TECHNICALLY DON'T HAVE TO PAY YOU BACK!
END

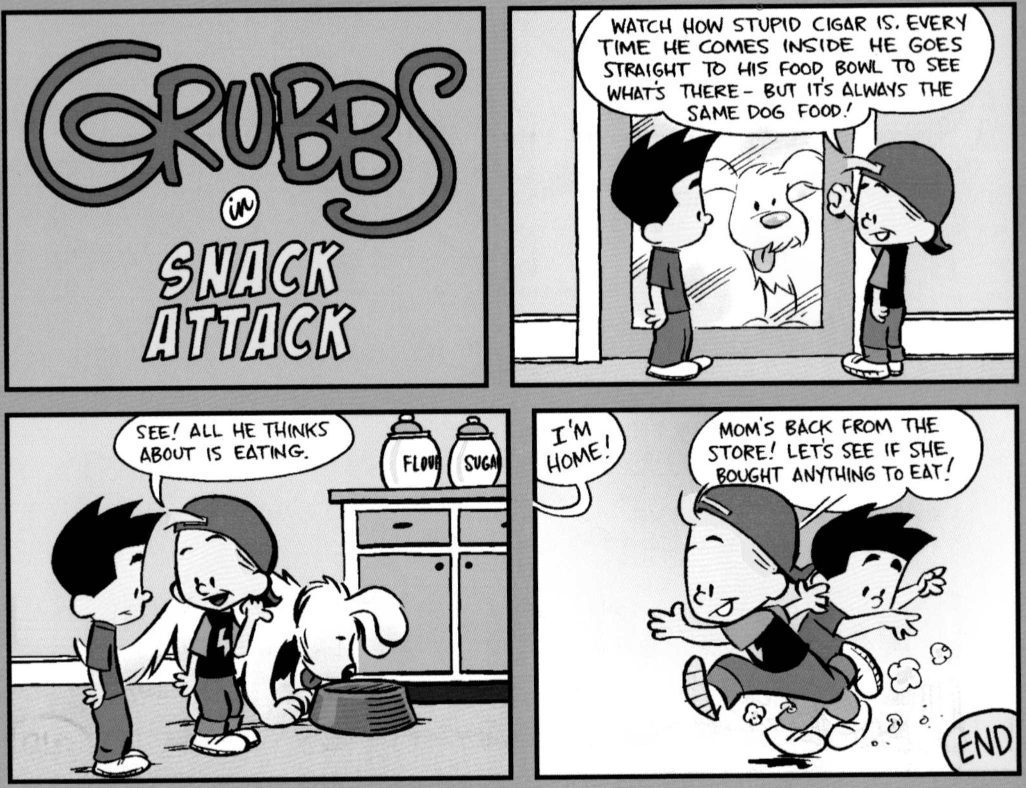
GRUBBS
in
SNACK ATTACK
WATCH HOW STUPID CIGAR IS. EVERY TIME HE COMES INSIDE HE GOES STRAIGHT TO HIS FOOD BOWL TO SEE WHAT'S THERE– BUT IT'S ALWAYS THE SAME DOG FOOD!
SEE! ALL HE THINKS ABOUT IS EATING.
FLOUR
SUGA
I'M HOME!
MOM'S BACK FROM THE STORE! LET'S SEE IF SHE BOUGHT ANYTHING TO EAT!
END

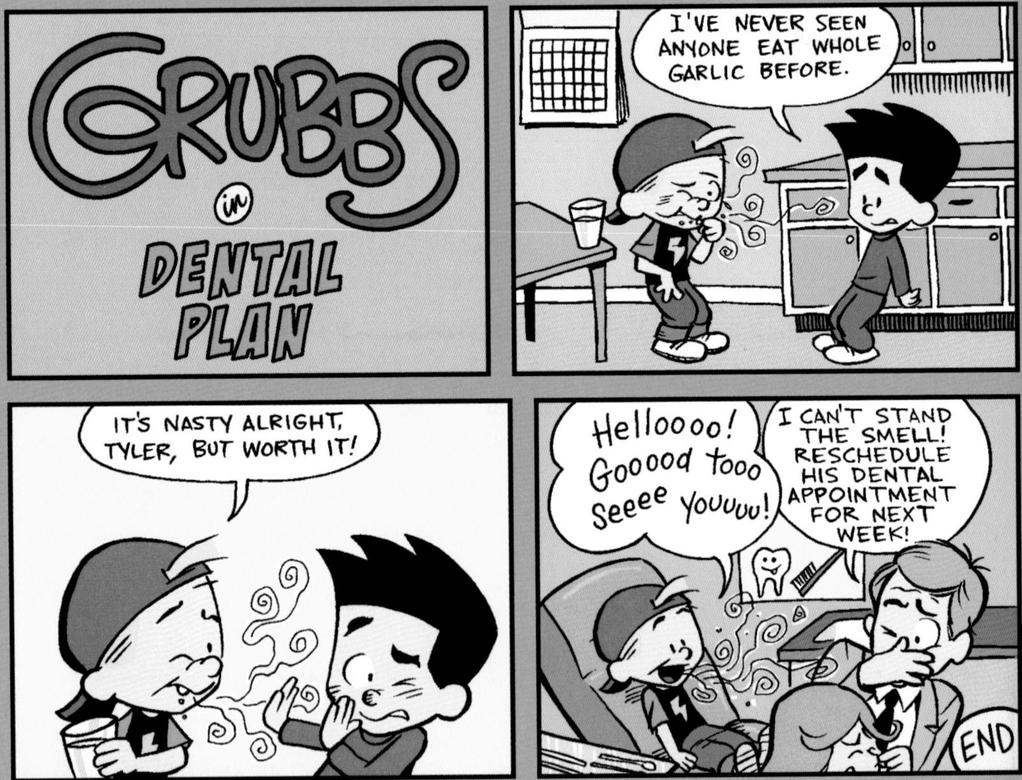
GRUBBS
in
DENTAL PLAN
I'VE NEVER SEEN ANYONE EAT WHOLE GARLIC BEFORE.
IT'S NASTY ALRIGHT, TYLER, BUT WORTH IT!
Hellooooo! Gooood tooo Seeee youuuu!
I CAN'T STAND THE SMELL! RESCHEDULE HIS DENTAL APPOINTMENT FOR NEXT WEEK!
END

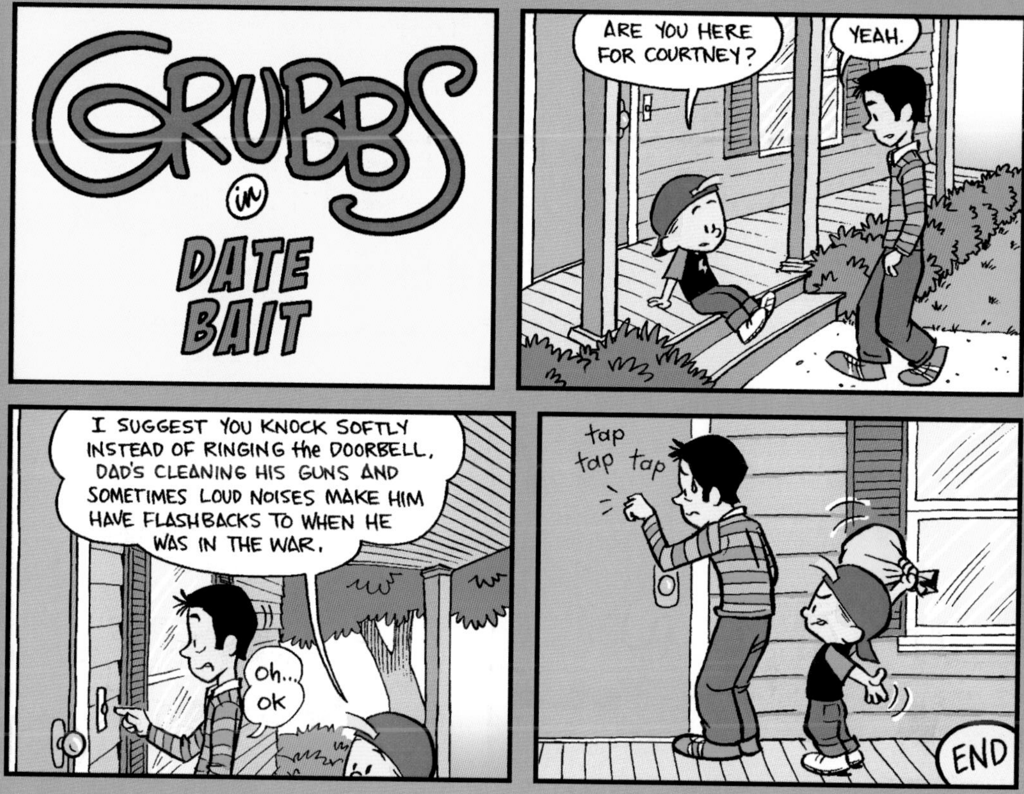
GRUBBS
in
DATE BAIT
ARE YOU HERE FOR COURTNEY?
YEAH.
I SUGGEST YOU KNOCK SOFTLY INSTEAD OF RINGING the DOORBELL. DAD'S CLEANING HIS GUNS AND SOMETIMES LOUD NOISES MAKE HIM HAVE FLASHBACKS TO WHEN HE WAS IN THE WAR.
oh... ok
tap tap tap
END

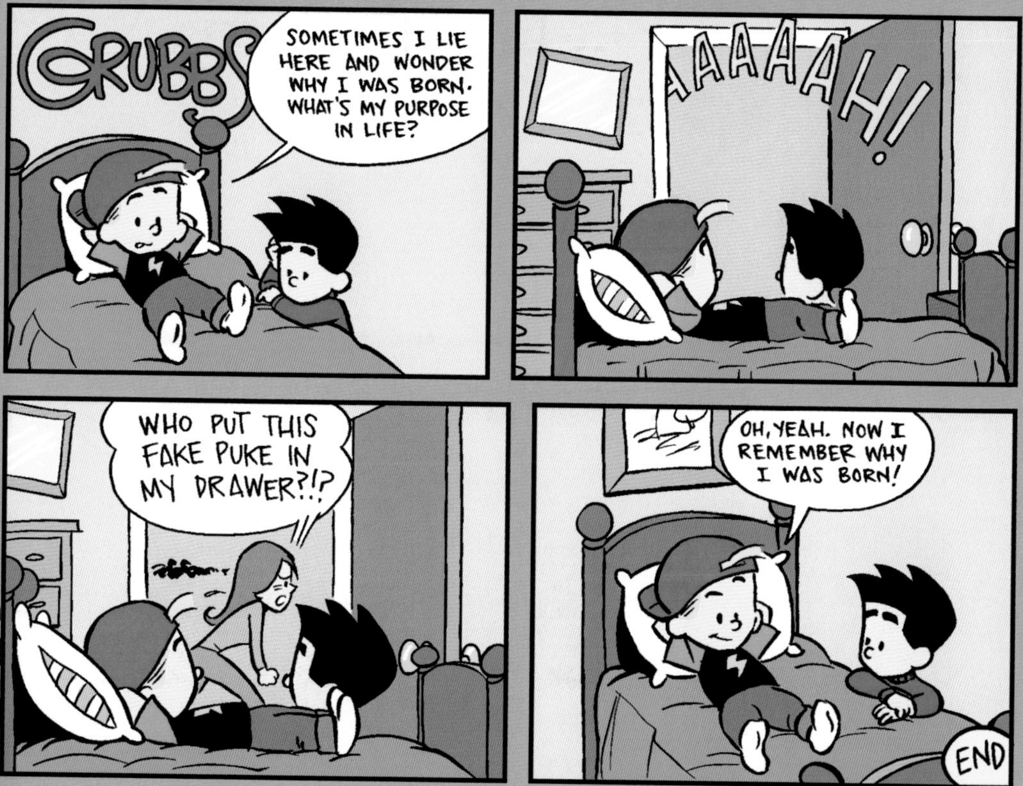
GRUBBS
SOMETIMES I LIE HERE AND WONDER WHY I WAS BORN. WHAT'S MY PURPOSE IN LIFE?
AAAAAH!
WHO PUT THIS FAKE PUKE IN MY DRAWER?!?
OH, YEAH. NOW I REMEMBER WHY I WAS BORN!
END

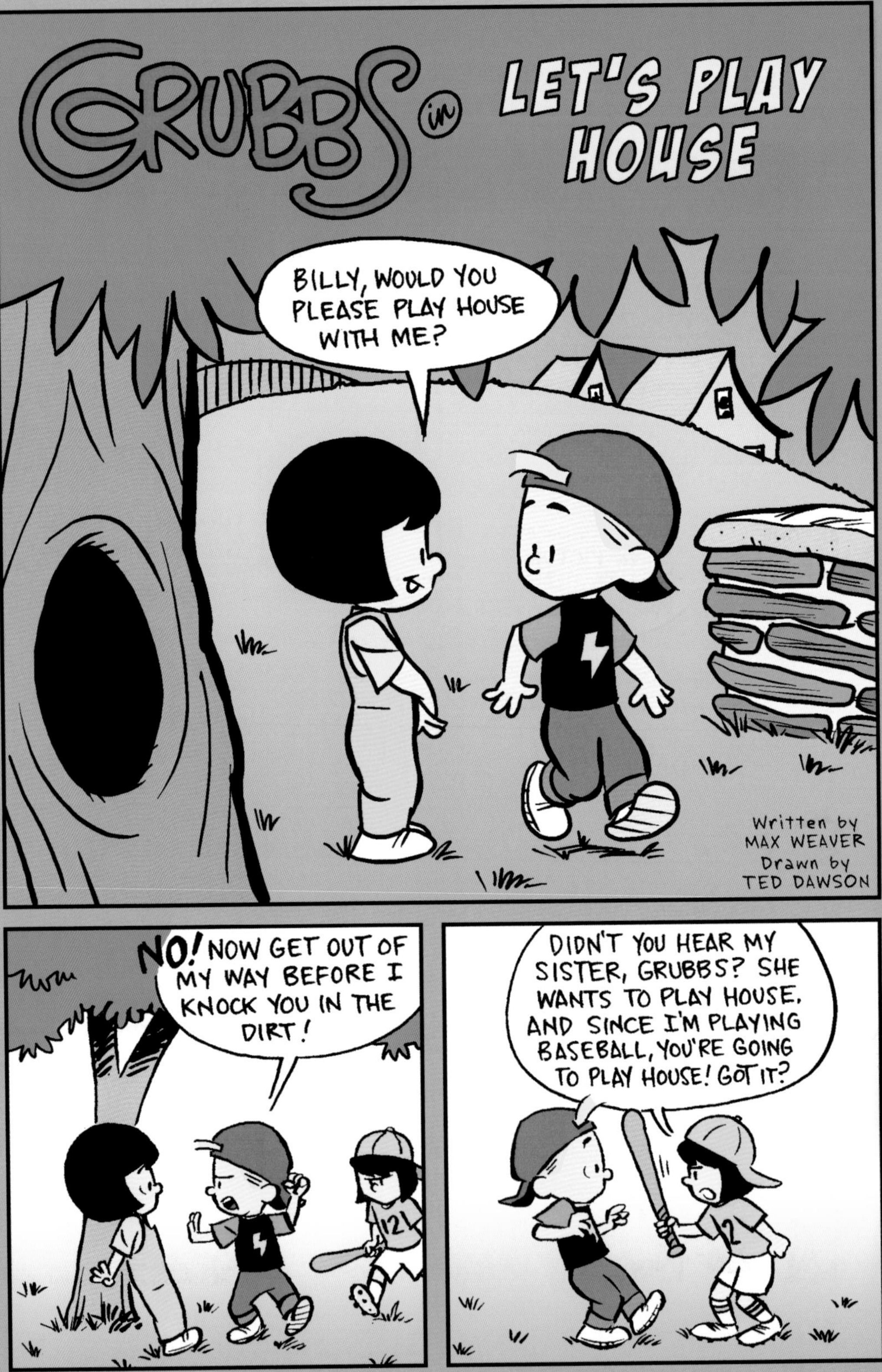
GRUBBS in LET'S PLAY HOUSE
BILLY, WOULD YOU PLEASE PLAY HOUSE WITH ME?
Written by MAX WEAVER
Drawn by TED DAWSON
NO! NOW GET OUT OF MY WAY BEFORE I KNOCK YOU IN THE DIRT!
DIDN'T YOU HEAR MY SISTER, GRUBBS? SHE WANTS TO PLAY HOUSE. AND SINCE I'M PLAYING BASEBALL, YOU'RE GOING TO PLAY HOUSE! GOT IT?

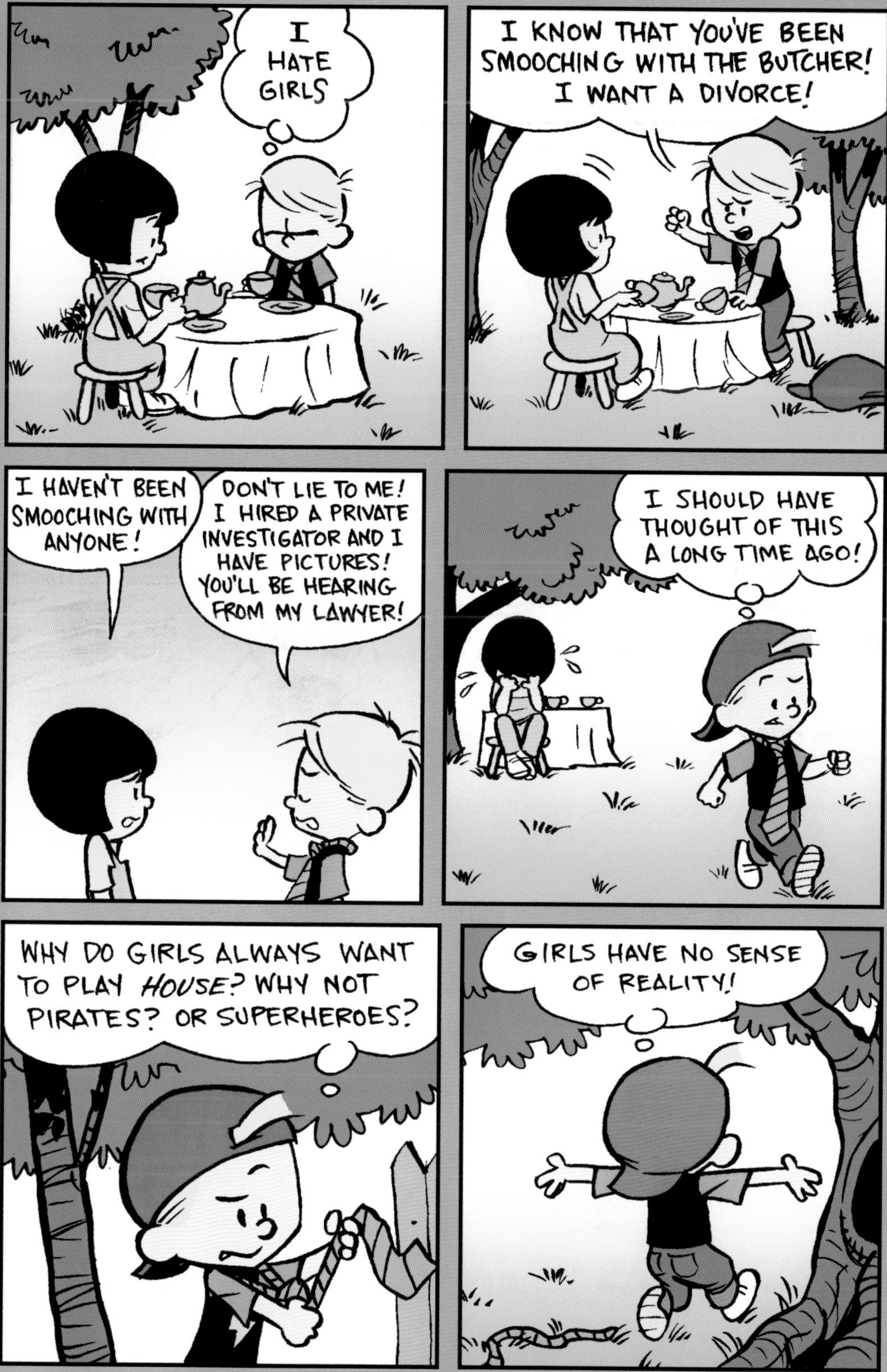

I HATE GIRLS
I KNOW THAT YOU'VE BEEN SMOOCHING WITH THE BUTCHER! I WANT A DIVORCE!
I HAVEN'T BEEN SMOOCHING WITH ANYONE!
DON'T LIE TO ME! I HIRED A PRIVATE INVESTIGATOR AND I HAVE PICTURES! YOU'LL BE HEARING FROM MY LAWYER!
I SHOULD HAVE THOUGHT OF THIS A LONG TIME AGO!
WHY DO GIRLS ALWAYS WANT TO PLAY *HOUSE*? WHY NOT PIRATES? OR SUPERHEROES?
GIRLS HAVE NO SENSE OF REALITY!

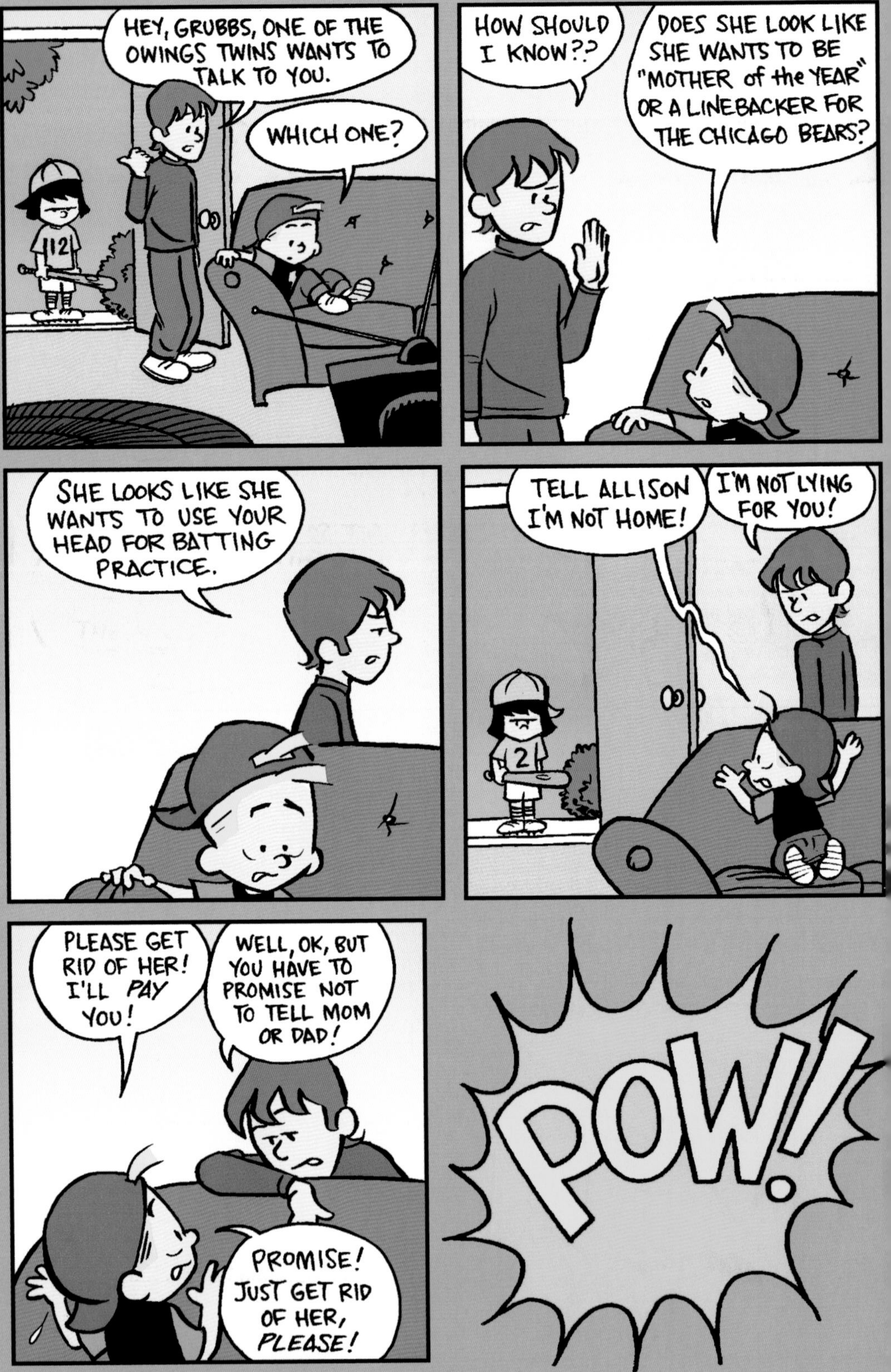
HEY, GRUBBS, ONE OF THE OWINGS TWINS WANTS TO TALK TO YOU.
WHICH ONE?
HOW SHOULD I KNOW?!?
DOES SHE LOOK LIKE SHE WANTS TO BE "MOTHER of the YEAR" OR A LINEBACKER FOR THE CHICAGO BEARS?
SHE LOOKS LIKE SHE WANTS TO USE YOUR HEAD FOR BATTING PRACTICE.
TELL ALLISON I'M NOT HOME!
I'M NOT LYING FOR YOU!
PLEASE GET RID OF HER! I'LL PAY YOU!
WELL, OK, BUT YOU HAVE TO PROMISE NOT TO TELL MOM OR DAD!
PROMISE! JUST GET RID OF HER, PLEASE!
POW!!

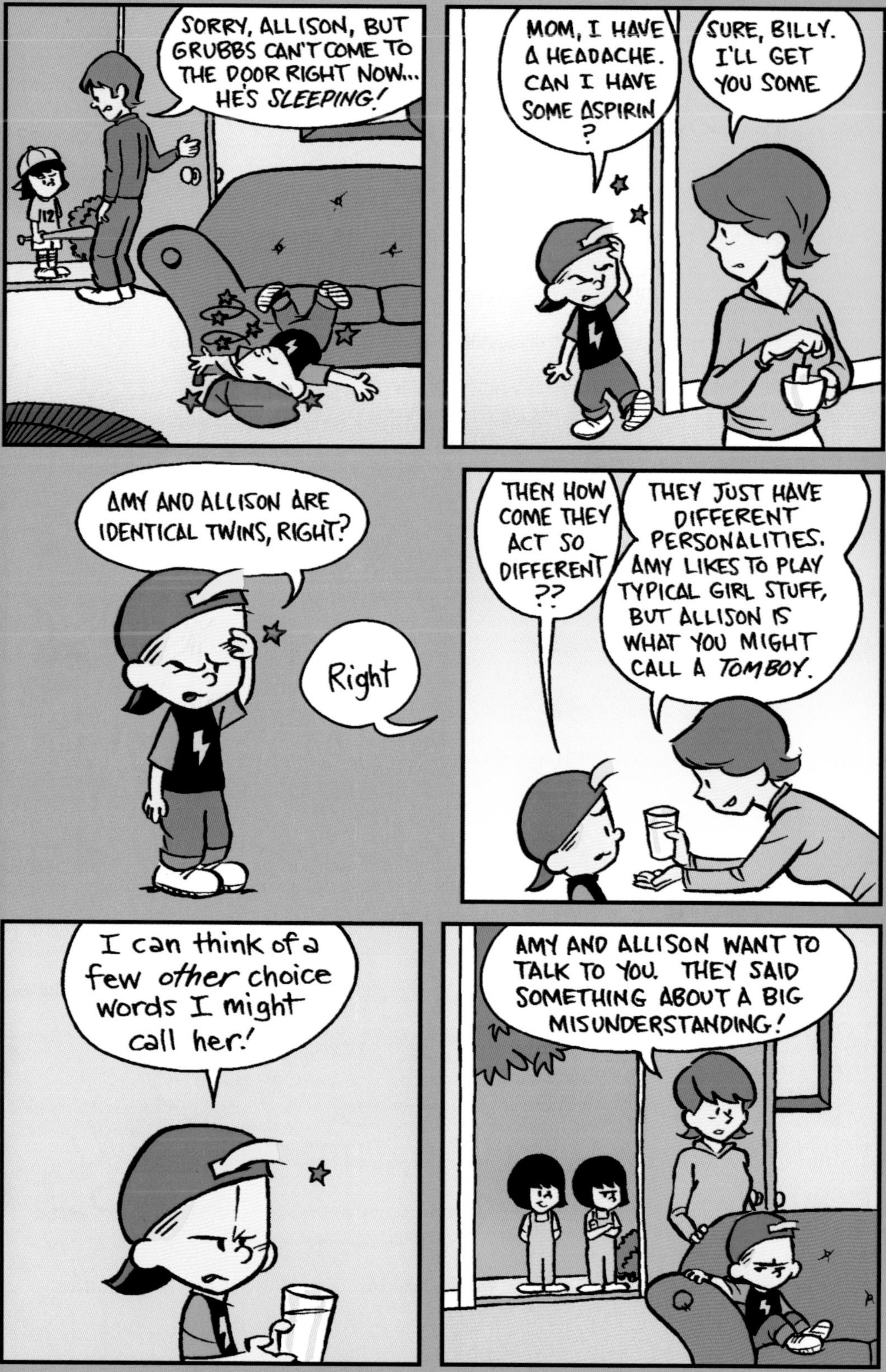
SORRY, ALLISON, BUT GRUBBS CAN'T COME TO THE DOOR RIGHT NOW... HE'S *SLEEPING!*
MOM, I HAVE A HEADACHE. CAN I HAVE SOME ASPIRIN?
SURE, BILLY. I'LL GET YOU SOME
AMY AND ALLISON ARE IDENTICAL TWINS, RIGHT?
Right
THEN HOW COME THEY ACT SO DIFFERENT??
THEY JUST HAVE DIFFERENT PERSONALITIES. AMY LIKES TO PLAY TYPICAL GIRL STUFF, BUT ALLISON IS WHAT YOU MIGHT CALL A *TOMBOY*.
I can think of a few *other* choice words I might call her!
AMY AND ALLISON WANT TO TALK TO YOU. THEY SAID SOMETHING ABOUT A BIG MISUNDERSTANDING!

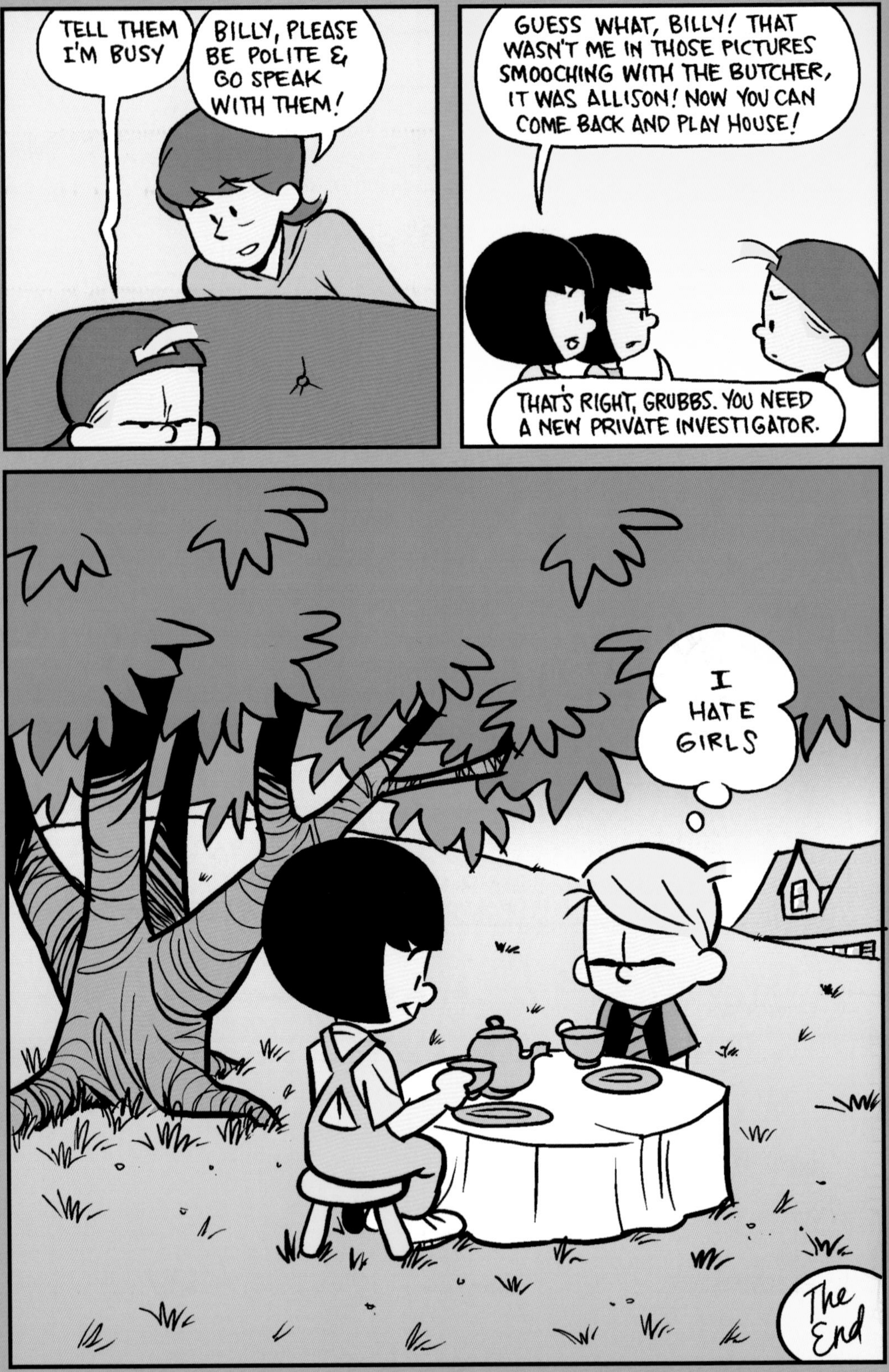
TELL THEM I'M BUSY
BILLY, PLEASE BE POLITE & GO SPEAK WITH THEM!
GUESS WHAT, BILLY! THAT WASN'T ME IN THOSE PICTURES SMOOCHING WITH THE BUTCHER, IT WAS ALLISON! NOW YOU CAN COME BACK AND PLAY HOUSE!
THAT'S RIGHT, GRUBBS. YOU NEED A NEW PRIVATE INVESTIGATOR.
I HATE GIRLS
The End

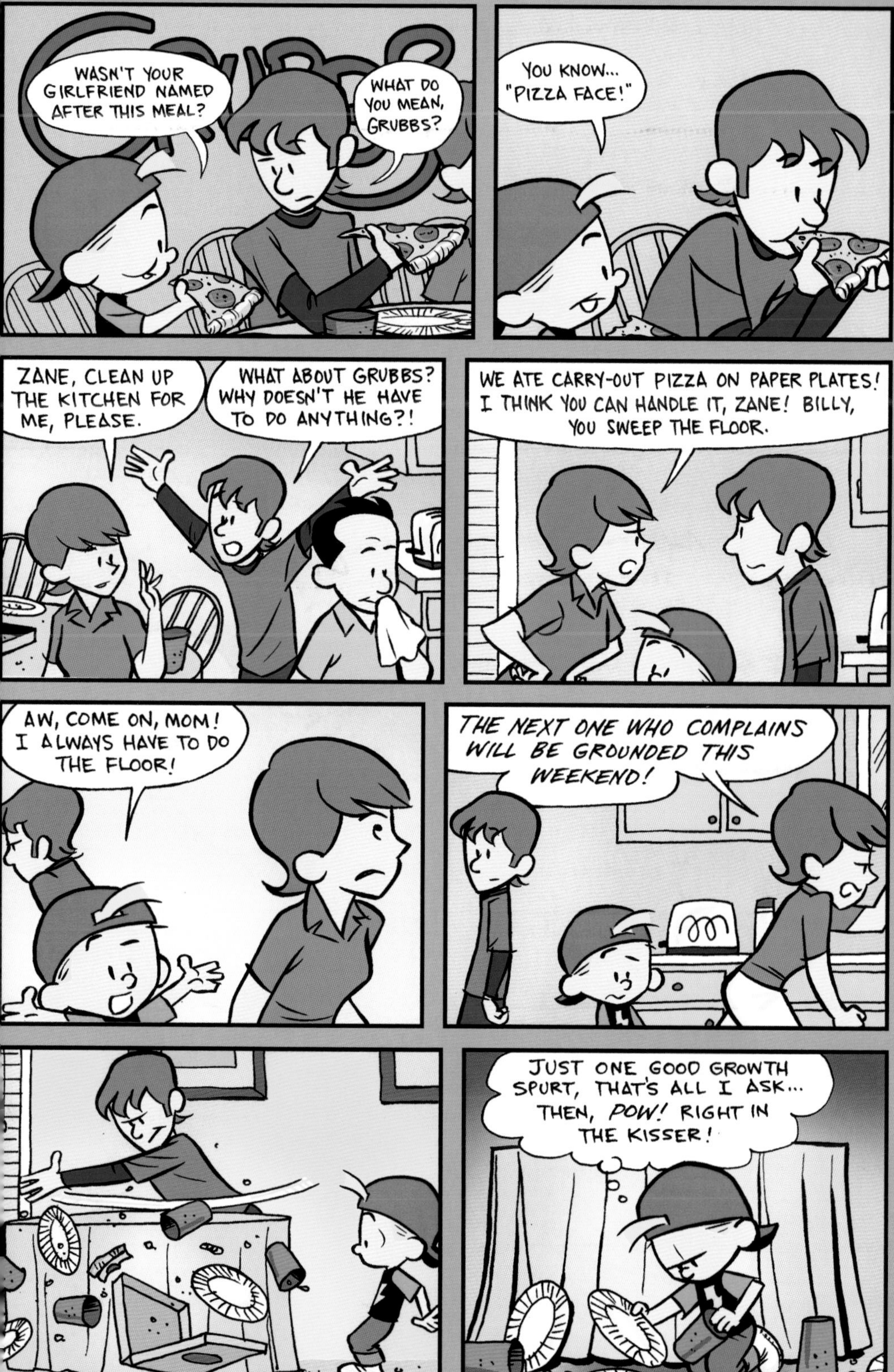
WASN'T YOUR GIRLFRIEND NAMED AFTER THIS MEAL?
WHAT DO YOU MEAN, GRUBBS?
YOU KNOW... "PIZZA FACE!"
ZANE, CLEAN UP THE KITCHEN FOR ME, PLEASE.
WHAT ABOUT GRUBBS? WHY DOESN'T HE HAVE TO DO ANYTHING?!
WE ATE CARRY-OUT PIZZA ON PAPER PLATES! I THINK YOU CAN HANDLE IT, ZANE! BILLY, YOU SWEEP THE FLOOR.
AW, COME ON, MOM! I ALWAYS HAVE TO DO THE FLOOR!
THE NEXT ONE WHO COMPLAINS WILL BE GROUNDED THIS WEEKEND!
JUST ONE GOOD GROWTH SPURT, THAT'S ALL I ASK... THEN, POW! RIGHT IN THE KISSER!

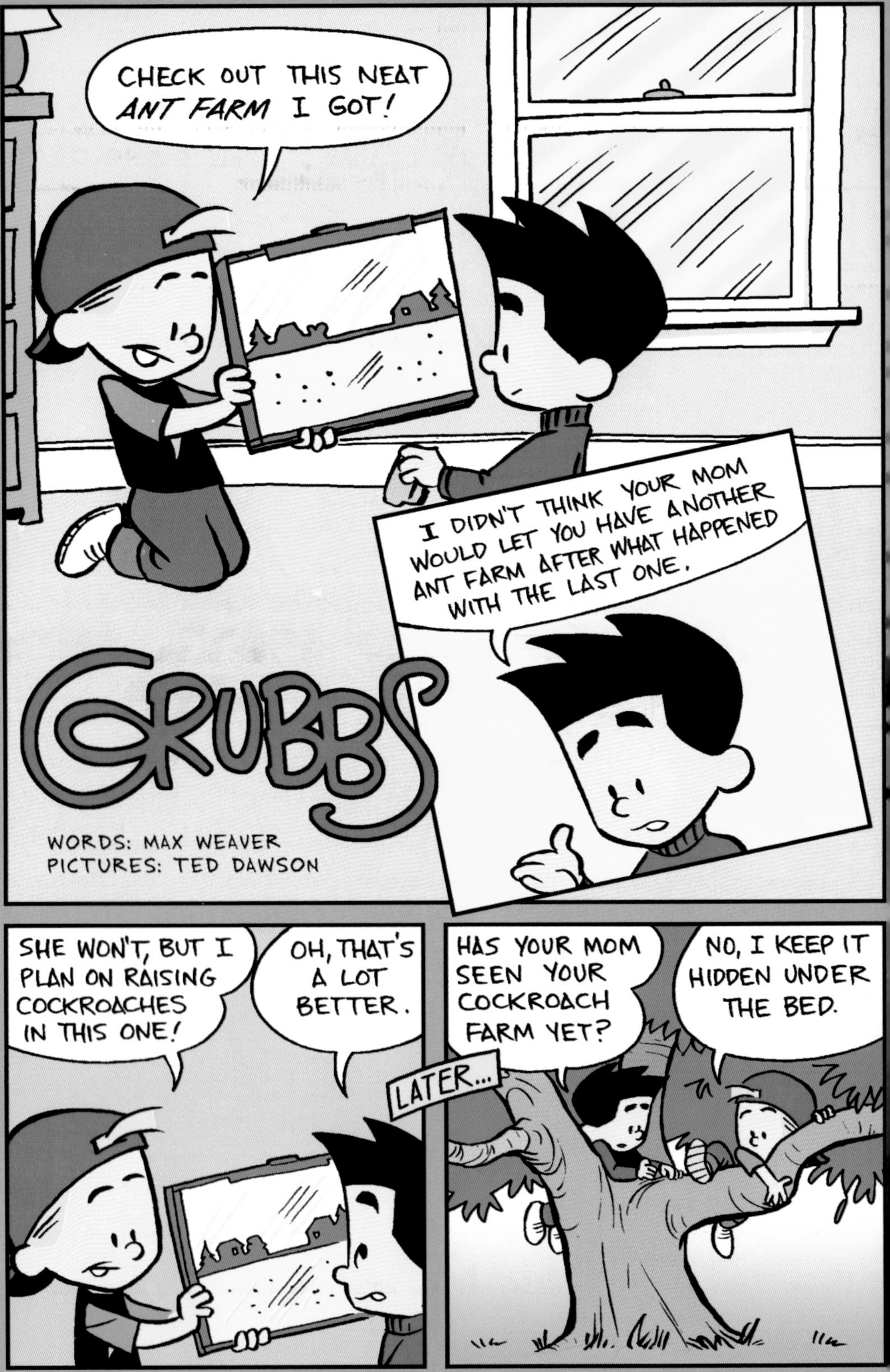
CHECK OUT THIS NEAT ANT FARM I GOT!
I DIDN'T THINK YOUR MOM WOULD LET YOU HAVE ANOTHER ANT FARM AFTER WHAT HAPPENED WITH THE LAST ONE.
GRUBBS
WORDS: MAX WEAVER
PICTURES: TED DAWSON
SHE WON'T, BUT I PLAN ON RAISING COCKROACHES IN THIS ONE!
OH, THAT'S A LOT BETTER.
LATER...
HAS YOUR MOM SEEN YOUR COCKROACH FARM YET?
NO, I KEEP IT HIDDEN UNDER THE BED.

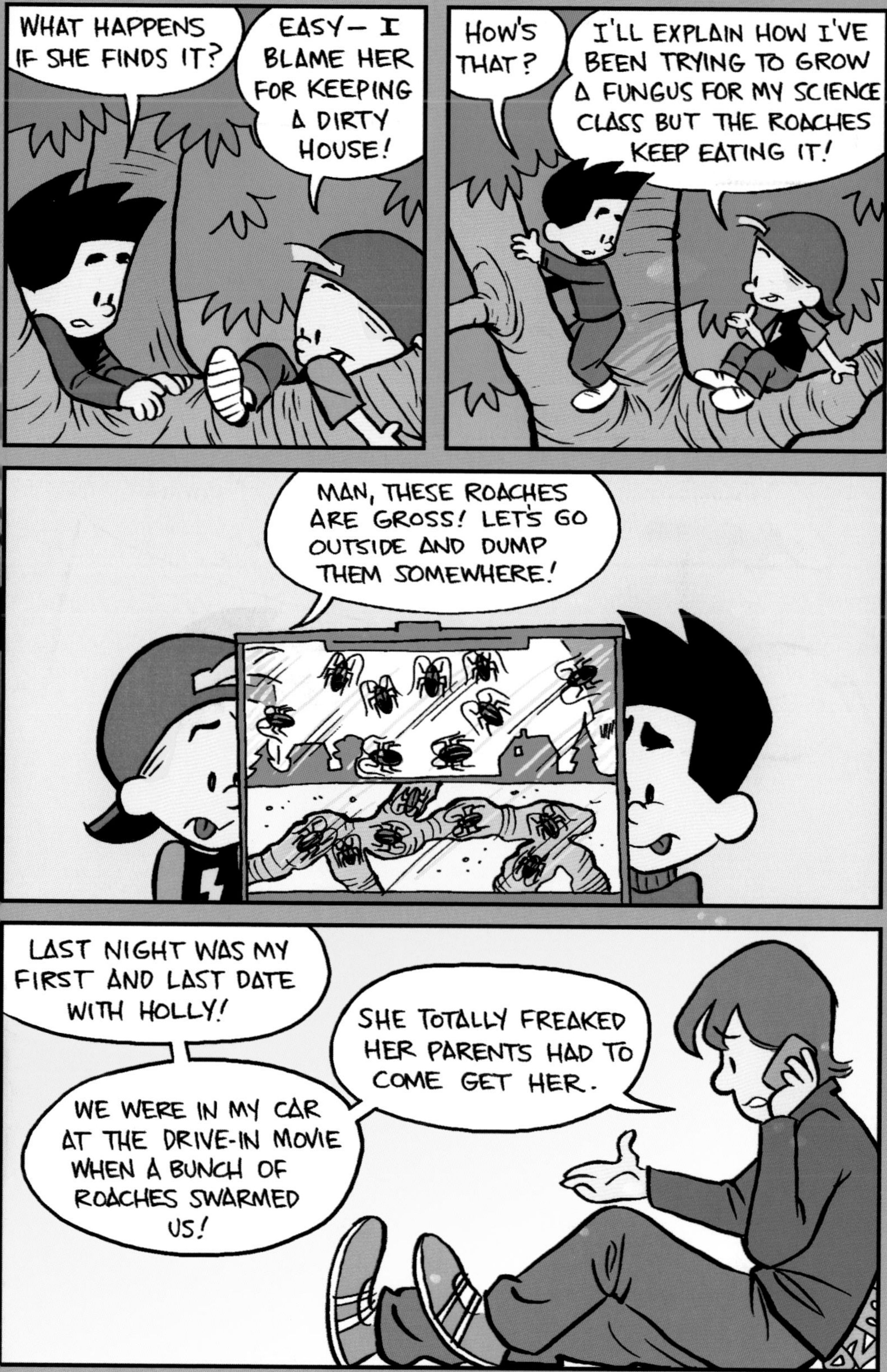
WHAT HAPPENS IF SHE FINDS IT?
EASY— I BLAME HER FOR KEEPING A DIRTY HOUSE!
HOW'S THAT?
I'LL EXPLAIN HOW I'VE BEEN TRYING TO GROW A FUNGUS FOR MY SCIENCE CLASS BUT THE ROACHES KEEP EATING IT!
MAN, THESE ROACHES ARE GROSS! LET'S GO OUTSIDE AND DUMP THEM SOMEWHERE!
LAST NIGHT WAS MY FIRST AND LAST DATE WITH HOLLY!
WE WERE IN MY CAR AT THE DRIVE-IN MOVIE WHEN A BUNCH OF ROACHES SWARMED US!
SHE TOTALLY FREAKED HER PARENTS HAD TO COME GET HER.

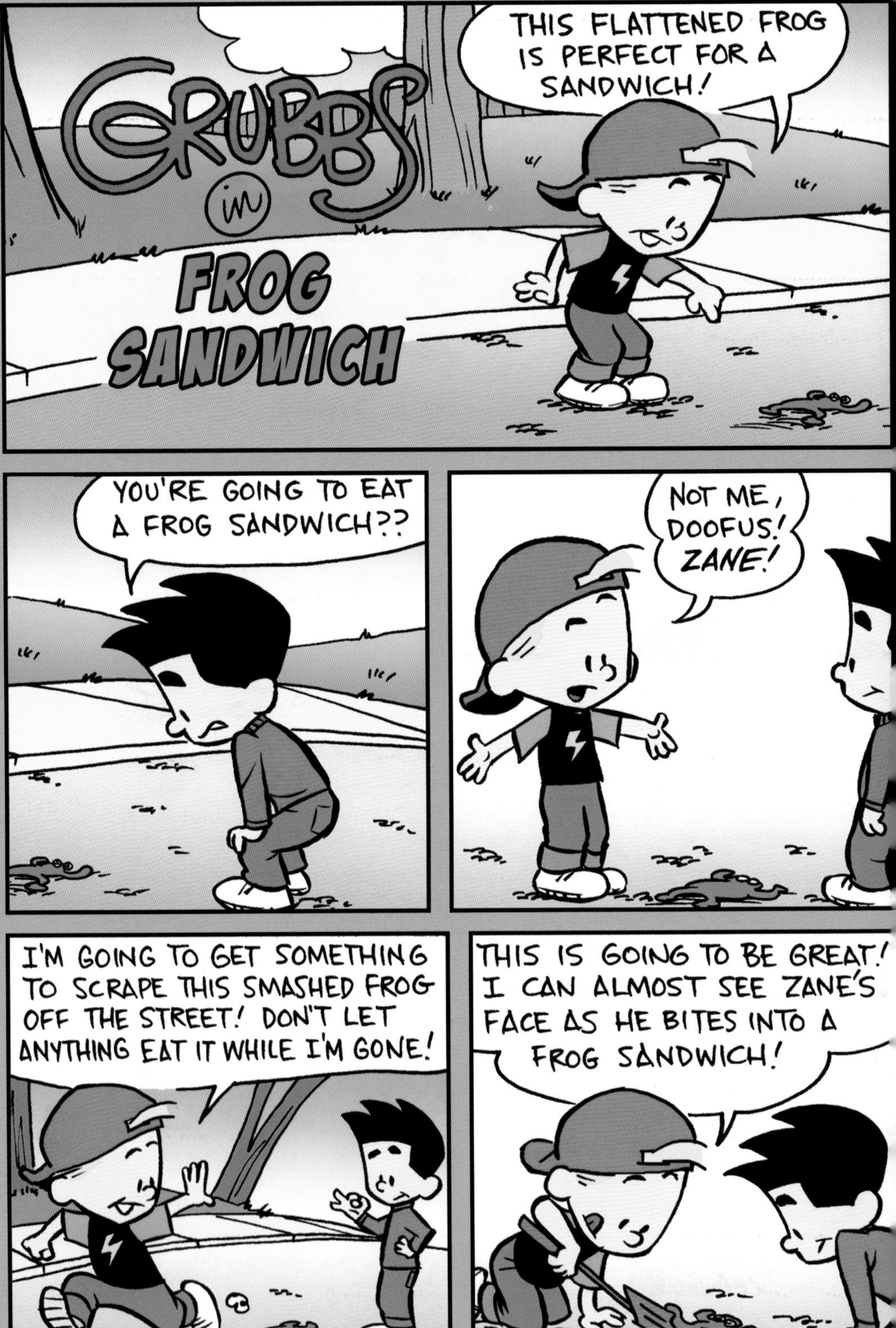
GRUBBS in
FROG SANDWICH
THIS FLATTENED FROG IS PERFECT FOR A SANDWICH!
YOU'RE GOING TO EAT A FROG SANDWICH??
NOT ME, DOOFUS! ZANE!
I'M GOING TO GET SOMETHING TO SCRAPE THIS SMASHED FROG OFF THE STREET! DON'T LET ANYTHING EAT IT WHILE I'M GONE!
THIS IS GOING TO BE GREAT! I CAN ALMOST SEE ZANE'S FACE AS HE BITES INTO A FROG SANDWICH!

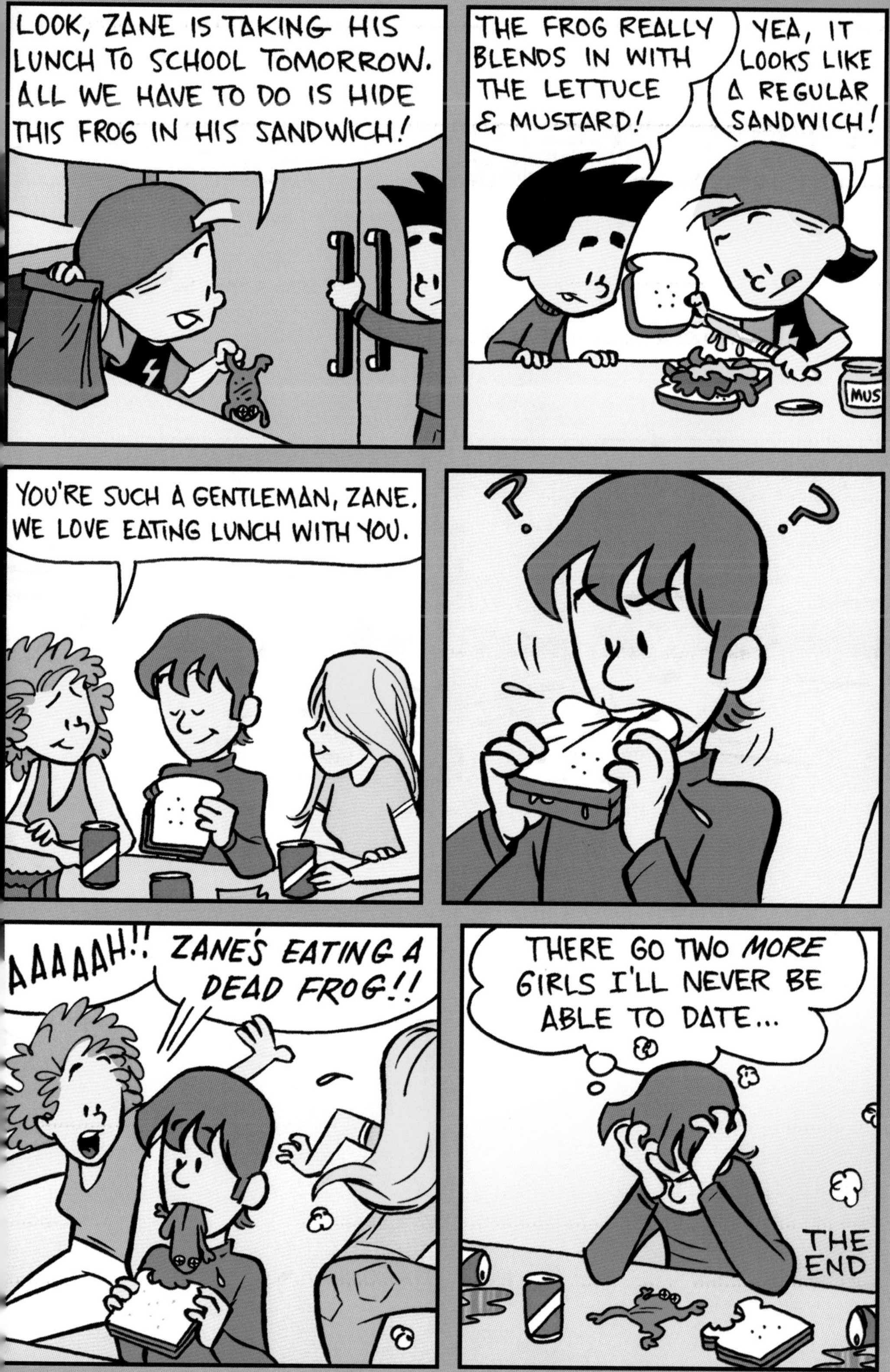
LOOK, ZANE IS TAKING HIS LUNCH TO SCHOOL TOMORROW. ALL WE HAVE TO DO IS HIDE THIS FROG IN HIS SANDWICH!
THE FROG REALLY BLENDS IN WITH THE LETTUCE & MUSTARD!
YEA, IT LOOKS LIKE A REGULAR SANDWICH!
MUS
YOU'RE SUCH A GENTLEMAN, ZANE. WE LOVE EATING LUNCH WITH YOU.
?
?
AAAAAH!!
ZANE'S EATING A DEAD FROG!!
THERE GO TWO MORE GIRLS I'LL NEVER BE ABLE TO DATE...
THE END

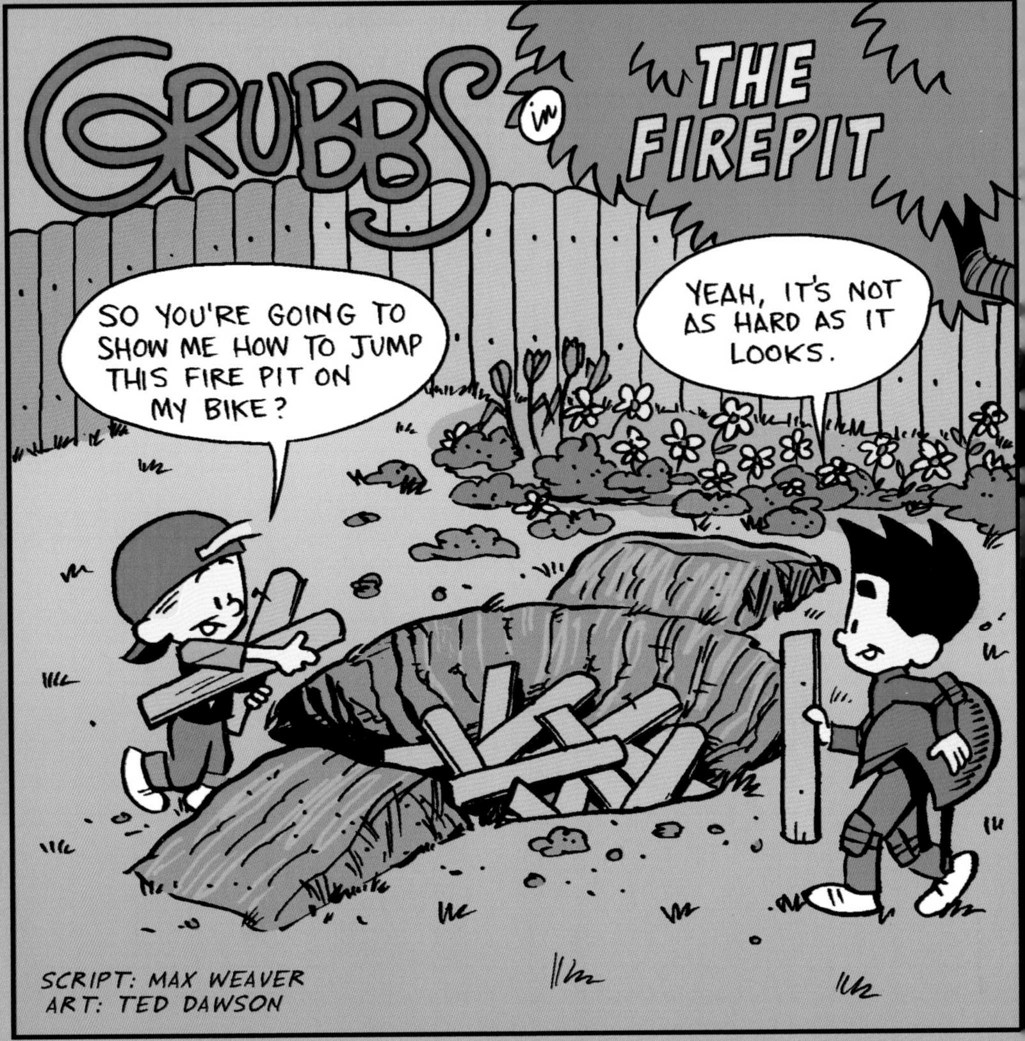
GRUBBS in THE FIREPIT
SO YOU'RE GOING TO SHOW ME HOW TO JUMP THIS FIRE PIT ON MY BIKE?
YEAH, IT'S NOT AS HARD AS IT LOOKS.
SCRIPT: MAX WEAVER
ART: TED DAWSON

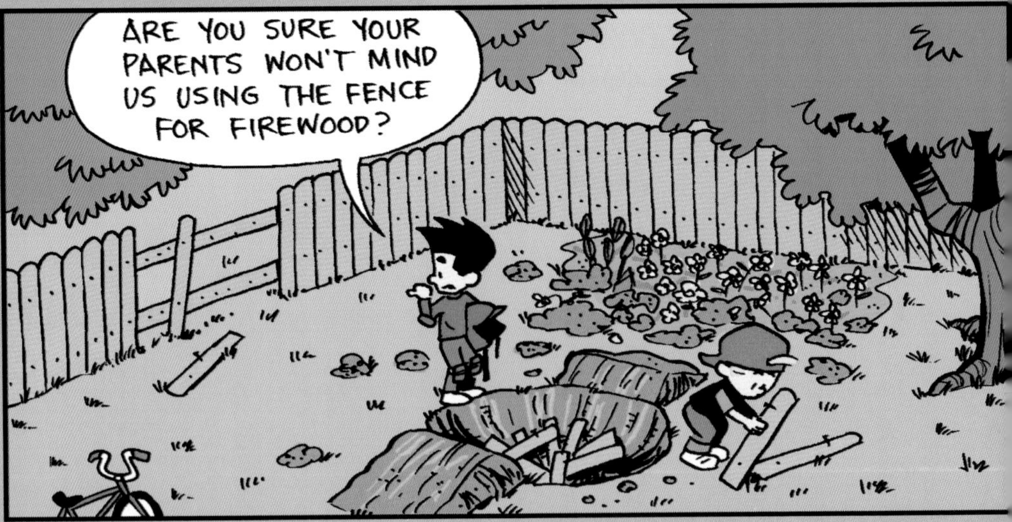
ARE YOU SURE YOUR PARENTS WON'T MIND US USING THE FENCE FOR FIREWOOD?

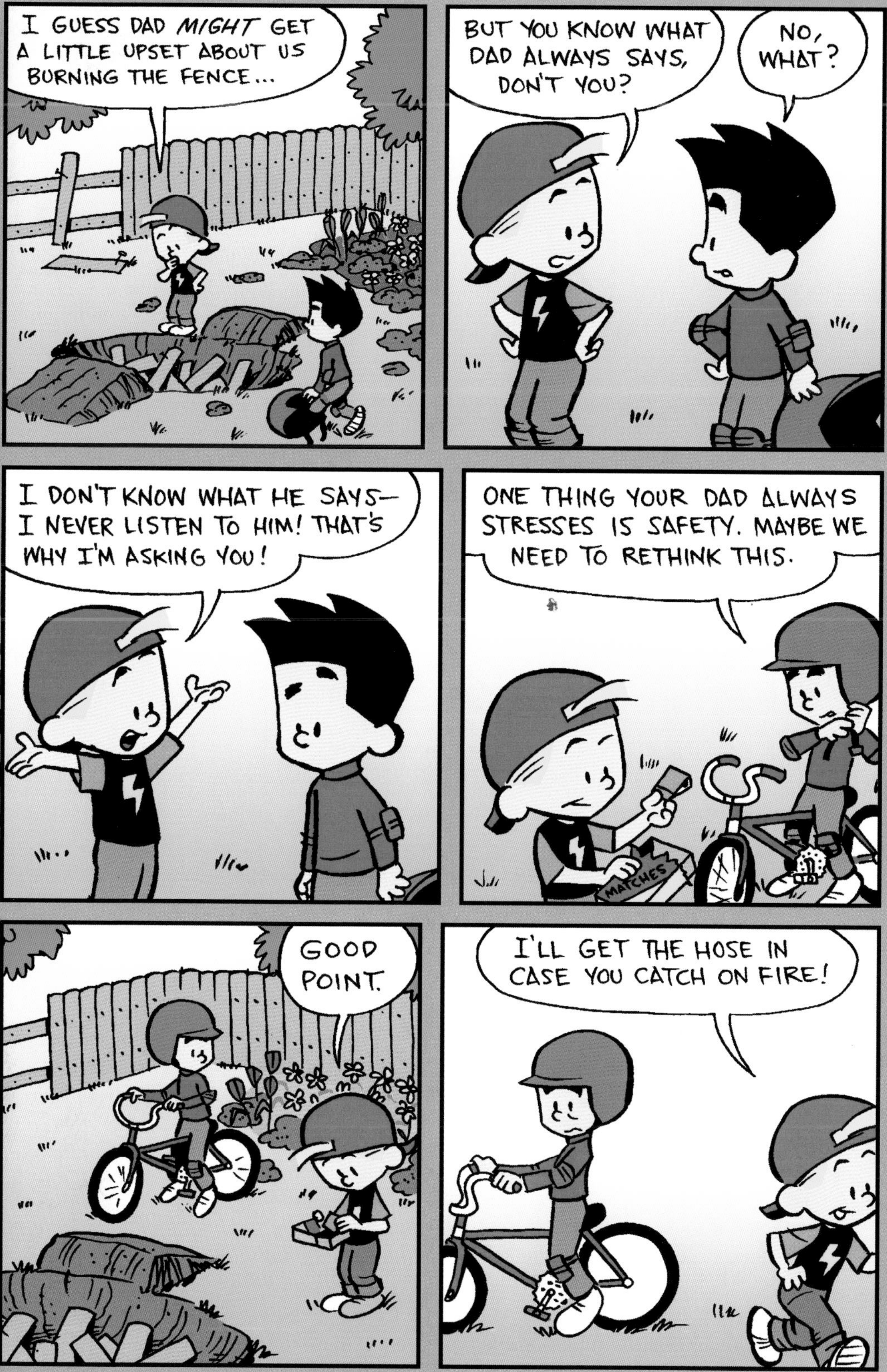
I GUESS DAD *MIGHT* GET A LITTLE UPSET ABOUT US BURNING THE FENCE...
BUT YOU KNOW WHAT DAD ALWAYS SAYS, DON'T YOU?
NO, WHAT?
I DON'T KNOW WHAT HE SAYS— I NEVER LISTEN TO HIM! THAT'S WHY I'M ASKING YOU!
ONE THING YOUR DAD ALWAYS STRESSES IS SAFETY. MAYBE WE NEED TO RETHINK THIS.
MATCHES
GOOD POINT.
I'LL GET THE HOSE IN CASE YOU CATCH ON FIRE!

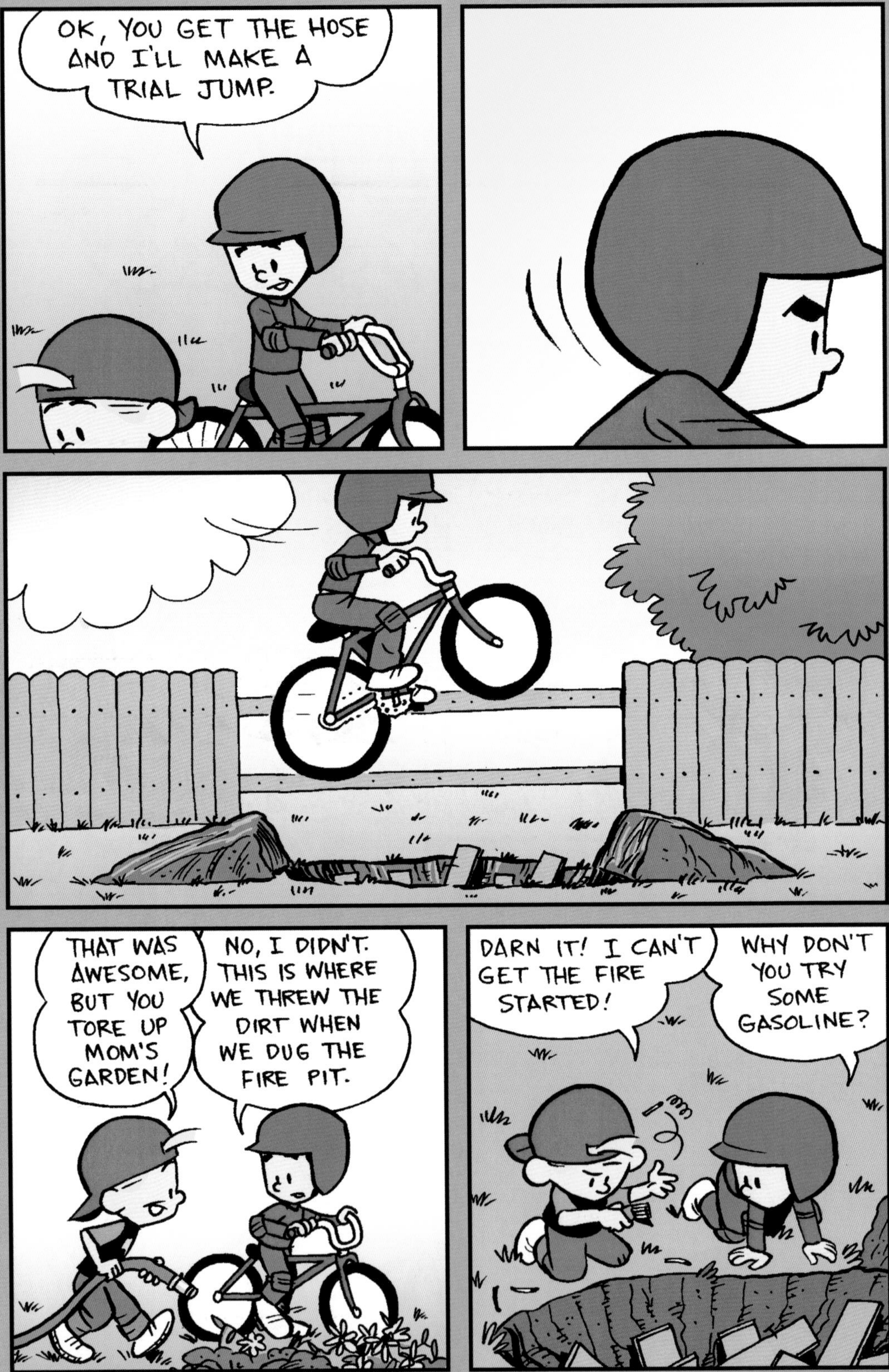
OK, YOU GET THE HOSE AND I'LL MAKE A TRIAL JUMP.
THAT WAS AWESOME, BUT YOU TORE UP MOM'S GARDEN!
NO, I DIDN'T. THIS IS WHERE WE THREW THE DIRT WHEN WE DUG THE FIRE PIT.
DARN IT! I CAN'T GET THE FIRE STARTED!
WHY DON'T YOU TRY SOME GASOLINE?

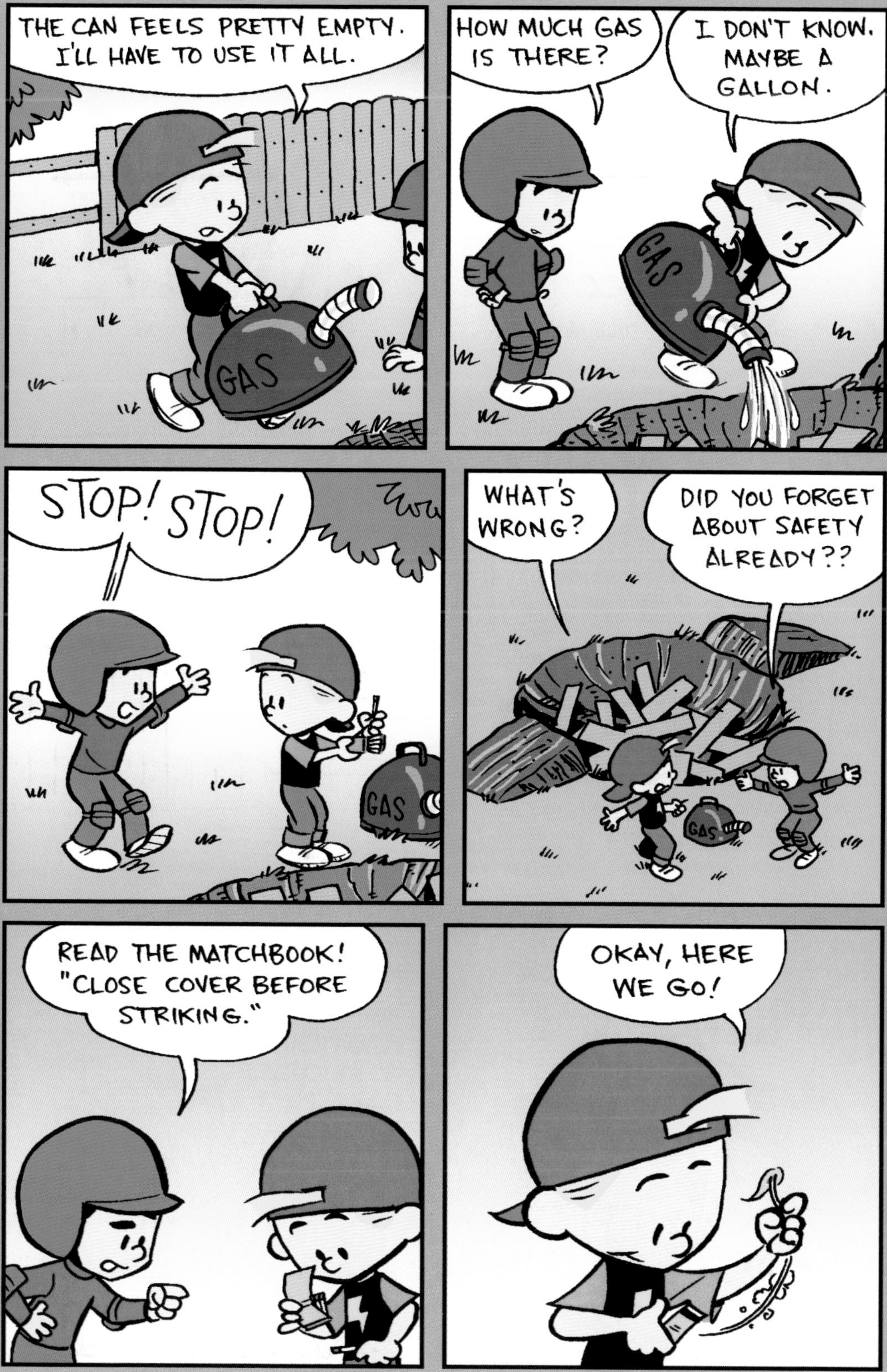
THE CAN FEELS PRETTY EMPTY. I'LL HAVE TO USE IT ALL.
GAS
HOW MUCH GAS IS THERE?
I DON'T KNOW. MAYBE A GALLON.
GAS
STOP! STOP!
GAS
WHAT'S WRONG?
DID YOU FORGET ABOUT SAFETY ALREADY??
GAS
READ THE MATCHBOOK! "CLOSE COVER BEFORE STRIKING."
OKAY, HERE WE GO!

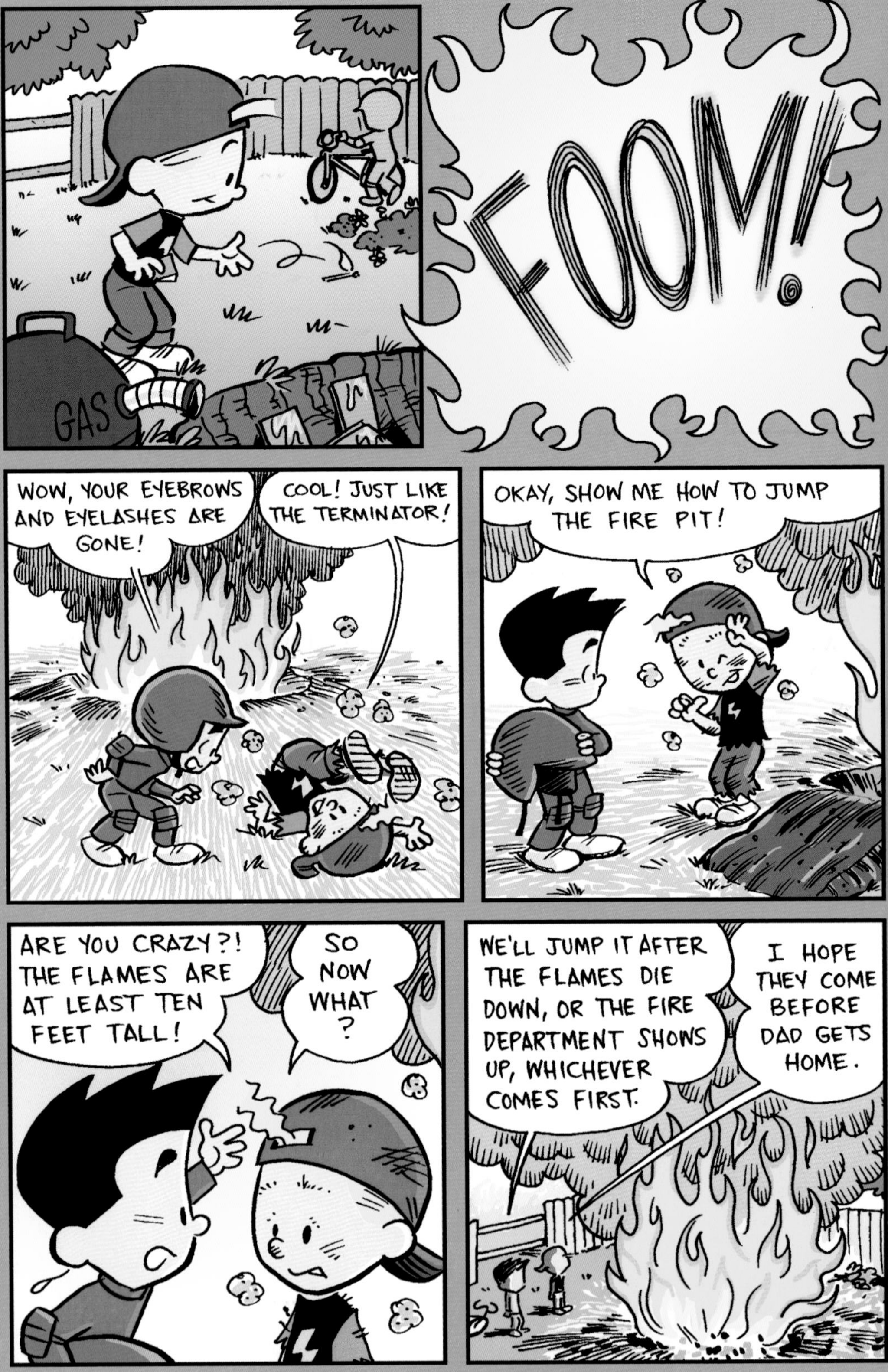
FOOM!
WOW, YOUR EYEBROWS AND EYELASHES ARE GONE!
COOL! JUST LIKE THE TERMINATOR!
OKAY, SHOW ME HOW TO JUMP THE FIRE PIT!
ARE YOU CRAZY?! THE FLAMES ARE AT LEAST TEN FEET TALL!
SO NOW WHAT?
WE'LL JUMP IT AFTER THE FLAMES DIE DOWN, OR THE FIRE DEPARTMENT SHOWS UP, WHICHEVER COMES FIRST.
I HOPE THEY COME BEFORE DAD GETS HOME.

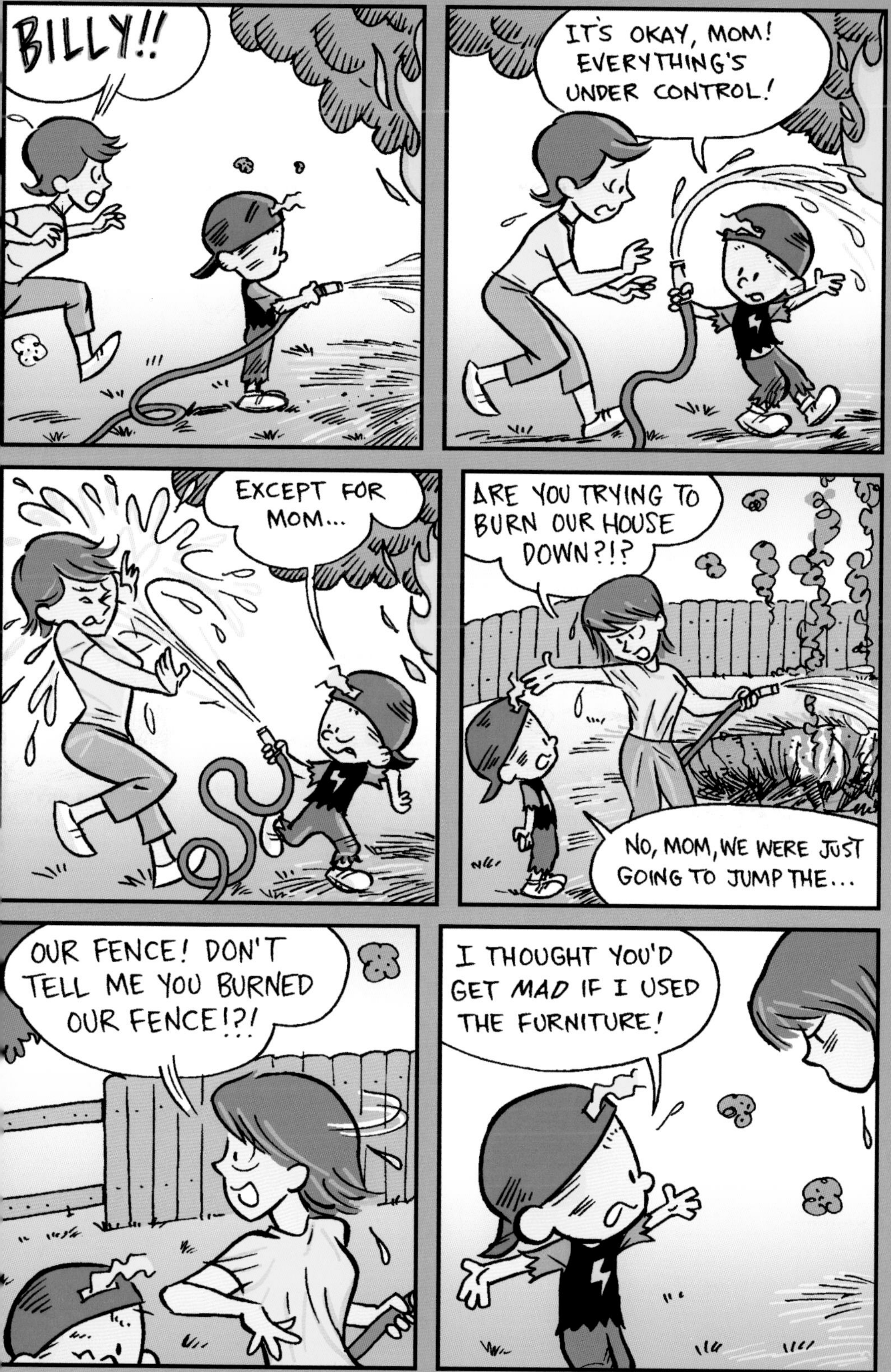
BILLY!!
IT'S OKAY, MOM! EVERYTHING'S UNDER CONTROL!
EXCEPT FOR MOM...
ARE YOU TRYING TO BURN OUR HOUSE DOWN?!?
NO, MOM, WE WERE JUST GOING TO JUMP THE...
OUR FENCE! DON'T TELL ME YOU BURNED OUR FENCE!?!
I THOUGHT YOU'D GET *MAD* IF I USED THE FURNITURE!

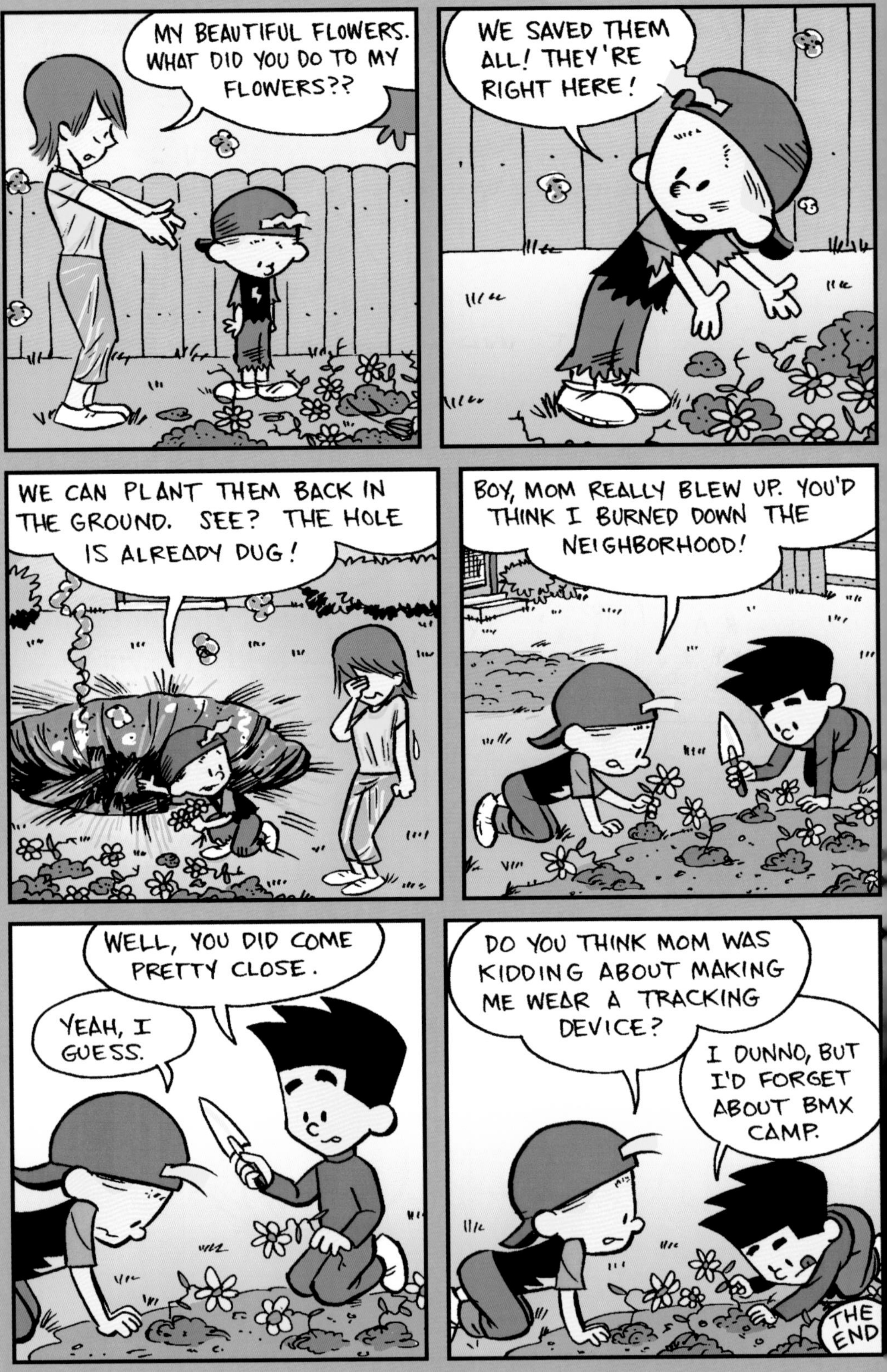
MY BEAUTIFUL FLOWERS. WHAT DID YOU DO TO MY FLOWERS??
WE SAVED THEM ALL! THEY'RE RIGHT HERE!
WE CAN PLANT THEM BACK IN THE GROUND. SEE? THE HOLE IS ALREADY DUG!
BOY, MOM REALLY BLEW UP. YOU'D THINK I BURNED DOWN THE NEIGHBORHOOD!
WELL, YOU DID COME PRETTY CLOSE.
YEAH, I GUESS.
DO YOU THINK MOM WAS KIDDING ABOUT MAKING ME WEAR A TRACKING DEVICE?
I DUNNO, BUT I'D FORGET ABOUT BMX CAMP.
THE END

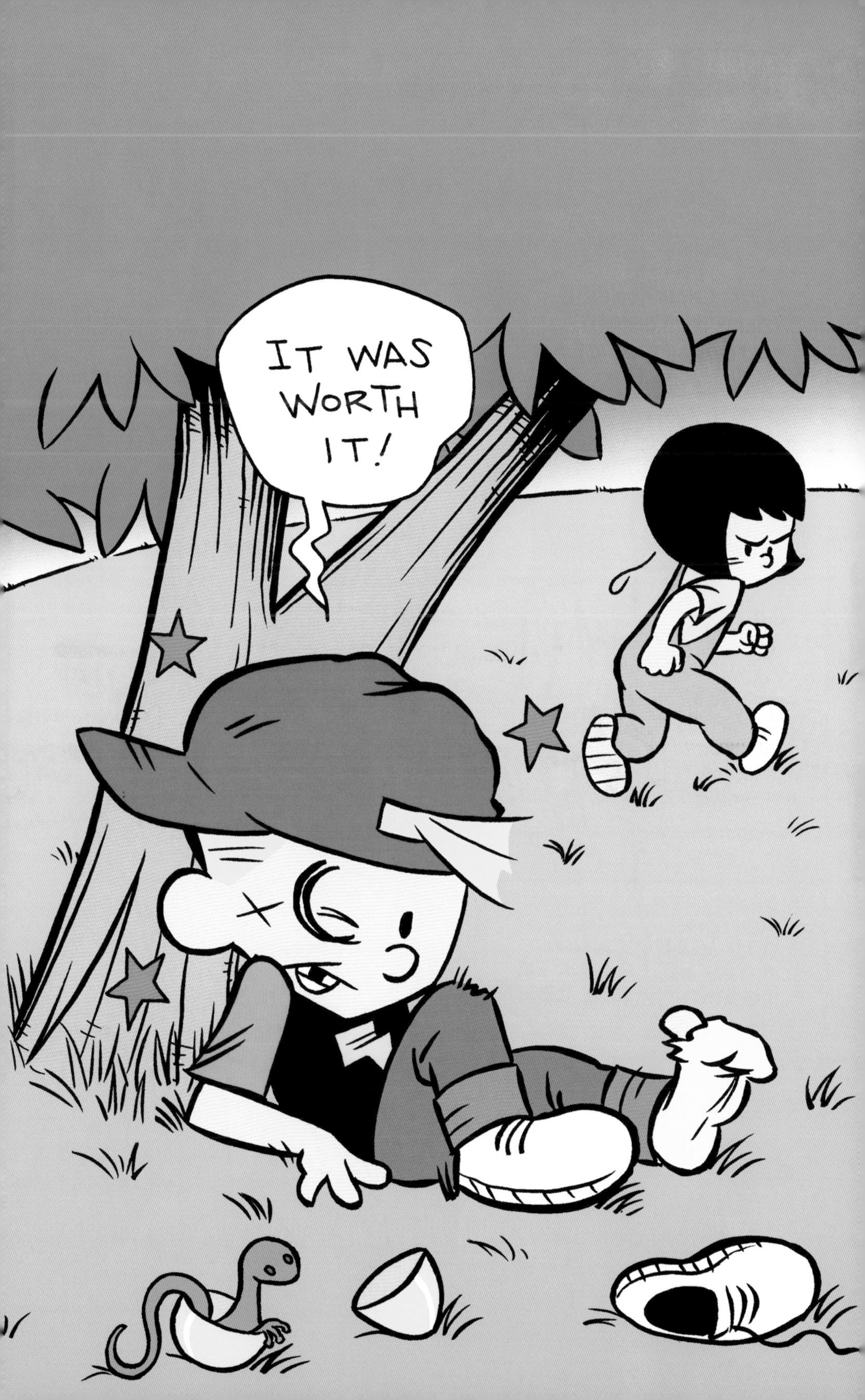
IT WAS WORTH IT!

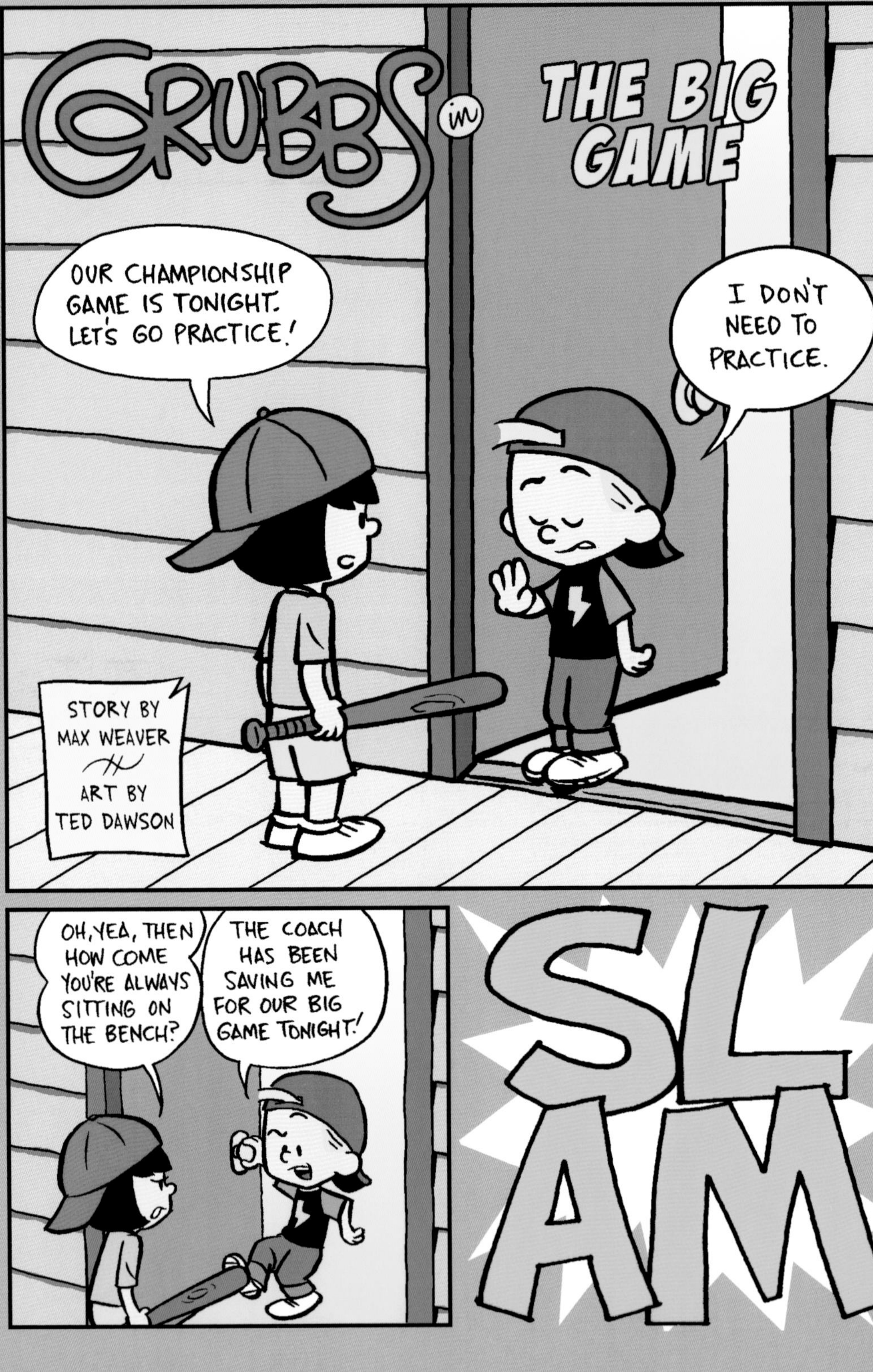
GRUBBS in THE BIG GAME
OUR CHAMPIONSHIP GAME IS TONIGHT. LET'S GO PRACTICE!
I DON'T NEED TO PRACTICE.
STORY BY MAX WEAVER
ART BY TED DAWSON
OH, YEA, THEN HOW COME YOU'RE ALWAYS SITTING ON THE BENCH?
THE COACH HAS BEEN SAVING ME FOR OUR BIG GAME TONIGHT!
SLAM

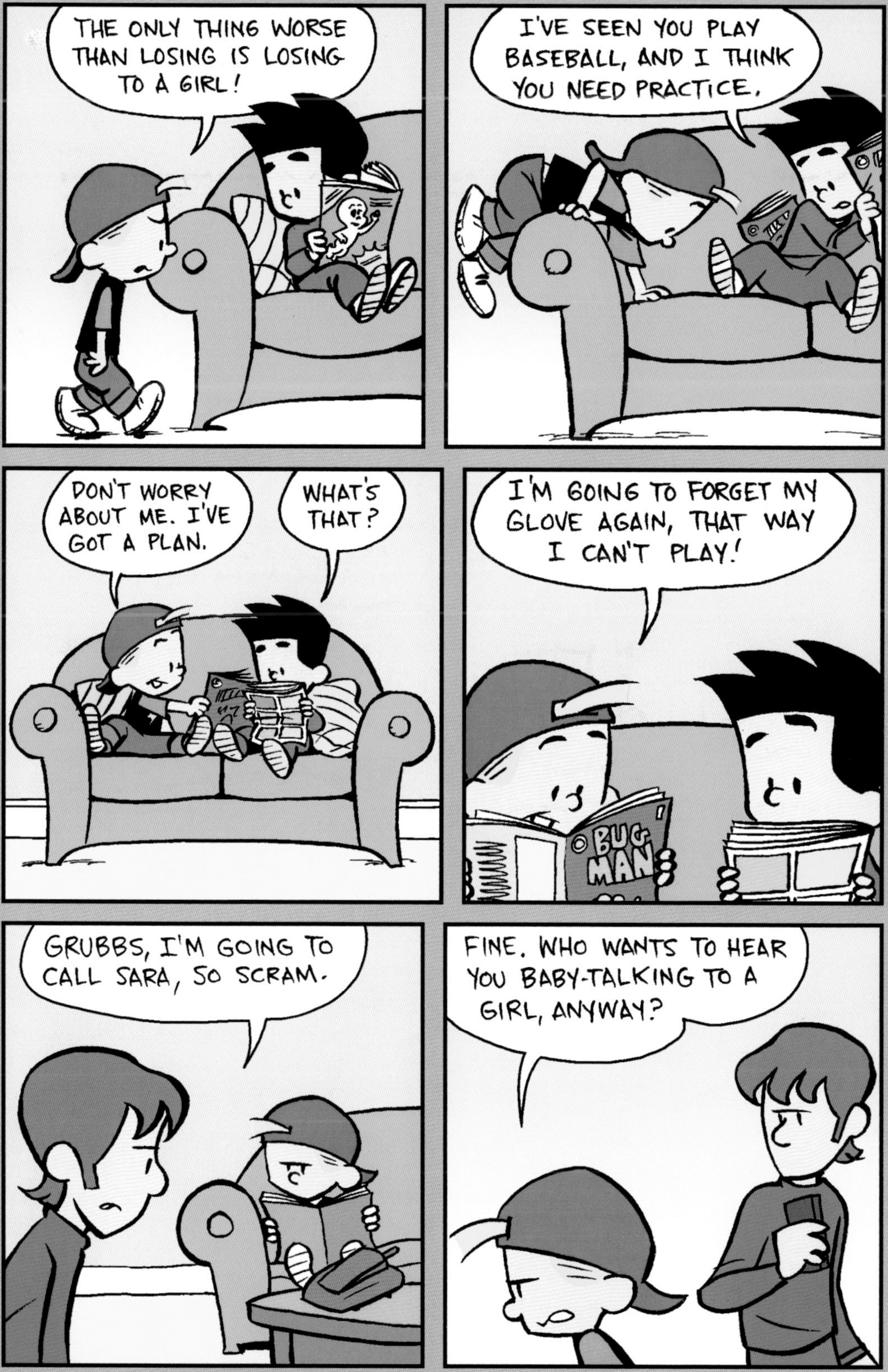
THE ONLY THING WORSE THAN LOSING IS LOSING TO A GIRL!
I'VE SEEN YOU PLAY BASEBALL, AND I THINK YOU NEED PRACTICE.
DON'T WORRY ABOUT ME. I'VE GOT A PLAN.
WHAT'S THAT?
I'M GOING TO FORGET MY GLOVE AGAIN, THAT WAY I CAN'T PLAY!
BUG MAN
GRUBBS, I'M GOING TO CALL SARA, SO SCRAM.
FINE. WHO WANTS TO HEAR YOU BABY-TALKING TO A GIRL, ANYWAY?

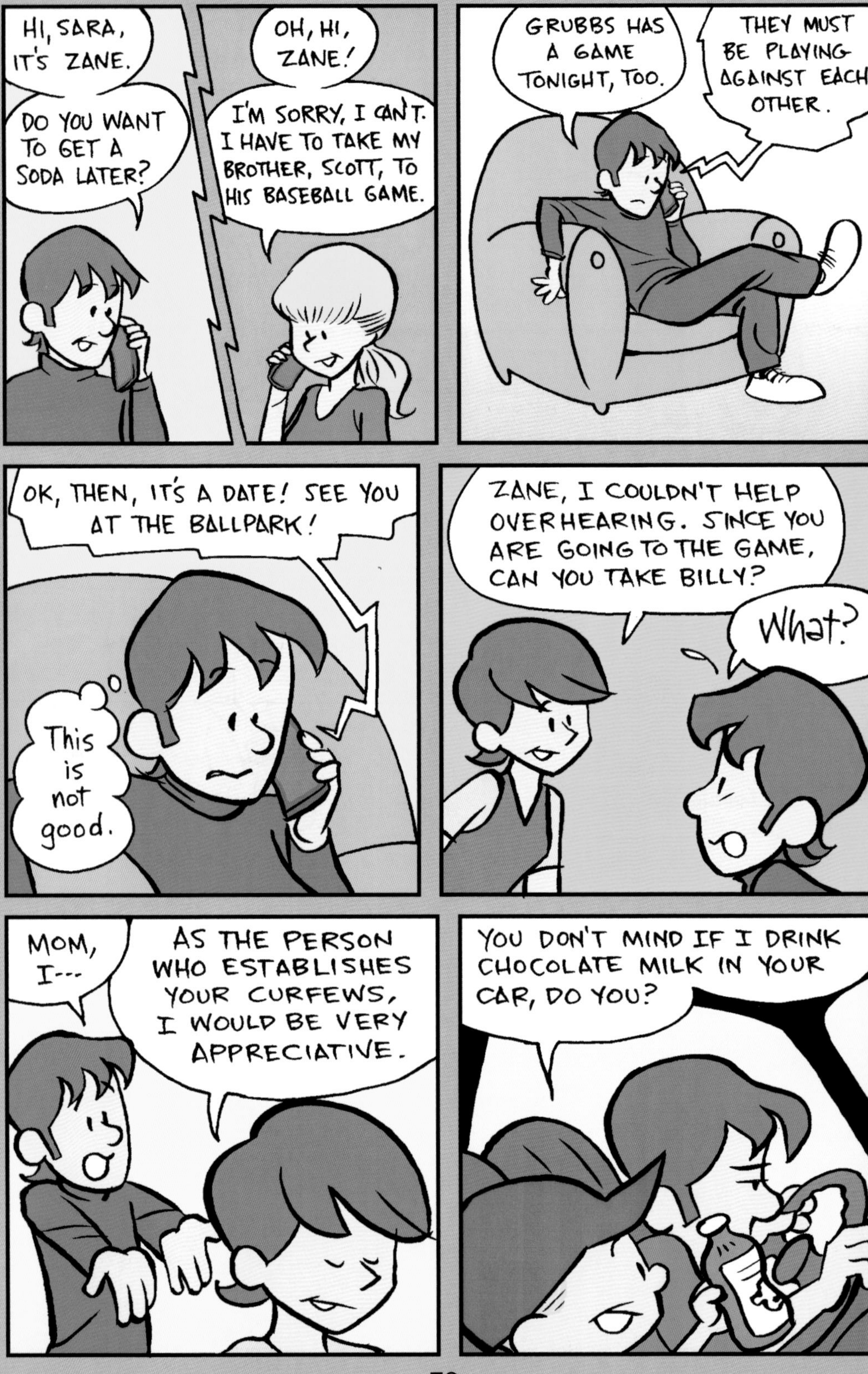
HI, SARA, IT'S ZANE.
DO YOU WANT TO GET A SODA LATER?
OH, HI, ZANE!
I'M SORRY, I CAN'T. I HAVE TO TAKE MY BROTHER, SCOTT, TO HIS BASEBALL GAME.
GRUBBS HAS A GAME TONIGHT, TOO.
THEY MUST BE PLAYING AGAINST EACH OTHER.
OK, THEN, IT'S A DATE! SEE YOU AT THE BALLPARK!
This is not good.
ZANE, I COULDN'T HELP OVERHEARING. SINCE YOU ARE GOING TO THE GAME, CAN YOU TAKE BILLY?
What?
MOM, I---
AS THE PERSON WHO ESTABLISHES YOUR CURFEWS, I WOULD BE VERY APPRECIATIVE.
YOU DON'T MIND IF I DRINK CHOCOLATE MILK IN YOUR CAR, DO YOU?

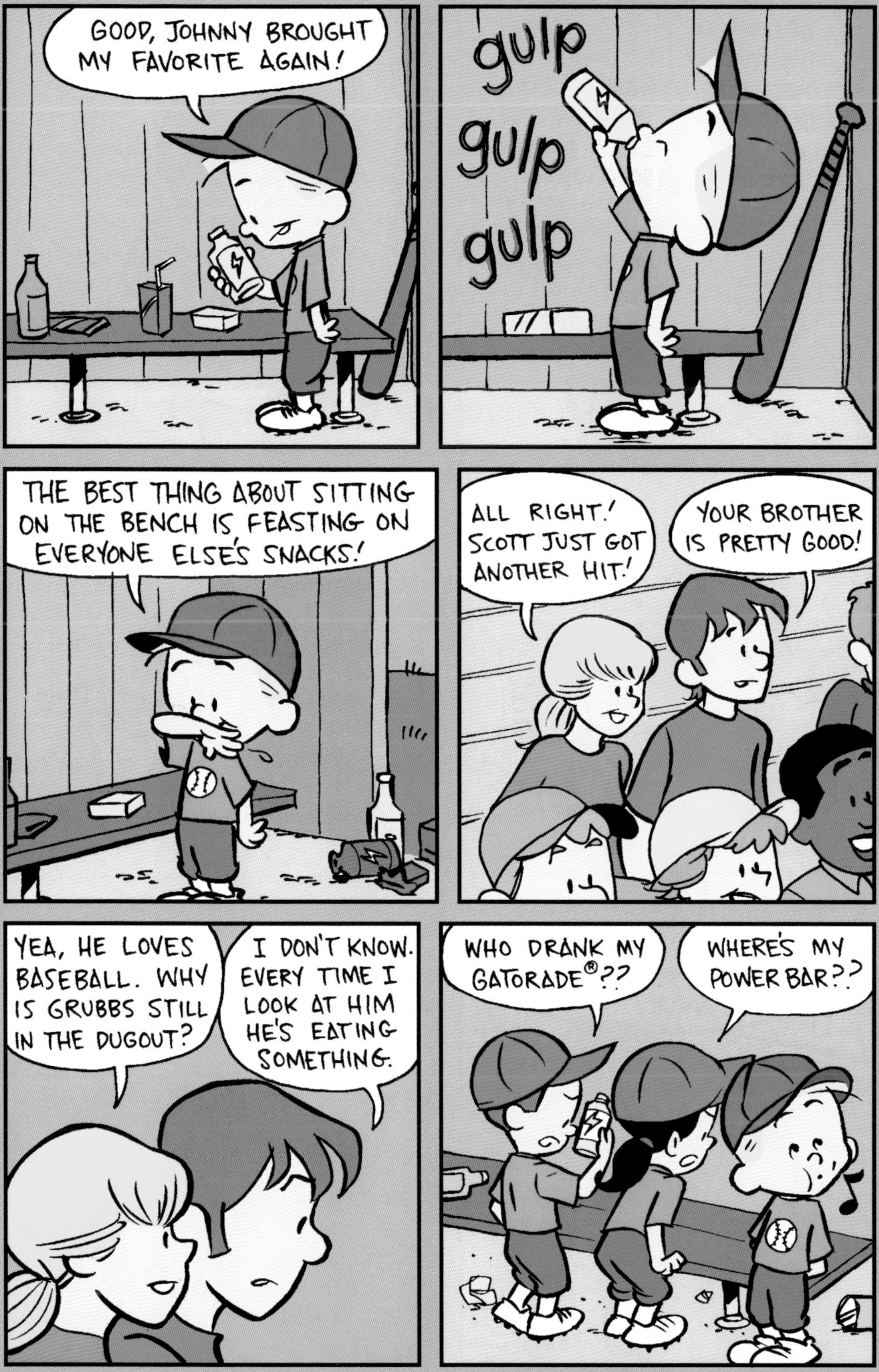
GOOD, JOHNNY BROUGHT MY FAVORITE AGAIN!
gulp gulp gulp
THE BEST THING ABOUT SITTING ON THE BENCH IS FEASTING ON EVERYONE ELSE'S SNACKS!
ALL RIGHT! SCOTT JUST GOT ANOTHER HIT!
YOUR BROTHER IS PRETTY GOOD!
YEA, HE LOVES BASEBALL. WHY IS GRUBBS STILL IN THE DUGOUT?
I DON'T KNOW. EVERY TIME I LOOK AT HIM HE'S EATING SOMETHING.
WHO DRANK MY GATORADE®??
WHERE'S MY POWER BAR??

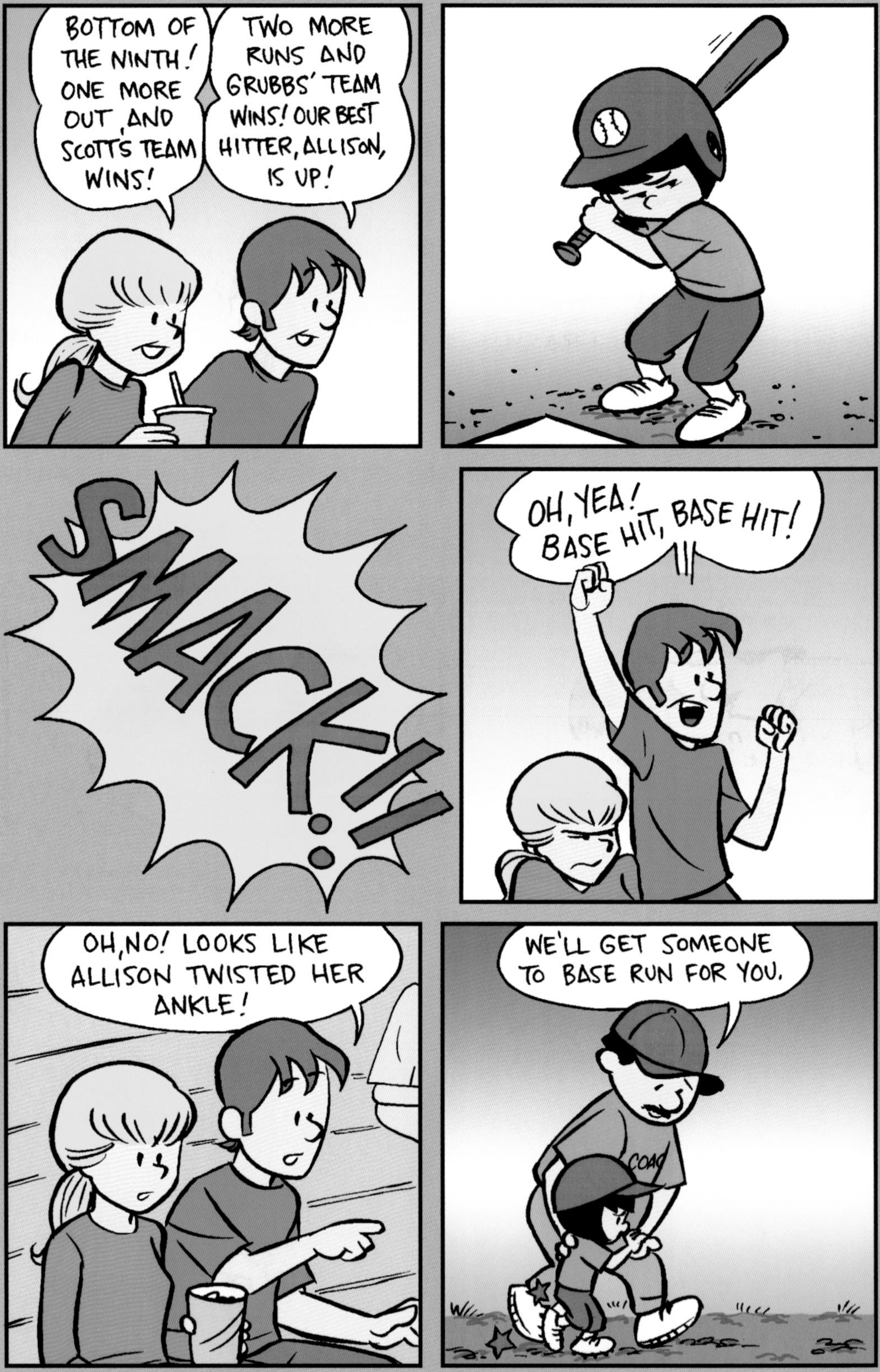

BOTTOM OF THE NINTH! ONE MORE OUT, AND SCOTT'S TEAM WINS!
TWO MORE RUNS AND GRUBBS' TEAM WINS! OUR BEST HITTER, ALLISON, IS UP!
SMACK!!
OH, YEA! BASE HIT, BASE HIT!
OH, NO! LOOKS LIKE ALLISON TWISTED HER ANKLE!
WE'LL GET SOMEONE TO BASE RUN FOR YOU.

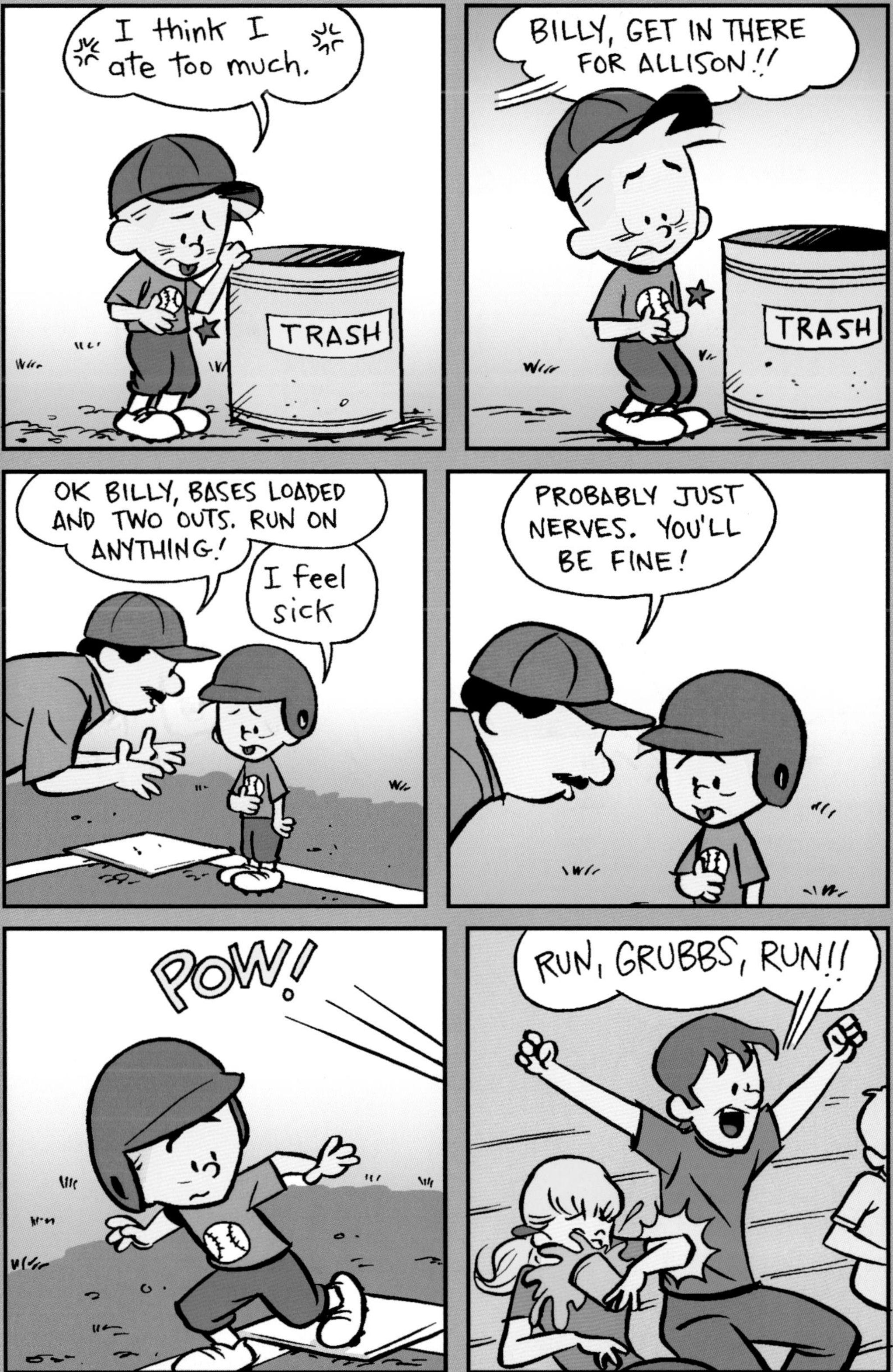
I think I ate too much.
BILLY, GET IN THERE FOR ALLISON!!
TRASH
TRASH
OK BILLY, BASES LOADED AND TWO OUTS. RUN ON ANYTHING!
I feel sick
PROBABLY JUST NERVES. YOU'LL BE FINE!
POW!
RUN, GRUBBS, RUN!!

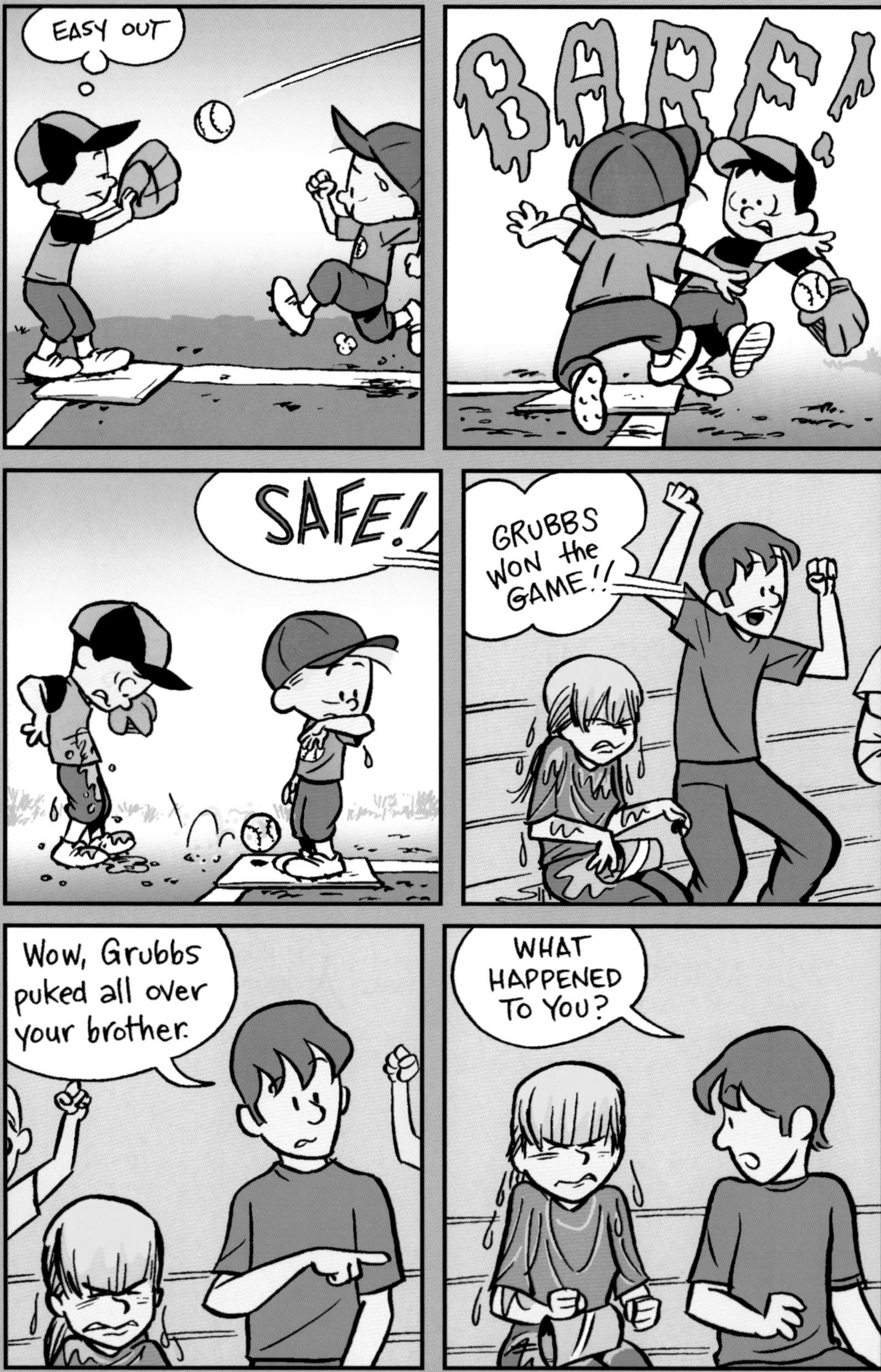
EASY OUT
BARF!
SAFE!
GRUBBS WON the GAME!!
Wow, Grubbs puked all over your brother.
WHAT HAPPENED TO YOU?

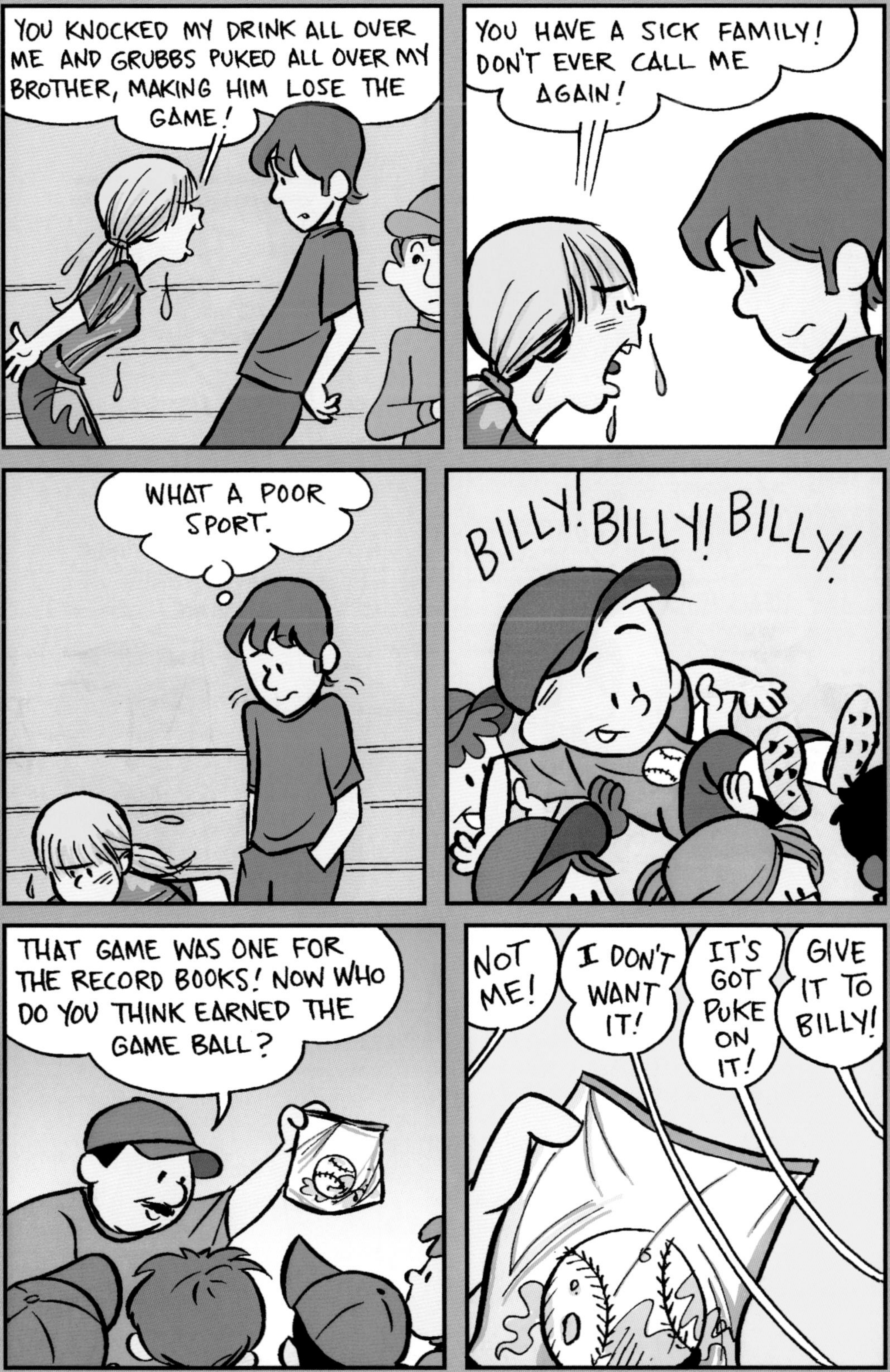
YOU KNOCKED MY DRINK ALL OVER ME AND GRUBBS PUKED ALL OVER MY BROTHER, MAKING HIM LOSE THE GAME!
YOU HAVE A SICK FAMILY! DON'T EVER CALL ME AGAIN!
WHAT A POOR SPORT.
BILLY! BILLY! BILLY!
THAT GAME WAS ONE FOR THE RECORD BOOKS! NOW WHO DO YOU THINK EARNED THE GAME BALL?
NOT ME!
I DON'T WANT IT!
IT'S GOT PUKE ON IT!
GIVE IT TO BILLY!

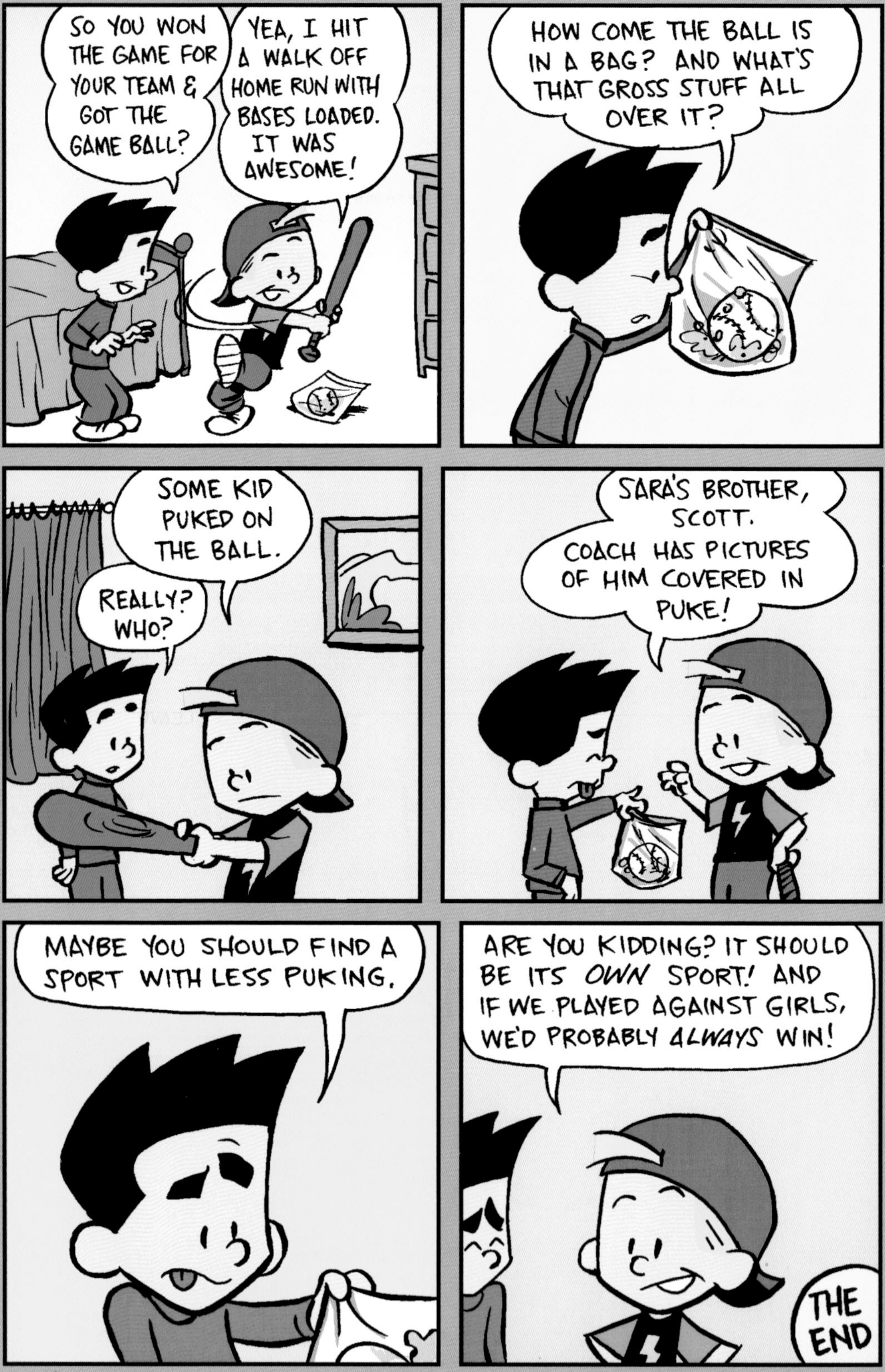
SO YOU WON THE GAME FOR YOUR TEAM & GOT THE GAME BALL?
YEA, I HIT A WALK OFF HOME RUN WITH BASES LOADED. IT WAS AWESOME!
HOW COME THE BALL IS IN A BAG? AND WHAT'S THAT GROSS STUFF ALL OVER IT?
SOME KID PUKED ON THE BALL.
REALLY? WHO?
SARA'S BROTHER, SCOTT. COACH HAS PICTURES OF HIM COVERED IN PUKE!
MAYBE YOU SHOULD FIND A SPORT WITH LESS PUKING.
ARE YOU KIDDING? IT SHOULD BE ITS OWN SPORT! AND IF WE PLAYED AGAINST GIRLS, WE'D PROBABLY ALWAYS WIN!
THE END

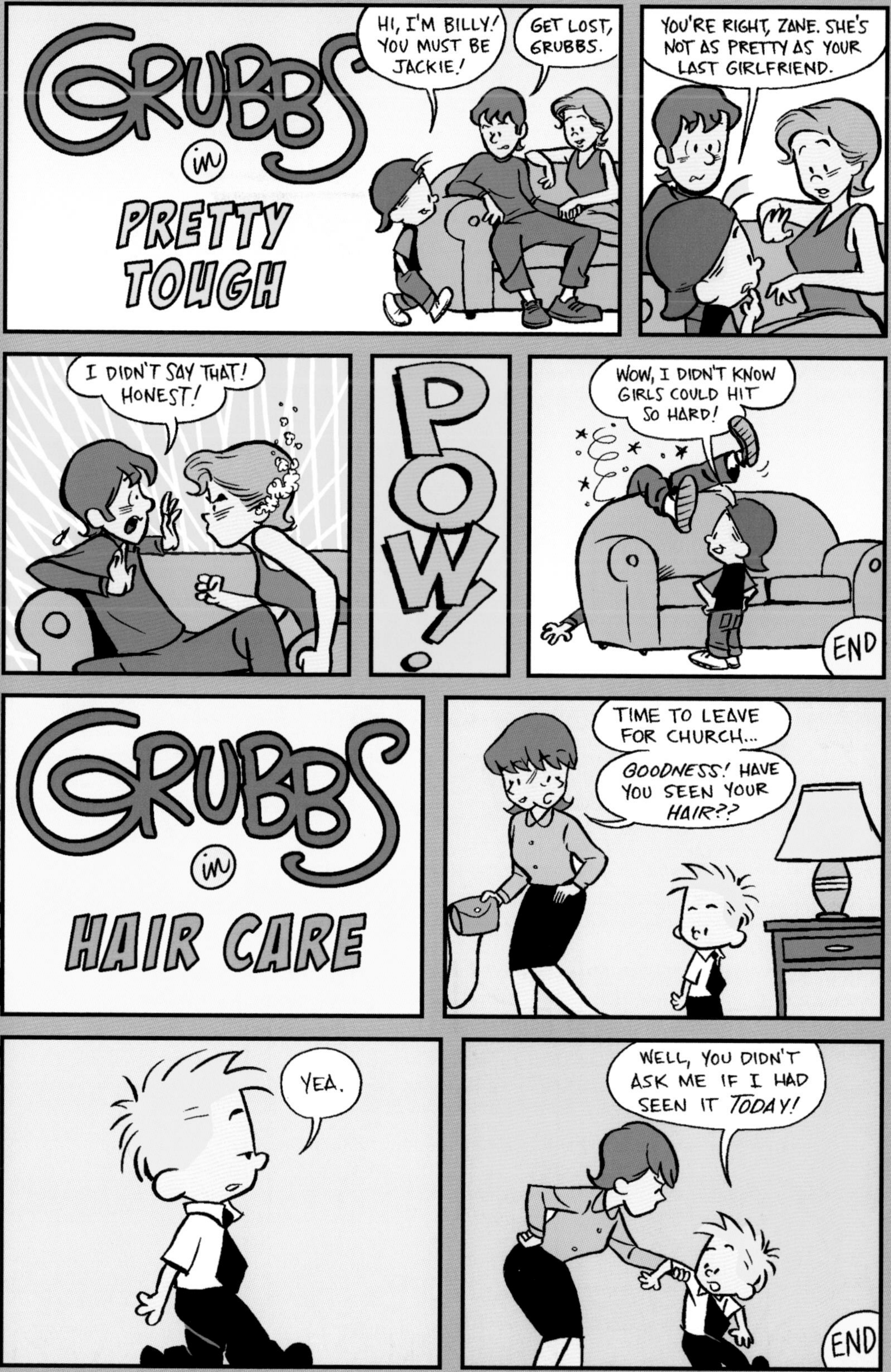
GRUBBS
in
PRETTY TOUGH
HI, I'M BILLY! YOU MUST BE JACKIE!
GET LOST, GRUBBS.
YOU'RE RIGHT, ZANE. SHE'S NOT AS PRETTY AS YOUR LAST GIRLFRIEND.
I DIDN'T SAY THAT! HONEST!
POW!
WOW, I DIDN'T KNOW GIRLS COULD HIT SO HARD!
END
GRUBBS
in
HAIR CARE
TIME TO LEAVE FOR CHURCH...
GOODNESS! HAVE YOU SEEN YOUR HAIR??
YEA.
WELL, YOU DIDN'T ASK ME IF I HAD SEEN IT TODAY!
END

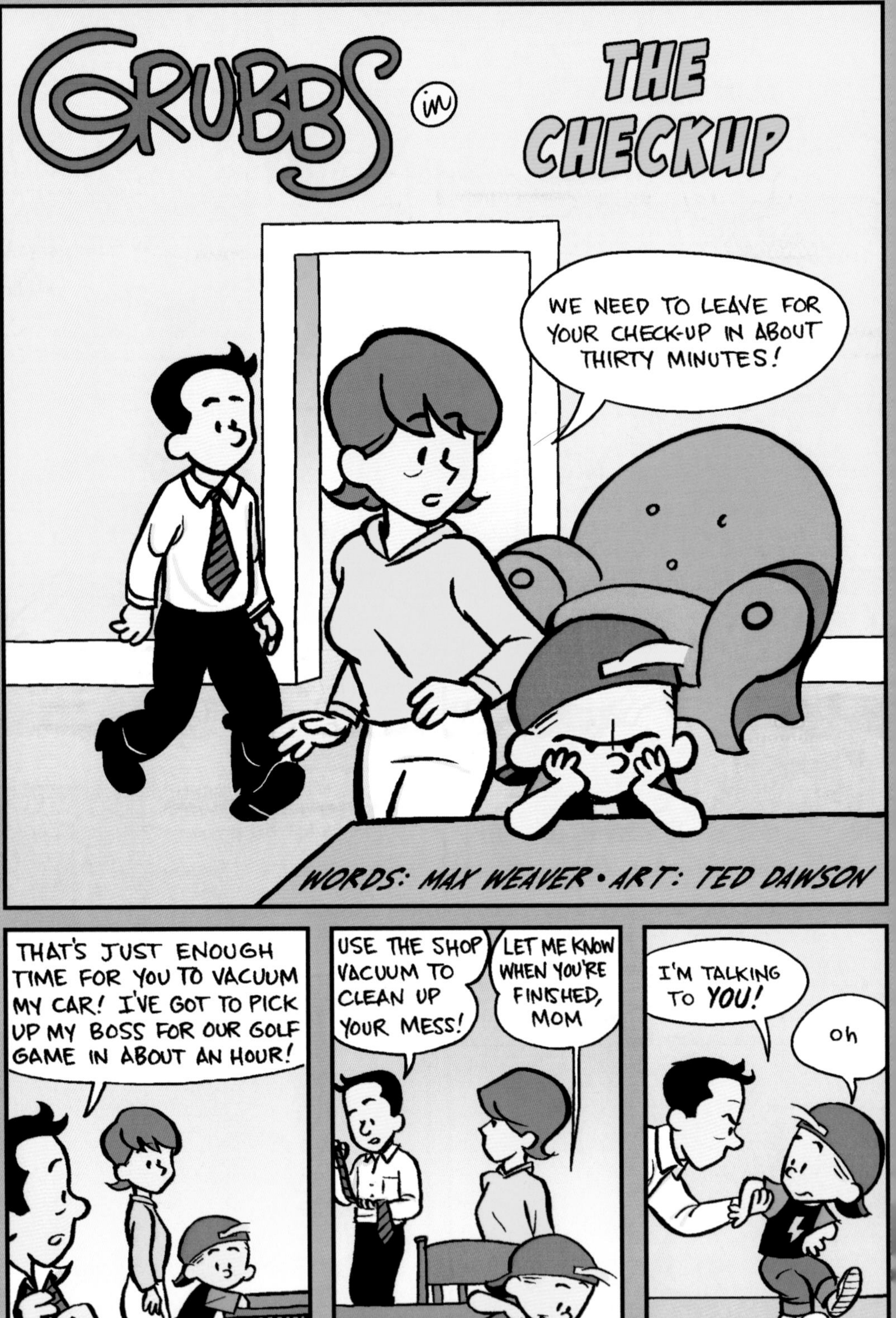
GRUBBS in THE CHECKUP
WE NEED TO LEAVE FOR YOUR CHECK-UP IN ABOUT THIRTY MINUTES!
WORDS: MAX WEAVER • ART: TED DAWSON
THAT'S JUST ENOUGH TIME FOR YOU TO VACUUM MY CAR! I'VE GOT TO PICK UP MY BOSS FOR OUR GOLF GAME IN ABOUT AN HOUR!
USE THE SHOP VACUUM TO CLEAN UP YOUR MESS!
LET ME KNOW WHEN YOU'RE FINISHED, MOM
I'M TALKING TO YOU!
oh

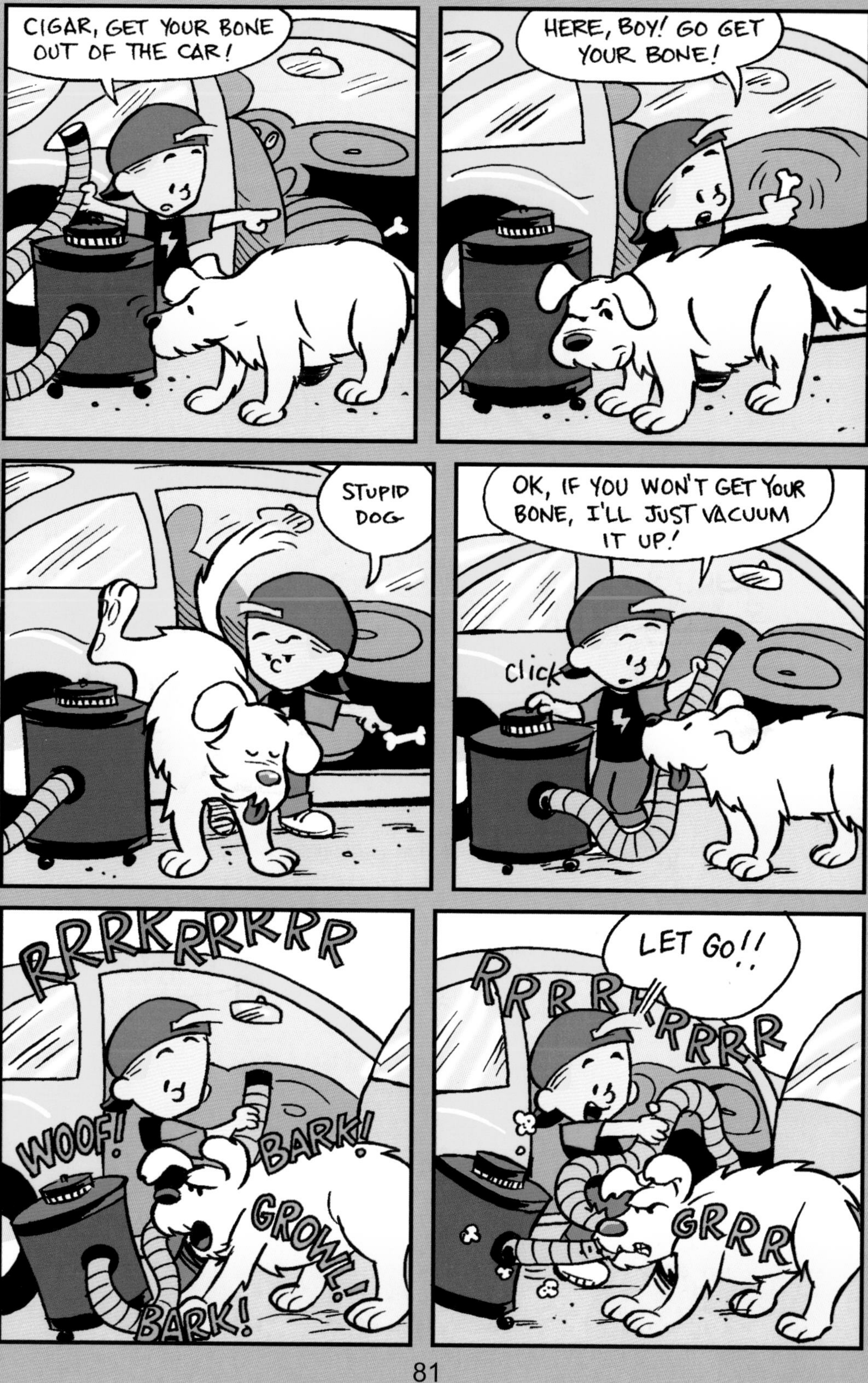
CIGAR, GET YOUR BONE OUT OF THE CAR!
HERE, BOY! GO GET YOUR BONE!
STUPID DOG
OK, IF YOU WON'T GET YOUR BONE, I'LL JUST VACUUM IT UP!
CLICK
RRRKRRRKRR
WOOF!
BARK!
GROWL!
BARK!
LET GO!!
RRRRRRRRR
GRRR

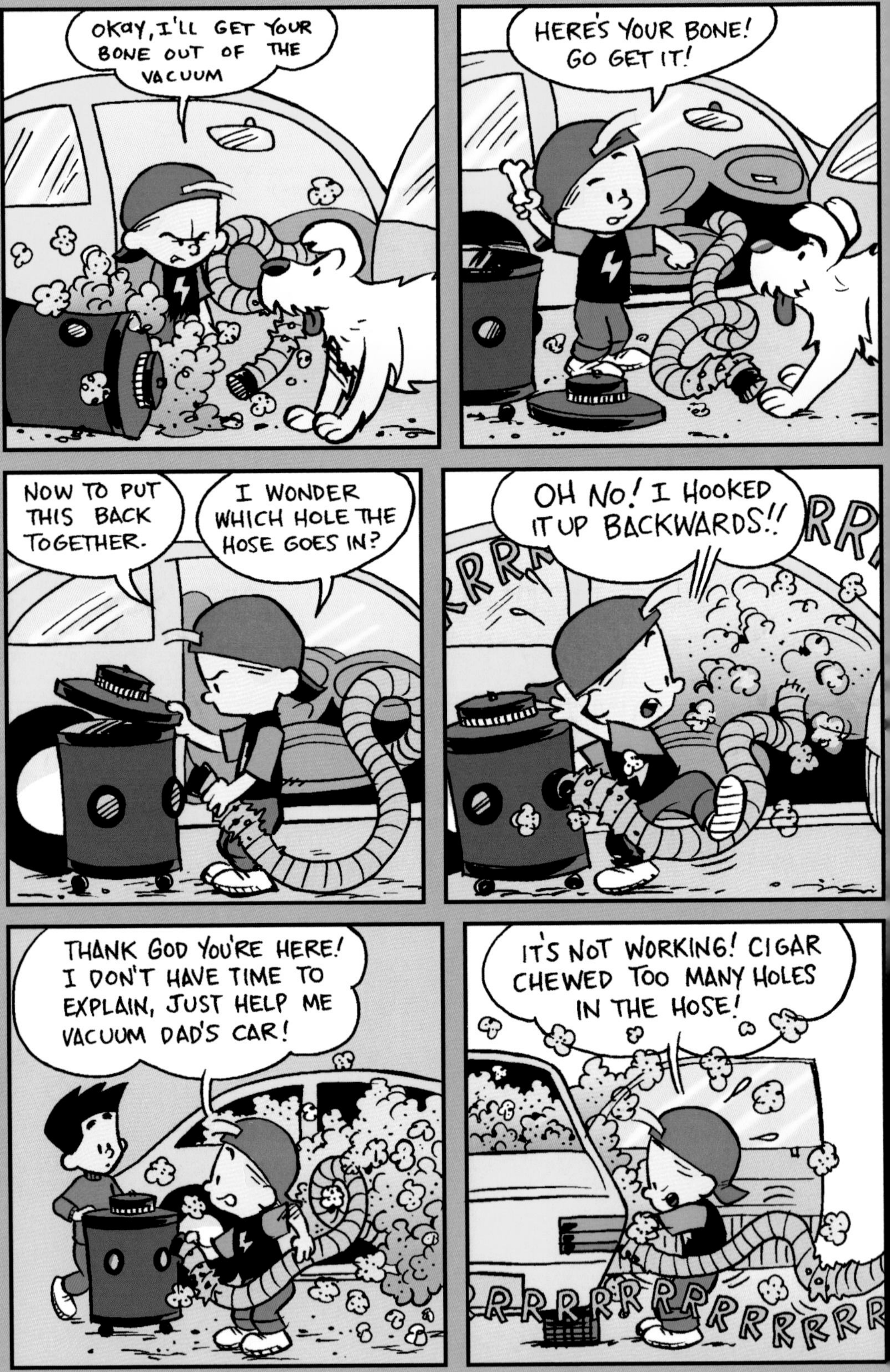
OKAY, I'LL GET YOUR BONE OUT OF THE VACUUM
HERE'S YOUR BONE! GO GET IT!
NOW TO PUT THIS BACK TOGETHER.
I WONDER WHICH HOLE THE HOSE GOES IN?
OH NO! I HOOKED IT UP BACKWARDS!!
RRRR
RR
THANK GOD YOU'RE HERE! I DON'T HAVE TIME TO EXPLAIN, JUST HELP ME VACUUM DAD'S CAR!
IT'S NOT WORKING! CIGAR CHEWED TOO MANY HOLES IN THE HOSE!
RRRRRRRRRRRRR

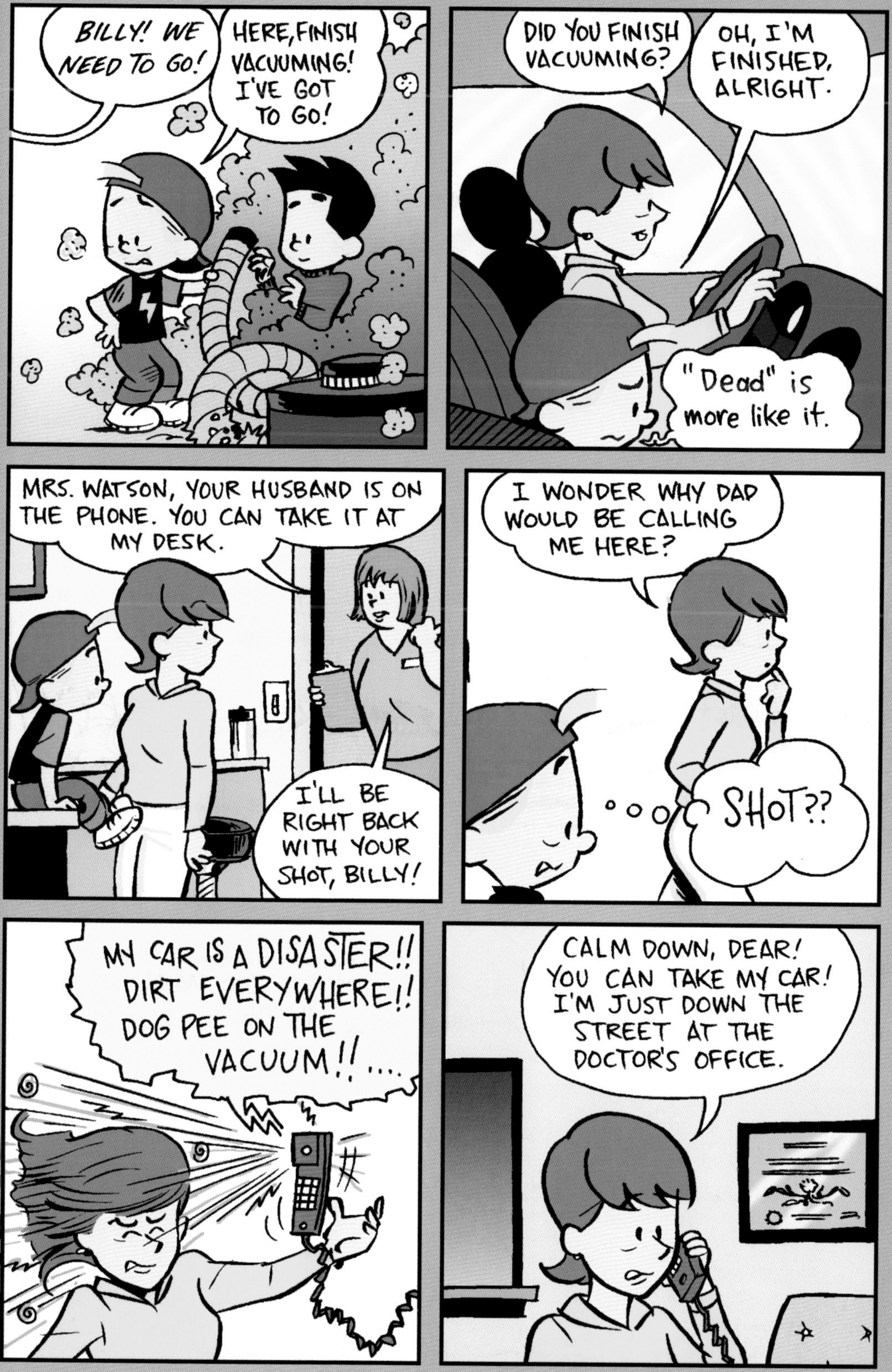
BILLY! WE NEED TO GO!
HERE, FINISH VACUUMING! I'VE GOT TO GO!
DID YOU FINISH VACUUMING?
OH, I'M FINISHED, ALRIGHT.
"Dead" is more like it.
MRS. WATSON, YOUR HUSBAND IS ON THE PHONE. YOU CAN TAKE IT AT MY DESK.
I'LL BE RIGHT BACK WITH YOUR SHOT, BILLY!
I WONDER WHY DAD WOULD BE CALLING ME HERE?
SHOT??
MY CAR IS A DISASTER!! DIRT EVERYWHERE!! DOG PEE ON THE VACUUM!! ....
CALM DOWN, DEAR! YOU CAN TAKE MY CAR! I'M JUST DOWN THE STREET AT THE DOCTOR'S OFFICE.

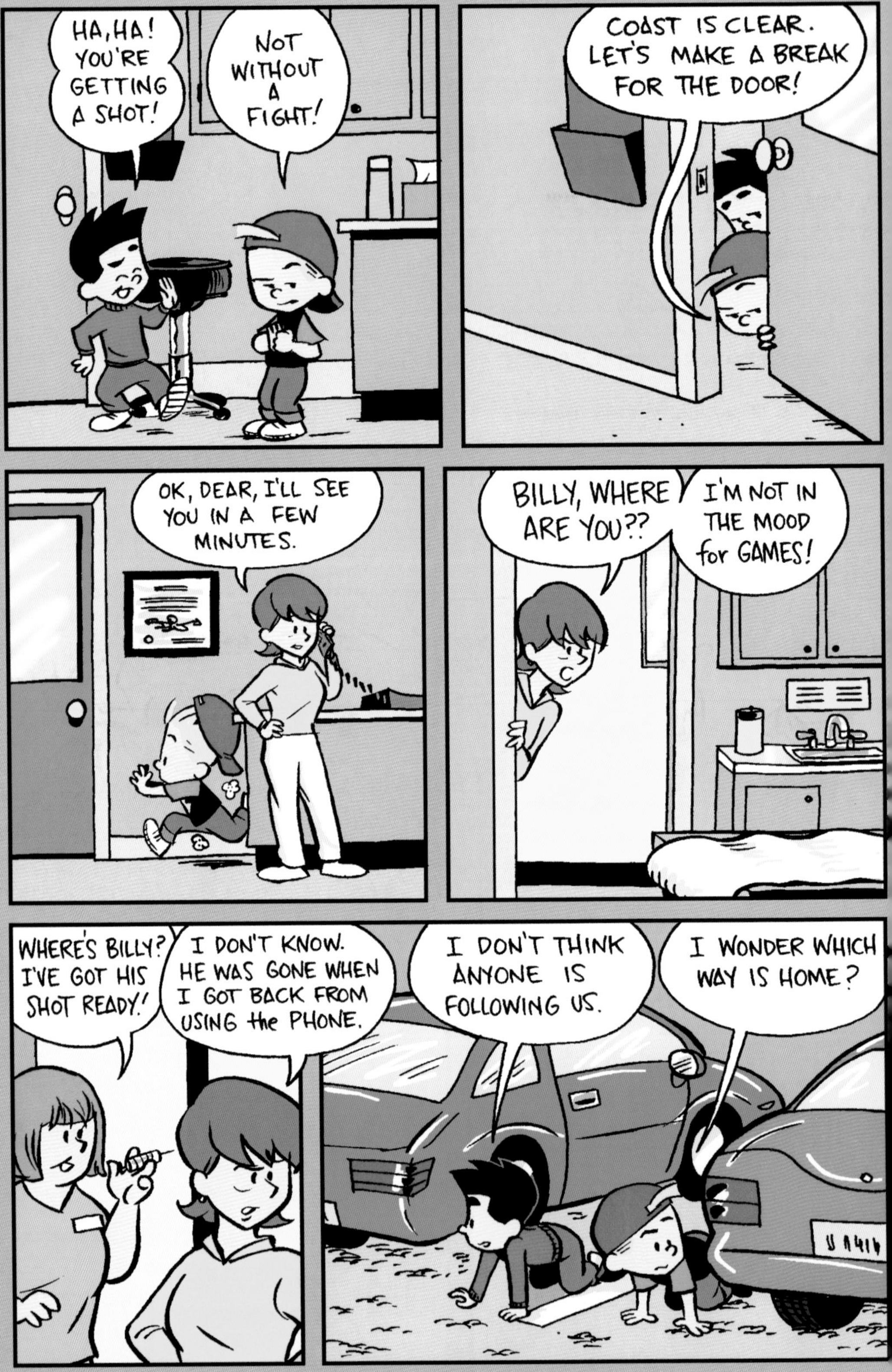
HA, HA! YOU'RE GETTING A SHOT!
NOT WITHOUT A FIGHT!
COAST IS CLEAR. LET'S MAKE A BREAK FOR THE DOOR!
OK, DEAR, I'LL SEE YOU IN A FEW MINUTES.
BILLY, WHERE ARE YOU??
I'M NOT IN THE MOOD for GAMES!
WHERE'S BILLY? I'VE GOT HIS SHOT READY!
I DON'T KNOW. HE WAS GONE WHEN I GOT BACK FROM USING the PHONE.
I DON'T THINK ANYONE IS FOLLOWING US.
I WONDER WHICH WAY IS HOME?

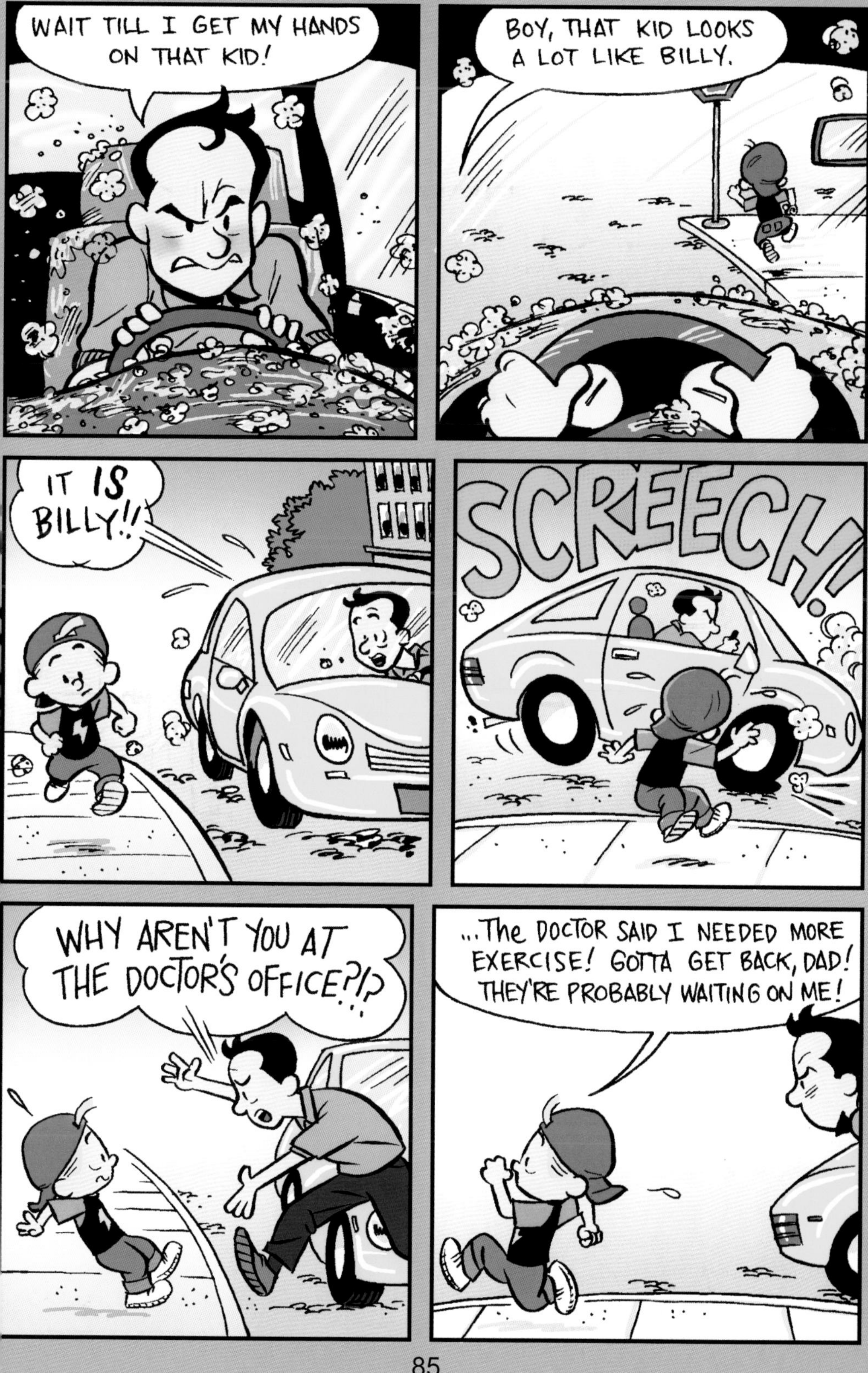
WAIT TILL I GET MY HANDS ON THAT KID!
BOY, THAT KID LOOKS A LOT LIKE BILLY.
IT IS BILLY!!
SCREECH!
WHY AREN'T YOU AT THE DOCTOR'S OFFICE?!?
...The DOCTOR SAID I NEEDED MORE EXERCISE! GOTTA GET BACK, DAD! THEY'RE PROBABLY WAITING ON ME!

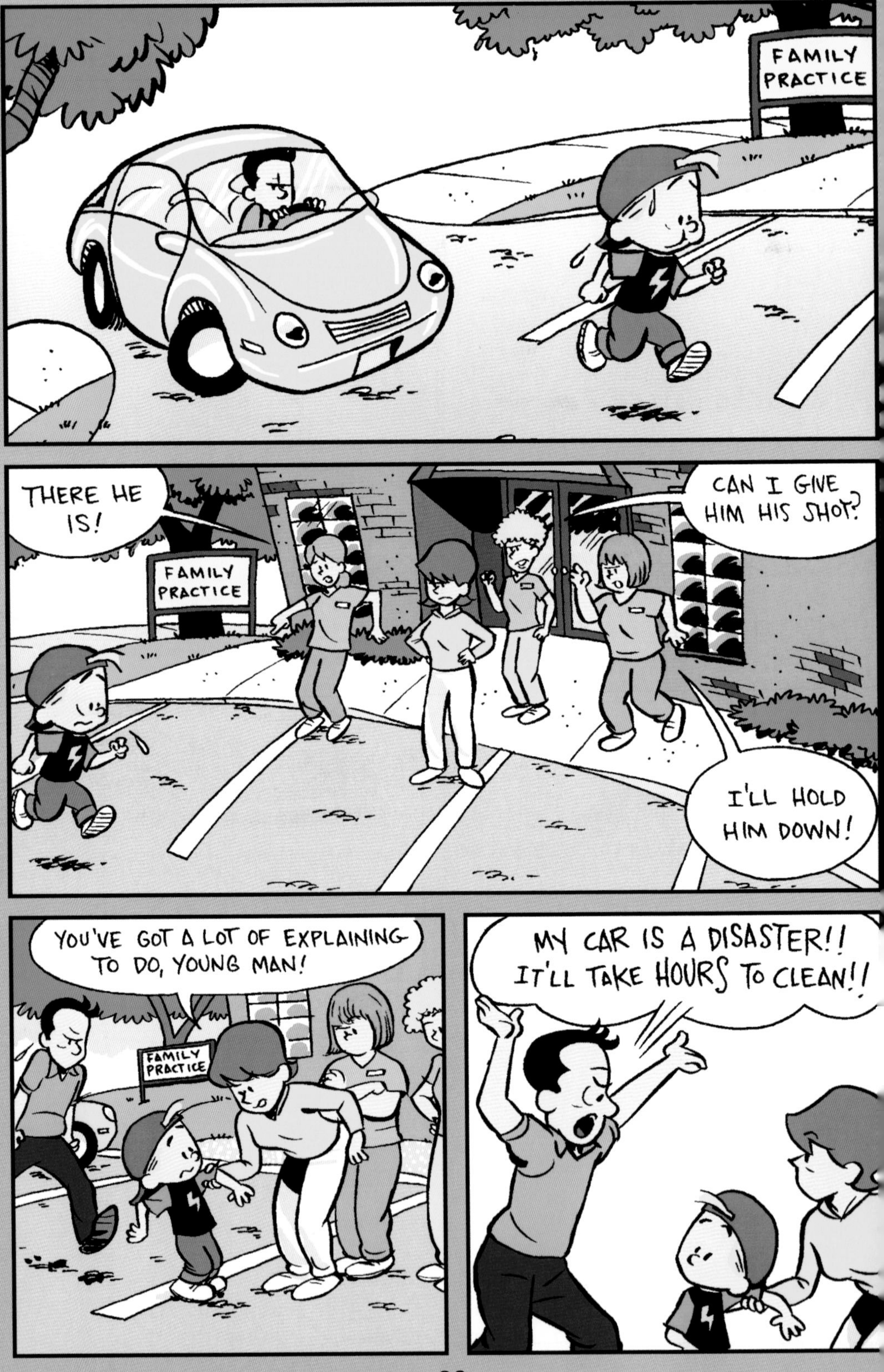
FAMILY PRACTICE
THERE HE IS!
FAMILY PRACTICE
CAN I GIVE HIM HIS SHOT?
I'LL HOLD HIM DOWN!
YOU'VE GOT A LOT OF EXPLAINING TO DO, YOUNG MAN!
FAMILY PRACTICE
MY CAR IS A DISASTER!! IT'LL TAKE HOURS TO CLEAN!!

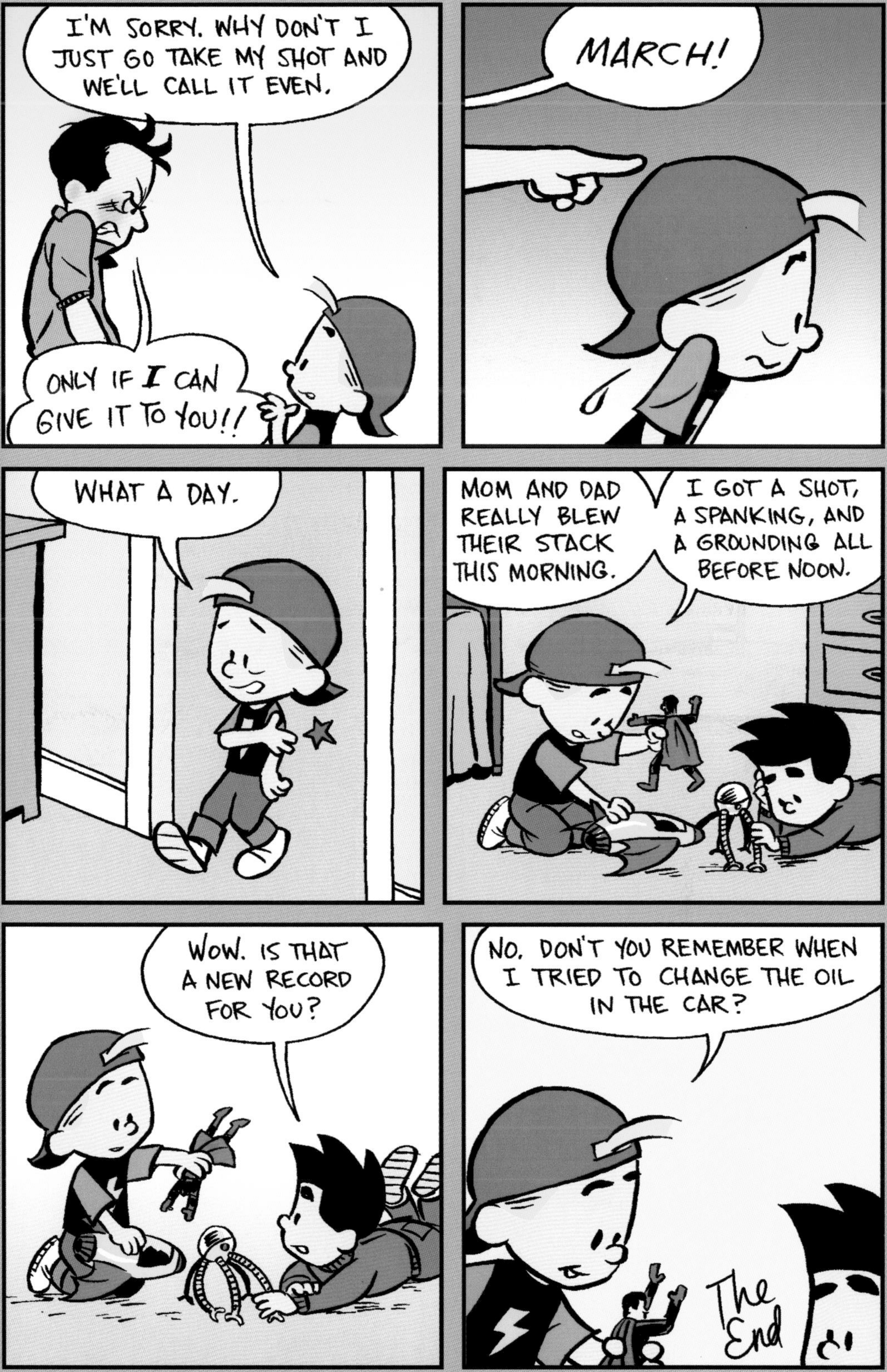
I'M SORRY. WHY DON'T I JUST GO TAKE MY SHOT AND WE'LL CALL IT EVEN.
ONLY IF I CAN GIVE IT TO YOU!!
MARCH!
WHAT A DAY.
MOM AND DAD REALLY BLEW THEIR STACK THIS MORNING.
I GOT A SHOT, A SPANKING, AND A GROUNDING ALL BEFORE NOON.
WOW. IS THAT A NEW RECORD FOR YOU?
NO. DON'T YOU REMEMBER WHEN I TRIED TO CHANGE THE OIL IN THE CAR?
The End

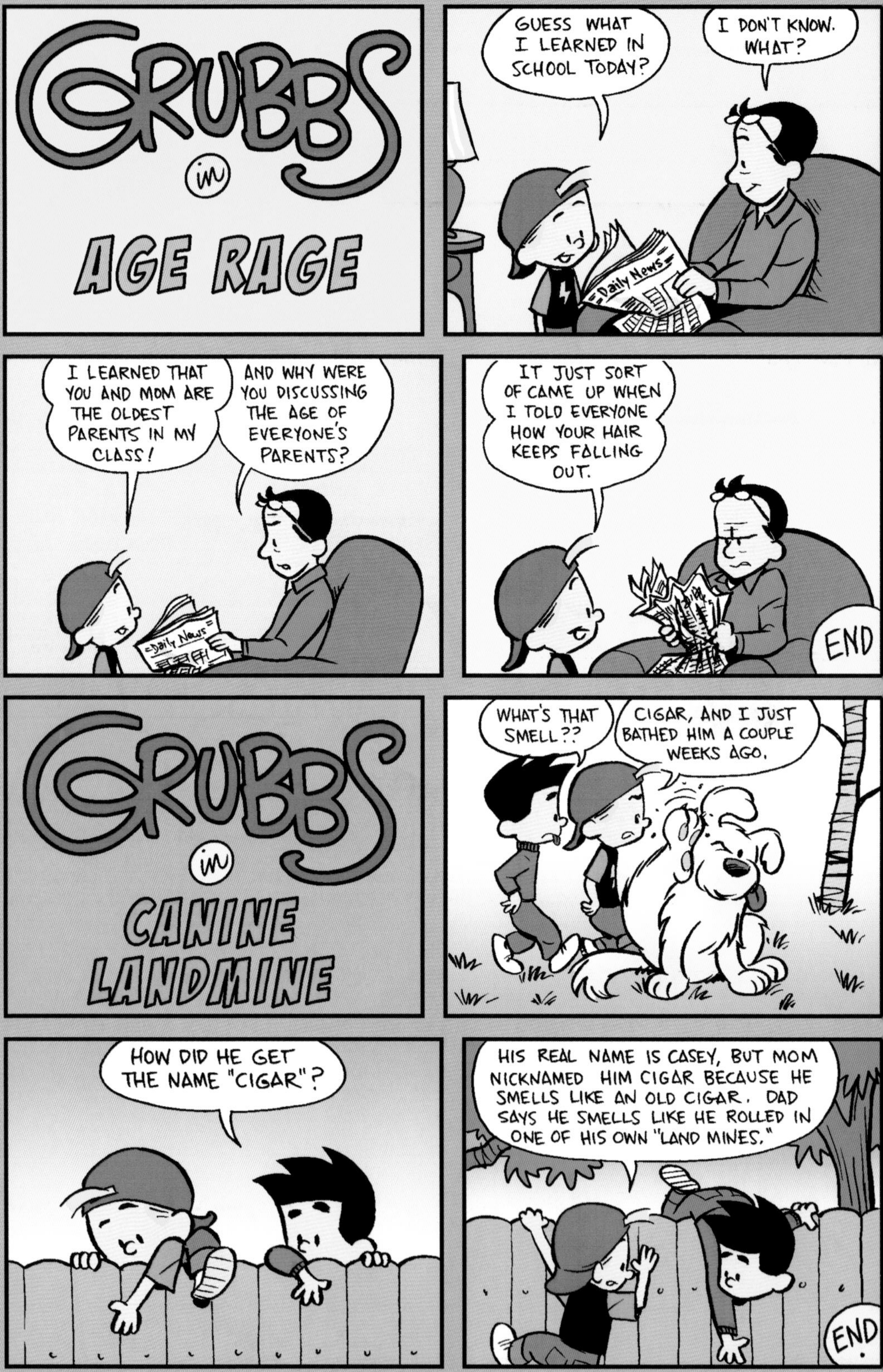
GRUBBS
in
AGE RAGE
GUESS WHAT I LEARNED IN SCHOOL TODAY?
I DON'T KNOW. WHAT?
Daily News
I LEARNED THAT YOU AND MOM ARE THE OLDEST PARENTS IN MY CLASS!
AND WHY WERE YOU DISCUSSING THE AGE OF EVERYONE'S PARENTS?
Daily News
IT JUST SORT OF CAME UP WHEN I TOLD EVERYONE HOW YOUR HAIR KEEPS FALLING OUT.
END
GRUBBS
in
CANINE LANDMINE
WHAT'S THAT SMELL??
CIGAR, AND I JUST BATHED HIM A COUPLE WEEKS AGO.
HOW DID HE GET THE NAME "CIGAR"?
HIS REAL NAME IS CASEY, BUT MOM NICKNAMED HIM CIGAR BECAUSE HE SMELLS LIKE AN OLD CIGAR. DAD SAYS HE SMELLS LIKE HE ROLLED IN ONE OF HIS OWN "LAND MINES."
END

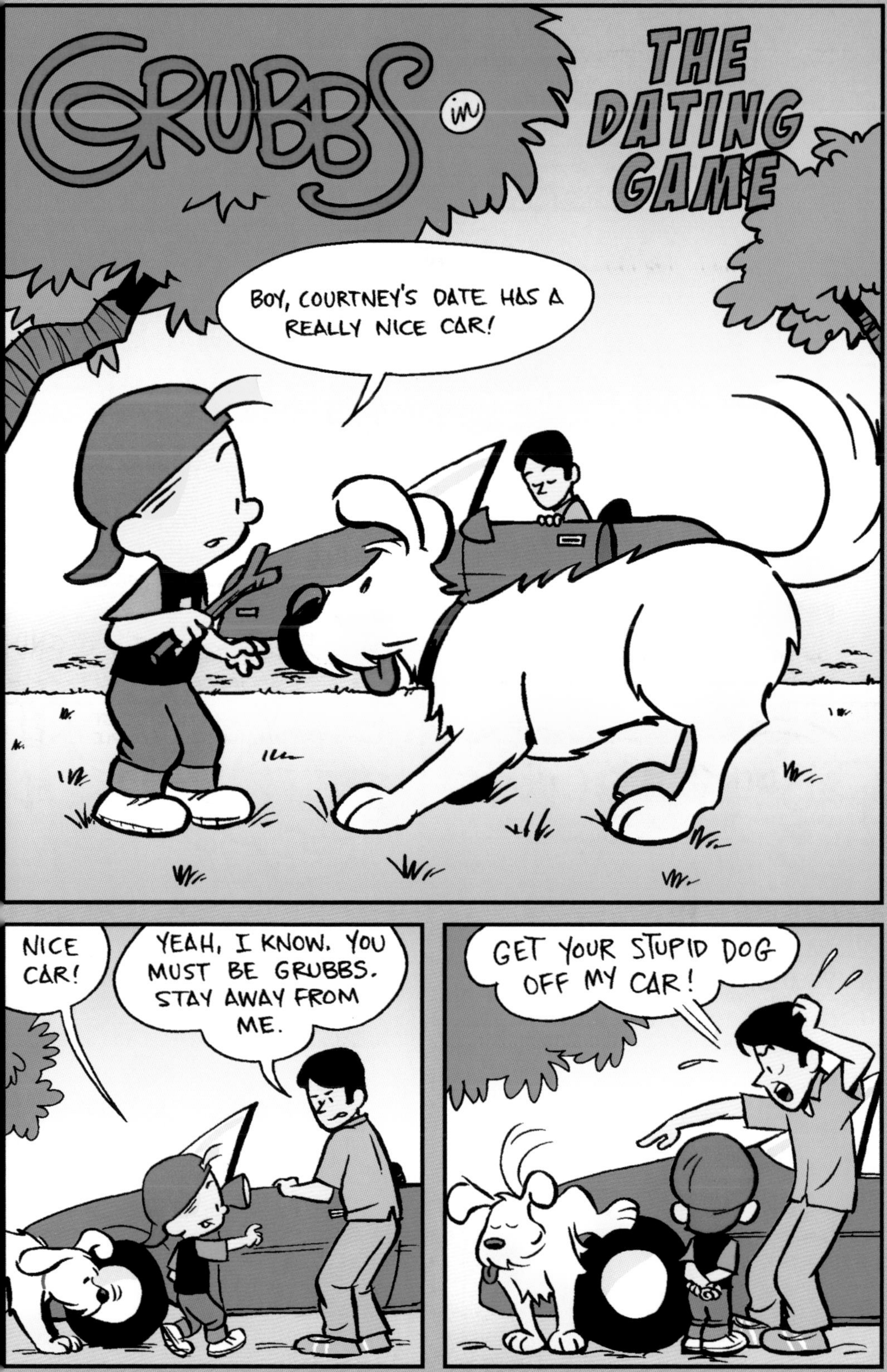
GRUBBS in
THE DATING GAME
BOY, COURTNEY'S DATE HAS A REALLY NICE CAR!
NICE CAR!
YEAH, I KNOW. YOU MUST BE GRUBBS. STAY AWAY FROM ME.
GET YOUR STUPID DOG OFF MY CAR!

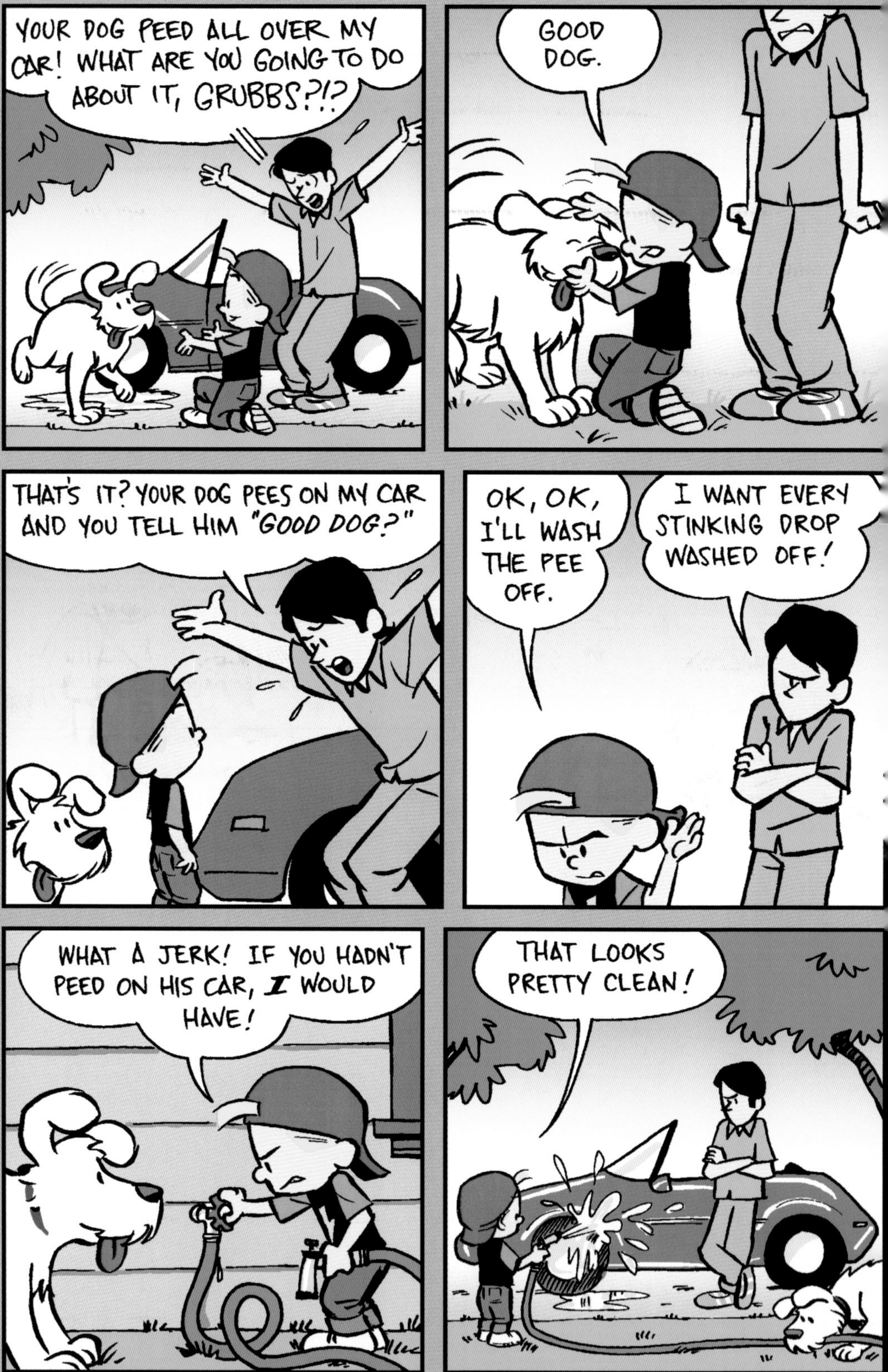
YOUR DOG PEED ALL OVER MY CAR! WHAT ARE YOU GOING TO DO ABOUT IT, GRUBBS?!?
GOOD DOG.
THAT'S IT? YOUR DOG PEES ON MY CAR AND YOU TELL HIM "GOOD DOG?"
OK, OK, I'LL WASH THE PEE OFF.
I WANT EVERY STINKING DROP WASHED OFF!
WHAT A JERK! IF YOU HADN'T PEED ON HIS CAR, I WOULD HAVE!
THAT LOOKS PRETTY CLEAN!

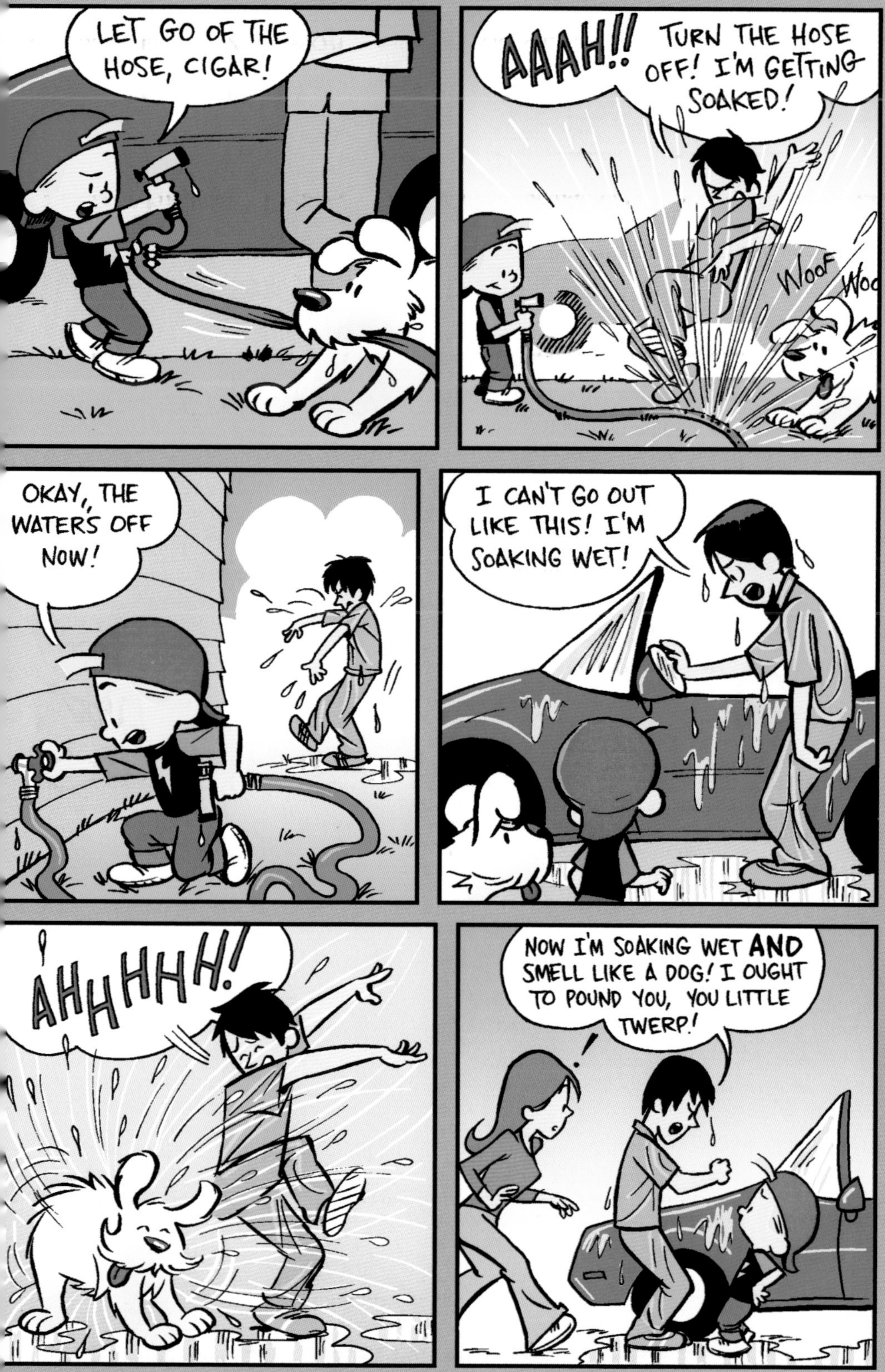
LET GO OF THE HOSE, CIGAR!
AAAH!!
TURN THE HOSE OFF! I'M GETTING SOAKED!
WOOF
WOO
OKAY,, THE WATER'S OFF NOW!
I CAN'T GO OUT LIKE THIS! I'M SOAKING WET!
AHHHHH!
NOW I'M SOAKING WET AND SMELL LIKE A DOG! I OUGHT TO POUND YOU, YOU LITTLE TWERP!

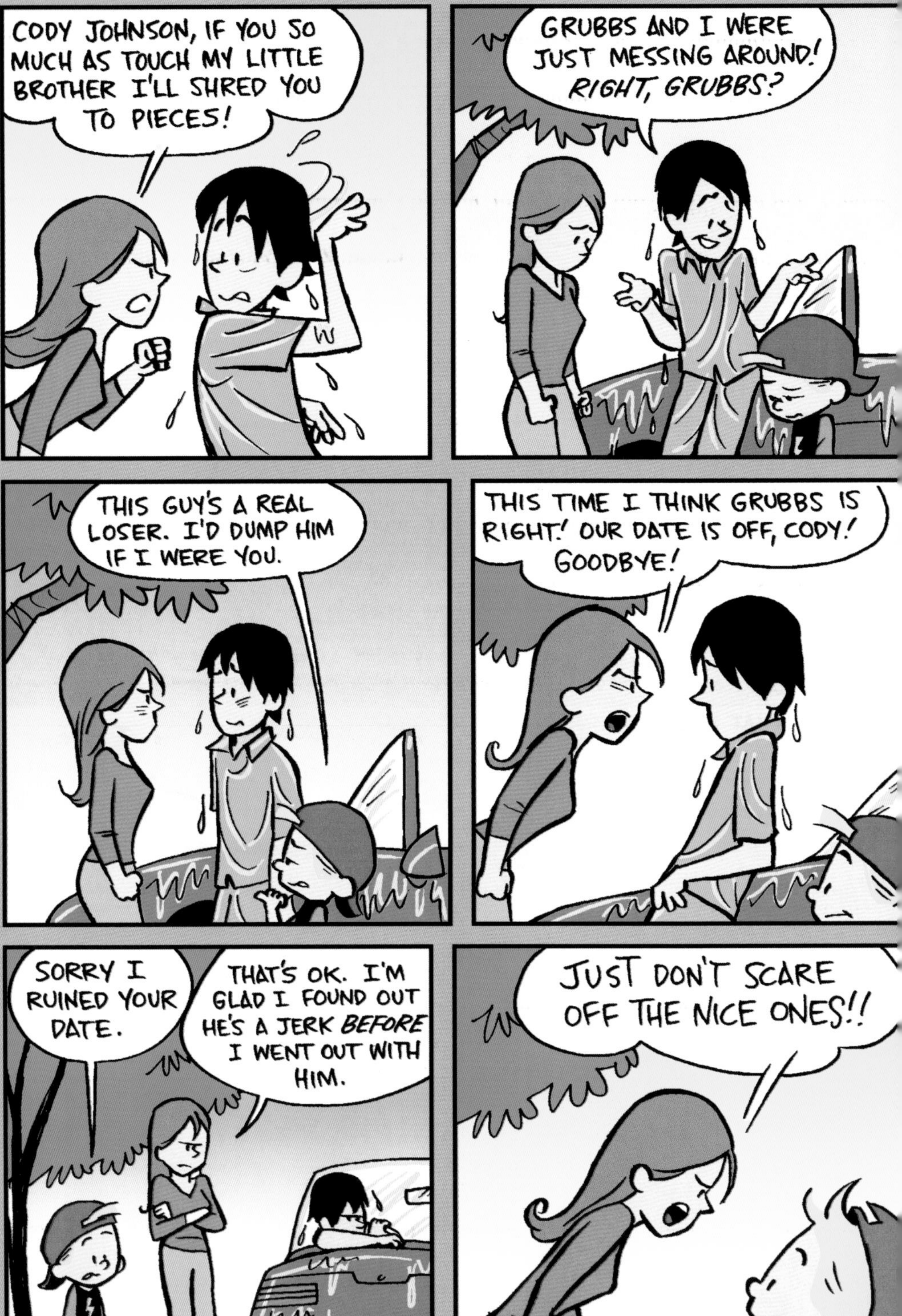
CODY JOHNSON, IF YOU SO MUCH AS TOUCH MY LITTLE BROTHER I'LL SHRED YOU TO PIECES!
GRUBBS AND I WERE JUST MESSING AROUND! *RIGHT, GRUBBS?*
THIS GUY'S A REAL LOSER. I'D DUMP HIM IF I WERE YOU.
THIS TIME I THINK GRUBBS IS RIGHT! OUR DATE IS OFF, CODY! GOODBYE!
SORRY I RUINED YOUR DATE.
THAT'S OK. I'M GLAD I FOUND OUT HE'S A JERK *BEFORE* I WENT OUT WITH HIM.
JUST DON'T SCARE OFF THE NICE ONES!!
FIN

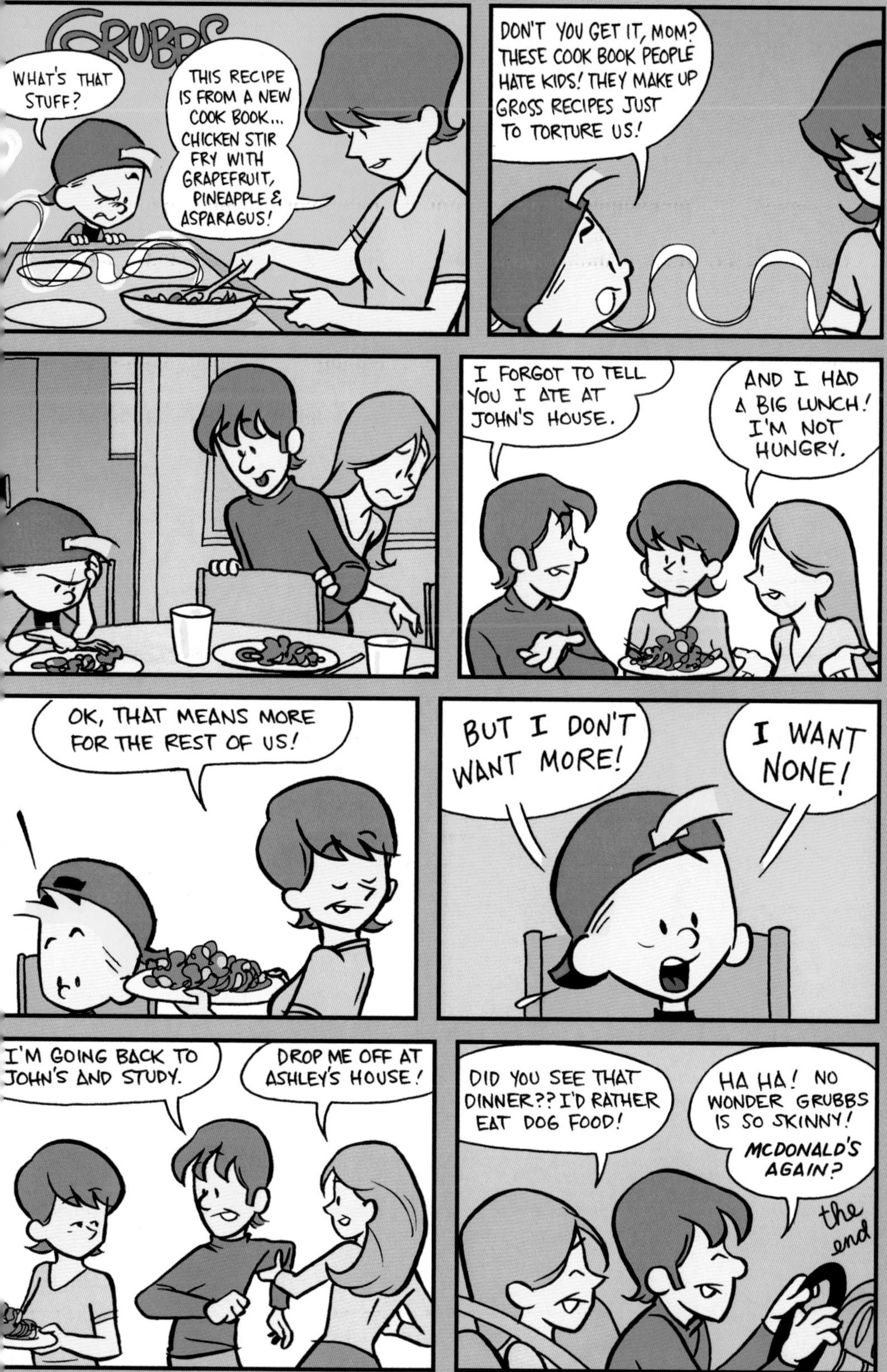
GRUBBS
WHAT'S THAT STUFF?
THIS RECIPE IS FROM A NEW COOK BOOK... CHICKEN STIR FRY WITH GRAPEFRUIT, PINEAPPLE & ASPARAGUS!
DON'T YOU GET IT, MOM? THESE COOK BOOK PEOPLE HATE KIDS! THEY MAKE UP GROSS RECIPES JUST TO TORTURE US!
I FORGOT TO TELL YOU I ATE AT JOHN'S HOUSE.
AND I HAD A BIG LUNCH! I'M NOT HUNGRY.
OK, THAT MEANS MORE FOR THE REST OF US!
BUT I DON'T WANT MORE!
I WANT NONE!
I'M GOING BACK TO JOHN'S AND STUDY.
DROP ME OFF AT ASHLEY'S HOUSE!
DID YOU SEE THAT DINNER?? I'D RATHER EAT DOG FOOD!
HA HA! NO WONDER GRUBBS IS SO SKINNY!
MCDONALD'S AGAIN?
the end

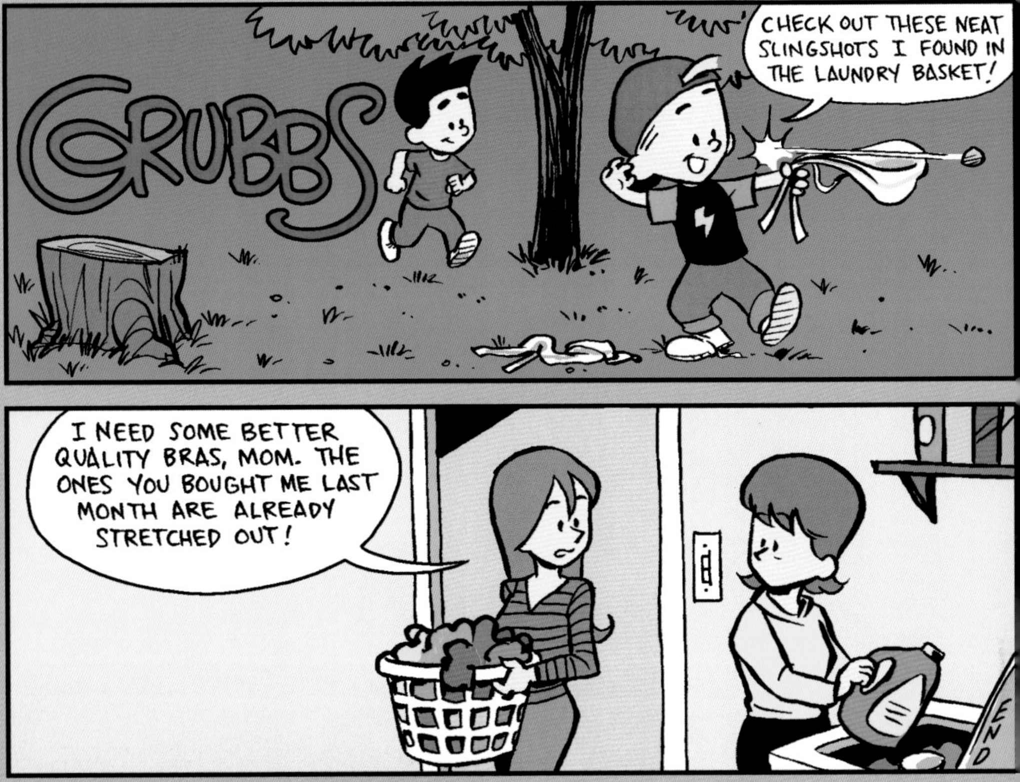
GRUBBS
CHECK OUT THESE NEAT SLINGSHOTS I FOUND IN THE LAUNDRY BASKET!
I NEED SOME BETTER QUALITY BRAS, MOM. THE ONES YOU BOUGHT ME LAST MONTH ARE ALREADY STRETCHED OUT!
END

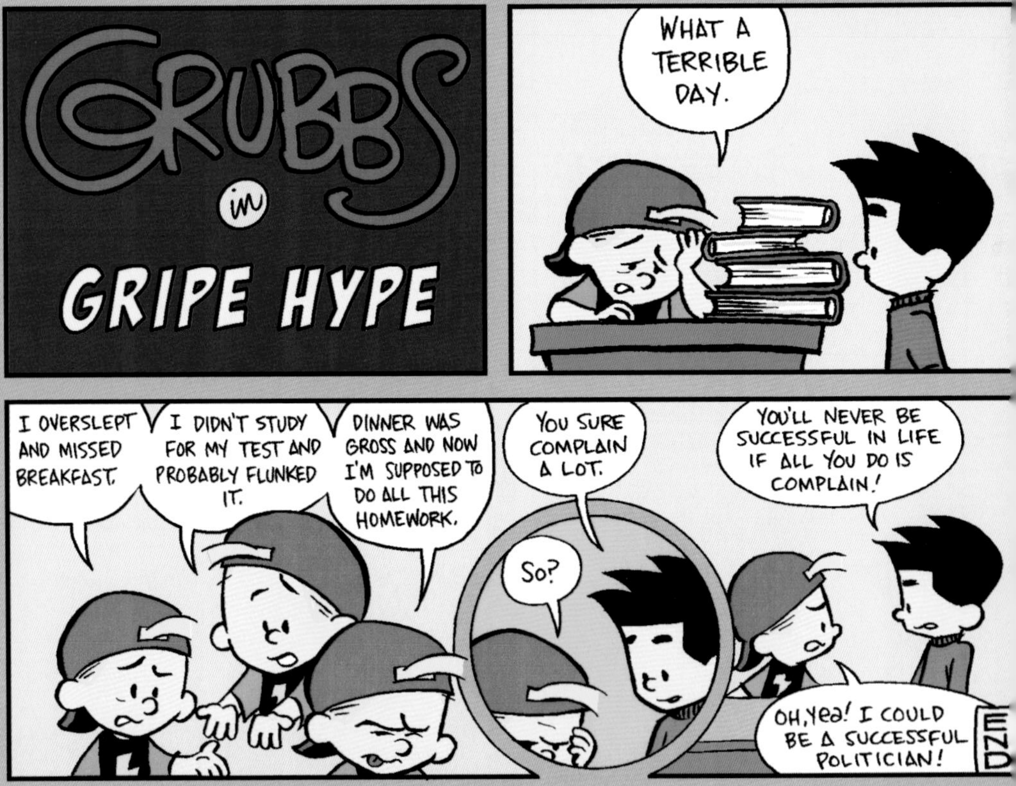
GRUBBS
in
GRIPE HYPE
WHAT A TERRIBLE DAY.
I OVERSLEPT AND MISSED BREAKFAST.
I DIDN'T STUDY FOR MY TEST AND PROBABLY FLUNKED IT.
DINNER WAS GROSS AND NOW I'M SUPPOSED TO DO ALL THIS HOMEWORK.
YOU SURE COMPLAIN A LOT.
So?
YOU'LL NEVER BE SUCCESSFUL IN LIFE IF ALL YOU DO IS COMPLAIN!
OH, YEA! I COULD BE A SUCCESSFUL POLITICIAN!
END

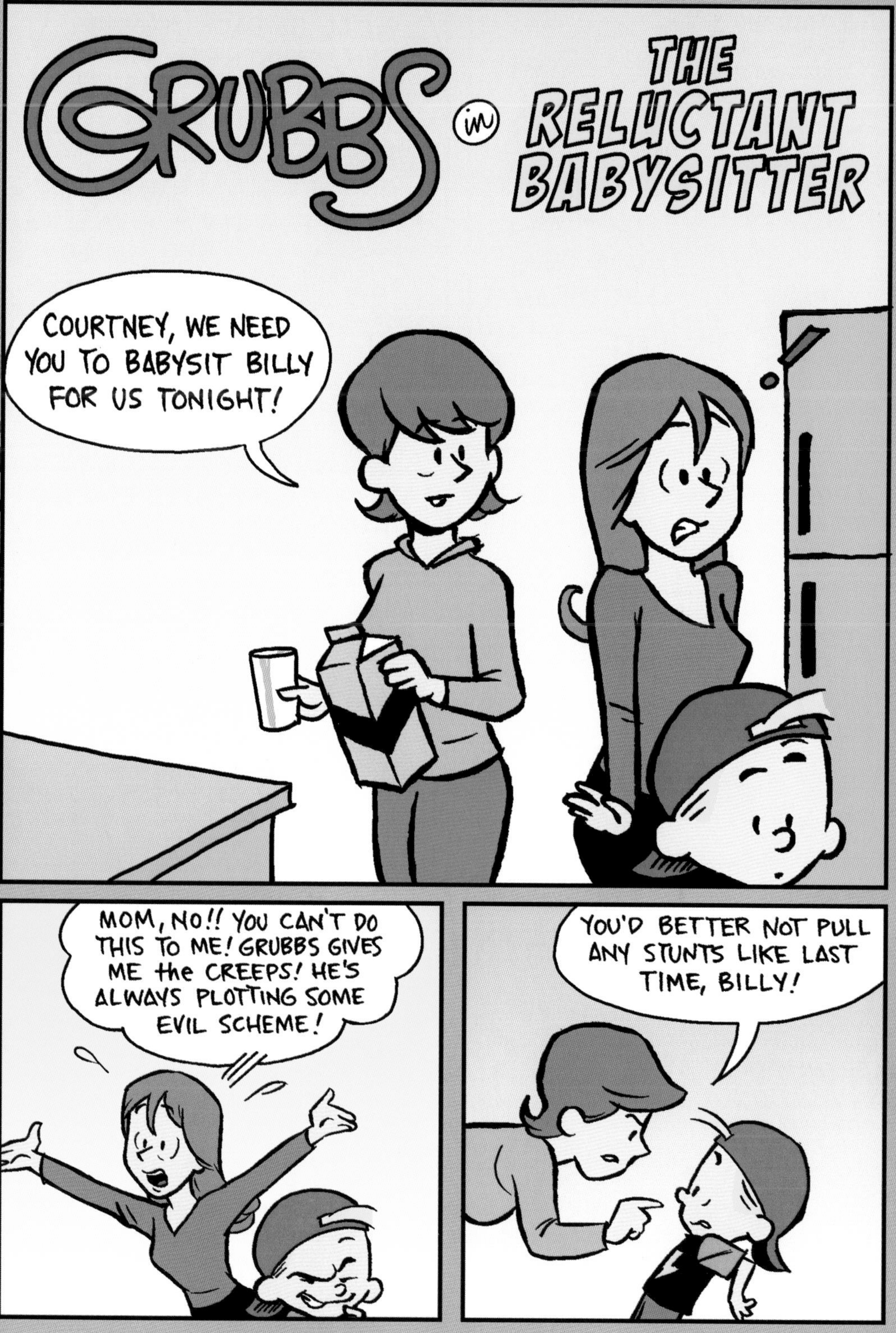
GRUBBS in THE RELUCTANT BABYSITTER
COURTNEY, WE NEED YOU TO BABYSIT BILLY FOR US TONIGHT!
MOM, NO!! YOU CAN'T DO THIS TO ME! GRUBBS GIVES ME the CREEPS! HE'S ALWAYS PLOTTING SOME EVIL SCHEME!
YOU'D BETTER NOT PULL ANY STUNTS LIKE LAST TIME, BILLY!

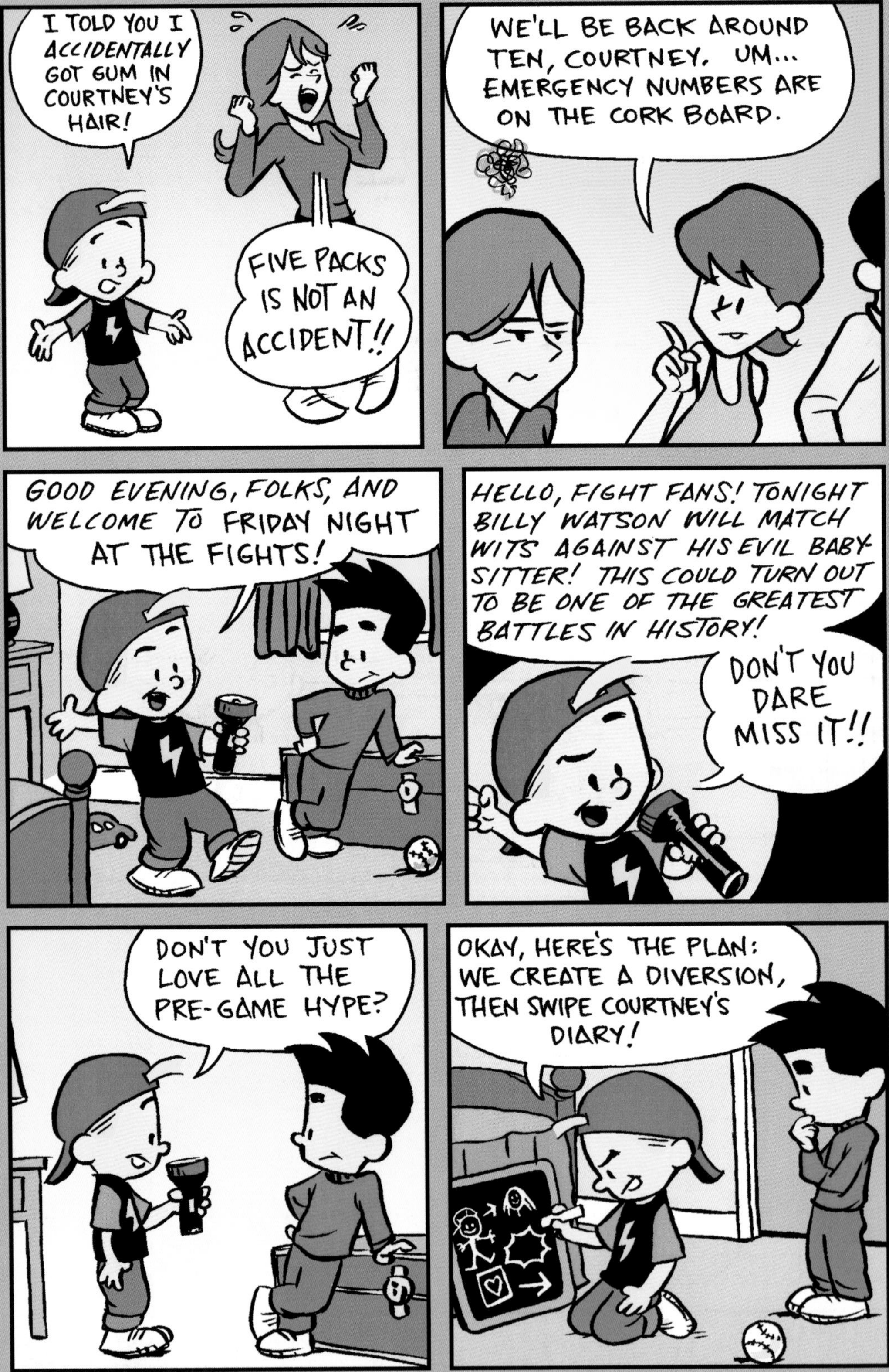
I TOLD YOU I ACCIDENTALLY GOT GUM IN COURTNEY'S HAIR!
FIVE PACKS IS NOT AN ACCIDENT!!
WE'LL BE BACK AROUND TEN, COURTNEY. UM... EMERGENCY NUMBERS ARE ON THE CORK BOARD.
GOOD EVENING, FOLKS, AND WELCOME TO FRIDAY NIGHT AT THE FIGHTS!
HELLO, FIGHT FANS! TONIGHT BILLY WATSON WILL MATCH WITS AGAINST HIS EVIL BABY-SITTER! THIS COULD TURN OUT TO BE ONE OF THE GREATEST BATTLES IN HISTORY!
DON'T YOU DARE MISS IT!!
DON'T YOU JUST LOVE ALL THE PRE-GAME HYPE?
OKAY, HERE'S THE PLAN: WE CREATE A DIVERSION, THEN SWIPE COURTNEY'S DIARY!

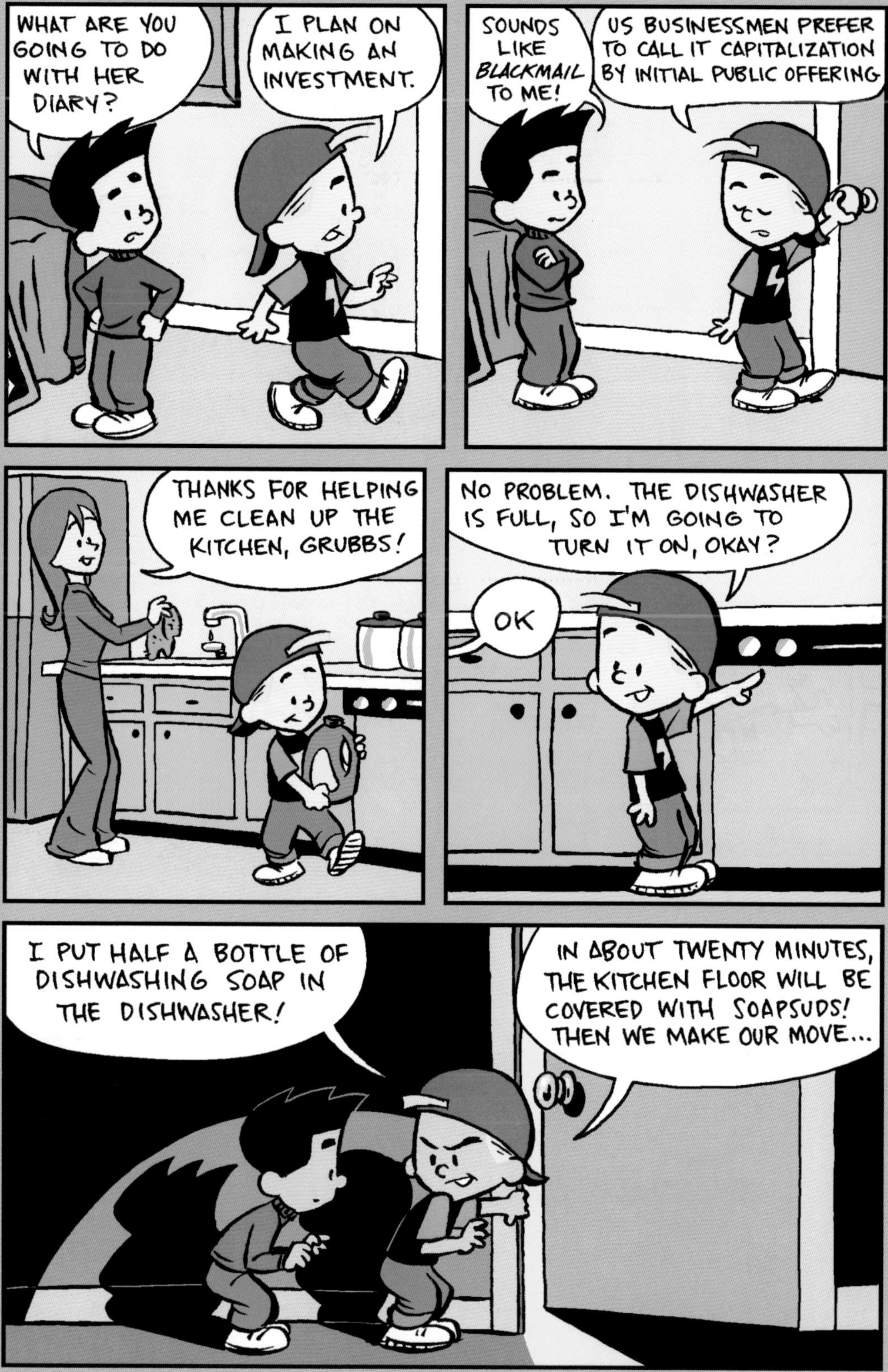
WHAT ARE YOU GOING TO DO WITH HER DIARY?
I PLAN ON MAKING AN INVESTMENT.
SOUNDS LIKE *BLACKMAIL* TO ME!
US BUSINESSMEN PREFER TO CALL IT CAPITALIZATION BY INITIAL PUBLIC OFFERING
THANKS FOR HELPING ME CLEAN UP THE KITCHEN, GRUBBS!
NO PROBLEM. THE DISHWASHER IS FULL, SO I'M GOING TO TURN IT ON, OKAY?
OK
I PUT HALF A BOTTLE OF DISHWASHING SOAP IN THE DISHWASHER!
IN ABOUT TWENTY MINUTES, THE KITCHEN FLOOR WILL BE COVERED WITH SOAPSUDS! THEN WE MAKE OUR MOVE...

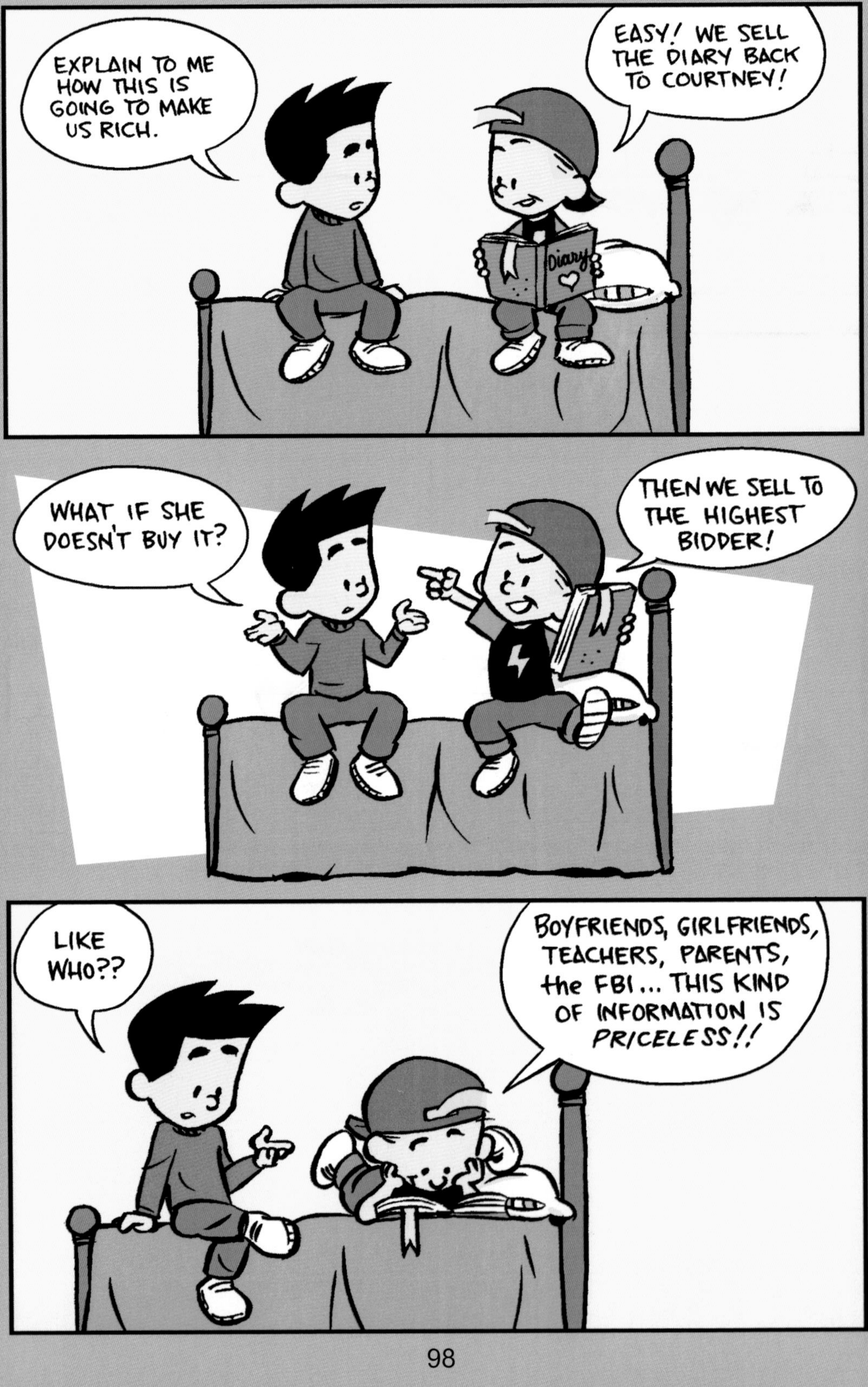
EXPLAIN TO ME HOW THIS IS GOING TO MAKE US RICH.
EASY! WE SELL THE DIARY BACK TO COURTNEY!
Diary
WHAT IF SHE DOESN'T BUY IT?
THEN WE SELL TO THE HIGHEST BIDDER!
LIKE WHO??
BOYFRIENDS, GIRLFRIENDS, TEACHERS, PARENTS, the FBI... THIS KIND OF INFORMATION IS *PRICELESS!!*

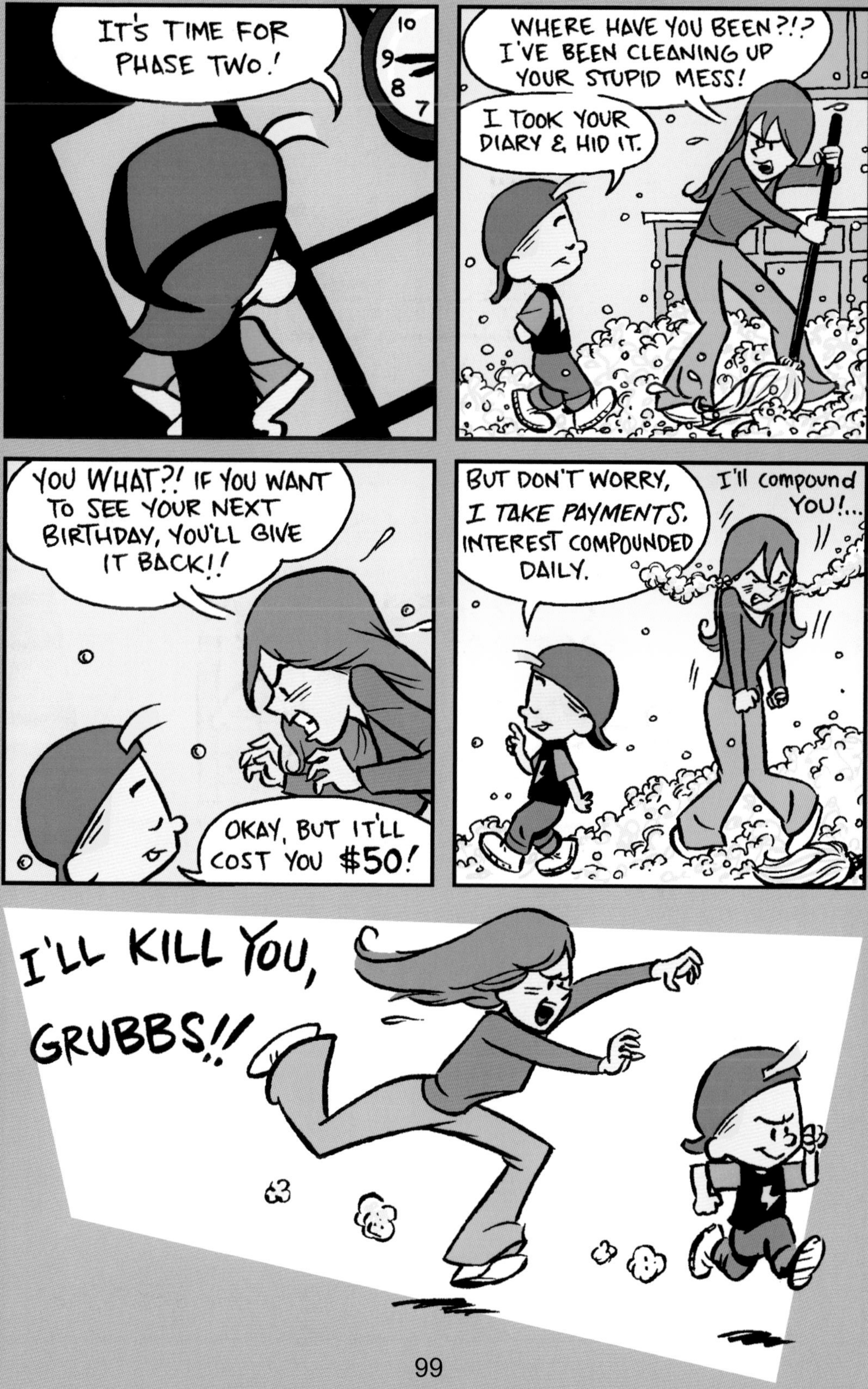
IT'S TIME FOR PHASE TWO!
WHERE HAVE YOU BEEN?!? I'VE BEEN CLEANING UP YOUR STUPID MESS!
I TOOK YOUR DIARY & HID IT.
YOU WHAT?! IF YOU WANT TO SEE YOUR NEXT BIRTHDAY, YOU'LL GIVE IT BACK!!
OKAY, BUT IT'LL COST YOU $50!
BUT DON'T WORRY, I TAKE PAYMENTS. INTEREST COMPOUNDED DAILY.
I'll compound YOU!...
I'LL KILL YOU, GRUBBS!!

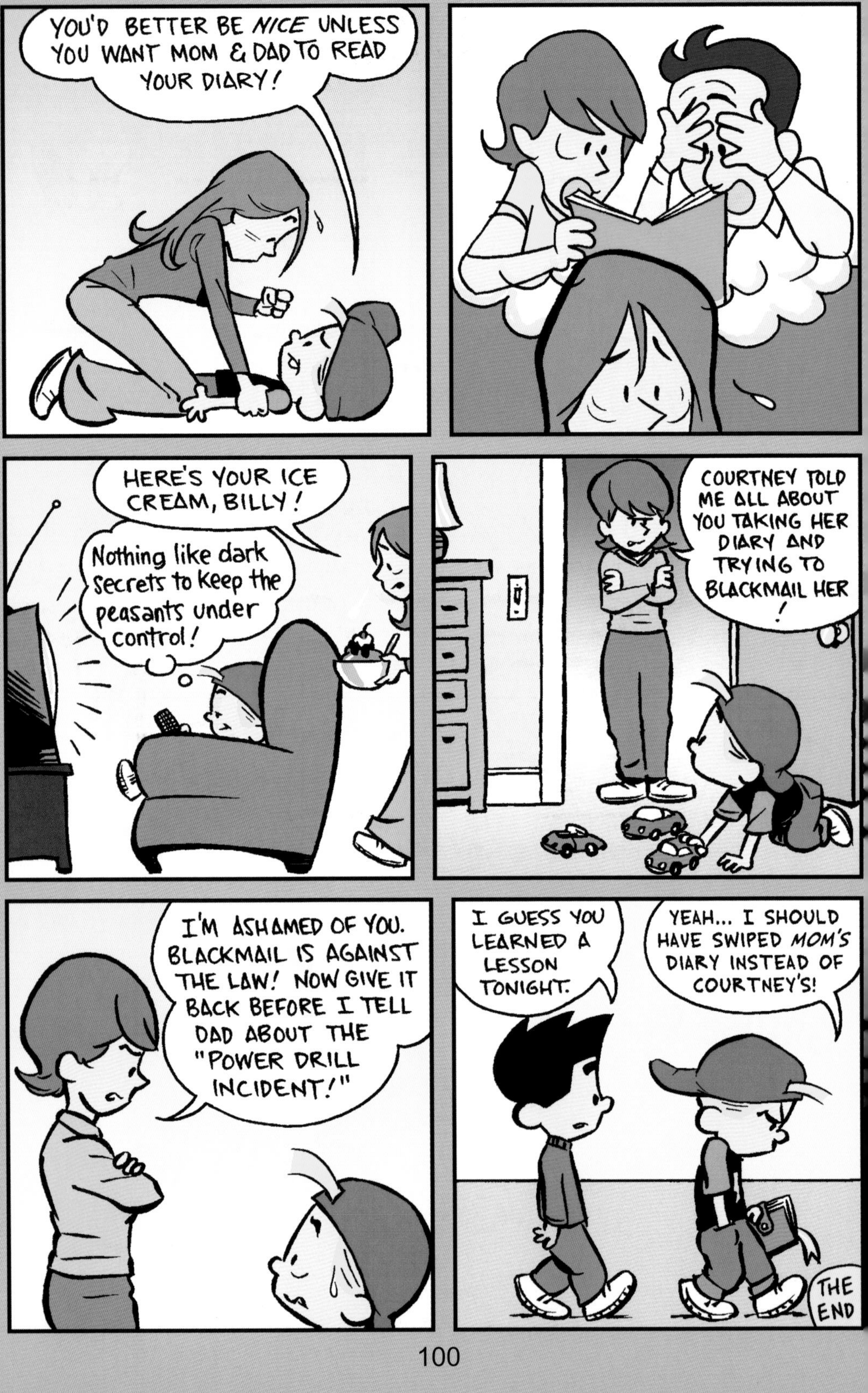
YOU'D BETTER BE NICE UNLESS YOU WANT MOM & DAD TO READ YOUR DIARY!
HERE'S YOUR ICE CREAM, BILLY!
Nothing like dark secrets to keep the peasants under control!
COURTNEY TOLD ME ALL ABOUT YOU TAKING HER DIARY AND TRYING TO BLACKMAIL HER!
I'M ASHAMED OF YOU. BLACKMAIL IS AGAINST THE LAW! NOW GIVE IT BACK BEFORE I TELL DAD ABOUT THE "POWER DRILL INCIDENT!"
I GUESS YOU LEARNED A LESSON TONIGHT.
YEAH... I SHOULD HAVE SWIPED MOM'S DIARY INSTEAD OF COURTNEY'S!
THE END

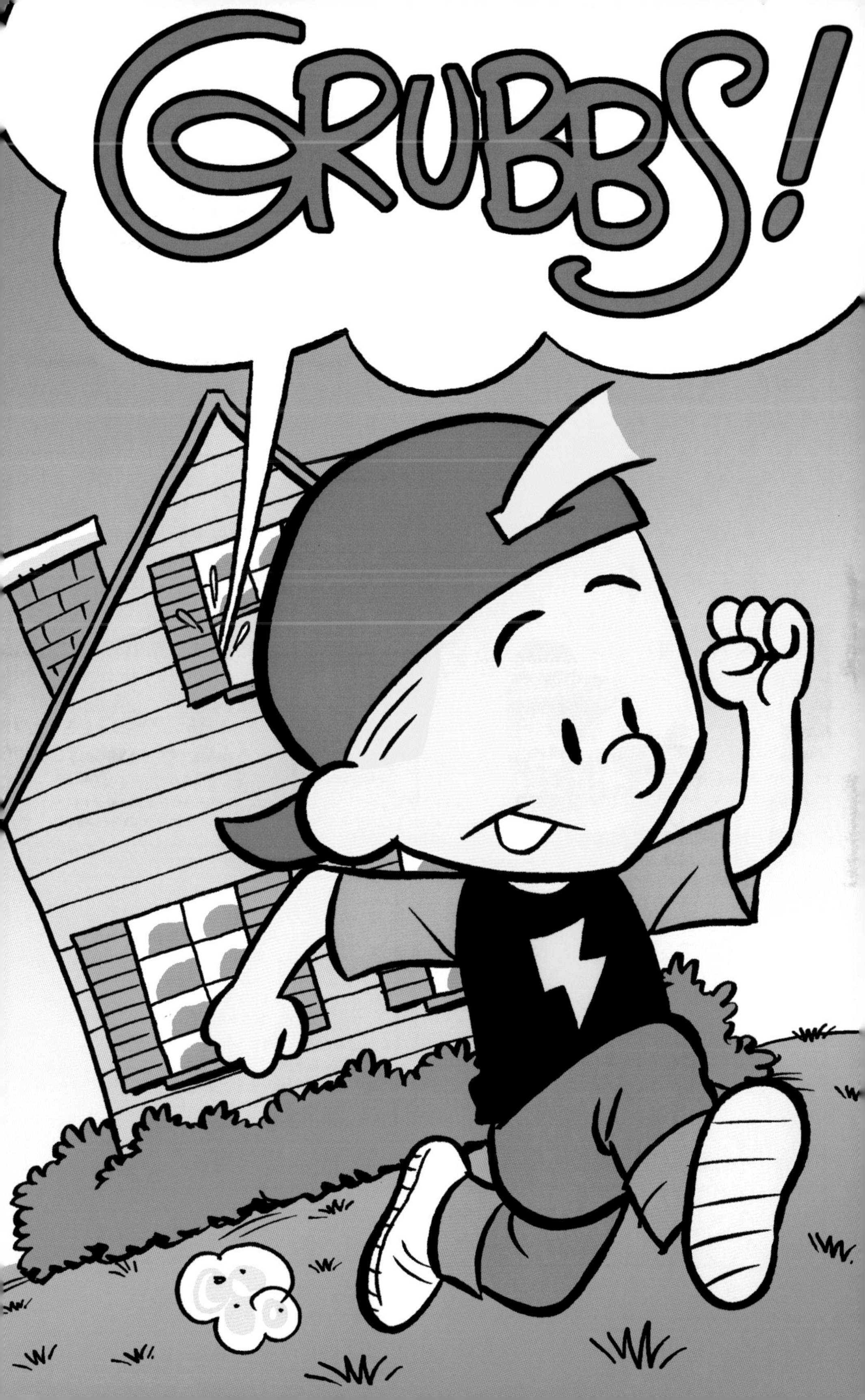
GRUBBS!

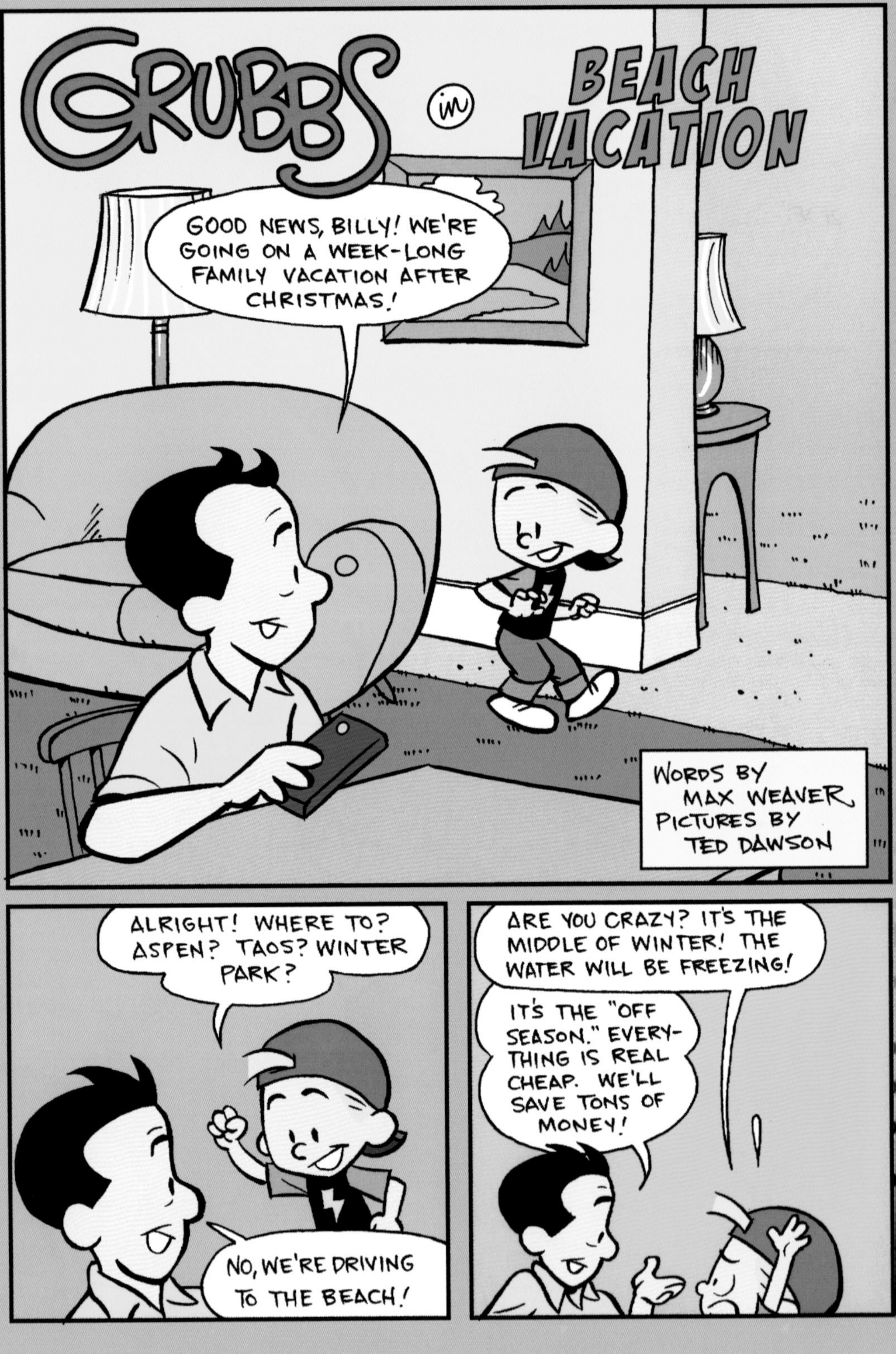
GRUBBS in
BEACH VACATION
GOOD NEWS, BILLY! WE'RE GOING ON A WEEK-LONG FAMILY VACATION AFTER CHRISTMAS!
WORDS BY MAX WEAVER PICTURES BY TED DAWSON
ALRIGHT! WHERE TO? ASPEN? TAOS? WINTER PARK?
NO, WE'RE DRIVING TO THE BEACH!
ARE YOU CRAZY? IT'S THE MIDDLE OF WINTER! THE WATER WILL BE FREEZING!
IT'S THE "OFF SEASON." EVERY-THING IS REAL CHEAP. WE'LL SAVE TONS OF MONEY!
!

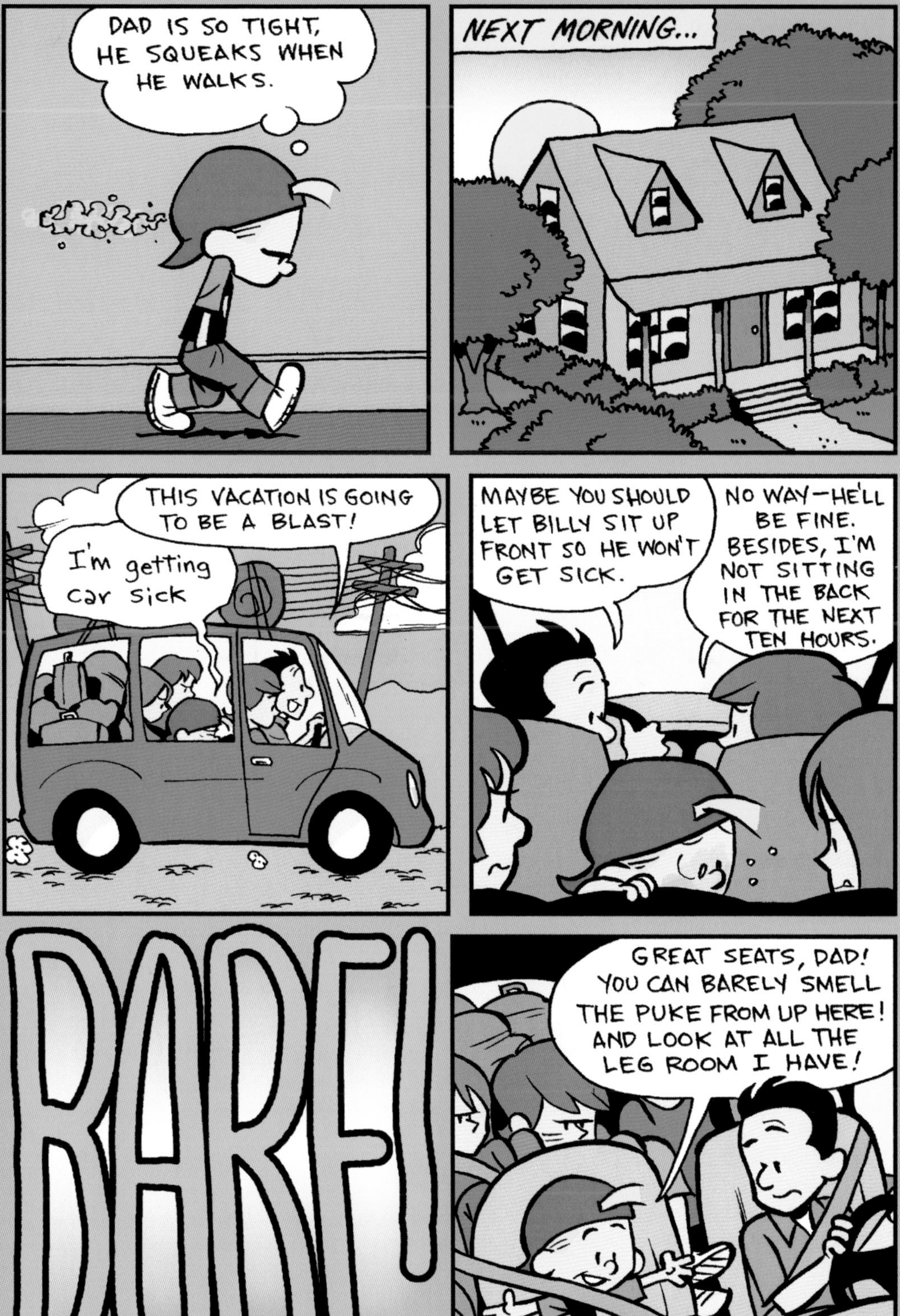
DAD IS SO TIGHT, HE SQUEAKS WHEN HE WALKS.
NEXT MORNING...
THIS VACATION IS GOING TO BE A BLAST!
I'm getting car sick
MAYBE YOU SHOULD LET BILLY SIT UP FRONT SO HE WON'T GET SICK.
NO WAY—HE'LL BE FINE. BESIDES, I'M NOT SITTING IN THE BACK FOR THE NEXT TEN HOURS.
BARF!
GREAT SEATS, DAD! YOU CAN BARELY SMELL THE PUKE FROM UP HERE! AND LOOK AT ALL THE LEG ROOM I HAVE!

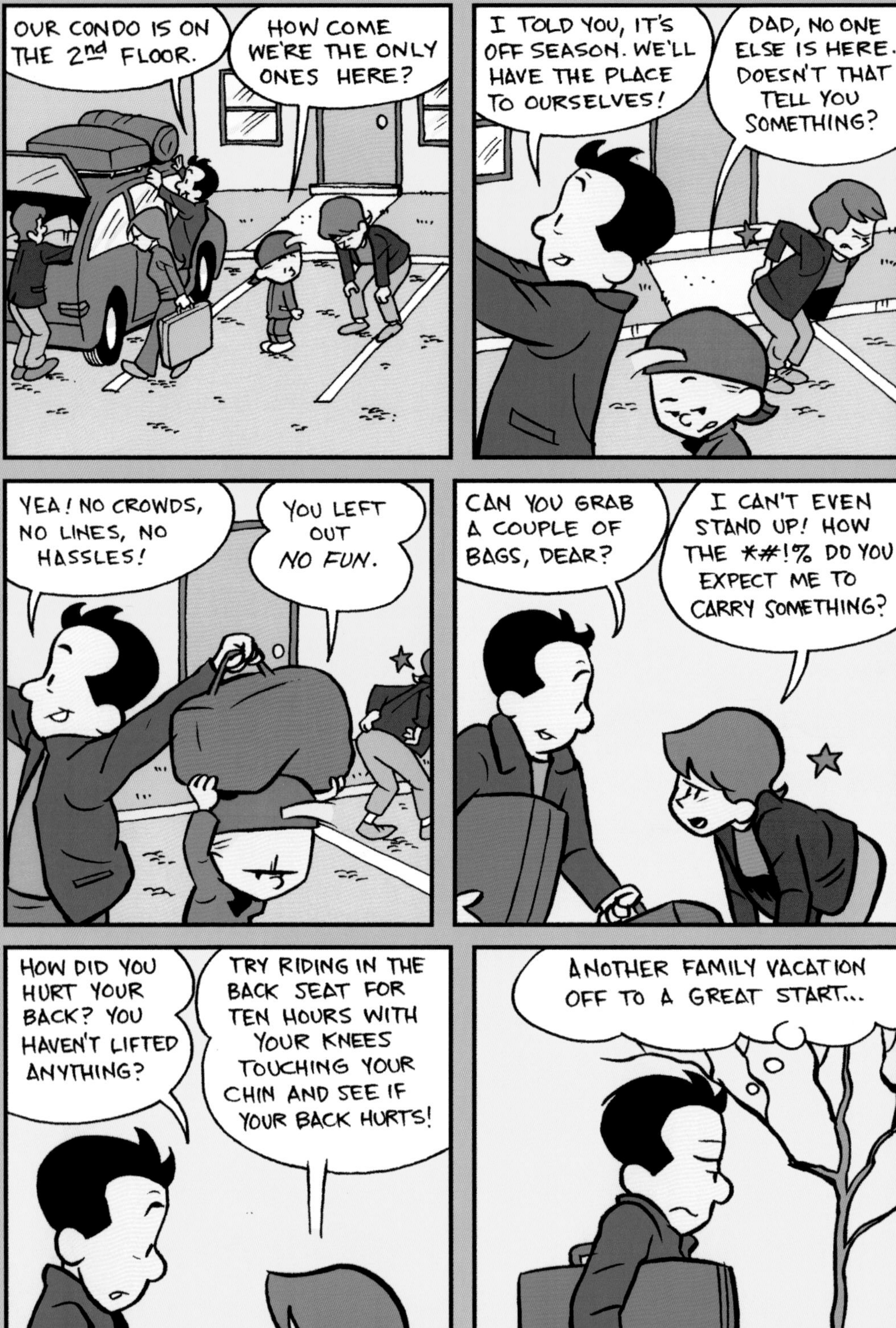
OUR CONDO IS ON THE 2nd FLOOR.
HOW COME WE'RE THE ONLY ONES HERE?
I TOLD YOU, IT'S OFF SEASON. WE'LL HAVE THE PLACE TO OURSELVES!
DAD, NO ONE ELSE IS HERE. DOESN'T THAT TELL YOU SOMETHING?
YEA! NO CROWDS, NO LINES, NO HASSLES!
YOU LEFT OUT *NO FUN*.
CAN YOU GRAB A COUPLE OF BAGS, DEAR?
I CAN'T EVEN STAND UP! HOW THE *#!% DO YOU EXPECT ME TO CARRY SOMETHING?
HOW DID YOU HURT YOUR BACK? YOU HAVEN'T LIFTED ANYTHING?
TRY RIDING IN THE BACK SEAT FOR TEN HOURS WITH YOUR KNEES TOUCHING YOUR CHIN AND SEE IF YOUR BACK HURTS!
ANOTHER FAMILY VACATION OFF TO A GREAT START...

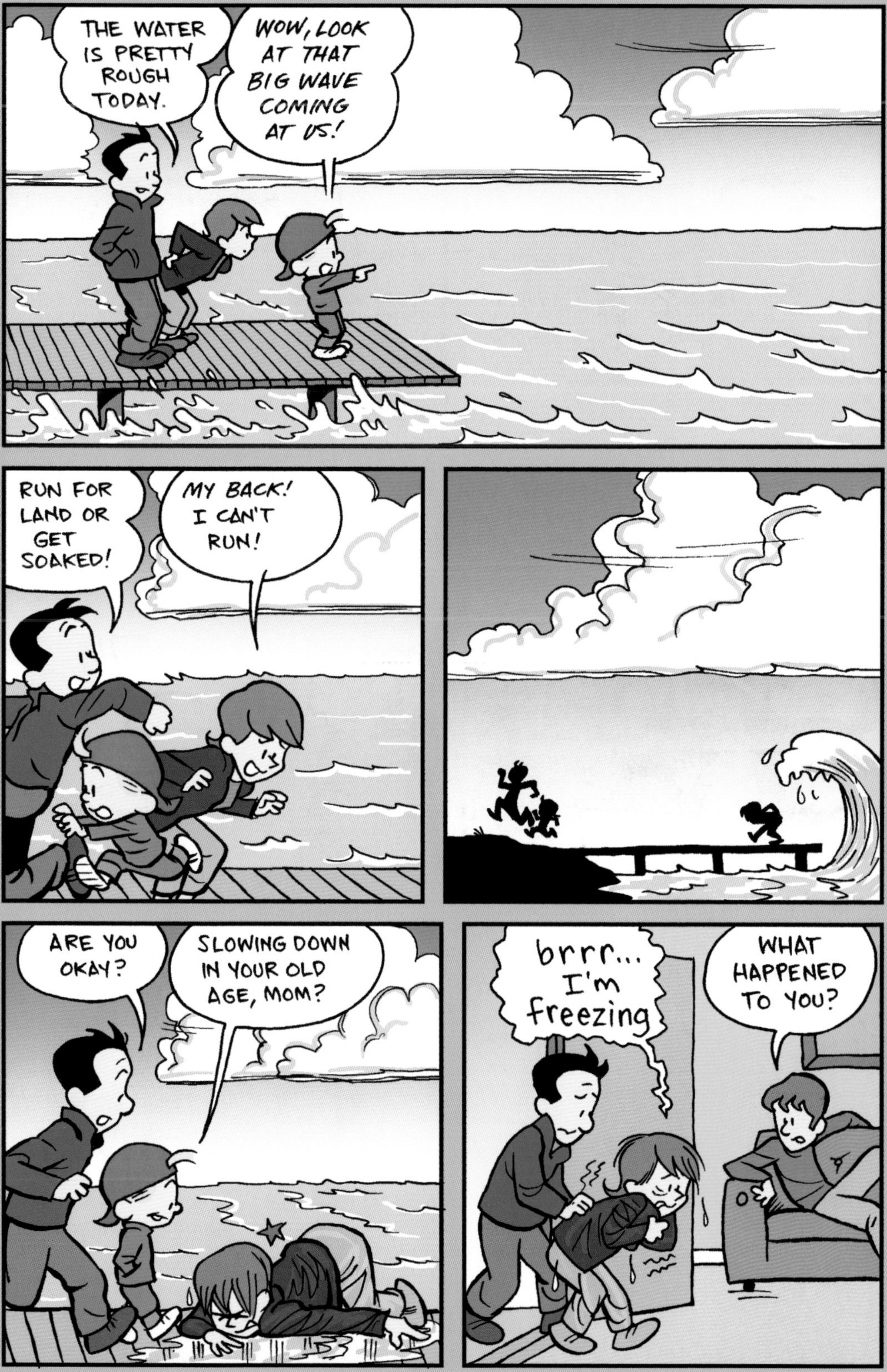
THE WATER IS PRETTY ROUGH TODAY.
WOW, LOOK AT THAT BIG WAVE COMING AT US!
RUN FOR LAND OR GET SOAKED!
MY BACK! I CAN'T RUN!
ARE YOU OKAY?
SLOWING DOWN IN YOUR OLD AGE, MOM?
brrr... I'm freezing
WHAT HAPPENED TO YOU?

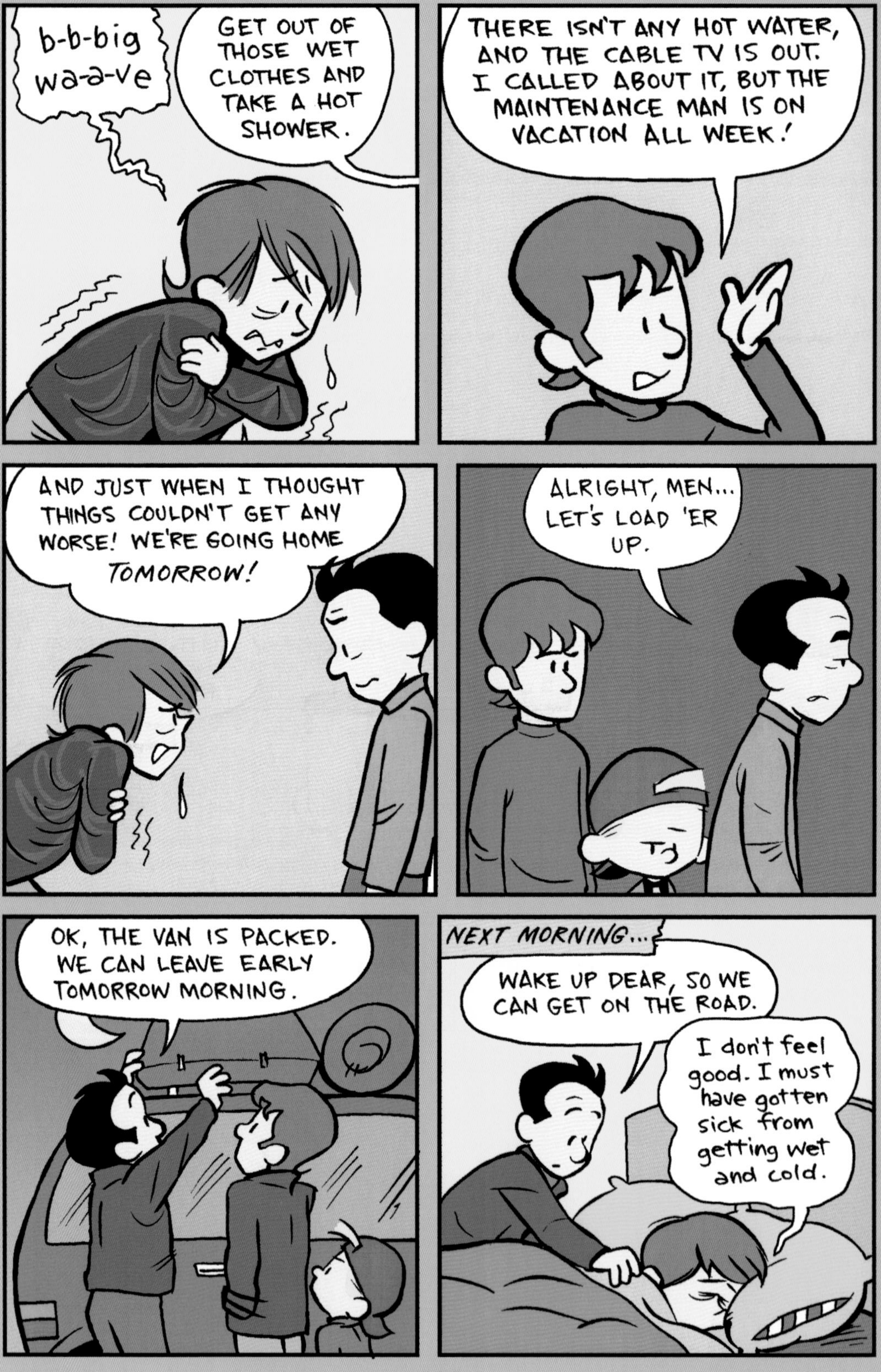
b-b-big wa-a-ve
GET OUT OF THOSE WET CLOTHES AND TAKE A HOT SHOWER.
THERE ISN'T ANY HOT WATER, AND THE CABLE TV IS OUT. I CALLED ABOUT IT, BUT THE MAINTENANCE MAN IS ON VACATION ALL WEEK!
AND JUST WHEN I THOUGHT THINGS COULDN'T GET ANY WORSE! WE'RE GOING HOME TOMORROW!
ALRIGHT, MEN... LET'S LOAD 'ER UP.
OK, THE VAN IS PACKED. WE CAN LEAVE EARLY TOMORROW MORNING.
NEXT MORNING...
WAKE UP DEAR, SO WE CAN GET ON THE ROAD.
I don't feel good. I must have gotten sick from getting wet and cold.

YOU'RE BURNING UP WITH FEVER! BETTER GO BACK TO SLEEP.

OK, WE'RE UNPACKED AGAIN...

I DON'T KNOW WHY WE CAN'T TRAVEL WHEN MOM'S SICK. I THREW UP AND WE STILL DROVE ALL THE WAY HERE!

I GUESS WE CAN'T GO HOME UNTIL MOM GETS WELL.

TOO BAD THE CABLE'S OUT.

OH, WELL, WE'LL JUST HAVE TO MAKE THE BEST OF THINGS.

THAT'S A GOOD ATTITUDE. WHAT DO YOU WANT TO DO? READ A BOOK?

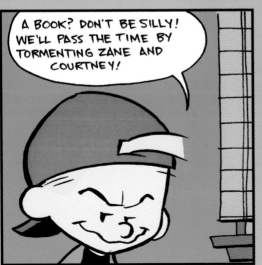

A BOOK? DON'T BE SILLY! WE'LL PASS THE TIME BY TORMENTING ZANE AND COURTNEY!

LET'S TAKE INVENTORY OF OUR PROPS SO WE CAN START PLAYING TRICKS ON ZANE AND COURTNEY.

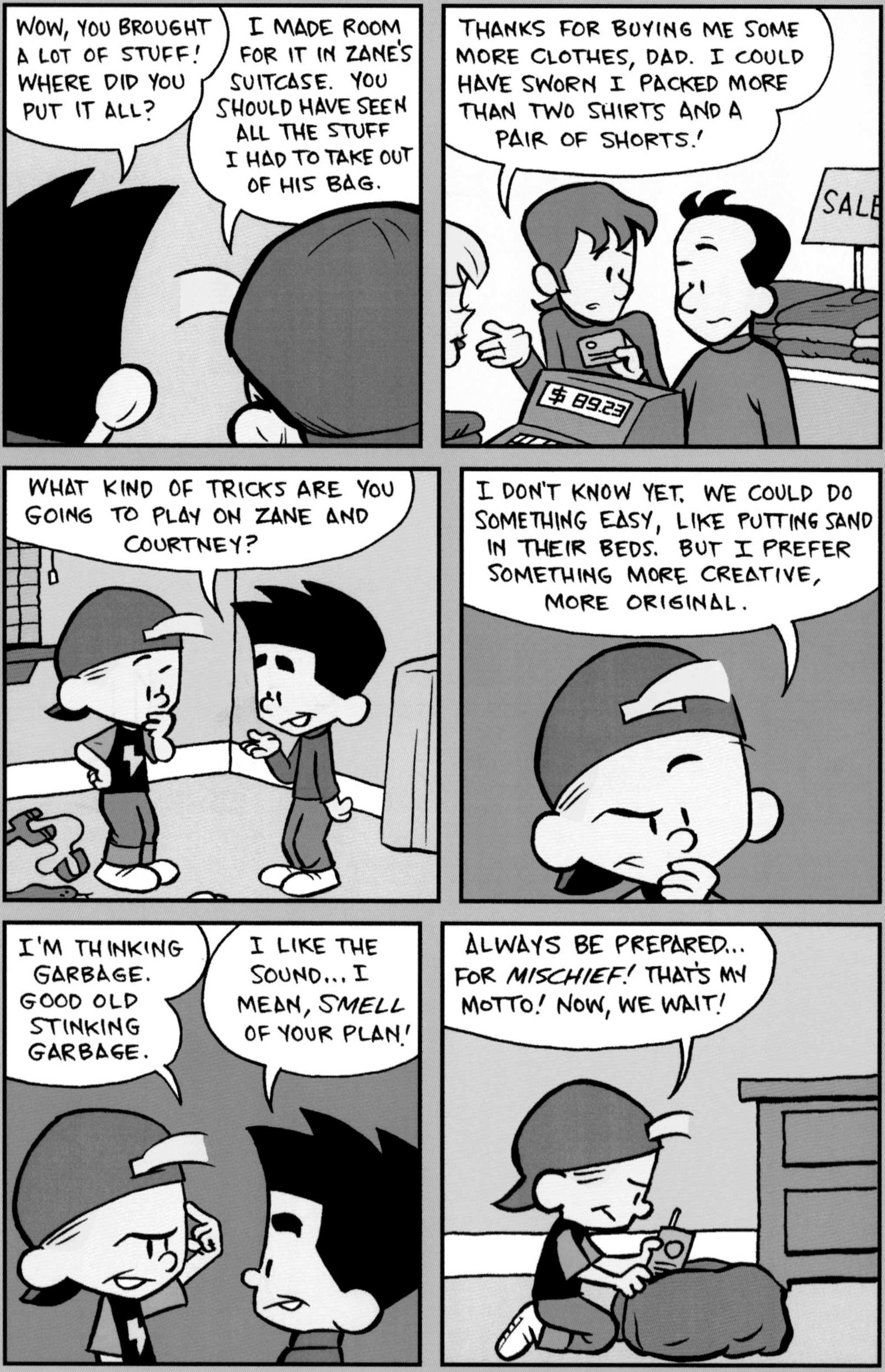
WOW, YOU BROUGHT A LOT OF STUFF! WHERE DID YOU PUT IT ALL?
I MADE ROOM FOR IT IN ZANE'S SUITCASE. YOU SHOULD HAVE SEEN ALL THE STUFF I HAD TO TAKE OUT OF HIS BAG.
THANKS FOR BUYING ME SOME MORE CLOTHES, DAD. I COULD HAVE SWORN I PACKED MORE THAN TWO SHIRTS AND A PAIR OF SHORTS!
SALE
$ 89.23
WHAT KIND OF TRICKS ARE YOU GOING TO PLAY ON ZANE AND COURTNEY?
I DON'T KNOW YET. WE COULD DO SOMETHING EASY, LIKE PUTTING SAND IN THEIR BEDS. BUT I PREFER SOMETHING MORE CREATIVE, MORE ORIGINAL.
I'M THINKING GARBAGE. GOOD OLD STINKING GARBAGE.
I LIKE THE SOUND... I MEAN, *SMELL* OF YOUR PLAN!
ALWAYS BE PREPARED... FOR *MISCHIEF*! THAT'S MY MOTTO! NOW, WE WAIT!

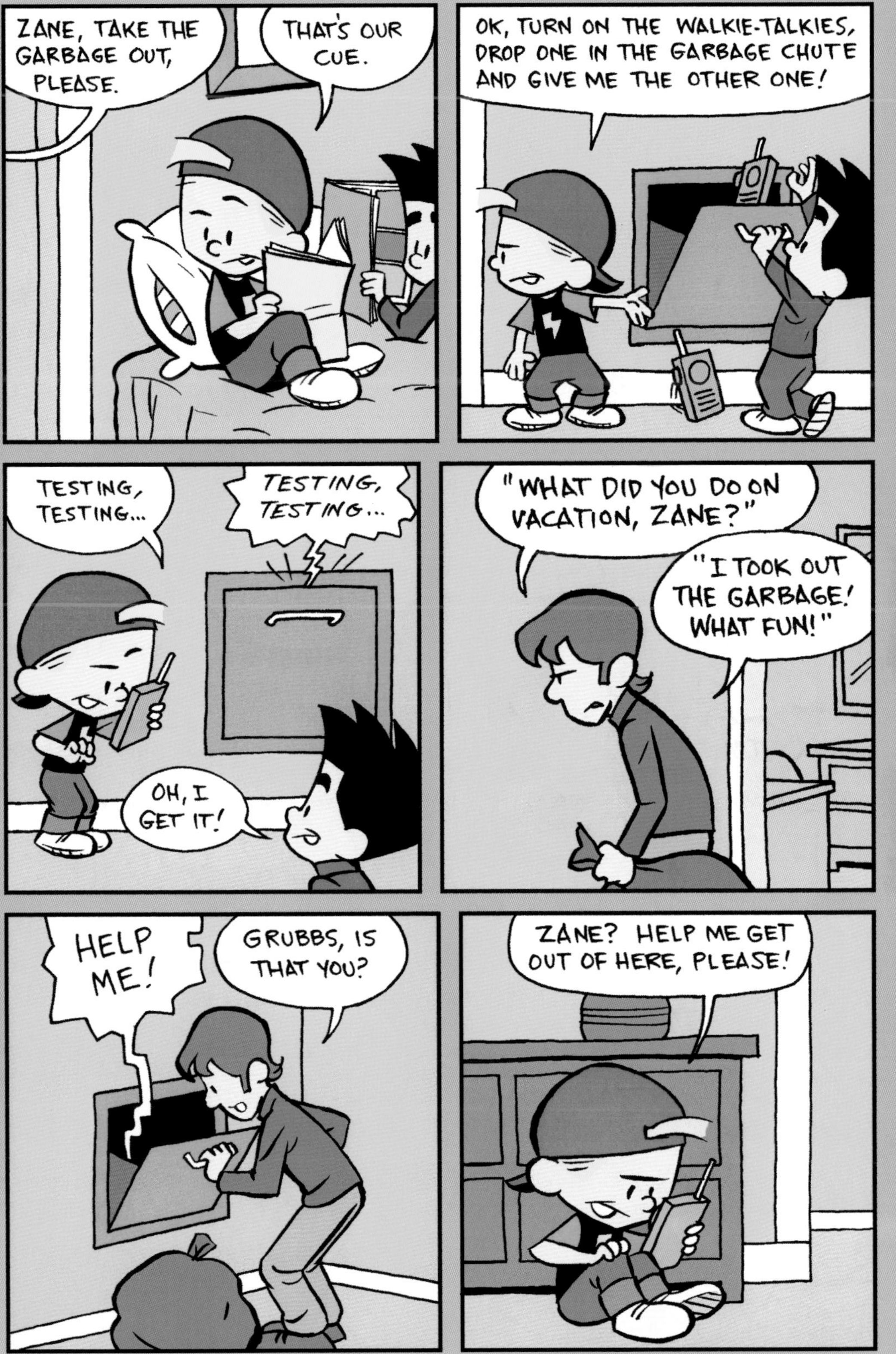
ZANE, TAKE THE GARBAGE OUT, PLEASE.
THAT'S OUR CUE.
OK, TURN ON THE WALKIE-TALKIES, DROP ONE IN THE GARBAGE CHUTE AND GIVE ME THE OTHER ONE!
TESTING, TESTING...
TESTING, TESTING...
OH, I GET IT!
"WHAT DID YOU DO ON VACATION, ZANE?"
"I TOOK OUT THE GARBAGE! WHAT FUN!"
HELP ME!
GRUBBS, IS THAT YOU?
ZANE? HELP ME GET OUT OF HERE, PLEASE!

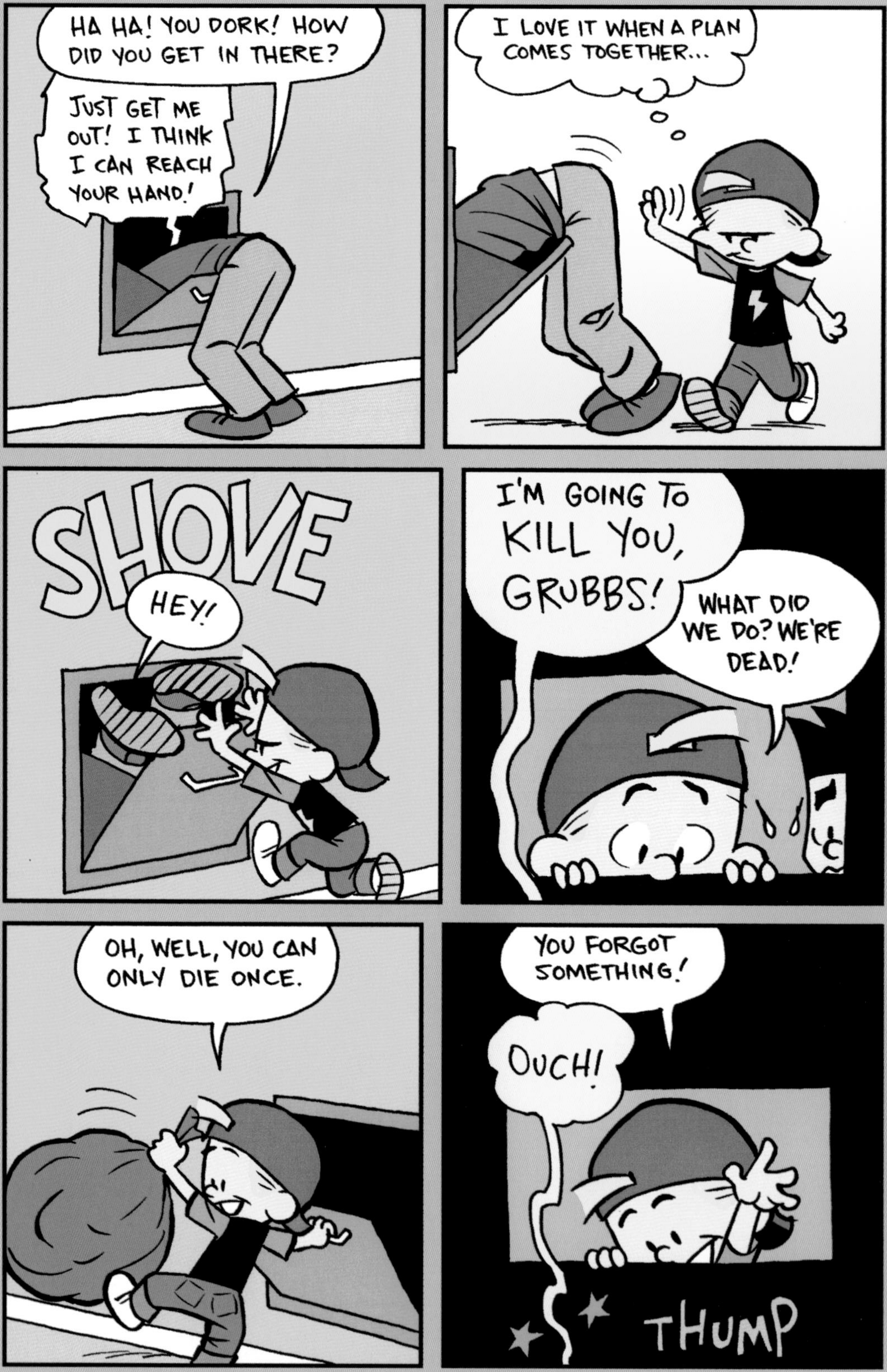
HA HA! YOU DORK! HOW DID YOU GET IN THERE?
JUST GET ME OUT! I THINK I CAN REACH YOUR HAND!
I LOVE IT WHEN A PLAN COMES TOGETHER...
SHOVE
HEY!
I'M GOING TO KILL YOU, GRUBBS!
WHAT DID WE DO? WE'RE DEAD!
OH, WELL, YOU CAN ONLY DIE ONCE.
YOU FORGOT SOMETHING!
OUCH!
THUMP

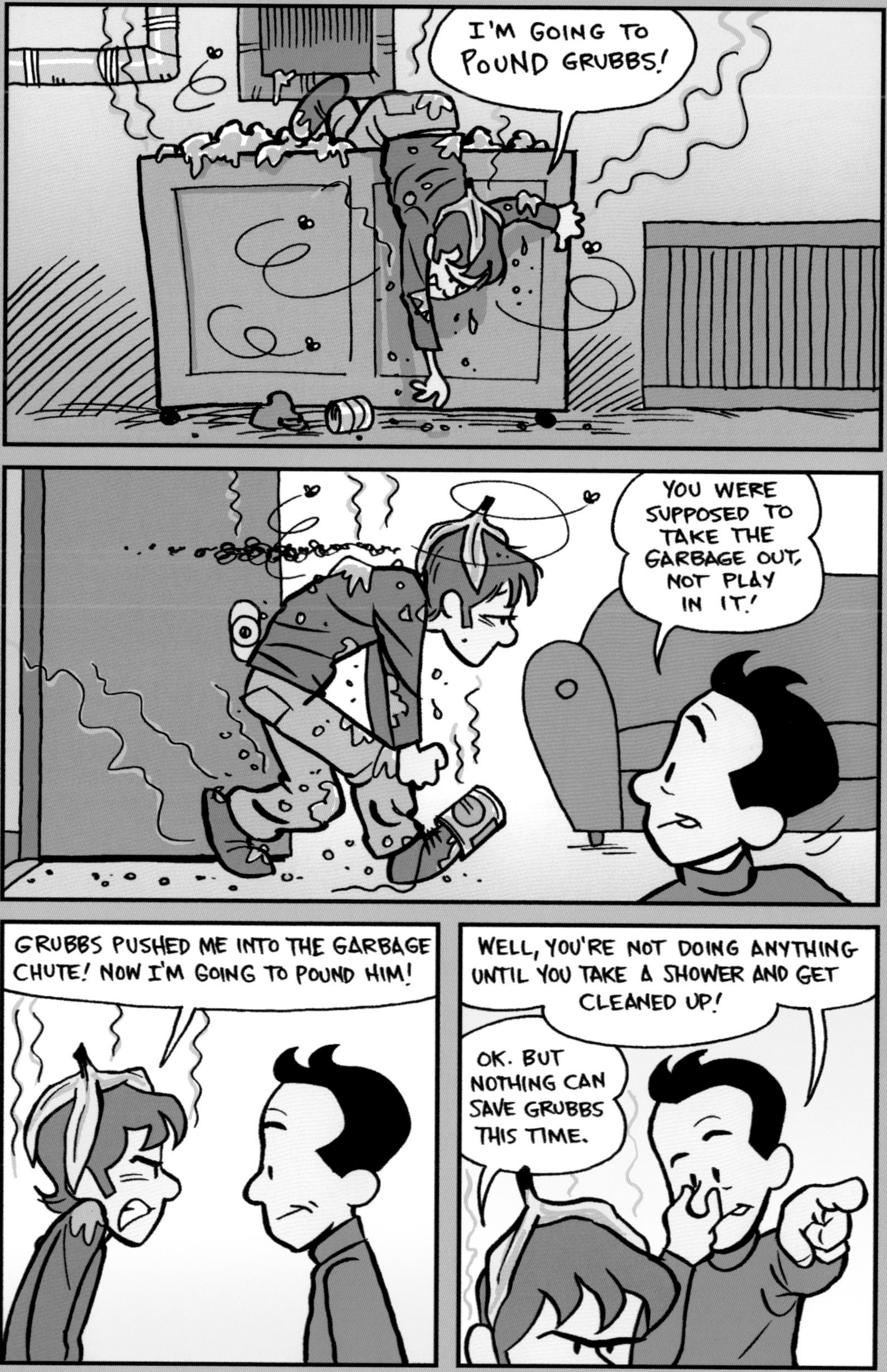
I'M GOING TO POUND GRUBBS!
YOU WERE SUPPOSED TO TAKE THE GARBAGE OUT, NOT PLAY IN IT!
GRUBBS PUSHED ME INTO THE GARBAGE CHUTE! NOW I'M GOING TO POUND HIM!
WELL, YOU'RE NOT DOING ANYTHING UNTIL YOU TAKE A SHOWER AND GET CLEANED UP!
OK. BUT NOTHING CAN SAVE GRUBBS THIS TIME.

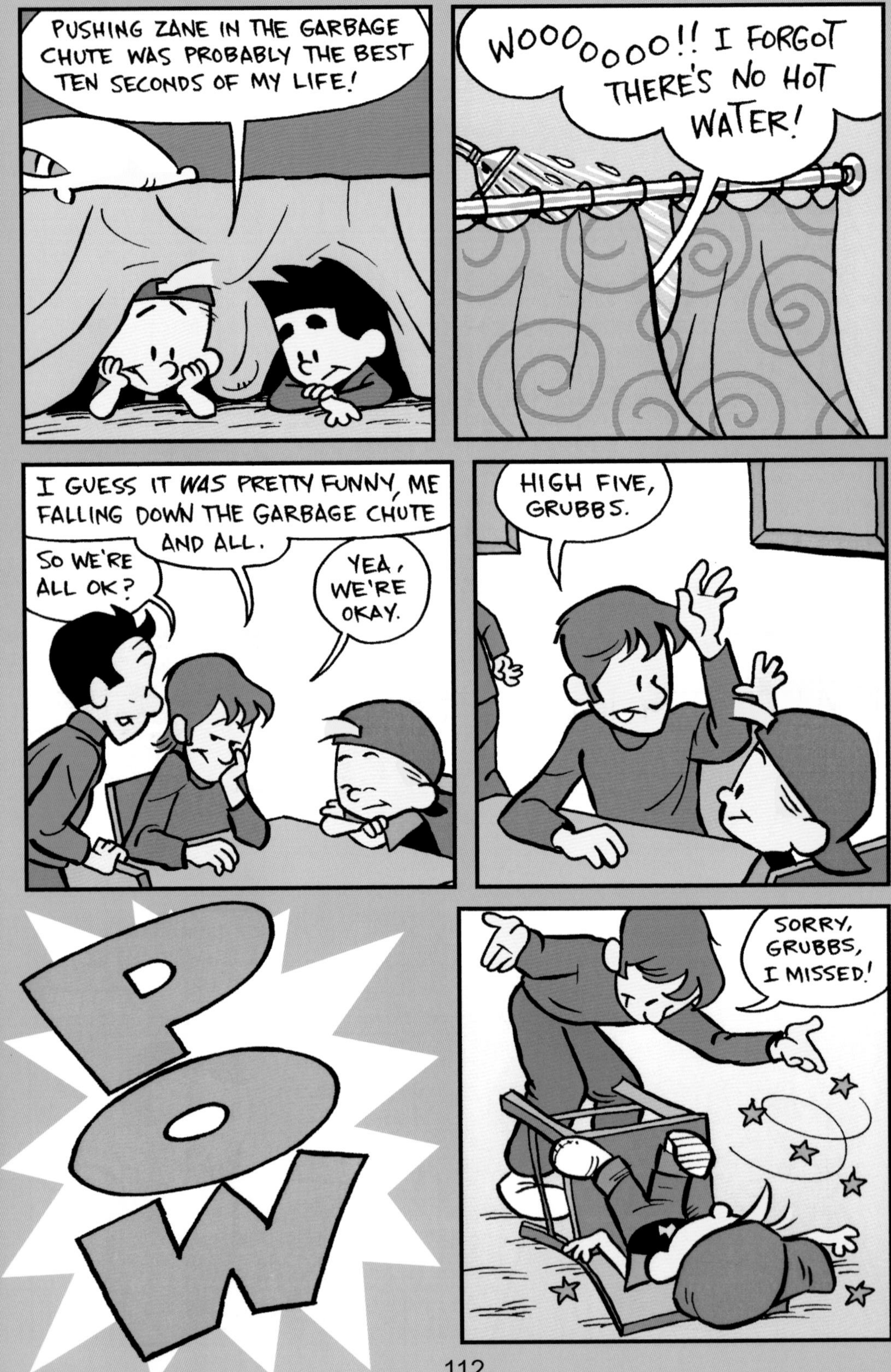
PUSHING ZANE IN THE GARBAGE CHUTE WAS PROBABLY THE BEST TEN SECONDS OF MY LIFE!
WOOOOOOOO!! I FORGOT THERE'S NO HOT WATER!
I GUESS IT WAS PRETTY FUNNY, ME FALLING DOWN THE GARBAGE CHUTE AND ALL.
SO WE'RE ALL OK?
YEA, WE'RE OKAY.
HIGH FIVE, GRUBBS.
POW
SORRY, GRUBBS, I MISSED!

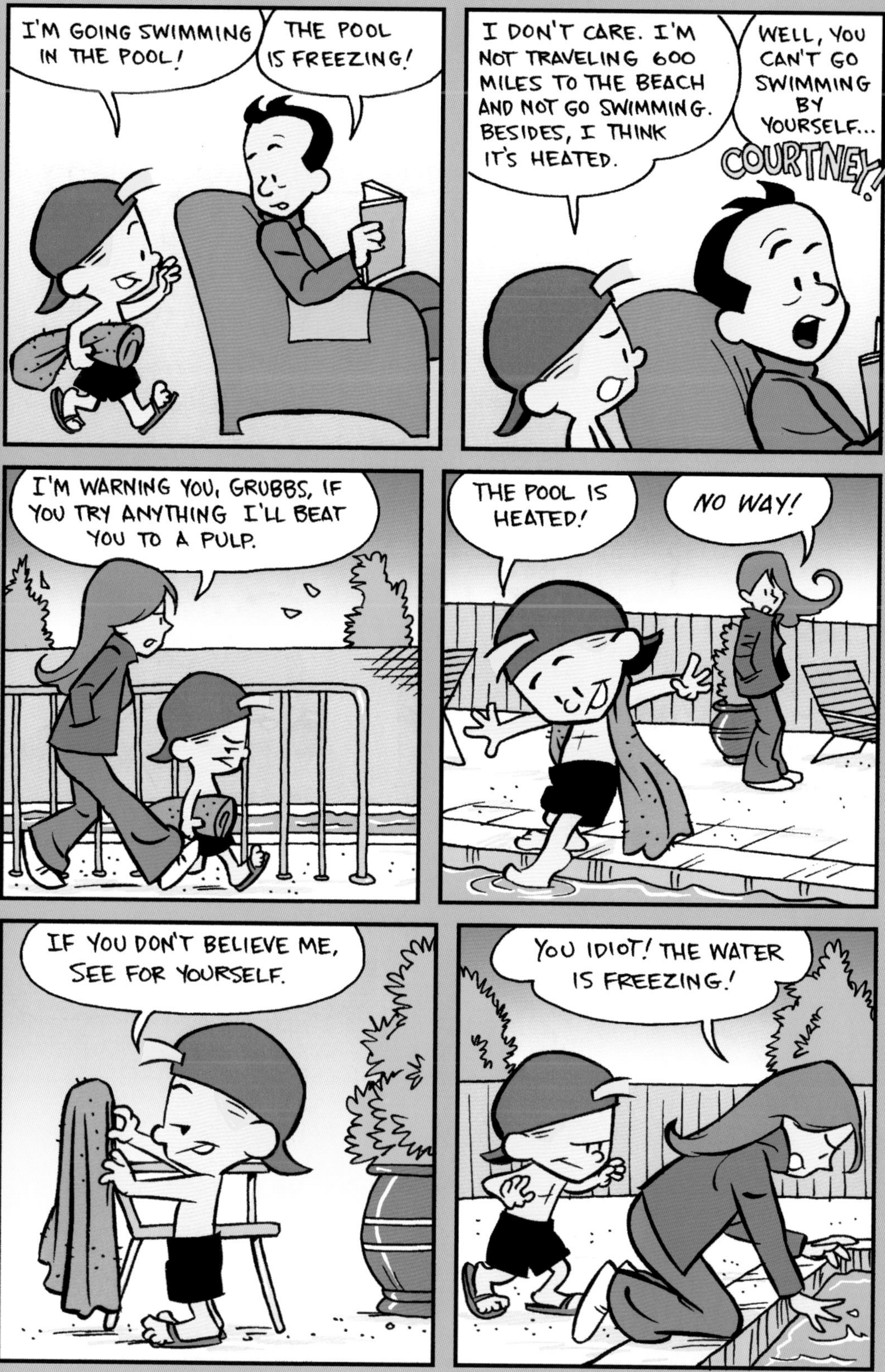
I'M GOING SWIMMING IN THE POOL!
THE POOL IS FREEZING!
I DON'T CARE. I'M NOT TRAVELING 600 MILES TO THE BEACH AND NOT GO SWIMMING. BESIDES, I THINK IT'S HEATED.
WELL, YOU CAN'T GO SWIMMING BY YOURSELF...
COURTNEY!
I'M WARNING YOU, GRUBBS, IF YOU TRY ANYTHING I'LL BEAT YOU TO A PULP.
THE POOL IS HEATED!
NO WAY!
IF YOU DON'T BELIEVE ME, SEE FOR YOURSELF.
YOU IDIOT! THE WATER IS FREEZING!

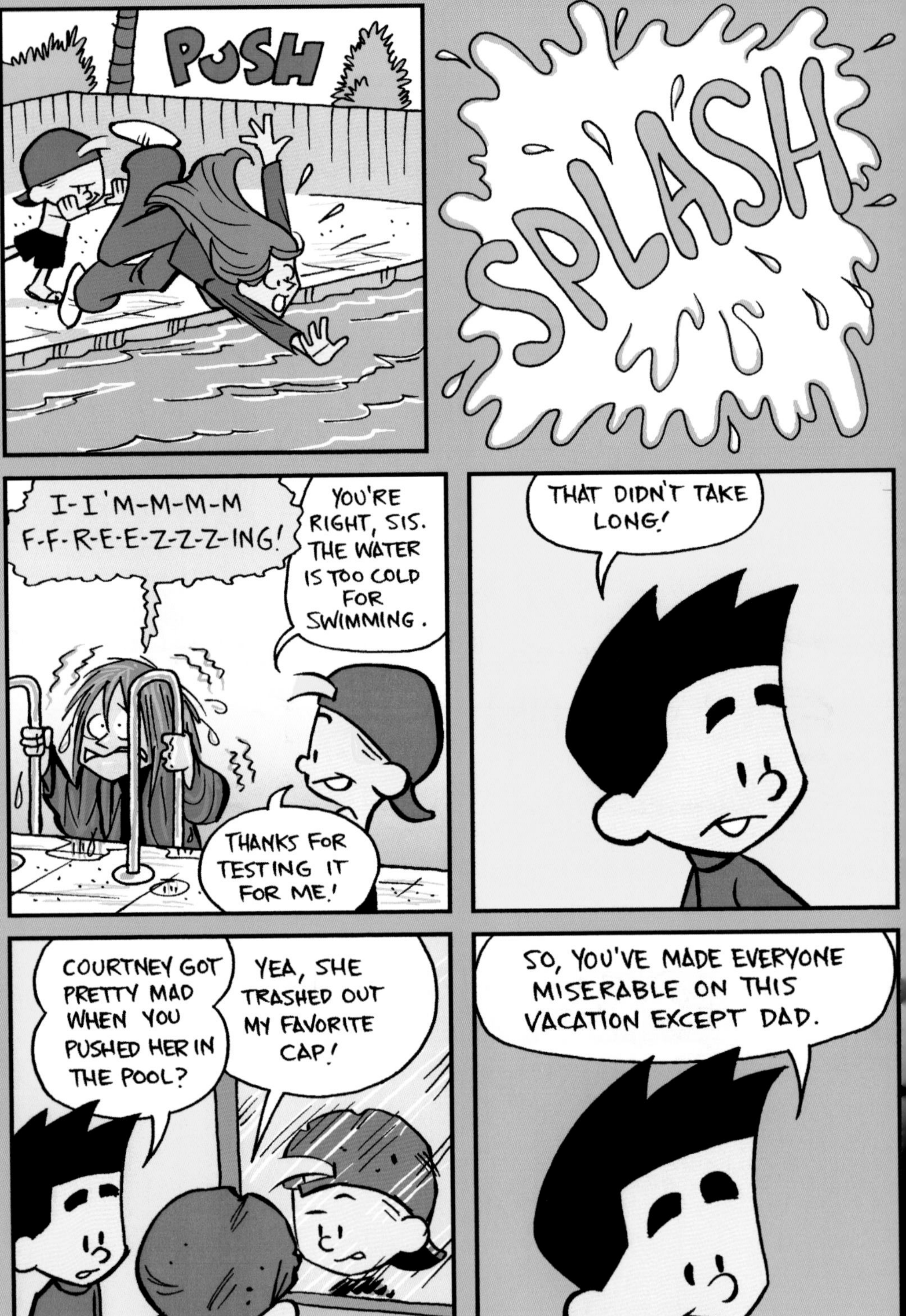
PUSH
SPLASH
I-I'M-M-M-M F-F-R-E-E-Z-Z-Z-ING!
YOU'RE RIGHT, SIS. THE WATER IS TOO COLD FOR SWIMMING.
THANKS FOR TESTING IT FOR ME!
THAT DIDN'T TAKE LONG!
COURTNEY GOT PRETTY MAD WHEN YOU PUSHED HER IN THE POOL?
YEA, SHE TRASHED OUT MY FAVORITE CAP!
SO, YOU'VE MADE EVERYONE MISERABLE ON THIS VACATION EXCEPT DAD.

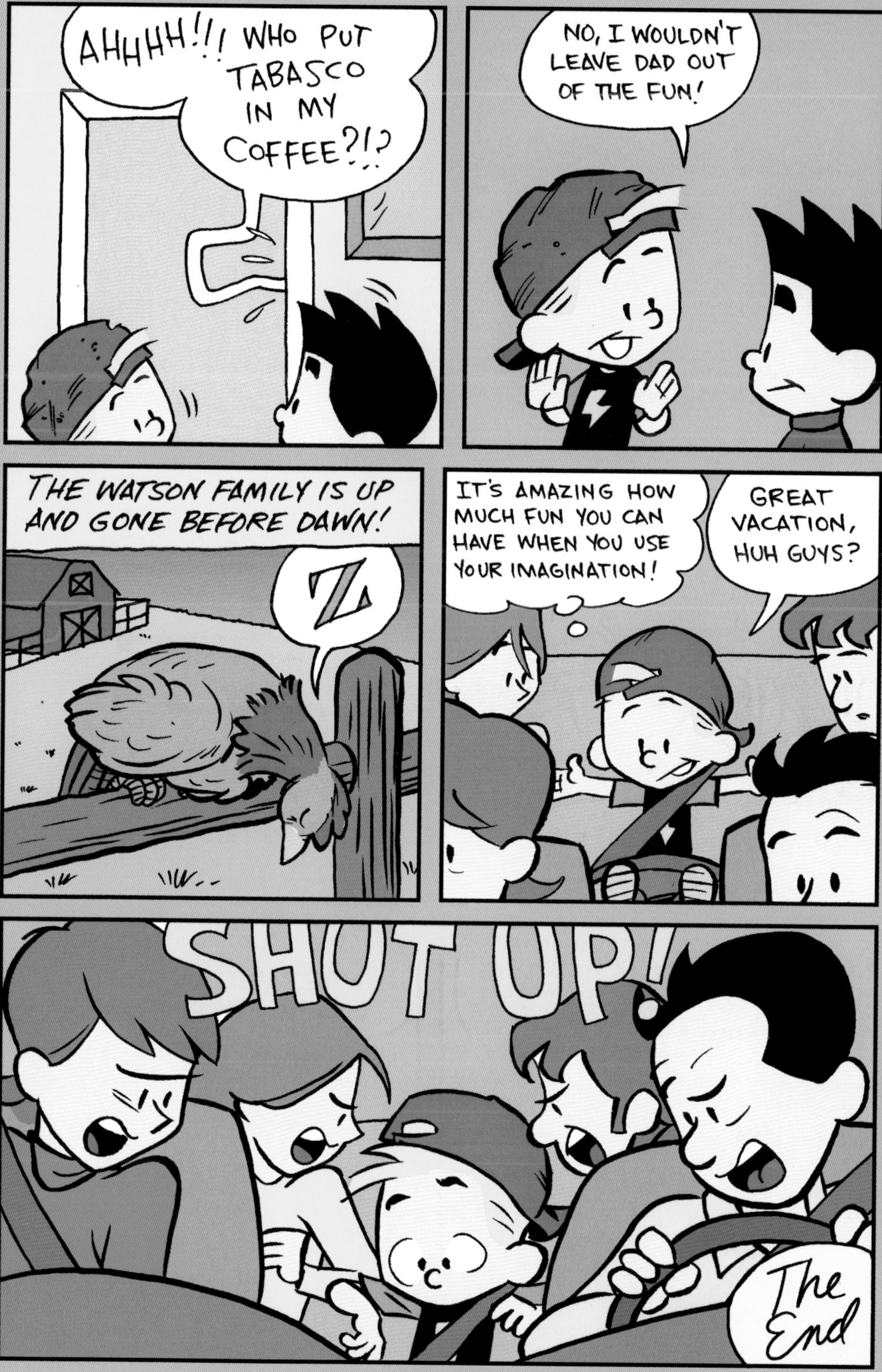
AHHHH!!! WHO PUT TABASCO IN MY COFFEE?!?
NO, I WOULDN'T LEAVE DAD OUT OF THE FUN!
THE WATSON FAMILY IS UP AND GONE BEFORE DAWN!
Z
IT'S AMAZING HOW MUCH FUN YOU CAN HAVE WHEN YOU USE YOUR IMAGINATION!
GREAT VACATION, HUH GUYS?
SHUT UP!
The End

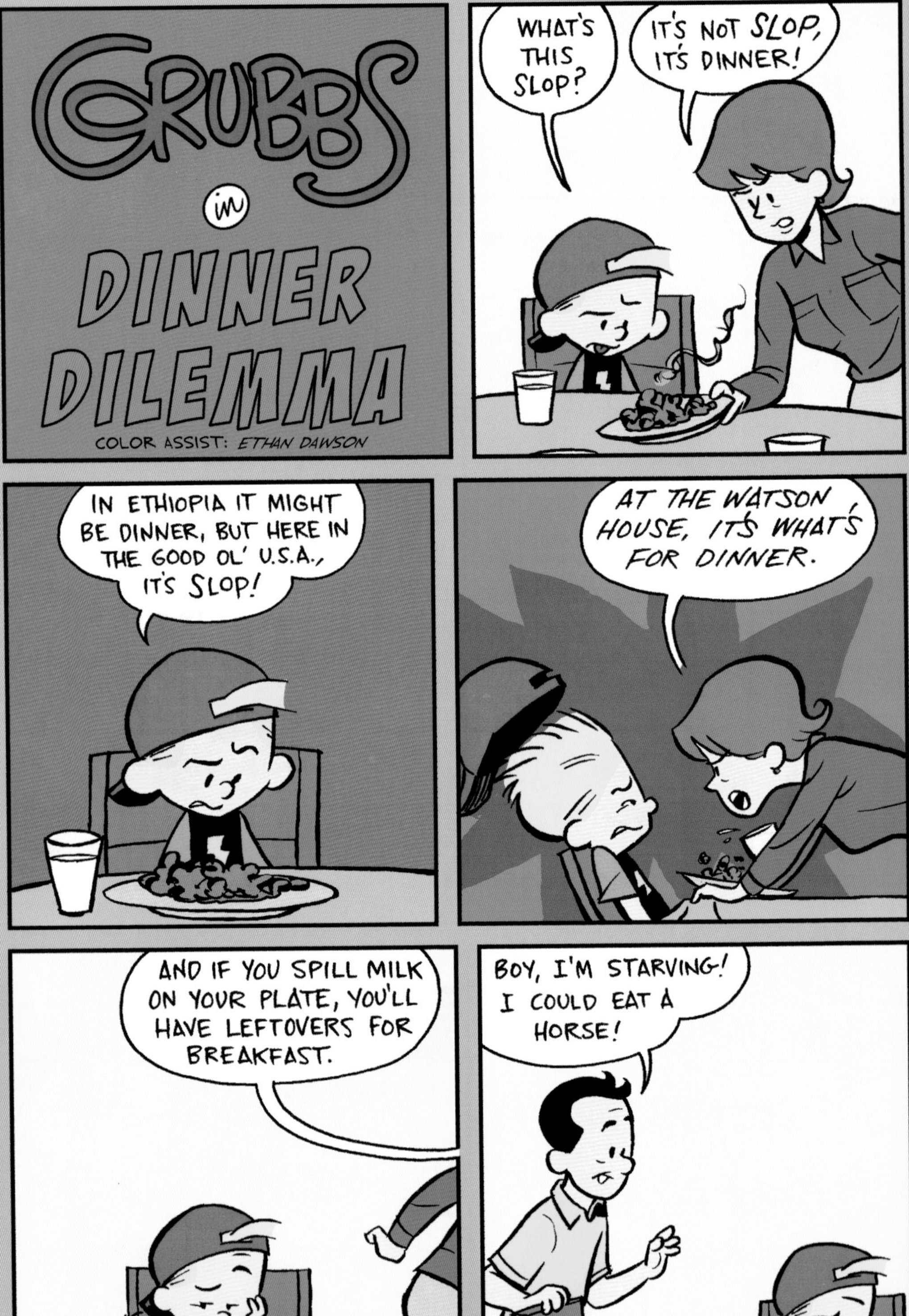
GRUBBS
in
DINNER DILEMMA
COLOR ASSIST: ETHAN DAWSON
WHAT'S THIS SLOP?
IT'S NOT SLOP, IT'S DINNER!
IN ETHIOPIA IT MIGHT BE DINNER, BUT HERE IN THE GOOD OL' U.S.A., IT'S SLOP!
AT THE WATSON HOUSE, IT'S WHAT'S FOR DINNER.
AND IF YOU SPILL MILK ON YOUR PLATE, YOU'LL HAVE LEFTOVERS FOR BREAKFAST.
BOY, I'M STARVING! I COULD EAT A HORSE!

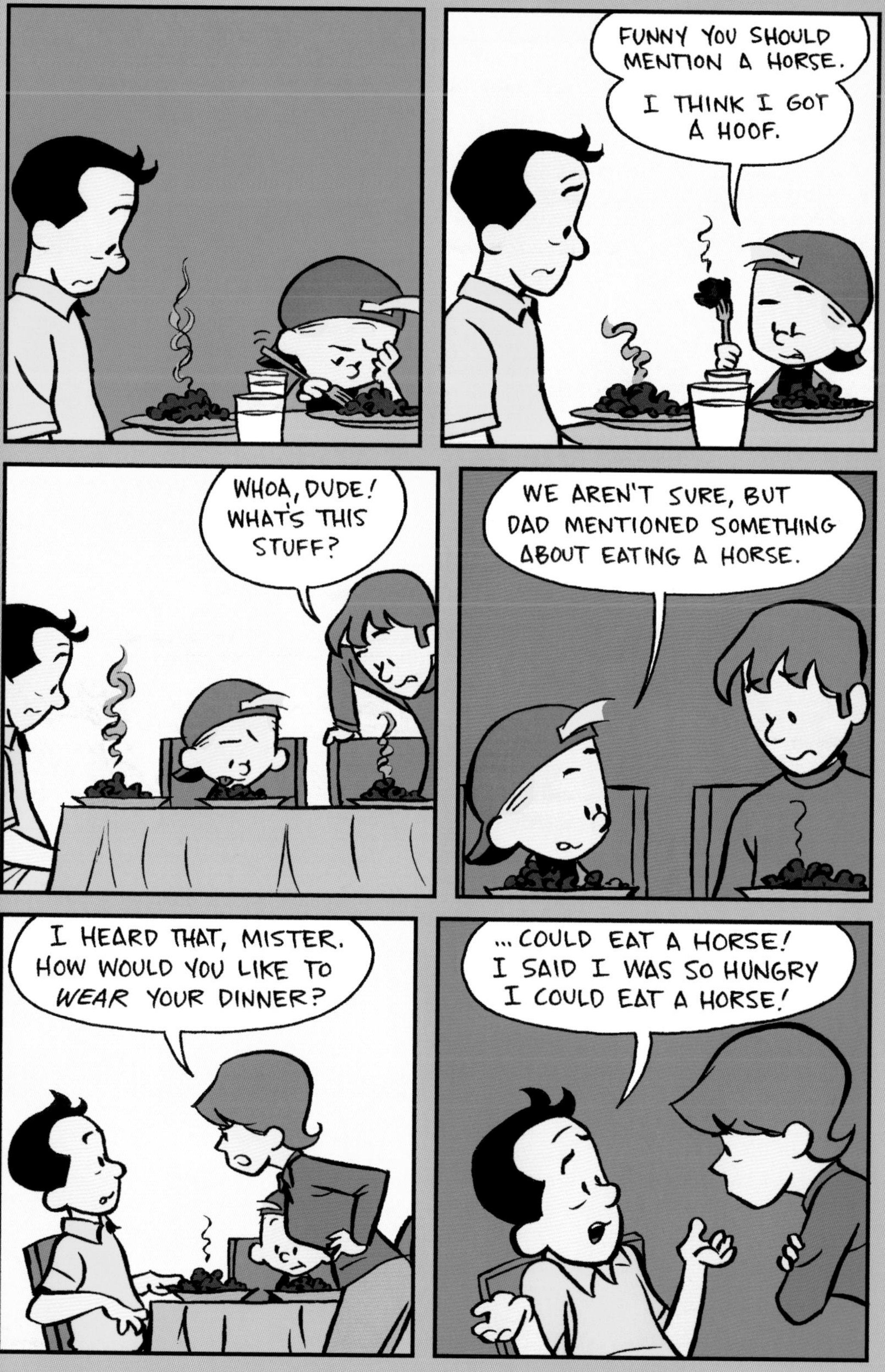
FUNNY YOU SHOULD MENTION A HORSE.
I THINK I GOT A HOOF.
WHOA, DUDE! WHAT'S THIS STUFF?
WE AREN'T SURE, BUT DAD MENTIONED SOMETHING ABOUT EATING A HORSE.
I HEARD THAT, MISTER. HOW WOULD YOU LIKE TO *WEAR* YOUR DINNER?
...COULD EAT A HORSE! I SAID I WAS SO HUNGRY I COULD EAT A HORSE!

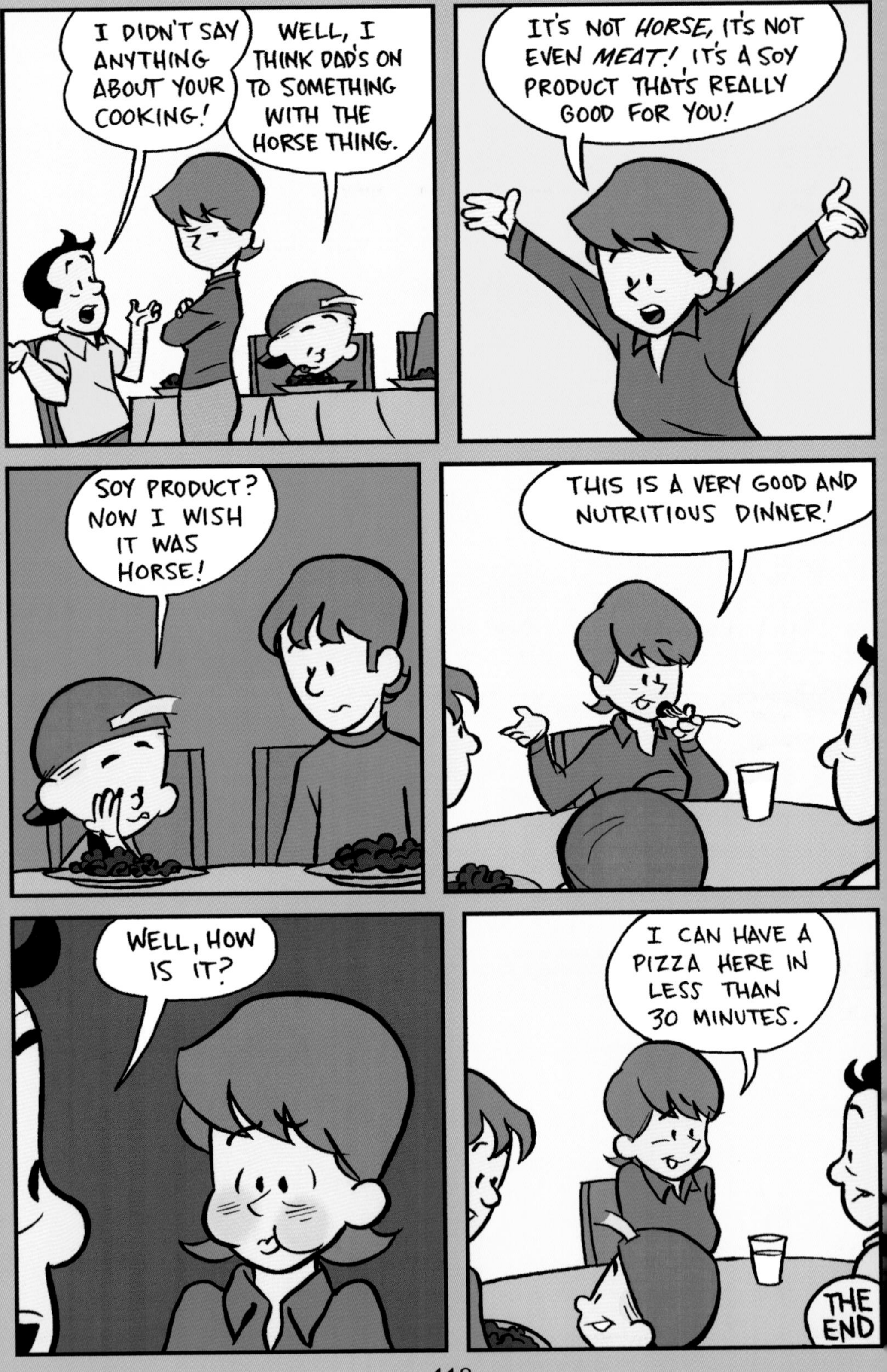
I DIDN'T SAY ANYTHING ABOUT YOUR COOKING!
WELL, I THINK DAD'S ON TO SOMETHING WITH THE HORSE THING.
IT'S NOT HORSE, IT'S NOT EVEN MEAT! IT'S A SOY PRODUCT THAT'S REALLY GOOD FOR YOU!
SOY PRODUCT? NOW I WISH IT WAS HORSE!
THIS IS A VERY GOOD AND NUTRITIOUS DINNER!
WELL, HOW IS IT?
I CAN HAVE A PIZZA HERE IN LESS THAN 30 MINUTES.
THE END

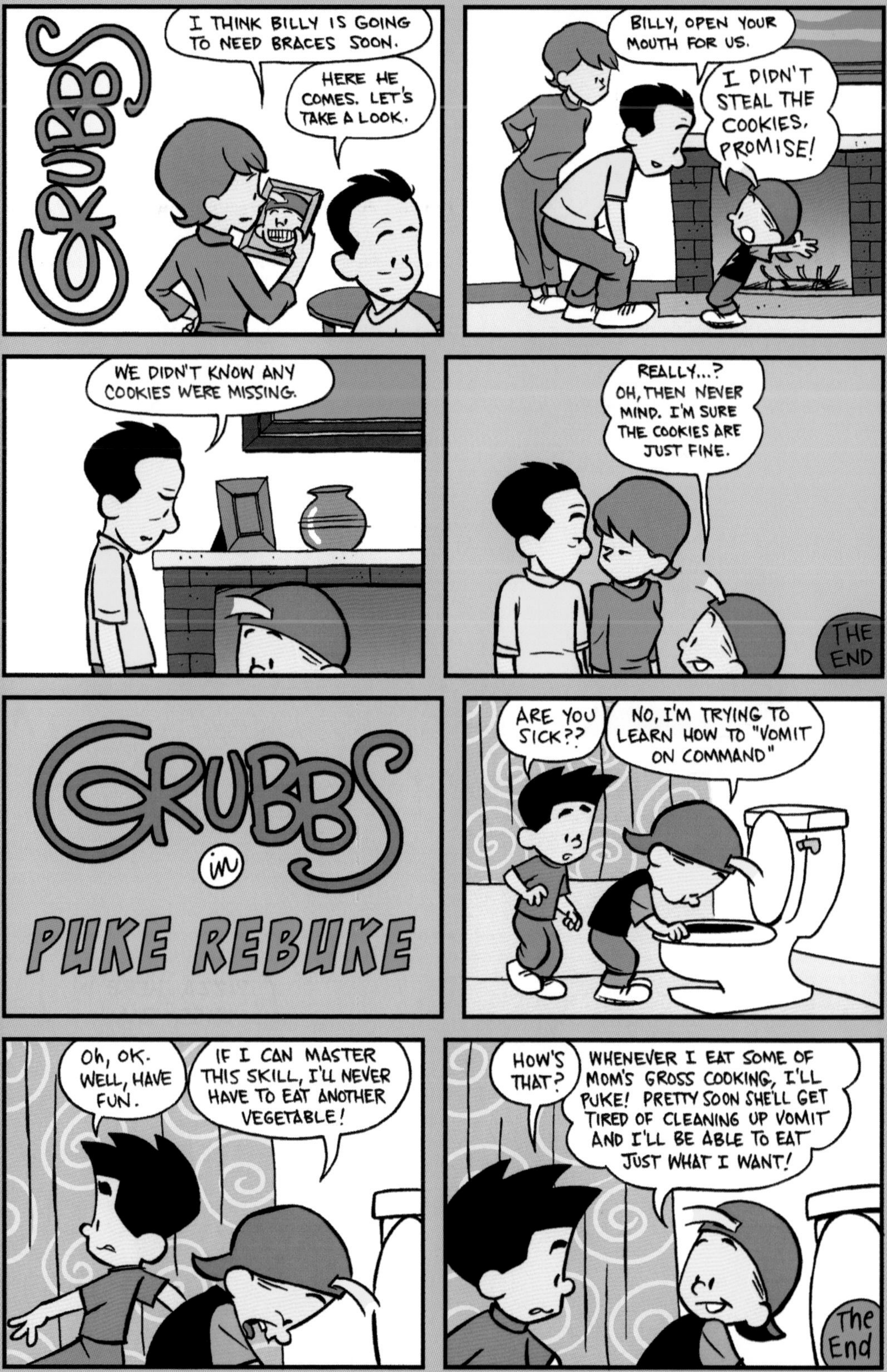
GRUBBS
I THINK BILLY IS GOING TO NEED BRACES SOON.
HERE HE COMES. LET'S TAKE A LOOK.
BILLY, OPEN YOUR MOUTH FOR US.
I DIDN'T STEAL THE COOKIES, PROMISE!
WE DIDN'T KNOW ANY COOKIES WERE MISSING.
REALLY...? OH, THEN NEVER MIND. I'M SURE THE COOKIES ARE JUST FINE.
THE END
GRUBBS in
PUKE REBUKE
ARE YOU SICK??
NO, I'M TRYING TO LEARN HOW TO "VOMIT ON COMMAND"
Oh, OK. WELL, HAVE FUN.
IF I CAN MASTER THIS SKILL, I'LL NEVER HAVE TO EAT ANOTHER VEGETABLE!
HOW'S THAT?
WHENEVER I EAT SOME OF MOM'S GROSS COOKING, I'LL PUKE! PRETTY SOON SHE'LL GET TIRED OF CLEANING UP VOMIT AND I'LL BE ABLE TO EAT JUST WHAT I WANT!
The End

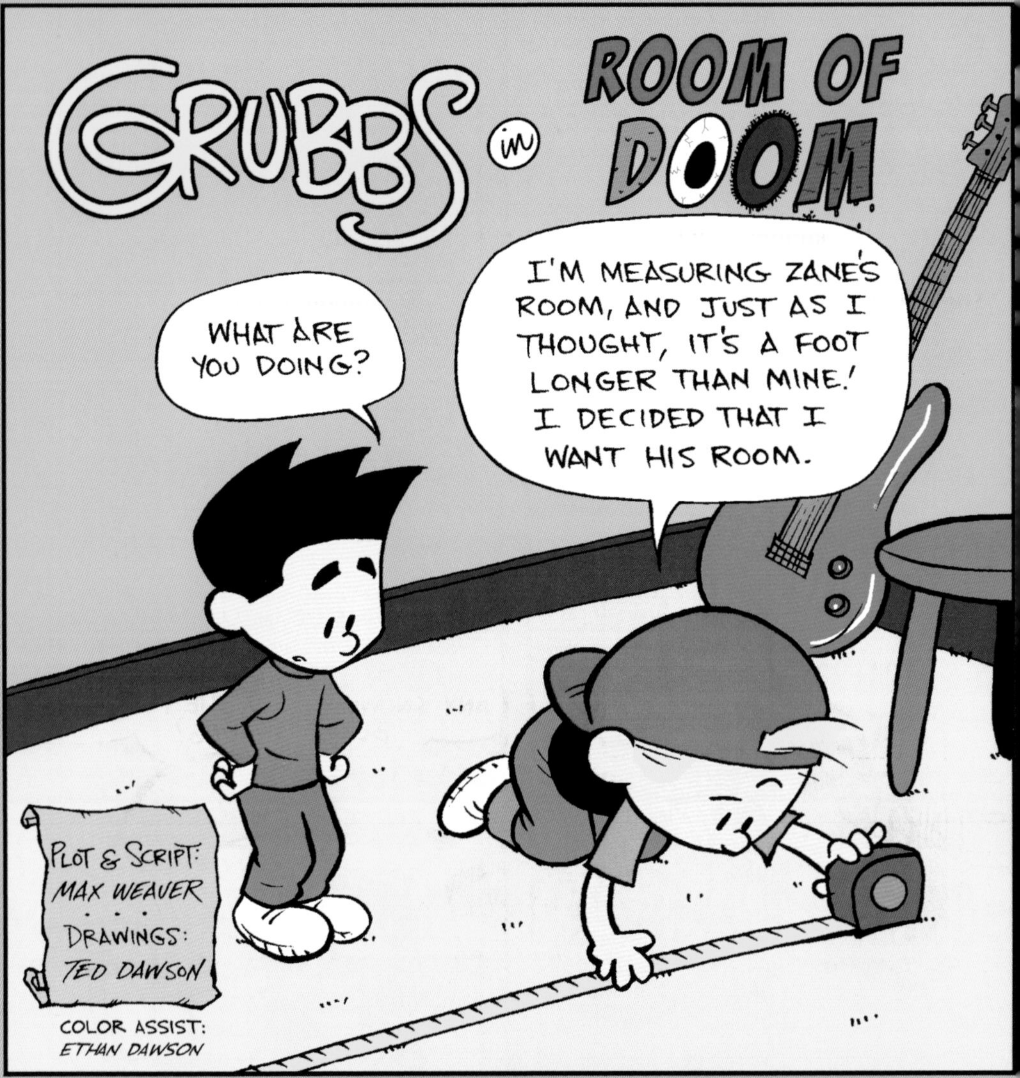
GRUBBS in ROOM OF DOOM
WHAT ARE YOU DOING?
I'M MEASURING ZANE'S ROOM, AND JUST AS I THOUGHT, IT'S A FOOT LONGER THAN MINE! I DECIDED THAT I WANT HIS ROOM.
PLOT & SCRIPT: MAX WEAVER
DRAWINGS: TED DAWSON
COLOR ASSIST: ETHAN DAWSON

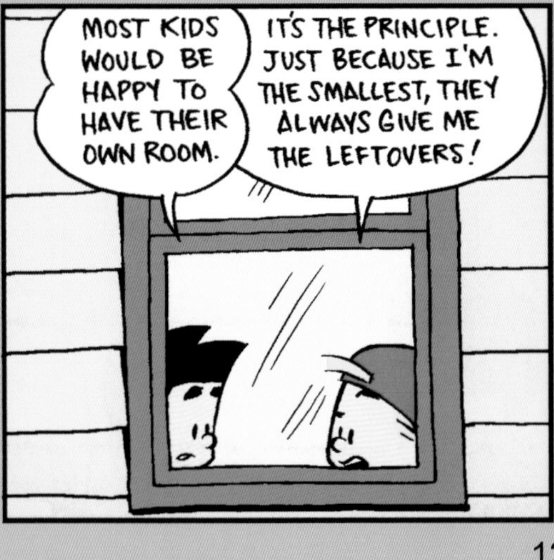
MOST KIDS WOULD BE HAPPY TO HAVE THEIR OWN ROOM.
IT'S THE PRINCIPLE. JUST BECAUSE I'M THE SMALLEST, THEY ALWAYS GIVE ME THE LEFTOVERS!

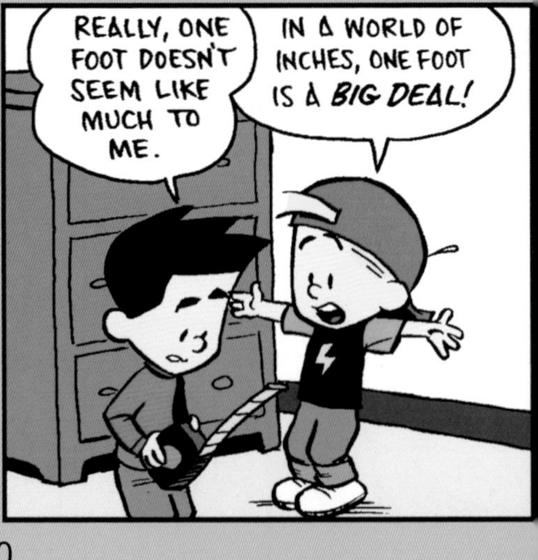
REALLY, ONE FOOT DOESN'T SEEM LIKE MUCH TO ME.
IN A WORLD OF INCHES, ONE FOOT IS A *BIG DEAL*!

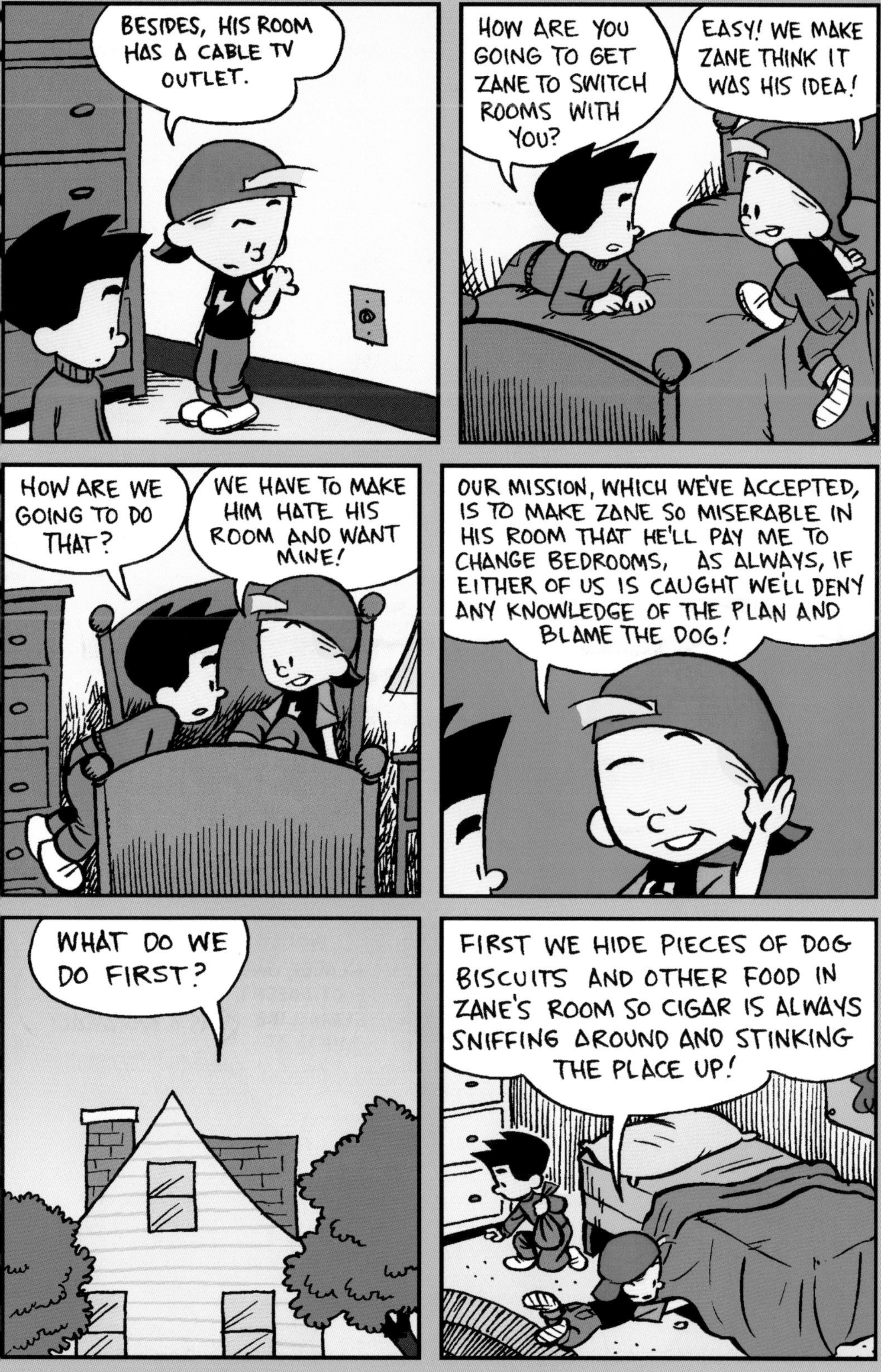
BESIDES, HIS ROOM HAS A CABLE TV OUTLET.
HOW ARE YOU GOING TO GET ZANE TO SWITCH ROOMS WITH YOU?
EASY! WE MAKE ZANE THINK IT WAS HIS IDEA!
HOW ARE WE GOING TO DO THAT?
WE HAVE TO MAKE HIM HATE HIS ROOM AND WANT MINE!
OUR MISSION, WHICH WE'VE ACCEPTED, IS TO MAKE ZANE SO MISERABLE IN HIS ROOM THAT HE'LL PAY ME TO CHANGE BEDROOMS. AS ALWAYS, IF EITHER OF US IS CAUGHT WE'LL DENY ANY KNOWLEDGE OF THE PLAN AND BLAME THE DOG!
WHAT DO WE DO FIRST?
FIRST WE HIDE PIECES OF DOG BISCUITS AND OTHER FOOD IN ZANE'S ROOM SO CIGAR IS ALWAYS SNIFFING AROUND AND STINKING THE PLACE UP!

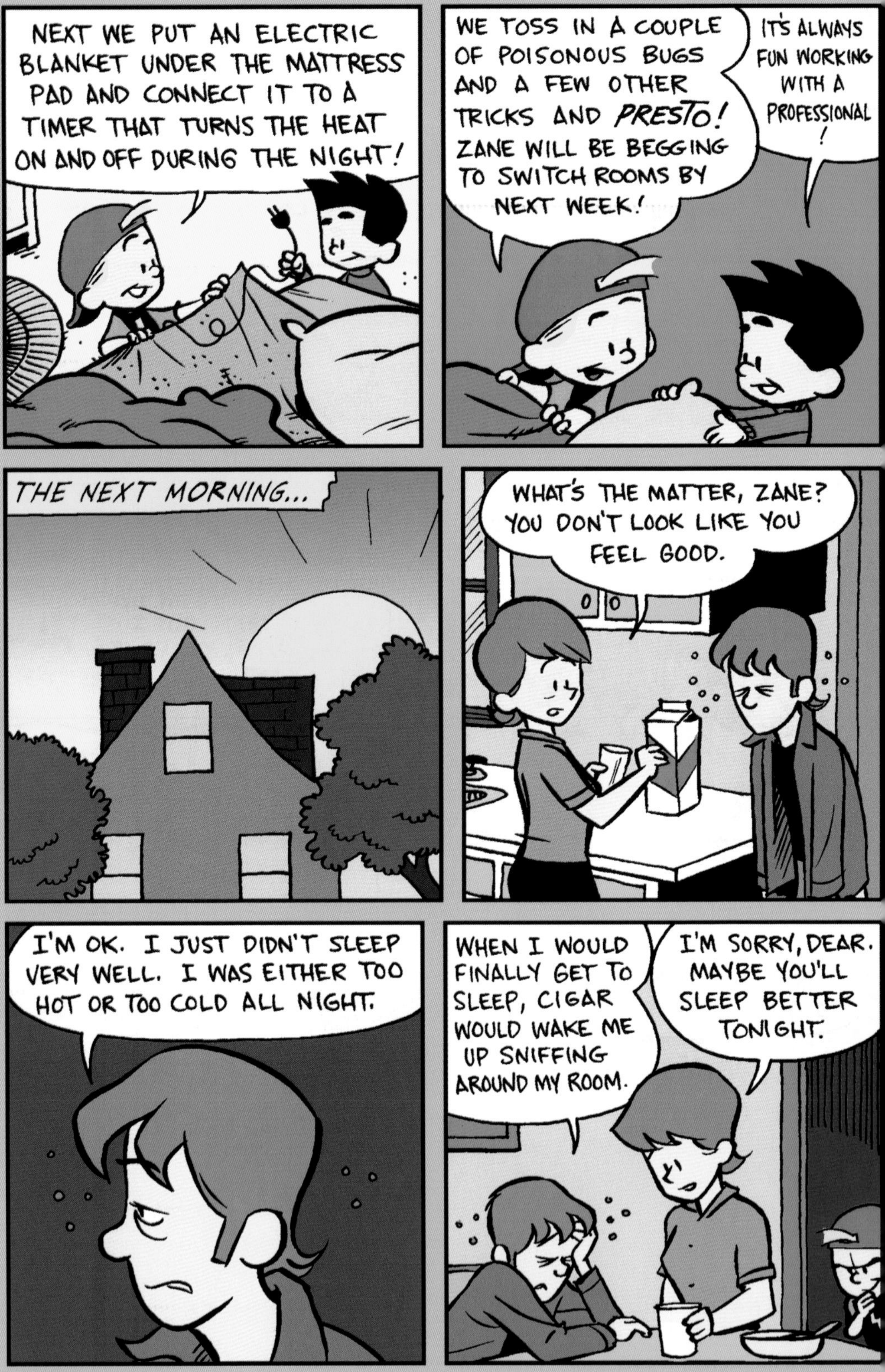
NEXT WE PUT AN ELECTRIC BLANKET UNDER THE MATTRESS PAD AND CONNECT IT TO A TIMER THAT TURNS THE HEAT ON AND OFF DURING THE NIGHT!
WE TOSS IN A COUPLE OF POISONOUS BUGS AND A FEW OTHER TRICKS AND PRESTO! ZANE WILL BE BEGGING TO SWITCH ROOMS BY NEXT WEEK!
IT'S ALWAYS FUN WORKING WITH A PROFESSIONAL!
THE NEXT MORNING...
WHAT'S THE MATTER, ZANE? YOU DON'T LOOK LIKE YOU FEEL GOOD.
I'M OK. I JUST DIDN'T SLEEP VERY WELL. I WAS EITHER TOO HOT OR TOO COLD ALL NIGHT.
WHEN I WOULD FINALLY GET TO SLEEP, CIGAR WOULD WAKE ME UP SNIFFING AROUND MY ROOM.
I'M SORRY, DEAR. MAYBE YOU'LL SLEEP BETTER TONIGHT.

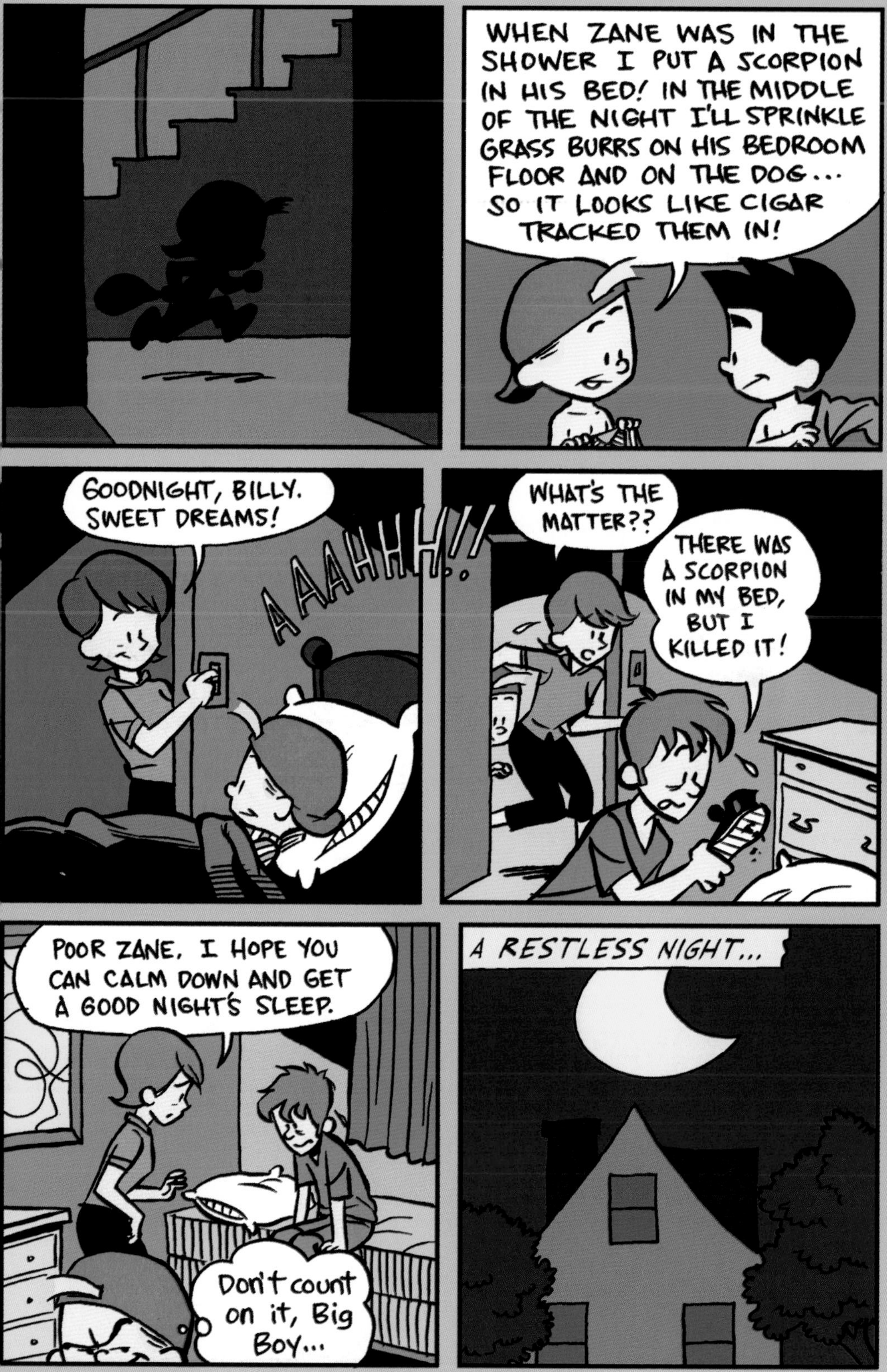
WHEN ZANE WAS IN THE SHOWER I PUT A SCORPION IN HIS BED! IN THE MIDDLE OF THE NIGHT I'LL SPRINKLE GRASS BURRS ON HIS BEDROOM FLOOR AND ON THE DOG... SO IT LOOKS LIKE CIGAR TRACKED THEM IN!
GOODNIGHT, BILLY. SWEET DREAMS!
AAAHHHH!!
WHAT'S THE MATTER??
THERE WAS A SCORPION IN MY BED, BUT I KILLED IT!
POOR ZANE. I HOPE YOU CAN CALM DOWN AND GET A GOOD NIGHT'S SLEEP.
Don't count on it, Big Boy...
A RESTLESS NIGHT...

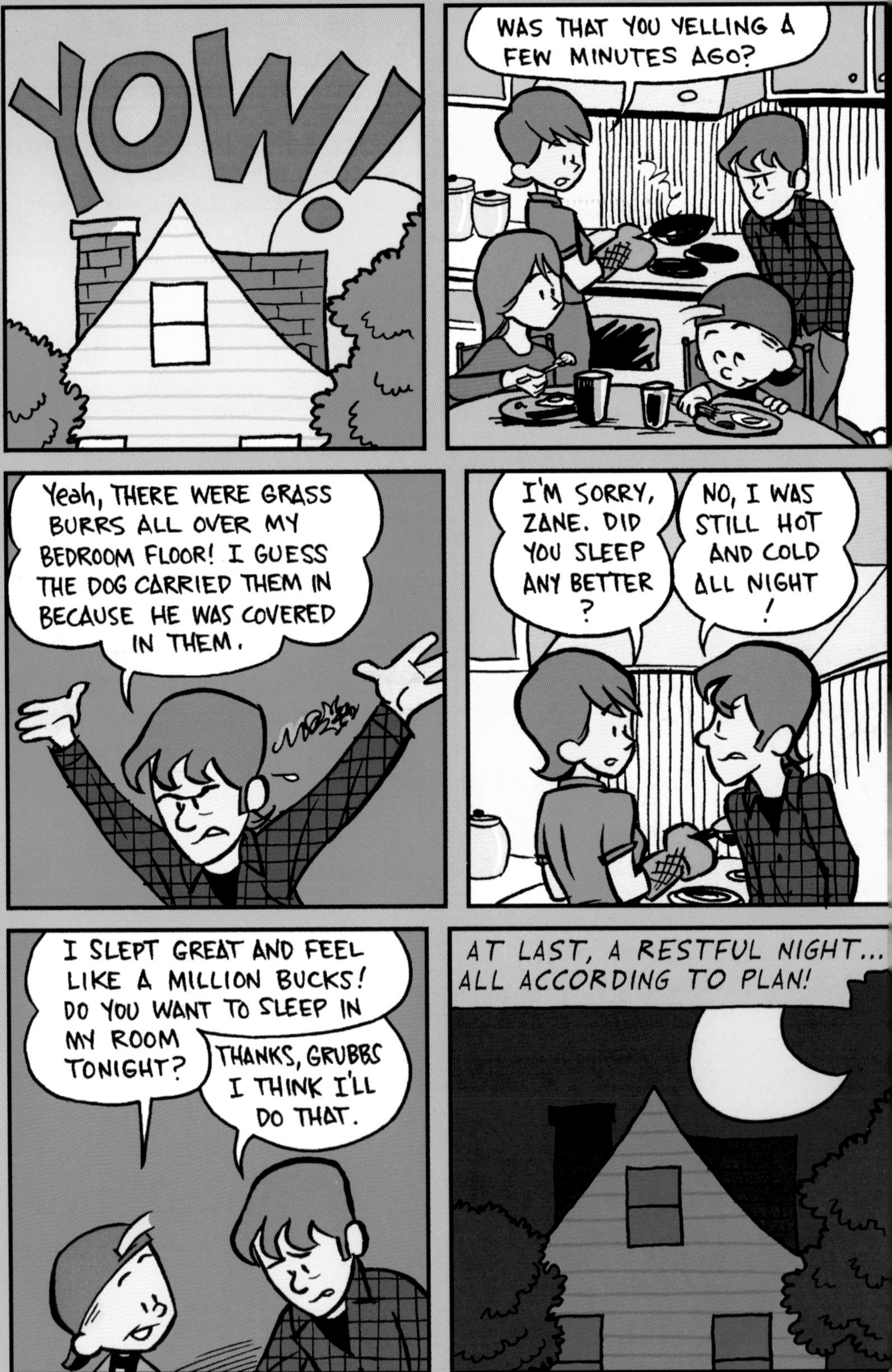
YOW!
WAS THAT YOU YELLING A FEW MINUTES AGO?
Yeah, THERE WERE GRASS BURRS ALL OVER MY BEDROOM FLOOR! I GUESS THE DOG CARRIED THEM IN BECAUSE HE WAS COVERED IN THEM.
I'M SORRY, ZANE. DID YOU SLEEP ANY BETTER?
NO, I WAS STILL HOT AND COLD ALL NIGHT!
I SLEPT GREAT AND FEEL LIKE A MILLION BUCKS! DO YOU WANT TO SLEEP IN MY ROOM TONIGHT?
THANKS, GRUBBS I THINK I'LL DO THAT.
AT LAST, A RESTFUL NIGHT... ALL ACCORDING TO PLAN!

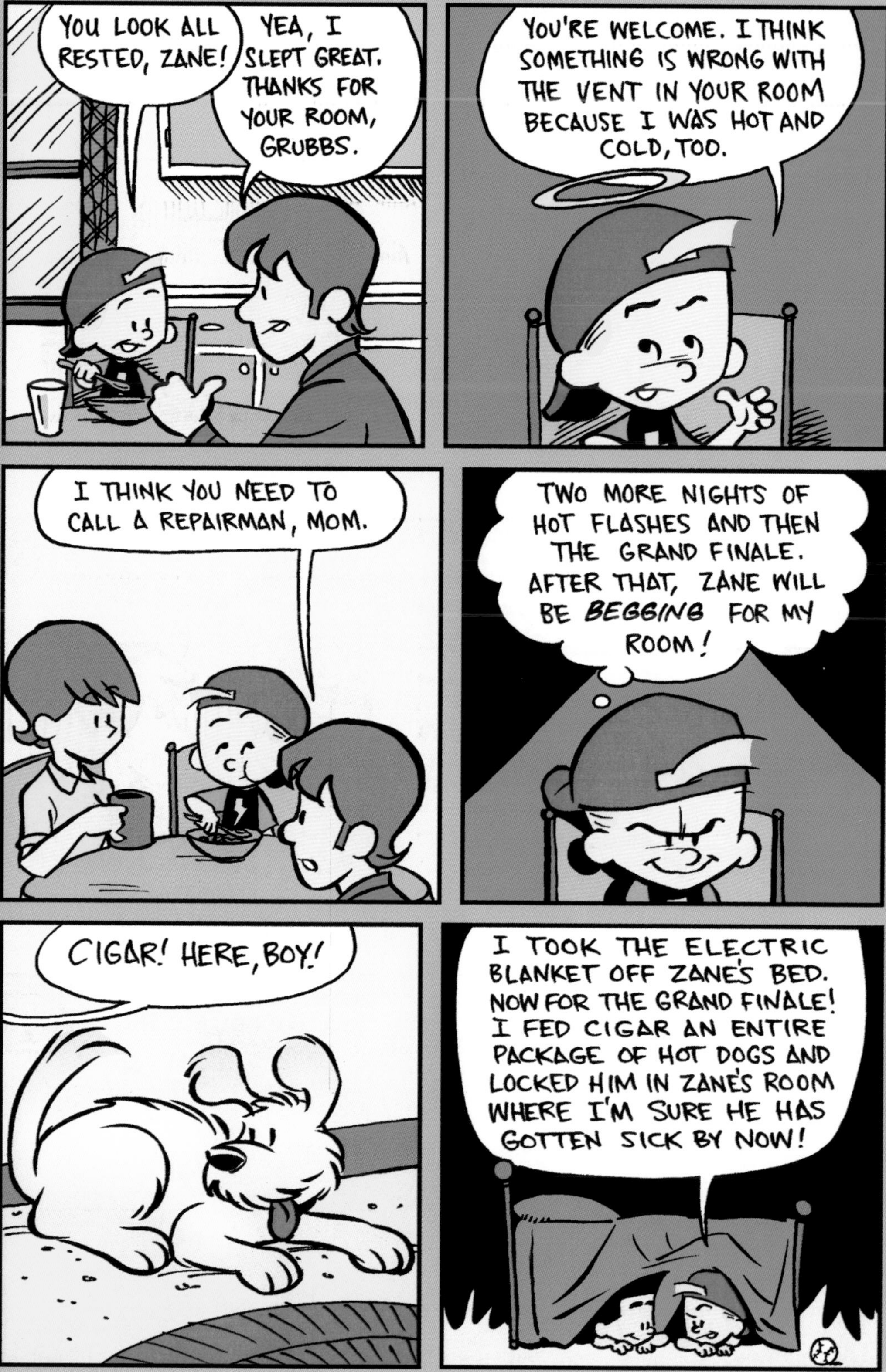
YOU LOOK ALL RESTED, ZANE!
YEA, I SLEPT GREAT. THANKS FOR YOUR ROOM, GRUBBS.
YOU'RE WELCOME. I THINK SOMETHING IS WRONG WITH THE VENT IN YOUR ROOM BECAUSE I WAS HOT AND COLD, TOO.
I THINK YOU NEED TO CALL A REPAIRMAN, MOM.
TWO MORE NIGHTS OF HOT FLASHES AND THEN THE GRAND FINALE. AFTER THAT, ZANE WILL BE *BEGGING* FOR MY ROOM!
CIGAR! HERE, BOY!
I TOOK THE ELECTRIC BLANKET OFF ZANE'S BED. NOW FOR THE GRAND FINALE! I FED CIGAR AN ENTIRE PACKAGE OF HOT DOGS AND LOCKED HIM IN ZANE'S ROOM WHERE I'M SURE HE HAS GOTTEN SICK BY NOW!

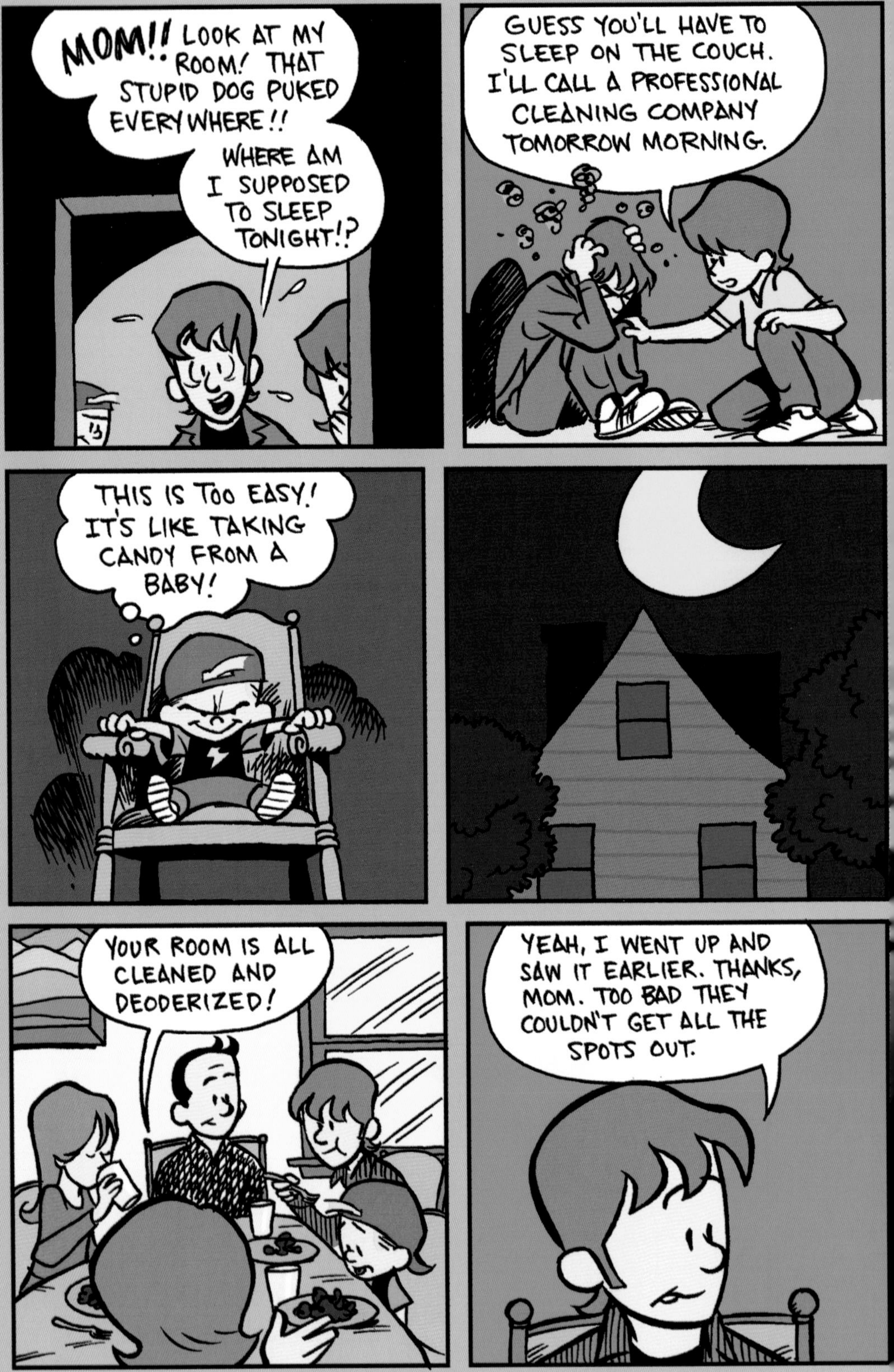
MOM!! LOOK AT MY ROOM! THAT STUPID DOG PUKED EVERYWHERE!!
WHERE AM I SUPPOSED TO SLEEP TONIGHT!?
GUESS YOU'LL HAVE TO SLEEP ON THE COUCH. I'LL CALL A PROFESSIONAL CLEANING COMPANY TOMORROW MORNING.
THIS IS TOO EASY! IT'S LIKE TAKING CANDY FROM A BABY!
YOUR ROOM IS ALL CLEANED AND DEODERIZED!
YEAH, I WENT UP AND SAW IT EARLIER. THANKS, MOM. TOO BAD THEY COULDN'T GET ALL THE SPOTS OUT.

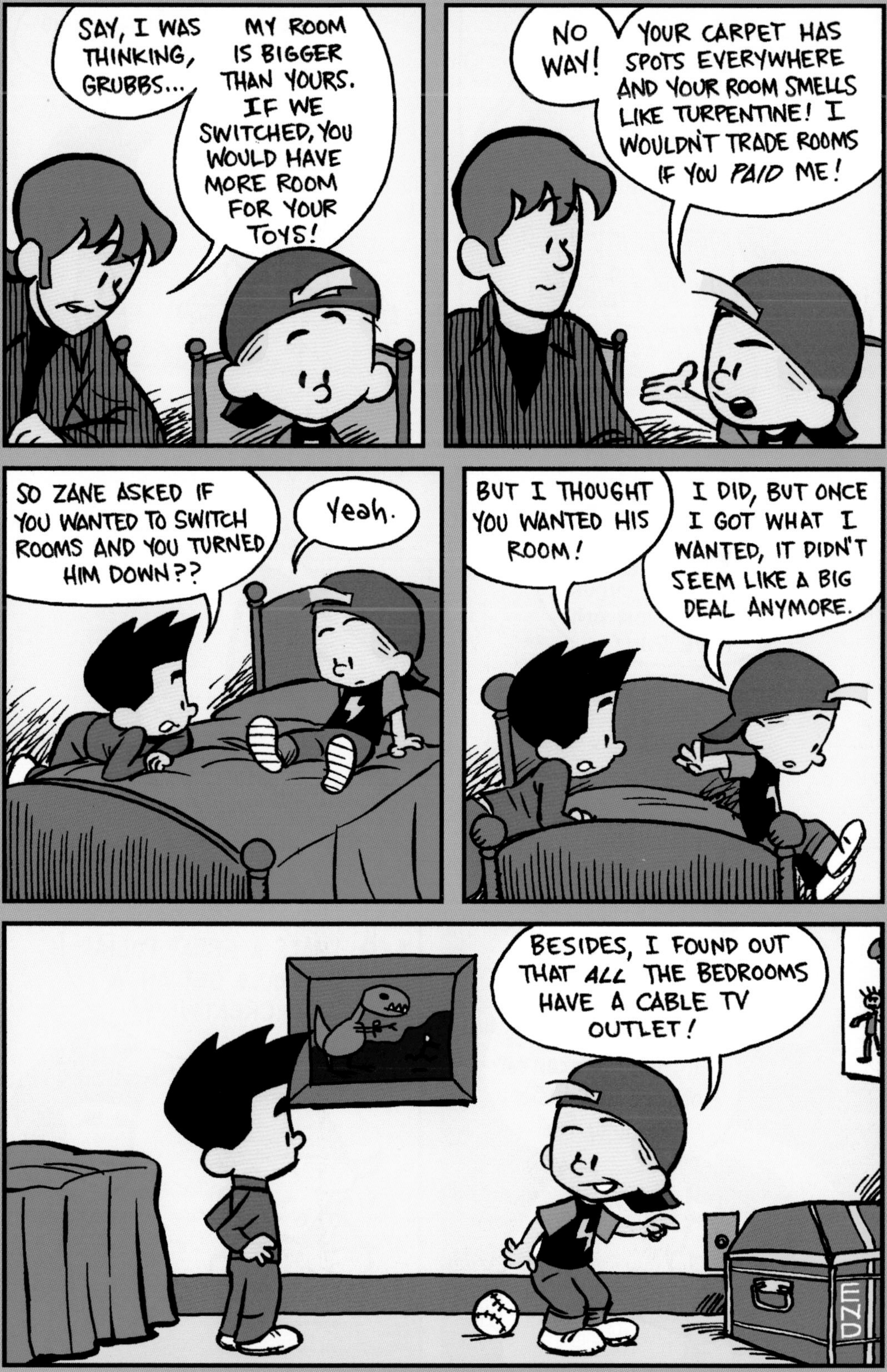
SAY, I WAS THINKING, GRUBBS...
MY ROOM IS BIGGER THAN YOURS. IF WE SWITCHED, YOU WOULD HAVE MORE ROOM FOR YOUR TOYS!
NO WAY!
YOUR CARPET HAS SPOTS EVERYWHERE AND YOUR ROOM SMELLS LIKE TURPENTINE! I WOULDN'T TRADE ROOMS IF YOU *PAID* ME!
SO ZANE ASKED IF YOU WANTED TO SWITCH ROOMS AND YOU TURNED HIM DOWN??
Yeah.
BUT I THOUGHT YOU WANTED HIS ROOM!
I DID, BUT ONCE I GOT WHAT I WANTED, IT DIDN'T SEEM LIKE A BIG DEAL ANYMORE.
BESIDES, I FOUND OUT THAT *ALL* THE BEDROOMS HAVE A CABLE TV OUTLET!
END

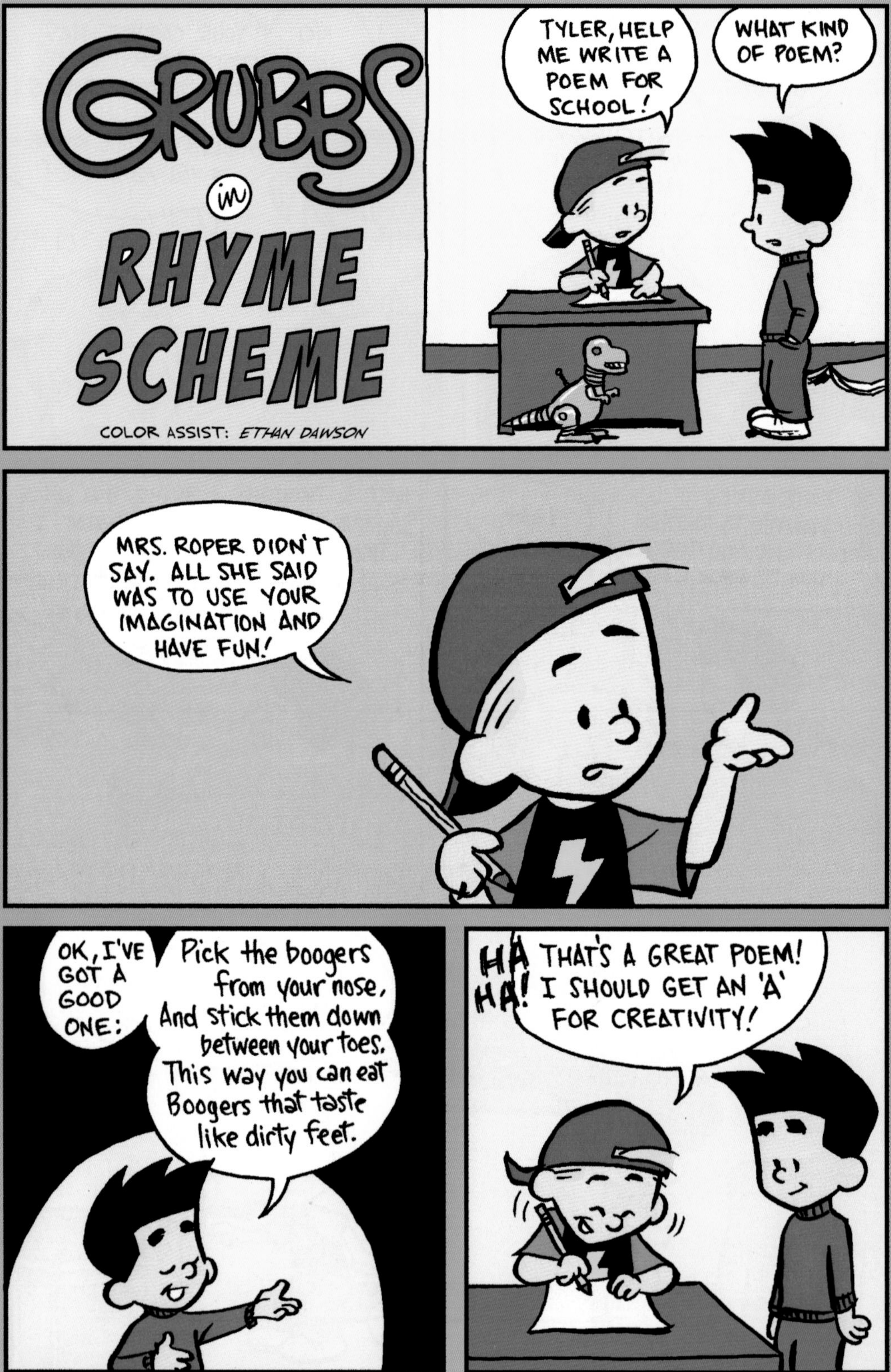

GRUBBS
in
RHYME SCHEME
COLOR ASSIST: ETHAN DAWSON
TYLER, HELP ME WRITE A POEM FOR SCHOOL!
WHAT KIND OF POEM?
MRS. ROPER DIDN'T SAY. ALL SHE SAID WAS TO USE YOUR IMAGINATION AND HAVE FUN!
OK, I'VE GOT A GOOD ONE:
Pick the boogers from your nose, And stick them down between your toes. This way you can eat Boogers that taste like dirty feet.
HA HA!
THAT'S A GREAT POEM! I SHOULD GET AN 'A' FOR CREATIVITY!

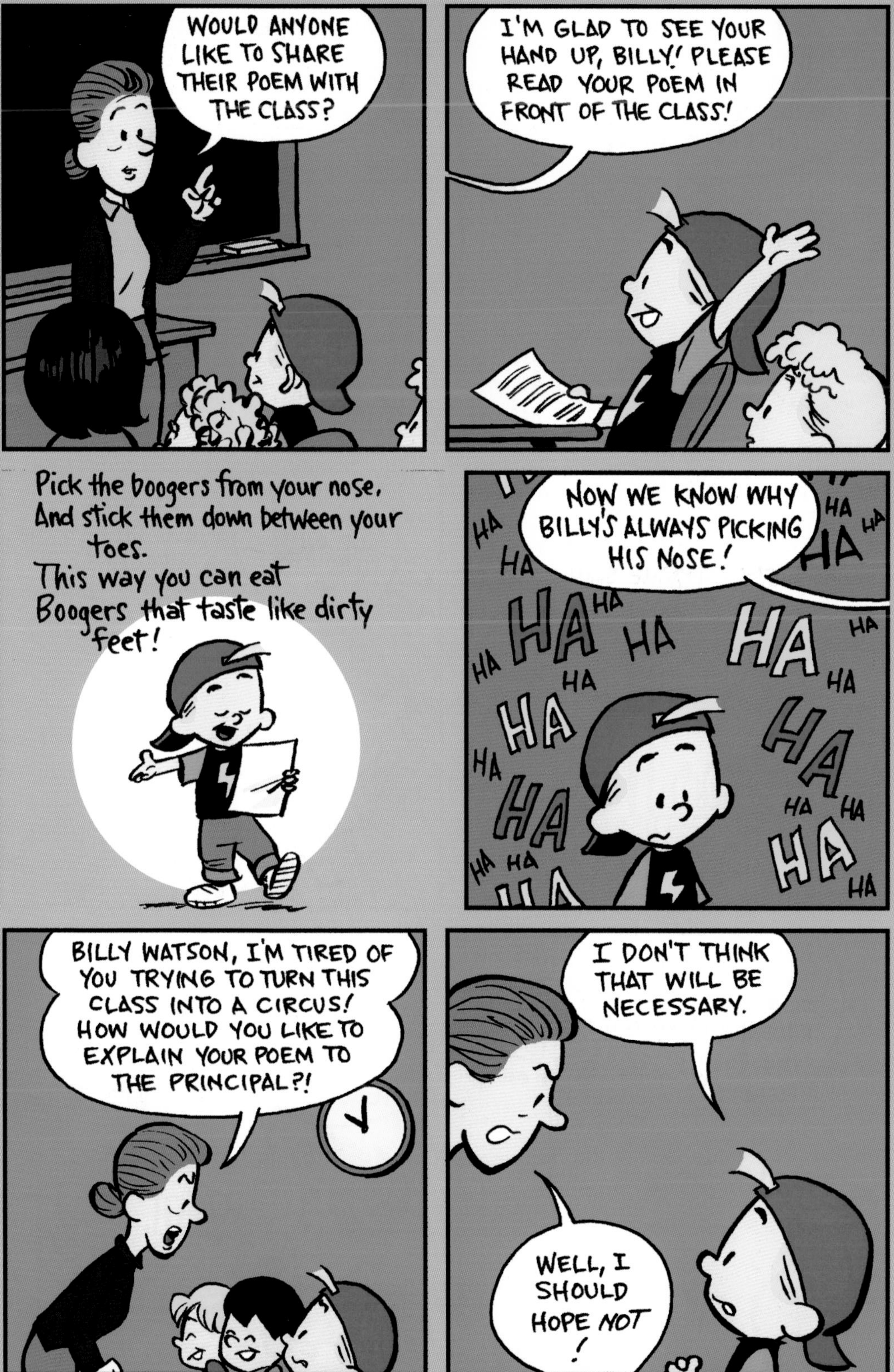
WOULD ANYONE LIKE TO SHARE THEIR POEM WITH THE CLASS?
I'M GLAD TO SEE YOUR HAND UP, BILLY! PLEASE READ YOUR POEM IN FRONT OF THE CLASS!
Pick the boogers from your nose,
And stick them down between your toes.
This way you can eat
Boogers that taste like dirty feet!
NOW WE KNOW WHY BILLY'S ALWAYS PICKING HIS NOSE!
HA HA HA HA HA HA HA HA HA HA HA HA HA HA HA HA HA HA HA HA HA
BILLY WATSON, I'M TIRED OF YOU TRYING TO TURN THIS CLASS INTO A CIRCUS! HOW WOULD YOU LIKE TO EXPLAIN YOUR POEM TO THE PRINCIPAL?!
I DON'T THINK THAT WILL BE NECESSARY.
WELL, I SHOULD HOPE *NOT*!

THE PRINCIPAL IS AN EDUCATED MAN. HE SHOULD BE ABLE TO UNDERSTAND IT WITHOUT AN EXPLANATION!

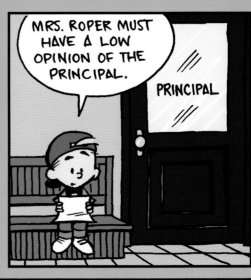

MRS. ROPER MUST HAVE A LOW OPINION OF THE PRINCIPAL.

PRINCIPAL

I RECEIVED A CALL FROM THE PRINCIPAL THIS AFTERNOON! HE READ ME A DISGUSTING POEM THAT YOU WROTE!

WHERE DO YOU COME UP WITH THIS STUFF ??

IT WAS ALL TYLER'S FAULT!

YOU EXPECT ME TO BELIEVE YOUR INVISIBLE FRIEND WROTE the POEM?

IT'S THE TRUTH, MOM!

ARE YOU SURE YOUR MOM SAID I HAD TO WRITE THE APOLOGY TO YOUR TEACHER?

YEAH, BUT SHE WANTS ME TO SIGN IT.

END

130

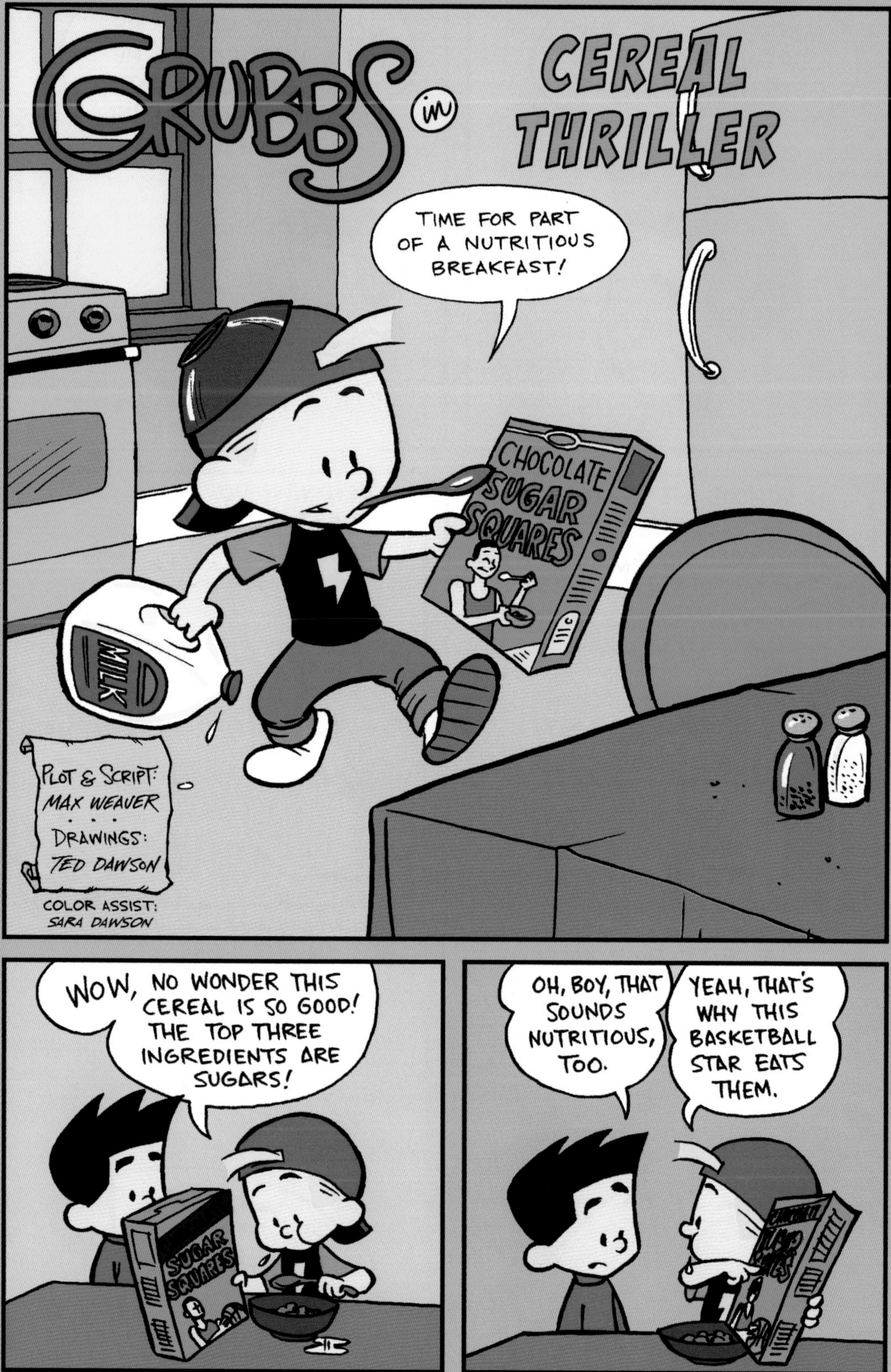

GRUBBS in
CEREAL THRILLER
TIME FOR PART OF A NUTRITIOUS BREAKFAST!
CHOCOLATE SUGAR SQUARES
MILK
PLOT & SCRIPT: MAX WEAVER
DRAWINGS: TED DAWSON
COLOR ASSIST: SARA DAWSON
WOW, NO WONDER THIS CEREAL IS SO GOOD! THE TOP THREE INGREDIENTS ARE SUGARS!
SUGAR SQUARES
OH, BOY, THAT SOUNDS NUTRITIOUS, TOO.
YEAH, THAT'S WHY THIS BASKETBALL STAR EATS THEM.

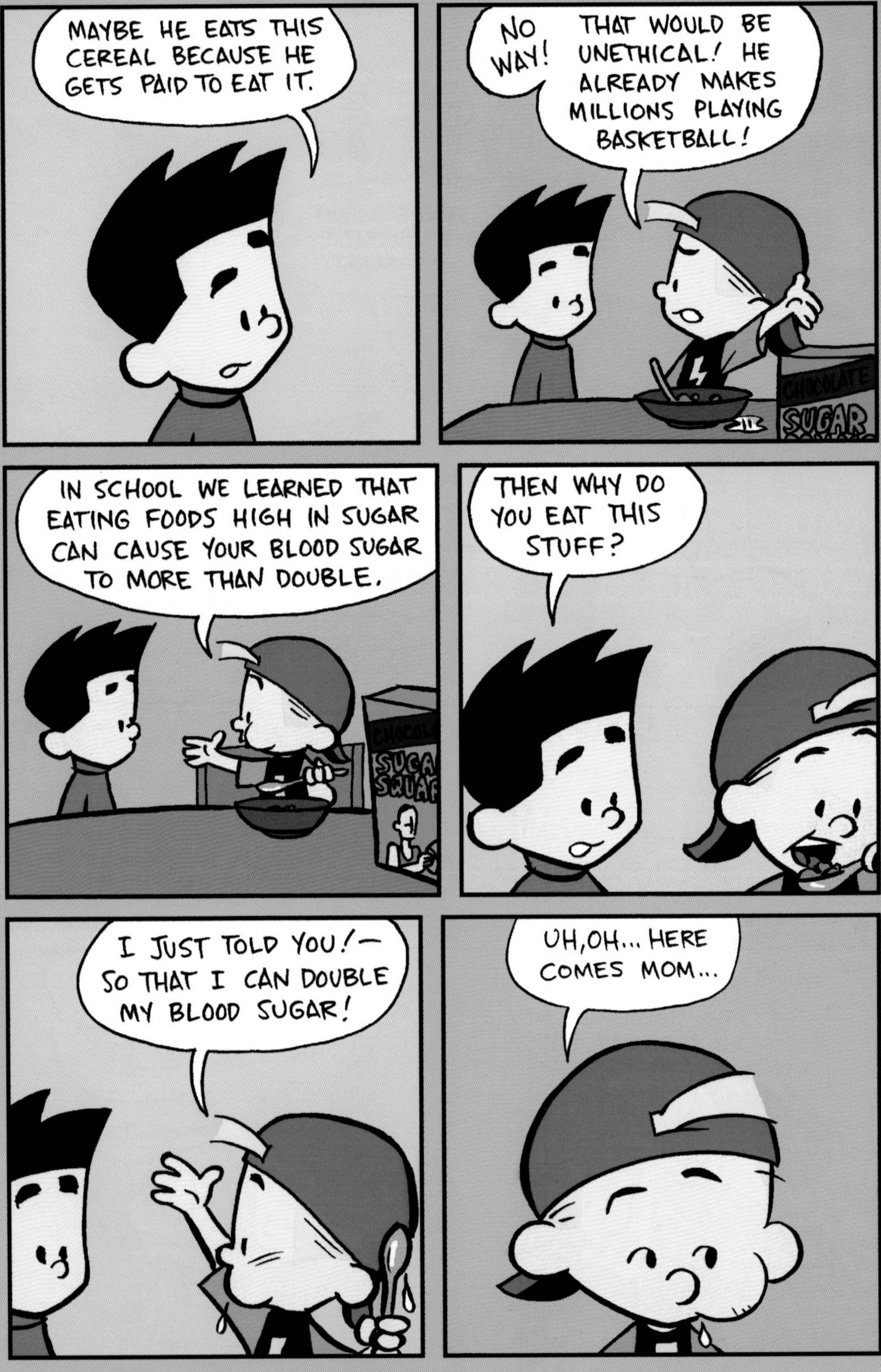
MAYBE HE EATS THIS CEREAL BECAUSE HE GETS PAID TO EAT IT.
NO WAY!
THAT WOULD BE UNETHICAL! HE ALREADY MAKES MILLIONS PLAYING BASKETBALL!
CHOCOLATE
SUGAR
IN SCHOOL WE LEARNED THAT EATING FOODS HIGH IN SUGAR CAN CAUSE YOUR BLOOD SUGAR TO MORE THAN DOUBLE.
THEN WHY DO YOU EAT THIS STUFF?
I JUST TOLD YOU!— SO THAT I CAN DOUBLE MY BLOOD SUGAR!
UH,OH... HERE COMES MOM...

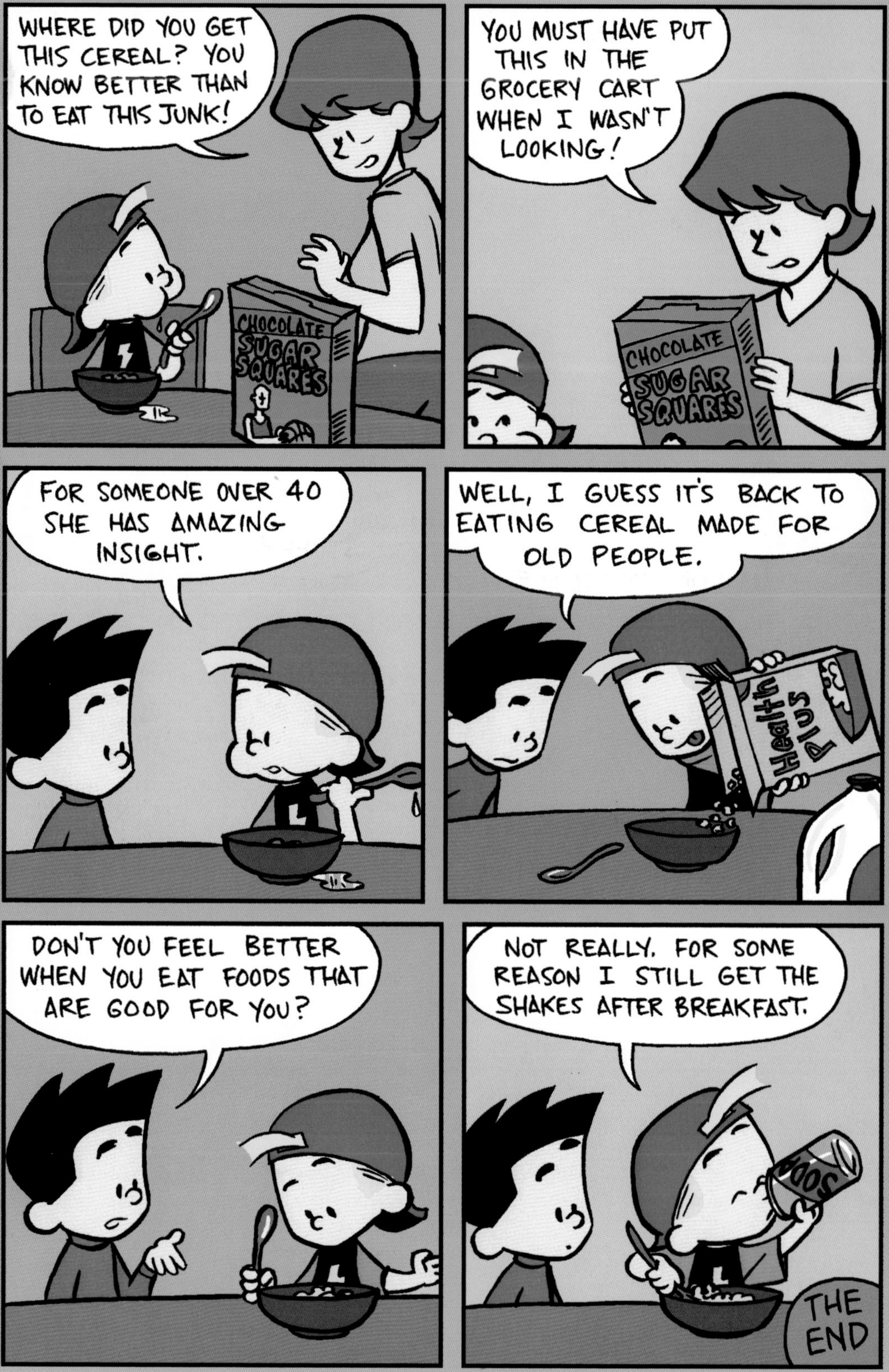
WHERE DID YOU GET THIS CEREAL? YOU KNOW BETTER THAN TO EAT THIS JUNK!
CHOCOLATE SUGAR SQUARES
YOU MUST HAVE PUT THIS IN THE GROCERY CART WHEN I WASN'T LOOKING!
CHOCOLATE SUGAR SQUARES
FOR SOMEONE OVER 40 SHE HAS AMAZING INSIGHT.
WELL, I GUESS IT'S BACK TO EATING CEREAL MADE FOR OLD PEOPLE.
Health PLUS
DON'T YOU FEEL BETTER WHEN YOU EAT FOODS THAT ARE GOOD FOR YOU?
NOT REALLY. FOR SOME REASON I STILL GET THE SHAKES AFTER BREAKFAST.
SODA
THE END

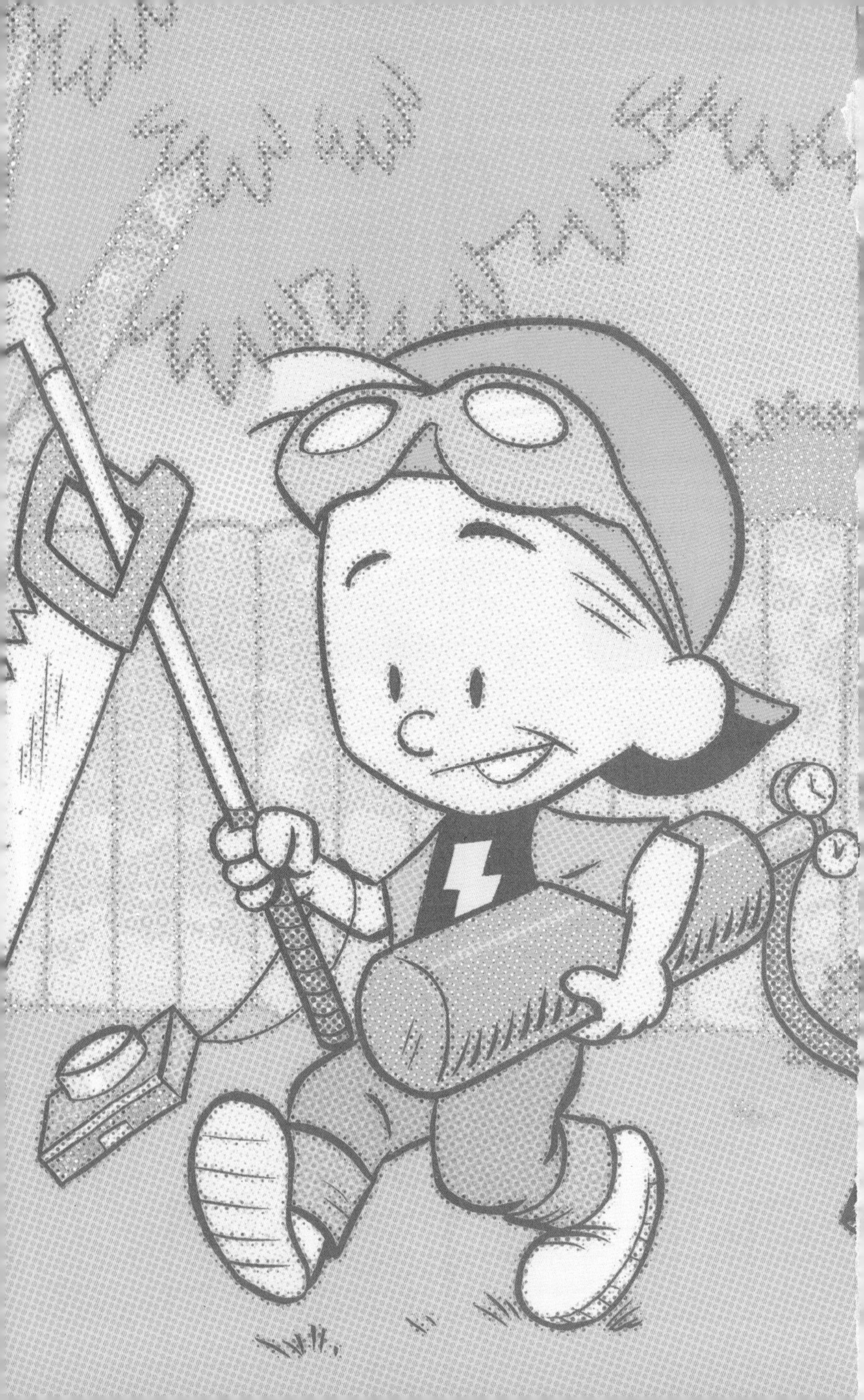